I0780102

Hear the Call

GREG ALLEN

Published by Builder of the Spirit Ministries
10465 West US Highway 136
Jamestown, Indiana 46147 USA
1.765.676.5014 www.builderofthespirit.org

ISBN: 979-8-218-40020-0
Published in the United States of America

Other books by: **_Greg Allen_**

Builder of the Spirit
War of the Heart
The Bored and the Cross

Contents

Dedication

This work is devoted to all those who aspire to a mind of entrepreneurship and Christlikeness.

I can remember beginning many a day at five in the morning at a young age. My vision of success was to deliver newspapers on a paper route for my first job. The occasional lemonade stand, raking leaves, shoveling snow, and the after-school job at the local grocery store isn't yet a fleeting memory either.

The realization of life's hardships then set in with adulthood, but like Martin Luther King Jr. once said, "I had a dream," and I began my own business.

Was the endeavor an easy one? *No.*

Was it enjoyable? *At times.*

But … was it in God's will?

"Beloved, I wish above all things that thou mayest prosper and be in health, even as thy soul prospereth." (3 John:2)

Prologue

We often times squander away God's true direction in our lives, be it for selfish fame and fortune, the pleasure of lust, or for the simple lack of faith.

All come into this world with nothing, we will exit with nothing, but poverty has never been God's plan. Understand that it's Satan, the thief, who comes to steal, kill, and destroy. *"But thou shalt remember the Lord thy God; for it is he that giveth thee power to get wealth."* (Deuteronomy 8:18)

Hear the Call is the echoing cry of God's heart. He whispers its spiritual message to many, but few recognize its significance or place of importance. Nathaniel Irwin will, in time, come to understand His voice, and the truth behind Christ's words, *"What good is it for a man to gain the whole world, yet forfeit his soul?"* (Mark 8:36)

Nathaniel was born rich. It didn't take long for him to gain billionaire status, but he never really earned any of it. He was just lucky enough to be the offspring of a family blessed with enormous wealth. Nathaniel's life-altering change comes after the death of his father. It's something money could never buy. When he makes the decision to sell it all for the seclusion of a cabin in the mountains, *Wall Street* reasons it as failure.

Nathaniel is a witness to all four seasons and God's continuous glory at a tiny place called *Lost Lake* tucked away in the heart of

Wyoming. In the end, it's the Creator who restores Nathaniel and his wealth while flooding his mind with the vision of feeding a starving world. God blesses a faithful heart, but we must *Hear the Call* - His divine, resolute invitation.

Chapter One

Prosperity

The seas grew heavy, the swells rolled with hellish force. Its constant motion churned with a devastating turmoil. The waves, some ten to fifteen feet tall, tossed the freighter about with a violent fury. The brutal wind drove a constant procession of whitecaps into the ship's side; many a wave crashing upon the vessel's deck with a battering blow. The Atlantic was relentless with its beating of the British craft. The fate of *The Queen's Pride,* her existence, her destiny, now rested in the hands of the Creator.

Rocked, a victim to this decreed of circumstance, the ship swayed violently back and forth as it was tossed to and fro in the vastness of the turbulent ocean waters. Her elderly wooden hull, and the integrity of her seaworthiness was now of grave concern to those fearful occupants aboard.

The ship's captain, some might say a pirate by nature, was a distant relative of the infamous *Blackbeard.* Although Captain Bry ran a legitimate shipping business, he wasn't above engaging in an occasional illegal activity or two; nor was he above committing a violent act when things didn't appear to be going his way. It wasn't his practice to rob, rape, or plunder upon the high seas, but he was indeed a thief of sorts.

The Captain and his crew of six were in sail from South Hampton, England to America. With a cargo hold full of brandy, wine, French champagne, and a vast assortment of other spirits, the bottom of the vessel also held a precious cargo of souls.

Captain Bry, a man in his 50's, was chiseled and well-worn with the passage of time. A tall ominous figure, he had been a sailor the vast majority of his life. His sinful pleasures were often the company of a prostitute and the intoxicating pride of a bottle.

When he was in port, the Captain loved to frequent the bars; his favorite being the *Sea Witch,* a sleazy English pub located along the north shore.

Niles Cavendish, a carpenter by trade and builder of small boats, was a brawny Irishman who also had been known to frequent the *Sea Witch* at times.

One night after work, Cavendish walked through the tavern's doors and took a seat, where he normally did, at the end of the bar. Sitting across from him, at an angle, was a drunken Captain Bry. After the Captain had poured a few more drinks down his throat, he boldly challenged the Irishman to an arm-wrestling match. It was a dual of sheer strength; one that would determine the master of superiority.

At first, Cavendish ignored the Captain's invitation. He reasoned it to be drunken foolishness. But soon after Cavendish had successfully liquored himself up, he accepted Bry's challenge. As both men prepared themselves for the feat, at a table in a dark corner of the room, excitement grew as word of the match quickly spread around the pub. Soon after, a small crowd gathered around the men. That's when the yelling started - a frenzy of wagers had begun.

Although the Captain was clearly the favorite, Cavendish won the match in relative short order. He also won the expressed gratitude of the winners who had placed a number of bets on him. After they had walked back over to their seats at the bar, Cavendish extended his hand to the Captain and offered to buy Bry a drink. Captain Bry shook his hand and accepted the drink. After downing it, the Captain said, "What do ya do for a livin', mate?"

Cavendish replied, "I'm a carpenter ... I build row boats."

The Captain's response was, "Ahhh ... I see. I captain *The Queen's Pride."*

Cavendish, after running his finger around the rim of his shot glass, spoke up to ask, "Do ya ever make way to that place called America?"

Captain Bry replied, "We set sail for Charleston next week ... Why?"

Cavendish was quick to elaborate on his much thought about intentions by asking, "Have ya ever took aboard passengers on that freighter, Captain?"

Bry slightly raised his head from where it now lay upon the bar, then raised his finger to say, "We had a stowaway once."

When the Captain didn't answer Cavendish's question of, "What happened to the stowaway?" Cavendish asked, "What would it cost me to get a one-way ticket to America?"

Raising his finger again slightly, the Captain said, "Now ... that would cost ya a hundred pounds!"

Cavendish replied, "I got three families in mind."

Captain Bry boasted, "That will cost ya seventy-five pounds then ... each ... not a pence less."

Cavendish knew it would deplete the life savings of all three families, but he told the Captain he would have the six hundred pounds Bry desired by next week.

The Captain's response was, "We sail Tuesday. Be on board by sunset, or we sail without ya!"

The Cavendishs, lrwins, and Smiths were all mutual friends who lived close to each other in the nearby village of *Lowshire.* All three of these families had long-standing dreams of making a new life for themselves in America. When Niles told the others of the opportunity they had everyone was eager to pull up stakes. They greeted this chance of a lifetime with great enthusiasm.

The Cavendish family, of Irish decent, consisted of Niles the father, Grace the mother, and Horatio their son. The Irwin family was of English heritage, as were the Smiths. Eli Irwin was a hard-working sheep farmer. He and his wife, Mary, had a son named Elias, but the Smiths had no children. Smith was an elderly shoemaker, who had had no previous desire for parenthood - something his spouse would quite often complain about.

Gathering their life savings, as well as their belongings, the group of eight kept their appointment with destiny the following week.

As they stepped aboard *The Queen's Pride,* excitement began to build within the group. Excitement would turn to concern shortly after they paid the Captain his bounty. They soon realized this trip wasn't going to be the much-anticipated adventure of a lifetime they had perceived as the crew locked them away in the belly of the ship. Forced to live in the isolation of the cargo hold at gunpoint, the dark, damp, musky bowels of the ship would now be their home for at least the next few weeks.

The group was convinced Niles had noble intentions. There was little doubt in their minds he had a desire to see a better life for them all, but his plan was about to take a tragic turn. It would not only bring heartache and sorrow to him and his family, but it would also prove quite costly for the others. The devastating consequences of this scheme would not only testify of a lack of judgment, but it would also be something that would affect them all, especially Niles. It would scar him the most, and for the rest of his life he would live with the haunting memory.

The first week at sea proved to be a rather calm one, as far as ocean conditions were concerned, but the sanitary conditions below deck grew worse by the day. Members of the crew would unlock the door that led to the cargo hold to hand down food and water every other day, but the living conditions down there were truly less than desirable. The frequent request for release by the captives would only fall upon the deaf ears of an indifferent crew.

The seas grew with steady intensity the second week, and the Smiths, who were already in their senior years when they decided to make the trip, became suddenly ill. The others could tell the Smiths were getting bad, but their repeated cries for help were just ignored by Captain Bry and his crew. Their complaints were instead rewarded with a rationing of food and water that were now only offered once every three days.

The seas grew worse the third week and the inevitable occurred, *The Queen's Pride* had sailed into the heart of a terrible storm. The turbulent atmospheric conditions would carry over into the fourth week of the voyage and last literally for days.

The group had seen rats on occasion before, but as the storm brewed it threw the rodents into a panicked frenzy and Grace Cavendish was bitten by one of the creatures when she accidentally stepped on one.

Grace died only six days later from the sustained effects of a high fever. The seas had calmed by then, but unfortunately, both Mr. and Mrs. Smith also perished during that terrible ordeal.

As he stared at the lifeless body of his wife, and the limp ones of his now deceased fiends, Niles couldn't help but notice the dejected look upon the faces of the living; he could sense the fear of hopelessness in their eyes. His heart began to beat rapidly as an uncontrollable rage began to build from within. His mind was then devoured by the self-imposed thoughts of conviction and guilt.

"We've left paradise to flounder about in the depths of hell, and it's my fault!" A confession that Niles would often times later ashamedly admit to.

With the encouragement of the others, Niles made the decision to confront the Captain and his crew. After he had climbed to the top of the stairway, Niles began to beat on the bottom of the door. The locked chains that held it moved only slightly with each effort. The hindrance was indeed a daunting obstacle.

Only after his fist grew bloody from all the pounding did two members of the crew open the door to hand down food and water. Momentarily blinded by an intense flood of bright light, Niles grabbed the rations and threw them upon the deck. Angered by Cavendish's actions, the crew members pushed him down the stairs then slammed the door shut and locked it.

Niles continued to beat on that door for the next four hours.

Frustrated by what he was doing, two other members of the crew finally opened the door. Once again shielding his eyes from the bright glare of the sun, Niles said, "We got dead down here!" The crew slammed the door, locked it, and did so with silent resolve. An hour or so later, the door was once again opened and Niles rushed to climb the stairs, but this time Captain Bry was standing at the top of the steps, with a gun in hand. Bry pointed the weapon at Niles, then yelled, "Stand back!"

Cavendish did, but reluctantly so.

The Captain then ordered two of his crew to go down into the cargo hold and retrieve the bodies. The sailors first picked up Mrs.

Smith, then carried her body up the steps to lay it upon the deck. The sailors then retrieved the body of Mr. Smith in like fashion. Then they removed Grace's body.

With no regard for his own safety, Niles climbed to the top of the steps and stood to stare at Bry; only a few inches would separate the two. The Captain quickly cocked the hammer back on his pistol and extended his arm forward to aim it at Cavendish.

Niles then shouted, "What are you doing?" soon after he heard a loud splash, followed by a series of two others. Puzzled by what he heard, Niles stood and stared at the vile Bry in contemptible silence; he did so with a glare full of disgust and disdain.

Slightly rubbing his beard, the Captain replied, "The sea can have 'em!" Bry then walked toward Cavendish and said, "Back away!" He then closed the door with his foot and chained it shut. Before walking away, Bry yelled, "Charleston's only a couple days from here. If the bunch of ya wanna live, I suggest you shut up!"

The Queen's Pride finally docked in Charleston, South Carolina on April 1st, 1868. The ship moored at mid-afternoon that day, but the captives would have to wait several more hours before the shackles that bound their path to freedom would eventually fall.

Once the vessel was secure, Captain Bry quickly formulated a plan then departed; his quest was the closest pub. His lustful habits were now driving him to the company of which he knew best, wine, women, and song. The sinful nature of the Captain, as it is with all sinners, was a custom that he acted upon with routine habitual practice. The desires of Bry's heart would in the end hold precedent above all else, even the safety of those left aboard. The captives would have to wait several more hours before the shackles that bound their path to freedom would eventually fall.

Captain Bry left strict, yet detailed, orders he wanted his crew to follow then he left. The two crew members, who had routinely given the captives food and water for the previous month, were given instructions to unlock the chains that held the cargo hold door shut at midnight in order to release the five who remained. Two other crew members were told to escort them from the ship, at gunpoint of course, to a destination north of there a little over three miles away. There the remaining members of the crew would wait with the spare horses they had stolen. The men were then instructed to bind the hands and feet of the adults and children with ropes after they hid them in the woods. With that accomplished, the sailors were to return to the ship under the cover of darkness. Bry and his crew would then set sail the following day; after *The Queen's Pride* had been unloaded of its cargo.

The Captain had spent the last few weeks devising this deliberate, what he thought was fool-proof, plan. Bry had spent those days convincing himself he wasn't guilty of anything, especially something like murder. If the authorities did pursue him and he was caught, he said he would fabricate a story that there were stow-a-ways on board his ship when it set sail and before he could discover it three of them had died. Naturally being so far from port, he would explain he had no choice but to give each decaying corpse a decent burial at sea. Bry made it a point to inform his crew of these intentions. He also made sure all transactions were made strictly through the untraceable use of cash.

The castaways would spend the next couple of days gazing at their wooded surroundings and a small nearby brook. They were unable to speak or cry out because they were bound by mouth, hand, and foot. A means of escape appeared to be void, seemingly lost in things that looked drastically hopeless. Surely it wasn't the end though, but they all thought it would be their demise. Niles soon found expectation in the form of all things, a small yet troublesomely dull stone.

Niles had his hands tied behind his back, but he was able to touch and then gather in that stone. His diligent effort of rubbing the rock against the bindings of his hands eventually paid off. After an exhausting two-day effort, Niles was able to break loose from those ties that bound him.

After Niles successfully released the others they all came to a mutual agreement, but only in the light of just one thing. The refreshing water of that alluring brook was just too tempting for them to overlook. The stench of their filthy bodies, a result of brutality and a month's worth of neglect at sea, was absolutely offensive and the smell just about too much for one to bear.

One by one, each removed their clothes to take a turn at bathing in a small pool while another sat on the bank with their backs turned. Guarding the view of naked bodies, the bather's privacy, was the concern. Eventually each would emerge from the stream refreshed, but puzzled by the events that had befallen them none the less.

A diabolical plot, fiendish scheme, is what the Captain had dreamed of then coerced into reality. His sinister plan was birthed out of a heart full of lies and deceit. It lead to the death and misfortune of those who had fallen into its devilish, and merciless grip.

Virtually penniless, lost and alone, this small group of five poor souls set out to find food as they tried to retrace their previous troddened steps from days before.

The ship's crew had been deliberately instructed to release the bound group, but into an unfamiliar land and that of a fearful darkness. Stranding them helpless was all part of the Captain's plan. It was an effort to buy the crew of *The Queen's Pride* just a little more time.

Within a few hours, the group gained direction as to where Charleston lay. It came in the form of friendly advice of a rider passing by. They walked back to the city, then to the docks. Much to their displeasure, the ship with its Captain and crew were long gone and already well under sail; far away from port.

It was the dawn of a new day, one in which the light of freedom was now shining, but everyone was too angry to know it. Talking among themselves, the group reasoned it would be a dangerous act to file a report. Informing the authorities of their grievous treatment was definitely out of the question. After all, they were strangers in a foreign land and they didn't dare speak of it - they were there perhaps illegally. They were left with no choice but to stay. They were now members of a new land; one that many called the home of the brave. Frustrated, and with little left to say, Niles smiled, then yelled, "Welcome to America!"

After he made that bold statement, everyone hung or shook their heads in silent disgust. It was after that they all looked around for some place to rest. A short distance away was a group of three broken down, old wooden benches - they looked quite inviting.

The group felt lost in a great big world, hungry, and alone. Never once did they give a single thought to that of a divine prayer. After the group sat down, they began to feel puzzled and helpless. They seemed to have no sense of direction, but before long Mrs. Irwin gave reason for their need of a plan. They would have to formulate their next move, one to devise a way of survival.

The group began to hear talk around town of vast fortunes to be made out west. The gold rush was on in states like California and Nevada. Numerous stories of the seemingly poor striking it rich greatly influenced both families so the Cavendishs and Irwins decided it was best to make their way westward.

Pooling their money together, what few British Pounds they had, Niles approached the only merchant in Charleston who was willing to exchange their currency for American Dollars. Feeling he had no choice Niles made the exchange, but the greedy merchant made out far better though. The merchant moved quickly to close the deal, but he never once gave it a second thought while he cheated those poor families. After all, for him, it was strictly business. In 1868, it took $6.83 to buy a single British Pound. The opportunistic merchant seized his chance to take advantage of those who were struggling and down on their luck. He smiled at Niles, then offered a measly exchange rate of only three dollars for each of their British Pounds.

Still strapped for cash, the group reverted to what they thought was drastic measures.

But everyone was in agreement that they must trade in their valuables and most of their belongings. That included their jewelry, personal effects, and even those gold wedding rings. Niles went as far as to have the local dentist pull his two golden teeth, and remove half-a-dozen gold fillings in exchange for cash. Niles thought to himself, "Why shouldn't I step forward to give this sacrifice. After all, I'm the biggest one to blame for this mess!"

Niles and Eli both decided it was best to approach the owner of the Livery Stable. It was their hope they could purchase some cheap transportation. The owner of the stable, who jokingly named it *The Silver Shoe,* had an old broken-down buckboard he was willing to part with. The wagon was in desperate need of repair, but a few rotten boards here and there didn't appear to be a big deal for Niles - he assured Eli it was something he could easily fix.

The only horse the stable owner had, that he would even consider for sale, was an old, worn out, worthless nag, he called, "Bell."

After a brief bit of conversation with the men, the stable owner began to look around, then he appeared to be lost in a moment of thought. He told Niles and Eli, "This place's been good to me ... I tell ya what! I'll sell ya the buckboard for twenty, and I'll even throw in *Bell* for four bits." (The equivalent of fifty cents)

Both men accepted the kindly businessman's offer.

It didn't take Niles long to repair the buckboard. He was fortunate enough to find all the lumber he needed in the form of scraps that had been thrown out by others. In the meantime, the rest of the group was busy purchasing the necessary provisions, all the supplies needed for a long and much anticipated trip.

Time passed quickly and everyone found it hard to believe the duration of three months had elapsed. The group had made the grueling, and often hazardous, venturesome way up through South Carolina. Then they traveled through Tennessee, Kentucky, and Indiana, but something happened on that bright July 4th day in Illinois - it would change their lives forever.

The group was forced to make camp near a small town called Burnt Plain. They could travel no farther because "Bell" got sick, laid down, and despite their best effort to persuade her, wouldn't get up. Old and tired, the horse eventually died within just a matter of a few hours.

Everyone pitched in to give the animal a decent burial. The boys made a make-shift cross out of a couple sticks and placed it at the head of the grave. Then they spelled out, with numerous small stones, "Here lays, Bell, a great old horse!"

As they sat, wondering what to do next, the group began to hear the sounds of celebration coming from what they knew to be was a nearby town. The echo of yelling and the loud pop of firecrackers going off, less than a mile away, was more than enough to arouse their curiosity and interest. Everyone then decided they should check out this unusual disturbance.

Once they reached the outskirts of Burnt Plain, they asked a young man, who they guessed to be nine or ten, playing in the street, what the celebration was all about. His response was, "It's July 4th! ... Are you kiddin'?"

The group wouldn't discover until much later what the significance, or meaning of this celebration called "The Fourth" was truly all about.

Stroding down the dusty streets of Burnt Plain was an all too similar experience for the Cavendishs and Irwins - It reflected shades of a previous experience in Charleston. The curious town folk welcomed the group with an occasional glance, followed then by a quick look away. A frequent controlled stare was the custom of the more hardened citizens, but the inconspicuous peer of discern from several windows was even more common. What an oddity these strangers appeared to be, walking, not riding into this town of only ninety-three. The group couldn't help but notice all the looks. They tried to ignore them, more important matters were of concern, but it wasn't easy.

Niles was the first to notice the Livery Stable was closed. The sign nailed on the door read, "Gone fishin'. See ya after the Fourth!"

The Land-Title Office was next door. Eli placed his hand on the back of Niles's neck, pointed at the building, and said, "Let's go in there!" Glancing over at his wife, Eli then said, "Mary, you stay here with the kids."

Approaching the men, in route from the General Store, was Walden Freedman, local farmer, rancher, and self-proclaimed part-time preacher. Curious, and fascinated by the strangers, Walden walked ever-so-slowly toward them, but kept a safe distance.

When Eli and Niles entered the Land-Title Office, Freedman quickened his pace and then stood outside to peer through the corner of the window. Walden did so only when he thought the Clerk, both men, Mary and the children weren't looking. The curious fellow did so all out of a simple need to eaves drop. When the Clerk glanced out the window, Freedman quickly sat down on the bench outside the storefront. The bench wasn't visible from inside the shop because the lower portion of the window's pane was covered by a curtain. Walden then removed a medium size block of wood and knife from his pocket as he normally did when he thought he was about to be confronted; ever so fearful of being caught in the act.

With keen ears, acutely affixed, and eager to listen, the nosy busy body strained to hear the conversation occurring within the office. Freedman did so while Mary and the boys were looking the other way.

Eli walked up to the counter, as his friend stood by, then he asked the Clerk if there was any land they could buy. The Clerk gave the two men a quick glance over, then replied, "Yeah ... some."

Eli gave Niles instructions to empty his pockets of all the money he had, and Eli did so as well. The grand total amounted to $36.90 - it was all they had left. After he had counted it, Eli glanced over at Niles. He then lowered his head slightly, briefly closed his eyes, nodded his head and said, "This is the right thing to do!"

Cupping his hand over the last of their life's savings, Eli slid the coins toward the Clerk. "We've come a long way, Sir... Can't see that we can go any farther. This place you call Illinois looks as good as any to settle upon. We'd like to purchase a wee bit of land." That was Eli's humble, yet simple request.

The Clerk laughed out loud, then said, "That won't even get ya a month's worth of room and board in a hotel!"

With a sense of urgency in his voice, Eli began to plead with the Clerk. "Our horse is dead. We're new to this country. We don't know what else to do!"

The unsympathetic Clerk said, "You're wastin' my time!" Pushing the money back toward Eli, the Clerk then shouted, "Go buy yourself another horse ... Get out of here!"

Freedman overheard every word.

After Eli and Niles had exited through the door, Walden began to whistle softly, then whittle a little more. Mary and the boys were curious and asked the men what happened, then they all stood in the middle of the street and whispered among themselves.

Freedman slowly raised his head to glance at the group. Then with a hidden inward smile, looked back downward to ask, "Got trouble?" as he continued with his carvings.

After a brief conversation among themselves, Eli walked over to the curious stranger, then said, "Yes ... we do!"

With a smile now upon his face, the farmer extended forth his hand, then said, "I'm Walden Freedman."

Eli was puzzled by this man's friendliness, but he extended his hand to shake the hand of the stranger - he did it out of simple response. "Eli ... Irwin" was his reply.

Freedman said, "I farm a little ... preach some too!"

Eli's response was one of silent wonder. It was reflected by the expression on his blank face.

"I hear you're lookin' for some land ... maybe settle down." Freedman inquired.

Eli's puzzled thoughts were now being substituted for ones of examination, inquiry, and investigating reason.

Walden hung his head and looked down when he realized Eli knew he had been eavesdropping. "I got a little over a hundred acres west of town." Whittling a little harder, Freedman said, "I can't possibly till it all!" Walden glanced up at Eli, then he looked over at the others who were standing in the street and stared. He could easily sense their fear and worry, their faces boldly revealed it. "I'll make you a deal ... I'll give you twenty acres ... You can split it up if you like. You pay the seven-dollar fee and I'll deed her over!"

With a hint of suspicion in his mind, doubt, and mistrust, Eli said, "What's the catch?"

Freedman replied, "There isn't one!"

No one in the group would ever know of Walden Freedman's dream, the one he had just the night before. It was something the farmer kept to himself for a lifetime; a secret he never once revealed, or made anybody else aware of.

God spoke to Walden in that dream. He told him two men, two young boys, and a woman, would appear in town, lost, the following day. The Lord said, "I am going to restore them, for they are strangers who have come a long way ... foreign to this land."

Freedman was instructed in the dream to give those strangers one-fifth of his land. In return, the Lord promised the farmer his obedience would reap a hundred-fold.

After Eli told the others of Freedman's generous intentions they all wondered why someone would do such a thing, but welcomed the gift with understandable reservation.

Walden walked into the Land-Title office with Niles, Eli, Mary, and the boys to sign over the best twenty acres of prime land he had on the northeast corner of the property. The Clerk knew

Walden, and he was somewhat taken back by all that. The farmer's puzzling act of kindness was strange to everyone present, but Eli went ahead and paid the seven-dollar fee. Within a matter of less than thirty minutes, the deed was finally ready. It was recorded and official, but simply read: "#36, Walden Freedman to Niles Cavendish / Eli Irwin, deed, 20a, Burnt Plain."

Walden took the group out to see the land that afternoon. Once there, Niles looked around, then said, "This is a beautiful place, Mr. Freedman. How can we thank you?"

Walden simply nodded his head a few times. It was like the farmer was saying, "Don't worry, you already have."

Eli convinced Niles it was best to stay there, make camp, then plan for the building of a home before winter hit. They spent the night camped out under the shade of a large oak, on what they thought was that of inherited good fortune. Both men were now in their late 40's. Luck, they thought, had smiled upon them both, for they were able to avoid participation in the country's Civil War. Little did they realize it was God's hand of direction that was guiding the circumstances of their lives.

Walden made arrangements to have the group's buck board delivered the following day. The group informed Freedman of their intentions, their plan, when he arrived. The Cavendishs would take the ten acres to the west, and the Irwins would take the other ten to the east. Both families planned to pick a suitable location on both plots to build themselves a cabin each, and elected to move forward rather quickly before cold weather approached - all that was perfectly acceptable to Walden.

Walden, his wife, and two sons dropped by to visit their new neighbors just three days later. The Freedmans had given it a lot of thought, and then volunteered to help build those cabins. Both families, the Cavendishs, as well as the Irwins, greeted the gracious and kindly offer with open arms and with tearful, reddened eyes of joyous acceptance. Less than a week later, Freedman arrived with his family, a team of horses, and a portable saw mill he had borrowed - a friend of Walden's in town had lent it, free of charge. Everyone then set out, with serious determination, to proceed with the construction of the family homes.

Located in a nearby woods was a large grouping of red oak trees. Those trees provided all the lumber for both projects. At times the workday began before the light of day and then ended with the setting of the sun, but with diligence, and a whole lot of hard work, both homes were completed in a little under five months - nearly a full week before Thanksgiving.

Over the course of time, the Cavendishs and Irwins became a welcome addition to the community. After Niles had settled in, he learned the trade of furniture making and set up shop in Burnt Plain, where he ran a profitable business. Eli pursued a career in the field of which he knew best, which was raising animals, and he became a successful cattle rancher.

Walden Freedman became a well-known leading member of *The Disciples of Christ* in the state, and before his death he would lay claim to more than 10,000 acres of prime tillable land. The land was a blessing, a gift from God, Walden would boast. A payment it was, the result of God's divine promise He had made, and that is what Walden had always faithfully perceived.

The air was crisp that fall day in early November of 1871. Only a few weeks before, the Southeastern Railroad company had laid track through the northern portion of White County and Mr. Freedman's property. The rail-line connected Evansville to St. Louis, then it ventured farther westward to points beyond.

Niles's son, Horatio, and the Irwin's son, Elias, were now the best of friends. Both boys were twelve and tall for their age. They loved to frequent Mr. Freedman's pond; a great fishin' hole. It was a small body of water that lay just south of the railroad tracks. The pond was filled with big, hungry catfish - the source of many a divine nightly meal.

That particular day, both boys acted upon a plan they had been devising for a long time. The scheme was one of skipping school. The Cavendish boy was successful in convincing his friend they needed a break. "Besides, what's it gonna hurt?" Horatio reasoned.

The one room school house they attended was run by an elderly woman. He was known to the community as Miss Lynch. She was nicknamed, "The Hangman," by Horatio because of her hard attitude, lack of humor, and love for the strict enforcement of rules.

The fish weren't biting very well that day, so the boys withdrew their lines from the muddy water when they heard a Locomotive in the distance that afternoon. They ran the entire 3/4 of a mile from the pond to the tracks, arriving just in time to see the *Illinois Central* roll past. Black billowing smoke filled the air; it rolled from the old steamer's stack. The dark cloud appeared to be hugging the ground and its sulphurous odor smelled of burning coal - the lingering effects were something difficult to escape.

As the massive locomotive's silhouette got smaller and smaller, minuscule in the distance, the distinctive *Chuka, Chuka* sound it made grew weaker and weaker. The train's whistle had blown several times, warning the boys of danger. The roar of its bellowing blow echoed across the landscape, signifying its intimidating presence, but now the locomotive's whistle was only a faint blast of steam that could be heard in the distance - a final expression of farewell from the train's engineer.

Horatio watched the train until it disappeared over the horizon. He then looked down at a rock and kicked the stone with his foot. With a great deal of seriousness in his voice, Horatio glanced over at Elias standing beside him and said, "I'm not gonna rot in this place like my old man ... I got big plans!" Horatio then placed his arm around the neck of his friend, smiled, and pointed in a westerly direction. His final statement was, "That's our ticket out of here, my friend ... The railroad is the future!"

Chapter Two
Way of the Rail

As people, we take transportation for granted. So why are we as a nation so dependent on the railroads? North America's railroads provide the dependable, low-lost, high-volume transportation that is essential to our mass production economy and high standard of living.

But our mass-production economy wasn't always that way. A century and a half ago, *The Iron Horse* began the revolution that linked railroads together with the diverse segments of this vast land so that together they might create the greatest economy the world has known.

New York to Philadelphia barely qualifies as a trip anymore. Morning business in one city and an afternoon conference in the other is commonplace. And yet, there was a time, little more than two centuries ago, when the journey was a long and hard three days by horse-drawn wagon over 90 miles of bumpy terrain. Transportation wasn't a flourishing industry then; it was an obstacle to be overcome.

For the early U.S. most trade was with Europe. Most important transportation was by ship. There were roads between the states, but they were poor specimens mostly made by simply widening an Indian or animal trail.

American pioneers were privy to the richness of the Americas, but reaping the potential rewards of this nation required a transportation system that could bridge the tremendous distances of a vast and unsettled land. Before the advent of railroads, the lack of efficient land transportation largely limited U.S. settlement to the "strip" areas adjacent to navigable waterways.

Railroads changed that picture. In 1830, there were fewer than 13 million people in the United States and its western territories. Nearly all of them lived east of the Mississippi River. The sprawl of land that lay beyond the Mississippi was like a locked door. With their fuel efficiency and hauling capability, railroads proved to be the key to unlocking that door, blazing a path for westward expansion to all the immense regions perfect for farming, mining, lumbering, and manufacturing.

Wherever railroads were laid, new towns sprang up and industry and commerce developed. Agricultural production increased and land values multiplied. Representing the best of the American pioneering spirit, railroads laid the foundation for new markets and stimulated an unprecedented expansion.

The first locomotive to run on rails in the United States was a small experimental engine built by Col. John Stevens and operated on a circular railway track in Hoboken, New Jersey in 1825, but it was never put to practical use.

The first locomotive to run on a standard railroad in the United States was the British built *Stourbridge Lion.* On August 8, 1829, the Lion, operated by Horatio Allen, a young civil engineer, was tested on a short wooden railroad in Pennsylvania. It proved to be too heavy for the rails.

In September, 1829, the *Tom Thumb,* an experimental locomotive built by Peter Cooper of New York, was given a trial run on a newly-built railroad in Baltimore, Maryland. That little engine, weighing about one ton, was the first American-built locomotive to run on a common carrier railroad in the U.S.

Meanwhile, another railroad experiment was getting underway in Charleston, South Carolina. In December, 1830, the first locomotive to pull a train of cars on an American railroad was the *Best Friend* of Charleston, built at the West Point Foundry in New York and shipped to Charleston by sailing vessel.

By 1835, there were 200 rail lines being planned or being built and operating on 1,098 miles of track. By 1850, trackage had grown ninefold and total investment had reached $372 million. By 1860, that total would be $1 billion, with one-fifth of that amount coming from European investors.

In the mid 1800's, what is now considered one of the nation's greatest assets, the sprawling heartland, represented a great challenge to the federal government. The government held 1.4 billion acres of land. It was apparent that without a dependable means of transportation, America's western riches were out of reach. Central to the development of the West, therefore, was the dependability and efficiency of the spreading railroad network.

In 1850, President Millard Fillmore made significant history by signing the first of the railroad land grants. More than 2.5 million acres were granted. The basic purpose of the land grant acts was to stimulate settlement and development of western lands. The land was not a gift because participating railroads were required to transport government personnel, property and mail at reduced rates.

In July 1862, with the nation mired in internal strife, President Lincoln signed the Pacific Railroad Act. In order to reach the Pacific by rail and bring the Western lands into settlement, the Act authorized two railroads to build the great line to the Pacific. The

Central Pacific was to head east from Sacramento and the newly chartered Union Pacific would drive westward from the Missouri River. So gigantic was the task, particularly in wartime, that it took three years of gathering investors and other preparations before the Union Pacific was able to put down its first rails beyond Omaha.

In 1866, with only 40 miles of track down, the stimulus of competition gave new spirit to the Union Pacific's westward drive. That June, Congress repealed earlier legislation forbidding the Central Pacific from building more than 150 miles east of the California/Nevada border. Since each railroad received 20 sections of land for each mile of track they laid, the great undertaking was transformed into a race.

Immigrants from China pushed the Central Pacific Eastward; while Irish immigrants often populated the Union Pacific crews pushing Westward. There were many problems along the way though, with weather, outlaws, and Indians.

But finally, on May 10, 1869, Central Pacific and Union Pacific locomotives sat a shovel toss of coal apart at Promontory, Utah, just north of the Great Salt Lake. Plans for the heroic joining had been laid well ahead of time. The Central Pacific president, Leland Stanford, who was also Governor of California, would join with Union Pacific Vice President Thomas C. Durant in driving home a final gold spike with a silver sledgehammer.

History would probably like to recall that both men applied mighty blows to the trembling spike, but truth is often far less dramatic. Neither man could even hit the spike, much less drive it home. It was left for Jack Casement to slam in the historic spike. The transcontinental railroad had been built!

It had taken more than half a century from the time the nation's first railroad was chartered to build a transcontinental railroad. It took only twelve more years to build the second, this one coming to a function in New Mexico and providing the first direct line to Southern California. In fact, during the 1870's and 1880's an unparalleled explosion of growth occurred for the railroads.

To stimulate business along the spreading network of rail lines, the railroads actively sought immigrants to "colonize" the Western regions. The potential of the American West was advertised widely, not only in the United States but in Europe as well. Industry opened along those rail lines. Towns and cities developed where before there had been only prairie, forest, or hills.

Along the way, railroads changed the way America kept time. Until November 18. 1883, every city and town across America had its own time determined by the sun! For example, when it was noon in Washington DC, it was 12:08 in Philadelphia, 12:12 in New York and 11:51 in Lynchburg. Virginia. When it was noon in Chicago, it was 12:31 in Pittsburgh; 12:24 in Cleveland; 12:09 in Louisville; 11:50 in St. Louis; 11:27 in Omaha, and 9:05 in Sacramento. The confusion for travelers and railroad operators alike was enormous. It was especially confusing for travelers. Between Maine and California, a traveler would have to change their watch twenty times.

That began to change in May of 1872, when an association of railroad officers met to arrange summer passenger train schedules. At that St. Louis meeting the group formed a permanent organization which was called the Timetable Convention then later the General Time Convention. Eventually that organization became the American Railway Association and finally the

Association of American Railroads.

At the General Time Convention of October 11,1883, Standard Time was adopted.

The plan was for five time zones, four in the United States, and one in the Eastern provinces of Canada. The directive was sent out to the railroads to change all railway clocks to the new standard on Sunday, November 18, 1883. Some critics said it was an attempt to put the sun out of a job - the 18th would become known as "the day of two noons." It was 35 years later when Congress made it official with the Standard Time Act of 1918.

The adjustment called for careful planning and preparation. Orders were issued on every division, instructing every officer and every employee as to what should be done. Train crews on line were instructed as to what change to make. The American people soon accepted Standard Time without question. The standardization movement gradually spread to other lands - today it is in almost universal use.

Wheels on rails move more easily than wheels on the ground. It was a simple concept that was made evident in the 19th century, but it holds continuing truth to this day. When steam boilers were put on wheels and those wheels were put on railroad tracks, the truth became undeniable. It is still the factor that makes railroads the backbone of national transportation.

Once Horatio caught a glimpse of his first locomotive he was hooked for life. His interest in them would be something that never-waivered. In his opinion, the machine was a magnificent feat of engineering know-how, a marvel, its sleek design captivated the young man. From front to back, the locomotive's shiny black streamlined grace was something to behold. It made a lasting impression upon the twelve-year-old. As he watched the locomotive speed past, Horatio thought, "That's a thing of beauty!"

The large light mounted on the front of the locomotive gave illumination; direction for the lighting of a dark path. Above that light were two smaller lanterns. Those were used for signaling purposes. Below those lanterns was a mounted plate. Engraved on the plate was the locomotive's assigned number. Quite noticeable, mounted on the front of the locomotive, hovering just above the tracks, was the "cow-catcher." Its triangular iron grated frame was used for the clearing of obstacles on the track. Four metal steps, mounted on both sides of the massive boiler, gave access to the top of the engine. The boiler, which made up more than half the length of the locomotive, was the heart of the machine. The boiler consisted of heavy steel plating; its rolled circular form was a riveted assembly used for the production of steam energy that powered the massive breast. A bell, used to signal the locomotive's slow approach, was also mounted directly atop the boiler and was just behind the machine's exhaust stack. Two large powerful pistons, mounted under the belly of the boiler, were linked to three sets of large iron spoked wheels by a set of connecting arms. Energy produced from the burning of coal was used to generate the extreme power needed to drive those wheels in acceleration of the massive piece of equipment. The wheels were mounted directly under the back portion of the boiler - their location gave the locomotive balance and support on the track. A smaller single set of wheels, located directly behind the "cow-catcher," guided the machine's direction. The Engineer's cabin, also engraved on both sides with a number for identification, featured a rounded metal roof to shed the elements of nature. The open design of the cabin's sides made it easier for visual inspection of the track ahead, but the Engineer's job could be quite cold in the winter; although the heat generated from the firebox did help somewhat. Mounted atop the boiler, directly in front of the Engineer's cabin, was a steam whistle; it was used primarily for warning. The coal car was affixed directly behind the Engineer's cabin; it held all the fuel needed to power the locomotive. Two medium size sets of wheels supported the coal car as it was pulled down the track by the engine, and on both sides of the car one could see the brightly colored, painted emblems of the Illinois Central Railroad - the engine's owner.

The passage of time had occurred rather quickly, for the year was now 1878. Seven years had passed since Horatio had his first chance to glance at destiny. He had just celebrated his 19th birthday only two days earlier. Elias would also celebrate his in a little over a month. They were now young men, no longer the freckled faced boys they once were. One longed for the bigger and better things in life, the other chose to take a more simple approach in view of what life had to offer.

Horatio had always held steadfast to his convictions. His firm belief was the railroads were his ticket out of poverty. When he turned nineteen, Horatio made good on his promise *to never rot in Burnt Plain* when he announced he was leaving home. Using his finally honed skills of persuasion, Horatio convinced his friend, Elias, that the real money was to be made in the big city - Chicago. After Horatio had exercised a continuous barrage of insistent

urges, and a few guilt provoking pleas upon his friend, Elias was finally compelled to accept his friend's proposal.
Horatio's repeated gest was, "It's you and me, Partner. We're gonna hit it big ... I can smell it!"

When the boys announced they were leaving it caught their parents off guard.

Needless to say, the decision to leave home didn't sit well with their families at first. The thought of their departure wore on the mind of Niles the hardest because he was a single parent.

Initially, he thought his son was making the right decision and Niles was eager to help Horatio out by giving him all the money he had on hand. "After all," He thought, "This is all for the best. I want Horatio to have a better life than me." But, as time passed, and days turned to months and months into years, Niles changed his mind. His attitude would eventually turn into cold and callous resentment once he came to the conclusion his son had abandoned him. His final assessment was, "I'm an old man, left all alone to fend for himself!" Niles developed a fondness for the companionship of a whiskey bottle - that habitual passion would fuel his anger, and thus a change of heart.

The Irwins were disappointed and heart broken by their son's decision as well, but they gave Elias their blessings, what savings they had, a good horse, and sent him on his way; hoping he would make a better life for himself than they had.

Although it took a few days to get to Chicago on horseback, the young men did have a routine trip and arrived in the city on October 8th. Of immediate concern to them upon arrival was their need for a place to stay. As luck, or fate would have it, they found a boarding house with rooms for rent on De Koven Street.

The sign in the front window of the home boldly said, "I got rooms!"

Elias didn't realize it at the time, but he and his friend were about to knock on the door of Gywnn McQue, and in a moment, that young man's life was about to change forever - the hand of destiny was ready to deal the cards for all to play.

Gywnn was a 25-year-old widow, struggling to raise her son. Edward, her seven-year old, was terminally ill. He had been suffering from the disabling effects of tuberculosis for some time.

That day wasn't one Gywnn cared to talk about or celebrate. For it marked the seventh anniversary of *The Great Chicago Fire*. The widow lost her husband in that fire. Her husband was a courageous man, a fireman, who lost his life while fighting those flames.

Several witnesses testified he saved many from a handful of burning buildings, but he died in his pursuit of saving others when a wall collapsed on him and the baby boy he was carrying. The city would mourn his loss and that of many others for a long time to come, for three hundred poor souls perished in the blaze.

The fire started on Sunday evening, October 8th, 1871, but it didn't die out until the early morning hours of Tuesday, the 10th. The blaze began in the barn of Patrick and Catherine O'Leary. The couple lived on Chicago's west side. The address was 137 De Koven. Oddly enough, their home was spared from the flames of destruction.

Although many buildings in the surrounding area had since been rebuilt, there were still tell-tale signs of where the fire had raged. The fire cut a destructive path through Chicago measuring some 3 1/3 square miles in size before it could be brought under control. The flames destroyed an estimated 192-million-dollars-worth of property, and left over 100,000 people homeless.

A board of Chicago Police and Fire Commissioners failed to ascertain the fire's cause, even after fifty different witnesses had been interviewed and over 1,100 pages of their handwritten testimony had been recorded.

The fire was later believed to have been started by a cow. Many believe, to this day, the blaze began when the animal kicked over a lit lantern. Could that be just a 19th century urban legend? Well, Chicago real estate records and other source materials of the period provide powerful evidence to demonstrate there may very well be some truth in that claim.

Gywnn opened the door soon after Horatio knocked on it. Then with an unassuming smile, she said, "Can I help you?"

Horatio replied, "My friend and I would like to rent a room."

"What's your names?" Gywnn inquired with a sense of relief and a broadened smile. She realized a double stroke of financial opportunity had come knocking on her needy household's door.

Pointing to himself, then to his friend, Horatio said, "I'm Horatio Cavendish ... this is my friend, Elias."

Gywnn offered her hand to greet Horatio first. After he shook her hand, she then extended her outstretched palm toward Elias. Elias stepped forward slightly from where he stood, then held Gywnn's hand for what seemed like a long time. Horatio couldn't help but notice what his friend was doing, and thought, "All right ... that's enough," then pushed Elias's hand gently away from Gywnn's.

Gywnn was intensely attractive, her beauty captivating, but Horatio didn't think so. Elias was unable to say much in response to her greeting, but he did manage to whisper under his breath, the words, "Glad to meet you."

Elias had a great deal of difficulty expressing himself because he was so fascinated with Gywnn. The thought, "She's the most beautiful woman I've ever seen," kept running through Elias's mind. The vision of her long brown hair, blue eyes, soft rosy cheeks, and 5' 3" shapely frame, was something to behold.

Horatio couldn't help but notice the rude behavior of his friend, and quickly stepped in front of Elias to ask how much rent would be. Gwynn replied, "It's three dollars a week ... if the two of you don't mind sharing a room, I'll make it fifteen a month."

Horatio said, "That'll be fine," and reached down in his pocket to retrieve the cash.

While Horatio was paying Gywnn her fifteen-dollar fee, Elias thought, "That'll be fine," as he shook his head slightly up and down in agreement as he stood beside their new landlady. The teen could only mustard a smile as he stared at the soft-spoken lady, but, by now, all words had eluded him.

Gwynn gave Elias and Horatio one of the rooms upstairs. She changed the linen on their beds once a week, brought them fresh water daily, and was faithful to cook three meals a day. If they were to eat, the young men had to go downstairs to eat with Gywnn and her son at the supper table. Since Elias and Horatio were her only boarders, Gywnn made that a requirement and long-standing house rule.

Neither Horatio or Elias had any difficulty settling in. Gywnn made them feel comfortable and quite at home. They adjusted well to their new environment - life in the big city. Horatio landed a job in less than a week, but Elias's efforts took a little longer and he was finally able to secure employment after three weeks.

Horatio began his career as a junior accountant for a local banker. Elias began his career in the engineering field as an architect's assistant.

Horatio and Elias were your typical roommates. They argued with each other on occasion, but both men had developed a strong friendly bond with each other over the past few years. Both had their share of bad habits though. Elias had the habit of snoring quite loudly. His snoring almost always woke Horatio up, but a properly placed pillow over his friend's mouth usually helped do the trick without even waking the bothersome fellow.

Horatio wasn't void of bad habits either. He would occasionally talk in his sleep and even walked around in his sleep a time or two. Horatio suffered through the horrifying experience of reoccurring nightmares often, and one in particular.

The dream would always begin with him being the only one in a funeral parlor. When he would walk over to the plain wooden coffin laying before him and open it, he always saw himself inside. Horatio would then realize he was dead, but also noticed the coffin to be full of money. The next portion of the dream would always fast forward to a cemetery. Again, Horatio was the only one in attendance and the grave would bear no headstone or markings of any kind. Horatio almost always woke up with night sweats after having that dream, but he just reasoned it to be foolish fancy and never told anyone.

Horatio's ambitious pursuit of success began quite early in

life. With some savings to his credit, he first approached his boss for a loan when he turned twenty. His vision was still focused on the railroads, but the defiant banker would deny all six attempts by Horatio to secure the needed capital for a new start-up company. Those rejections and repeated denial never really discouraged the young man, they actually fueled his passion to try harder.

Elias and Horatio had always been different from each other. Their personalities varied greatly, but their social lives were also becoming vastly uncharacteristic of each other. Horatio worked long hours and found little time for anything except the pursuit of his vision - wealth. Elias on the other hand, rarely worked past ten hours a day. He had a habit of bringing food home, as well as flowers once in a while, and placing them on the kitchen table for Gywnn. Elias's love for Gywnn was growing, but he never told her how he felt or who was responsible for all those numerous gifts of kindness - although she obviously knew who it was.

Unfortunately, Gywnn's son, Edward, died as a result of his long struggle with "TB" in the spring of' '79. Gywnn took the loss quite hard. Horatio was never around much anymore, so Elias took it upon himself to spend more time with Gywnn in an effort to comfort her as she mourned the loss of her son.

Elias's feelings for Gywnn had developed into something more than just friendship a long time ago, but it took Gywnn a long time to realize he was in love with her. After Edward's death, she began to see his affection for her in a more pronounced way. She finally realized his feelings for her were advanced past friendship when a letter arrived for Horatio only days before Thanksgiving - the letter was from Burnt Plain.

The note read:

Niles began to blame himself for their deaths once the Irwins were laid to rest, just like he did at sea when the Smiths perished along with his wife. That burden of self-imposed guilt now weighed heavily upon his shoulders, it would for the rest of his life, for Niles reasoned the Irwins died while on their way to visit him.

In reality, the Irwins were indeed on their way to visit their friend. Their food supply was dangerously low and they thought it would be best to stay with Niles until the storm blew over when they could resupply themselves. The distance between both homes was a short walk the Irwins had made many times before, and in all kinds of weather, but they failed to realize how severe the conditions outside truly were and gravely underestimated the storm's ferocity. Before they could reach Niles's home Eli suffered a heart attack.

When he insisted Mary should go for help, she refused. She
argued with Eli that she'd have difficulty finding her way to
Niles's place in the dark and feared getting lost in that blinding
snow, so she decided it was best not to leave her husband alone
in the cold. It was a fateful decision that would ultimately cost
them both their lives.

Almost everyone who lived in or around Burnt Plain knew
the Irwins were prepared for what lay in store for them after
death. Thanks to Walden Freedman, and his persistent sermons
on hellfire and brimstone, both Eli and Mary had openly
embraced the Christian faith several years before and many
believed heaven was now their eternal home - all except for
Niles.

In spite of the numerous efforts made by his friends to lead
him to a saving knowledge of Jesus Christ, Niles refused to
believe in God at all. He would eventually die in that hopeless
pool of self-pity he created for himself and perish a poor drunk
who also gave God a share of the blame for the death of his wife
and friends.

Horatio believed, as his father did, that God didn't exist.

On the other hand, Elias believed in God, but he wasn't
committed to leading a sustained Christian life as his parents did.
He was always of the opinion God doesn't control the
circumstances of life - we do. His firm belief was, to get anywhere
in life one must become their own *self-made man.*

Elias loved his parents, and their death was a difficult thing for
him to accept. He chose to travel back to Burnt Plain for the
funeral, but when Elias asked his friend to accompany him on the
trip Horatio declined the invitation and elected to stay in Chicago.

Before he left, Elias hugged Gwynn tightly, then told her, "I have nothing left except you and Horatio." He felt now was the best time to pose the question he had been contemplating for weeks, so Elias dropped to one knee, grabbed Gywnn's hand, then said, "Gywnn, I love you ... I always have ... I don't know how else to say this, but ... will you marry me?"

Needless to say, Gywnn was caught totally off guard by that. After she pulled her hand from his, Gywnn walked over to sit down on a nearby chair. After she had given Elias's proposal a few brief moments of thought, she politely turned him down. Her reasoning was, "It's just simply too soon."

Elias spent nearly the entire month of December in Burnt Plain, but he was able to make it back in time for Christmas.

A couple days before the holiday, Horatio took the afternoon off to get a haircut. Fred O'Brien was Horatio's favorite barber. He owned the local barber shop on the comer across the street from the bank where Horatio worked. Fred was having a slow day that day and since there were no customers waiting in line when Horatio walked in, the barber told him, "Have a seat!"

After Horatio sat down, Fred began to trim his hair and then the front door blew open. The rush of cold frigid air left a noticeable chill in the room. That's when Fred shouted, "Shut the door!"

An older gentleman stepped through the door, shut it behind himself, then said, "I apologize ... the wind blew the door right out of my hands when I tried to open it."

Fred looked up to make eye contact with the man, then silently nodded his head as to say, "I understand," and went back to trimming Horatio's hair.

The customer hung his coat, hat, and gloves on the old
wooden circular coat rack that stood in the corner of the tiny
room. The elderly gentleman then shuffled his way over to the
chairs that lined the wall directly across from the barber's chair and
sat down. Fred told the customer, "Make yourself comfortable, I'll
be right with ya ... after I finish with Horatio here."

As soon as Fred said that, the gray-haired gentleman appeared
to be lost for a moment in his thoughts. He then said, "Horatio? ...
You wouldn't happen to be that same Horatio who works for my
banker friend across the street, would you?"

With a puzzled, yet curious look upon his face, Horatio replied,
"I work at the bank across the street ... that's right ... my name's
Horatio Cavendish." Looking down his nose at the man, Horatio
said, "Do I know you?"

The elderly, soft-spoken, man said, "I'm Lourse O'Grady ... I've
heard a lot about you … young man!"

Horatio had never met Mr. O'Grady in person before, but he
sure did recognize the name. Lourse O'Grady was a very
important businessman in those days. He owned a large amount
of property in and around the city of Chicago. O'Grady was a very
wealthy man; he acquired those riches through the transactions of
buying and selling real estate.

Once Fred finished trimming Horatio's hair, it was Lourse's
turn to have a seat in the barber's chair. Horatio paid O'Brien for
his services, then he walked over to the coat rack in the comer to
don his coat and gloves. Before he opened the door to leave,
Horatio hesitated for a moment when he grabbed the door handle.
He then turned and nervously made his way towards the wealthy
businessman. Horatio removed his glove, extended his hand

toward Lourse, and said, "It's been a pleasure to meet you, Sir!"

O'Grady extended his hand toward Horatio, and with a firm grip shook hands with the young man. Lourse then said, "I'm throwing a party at my office on New Year's ... why don't you stop by ... I've got some friends I'd like you to meet."

Horatio tried to conceal the excitement that boiled within him with a disguise of professionalism; he pulled the feat off by keeping a straight face and acting dignified. He said, "I'll be there," but his emotions were hard to contain. Afterall, never in his wildest dreams would Horatio ever envision the richest man in Chicago inviting him to a private party, especially one in which the rich and famous would surely attend.

Horatio was quite nervous about attending a Lourse O'Grady's party, for he had some serious inner reservations about it, but he kept his promise and arrived at the businessman's office at 8 O'clock on New Year's Eve.

When he got there, Horatio couldn't help but notice the expensive furnishings O'Grady had in his lavish penthouse office; it was obvious no expense had been spared. Even Lourse himself would later comment, with a great deal of boldness, "This place is decorated with nothing but the best!"

As soon as Horatio stepped inside the door he was asked, "May I take your garment, Sir?" by a male servant who was dressed in all white attire who waited upon the guests when they arrived. After he surrendered his coat and gloves to the kind and helpful man, Horatio walked down a long hall toward a large open room where he could hear others talking and laughing.

His mind was quickly filled with a host of pondering thoughts. "Who's really in that room?" He tried to guess with foolish

reason. "The Mayor is in there ... I just know it ... the Chief of
Police is probably in there too." Horatio thought.

Horatio was nervous, but he was also quite anxious to meet
some important people that night. As he walked down the hall,
Horatio tried to rehearse the responses he would give if anyone
dared speak to him. Before he could enter the room, Horatio was
distracted by the presence of a young, beautiful, female hostess
who was standing just outside the doorway. Horatio was indeed
nervous, but he convinced himself what she had to offer was just
too tempting to pass up and approached the young lady. In a soft
voice, she inquired of Horatio, "Drink, Sir?" He then took one
of the alcoholic beverages from the tray she held and downed it
in short order. Horatio wiped his lips with his fingers, placed the
empty glass back on the tray, then mustered up the courage to
walk into that room.

Once inside the room, Horatio tried to keep to himself and hide
in the shadow of everyone else's conversations.

Horatio's strategy didn't work for long though, for Lourse soon
recognized him among the crowd.

The elderly O'Grady shuffled his way over toward Horatio,
then Lourse asked the young man to come with him. After they
stepped away from the party, the wealthy businessman led
Horatio to his private office. Once they were inside the office,
Lourse said, "Shut the door." Horatio closed the door, then
Lourse said, "Have a seat, son."

After Horatio made himself comfortable in one of the
expensive overstuffed chairs across from O'Grady's desk, he
said, "I feel so out of place wearing just a necktie," as he looked
down to play with it for a moment with his fingers. "The women

look so beautiful in those evening dresses ... and the men ... those dinner jackets!"

Lourse responded by placing his hands behind his head and leaning slightly backward in the chair. "I want you to have a good time tonight ... don't worry ... most of those people won't even notice after they've gotten a few drinks in their bellies."

Horatio then curiously asked, "Sir, why did you invite me down here?"

Lourse replied, "That's what I'd like to speak with you about." As Horatio listened with intent, O'Grady went on to say, "You remind me of myself as a young man ... when I first got into business. Your boss tells me you're a whiz with the books. He said you've tried several times to secure a loan from him. He says you think railroads are big business ... is that true?"

Horatio replied, "Yes ... I think there's a lot of money to be made out there ... I just need a chance to prove it."

The businessman's countenance got a bit more serious. Lourse leaned forward in his chair, then placed his elbows on the desk and began to slightly tap all of his fingers together. After a brief moment of thought, he said, "I hear he turned you down every time. He's a good man, son, but he's a lot more conservative than me. Horatio ... I admire your determination. I tell you what, let's don't beat around the bush any longer, shall we? I've got a business proposal for you."

"What might that be, Sir?" Horatio replied.

"First of all, don't call me, Sir. My business partners call me Lourse."

Horatio was quick to reply, "I don't understand."

"Here's the deal, Horatio. I'll see to it you get all the capital

you need to start that railroad. It'll be a loan of course ... we'll
work out the details on that later." After he hesitated for a
moment, Lourse then went on to say, "Hey ... I've got a real nice
building in Mt. Prospect ... it's not too far from here. It would
make a great office for you. I'll rent it to you till you're in a
position to buy."

Horatio couldn't believe O'Grady was offering such an
opportunity. He then asked of the businessman, "Why are you
doing this?"

"You gotta start somewhere, Horatio ... believe me, if I didn't
think it would make me money, I wouldn't go to the trouble."

Horatio replied, "I don't know what to say!"

Lourse smiled as a result of that comment and got up from
behind his desk to make his way toward Horatio. He placed his
hand on the young man's shoulder, then said, "Don't say a thing,
just make us a pile of money ... You'll need to consider going
public with the company though. I can be pretty persuasive. I'm
sure I can talk a few of my friends into investing in a new business
adventure ... I'd be the first to buy those shares! Besides, we Irish
need to stick together ... right ... now …let's go back to that party
… shall we?"

Horatio later told Elias of what the businessman had offered,
and then asked his friend to become his partner. Elias was truly
grateful Horatio had thought of him, and he accepted his friend's
proposal.

With the help of Lourse O'Grady, and a number of
other investors, *The Irwin ~ Cavendish Company* successfully
opened its doors for business on March 15th, 1880. Horatio and
Elias had worked long and hard for the establishment of that new

railroad, and the *C - I Line* was a result of their efforts. Both men were in full agreement the corporate headquarters should be based in that rented office building located in the Chicago suburb of Mt. Prospect, Illinois as well.

Horatio had six manufacturers to choose from who produced Locomotives at the time. Two were located in Patterson, New Jersey. Those companies were the Grant Locomotive Works and the Rogers Locomotive & Machine Works. Two other manufacturers were headquartered in Pennsylvania. They were the Dickson Manufacturing Company of Scranton and the Baldwin Locomotive Works - owned by the Burnham, Parry, & Williams Company of Philadelphia. The Schenectody Locomotive Works located in Schenectody, New York and the Tournton Locomotive Manufacturing Company of Toumton, Massachusetts were also producers of engines as well.

The first Locomotives Horatio purchased for the company were a pair of second hand Dicksons. Those engines were a great deal of trouble though; they simply weren't reliable. They were constantly breaking down and always seemed to require the type of repair that was expensive.

Within a matter of a few short months, Horatio decided it was time to purchase additional engines - his assessment was they would be better off buying new equipment. He then narrowed the competitors down to the Grant and Baldwin Companies for they offered the benefit of "Interchangeable Parts." He eventually decided on the purchase of four Grant engines, followed by the purchase of an additional four Baldwin Locomotives later. The Baldwin engine seemed to produce the best results for the money, and they broke down less often, so Horatio purchased all of the company's remaining Locomotives from The Baldwin Works in Philadelphia. Horatio always ordered five engines at a time. He did that on thirty-five different occasions until *The C & I Line* eventually obtained a fleet of eighty Locomotives.

Chapter Three
The Golden Spoon

Horatio and Elias had been in business almost two years now, and a sense of excitement could be felt there in the Mt. Prospect air. An atmosphere of celebration lay hold of Elias's heart, for the holiday season was here once again.

Although Elias thought of Gywnn often, he never took it upon himself to visit her again after he and Horatio moved from her residence. Christmas was only a week away and Elias told his partner he planned to spend the following day in Chicago. He had convinced Horatio he was going to the city in order to buy presents for the holiday, but Elias had something different in mind. He did plan to purchase a few gifts, but the true reason for making the trip was he wanted to visit that home on De Koven Street once more.

Elias loved Gywnn, he always had. His actions were being driven by the motivation of a deeply passionate heart, one full of affection for a woman of breath-taking beauty.

The sensitization that stimulated his heart was something much too difficult to resist. From the first day Elias met Gywnn he knew he loved her. That feeling of delight never died with the passing of time. As the days, months, and years flew by, his love for Gywnn grew even more profound from within.

That much anticipated day had indeed come. Elias had just finished purchasing a small handful of gifts before he arrived at Gywnn's residence. Elias was enthusiastic, but also quite nervous as he walked up those front steps. The steps, as well as the porch, were covered with several inches of snow - it appeared no one cared to clean them. Elias waded through the crusty drifts and stood before the window to remove a glove. He then gently rubbed the palm of his hand across the frozen pane to remove a bit of frost to peer inside. Elias noticed an illumination of light from within. A kerosene lamp sitting on the table lit the room, giving the curious fellow a clear view. Elias decided it was best to then knock, and did so several times, as he stood anxiously by. Elias's mind then began to fill with the thought of, "I hope this works!" as anticipation grew while he nervously chewed on his lower lip and waited for Gywnn to answer the door.

Elias's wait was a short one, but in his mind it was a frightening ordeal just the same. It was only a brief moment or so after he knocked when Elias saw a finger slowly move the window curtain to the side. It was obscure, but Elias was able to catch a glimpse of Gywnn's face through the frosted pane. Her facial expression first revealed the emotion of curiosity, then worry, then finally the indication of perplexity. Once Gywnn recognized it was Elias she opened the door, then her facial features reverted to a smile.

"I'm surprised to see you ... come on in!" Gywnn said with a broad grin. While Elias gently tapped his shoes on the floor rug to remove the snow from his feet, Gwynn extended her hand, then said, "Here ... let me take your coat!"

Elias removed his hat, coat, and gloves, and handed them to Gywnn, then responded to her kindness by saying, "Thank you."

After she hung the garments up, Gywnn said, "What brings you by these parts?"

Elias replied, "Oh ... I just happened to be in the neighborhood ... thought I'd pay a visit."

Gwynn extended her hand, then pointed towards the dining room table and said, "Won't you please have a seat ... I'll make us a cup of tea."

Elias said, "I'd like that" then took a seat and proceeded to make himself comfortable.

After Gywnn returned with the tea, she sat down and both individuals began to strike up further conversation.

Elias first asked, "How have you been?"

Gywnn responded by saying, "Good," but that was a contradiction of the truth. She replied by using only a single word, but it was given to mislead Elias, to deceive him, and carefully hide the true circumstances that surrounded her. Gywnn wasn't fine at all. She was several months behind on her mortgage payments and the flow of boarders had since dried up as well. Gywnn was indeed surprised to see Elias at her door, for she thought that knock would surely be her banker. She had been anticipating his arrival and dreaded the day for quite a while. Gywnn was convinced he was coming soon and the banker would bring news of repossession, then eviction.

Elias had been visiting about half an hour or so when he decided to gather his courage and tell Gywnn the true reason why he was there. Gywnn could sense the conversation was turning serious by now, so she sat quietly by as Elias revealed what he had to say. Reaching across the table to hold Gywnn's hand, Elias carefully chose his words, stared at Gywnn for a moment, then said, "Gywnn ... I have to be honest with you ... I didn't really just happen to be in the area. I came by to ... Gywnn ... I don't know how else to say this ... I love you. I always have! I decided, since it's the holidays and all ..." Elias looked down, then hesitated for a moment and said, "Well ... I realize it's been a long time, but I decided to try once more ... " A tear began to well in the comer of Elias's eye as he said, "To see if you'd marry me!"

Gywnn sighed with relief; then she began to cry.

Worried and troubled by that response, Elias gripped Gywnn's hand a little tighter, then he began to reason with her in an effort to settle what he thought was her obvious concerns about the proposal. "Horatio and I are doing really well, business is booming!" After a brief moment of hesitation, Elias said, "I'll be a good provider ... I'll make you a great husband, I promise ... I'll see to it you'll never lack for anything. I swear!"

Wiping the tears from her eyes in an effort to regain her composure, Gwynn squeezed Elias's hand, then said, "Oh, Elias ... I've been a foolish woman ... I was crazy to say no. I loved the way you played with Edward and the way you cared for me." With a smile, Gwynn said, "You were always so kind." After a brief moment of hesitation, Gwynn went on to say, "I was concerned the neighbors would think badly of me for marrying a younger man ... I was a fool for saying no."

Elias continued to hold Gywnn's hand and quietly listened to her response with a half-hearted smile as he sat there in anticipation of a positive answer that was hopefully forthcoming.

Gywnn reached across the table to gently place her free hand around the back of Elias's neck, then she gave him a passionate kiss on the cheek. Gwynn then gripped Elias's hand a little tighter as she asked, "Can you ever forgive me?"

Elias nodded his head as to silently say yes, but he was really puzzled by now. He just wanted a quick and simple answer to the question, but he was beginning to think Gwynn was going to reject his marriage proposal for the second time.

Gywnn was then overcome by the emotions that had been building from within as she began to cry even more. "I loved you too ... but I could never say it. I love you, Elias Irwin ... I always have!" As the tears began to trickle down Elias's cheeks, Gywnn sighed once again, then said, "If you dare to spend the rest of your life with me ... well ... the answer would have to be Y-E-S!"

To say Elias was elated with Gywnn's positive response would be rather something of an understatement. The emotion he felt at that moment gripped the very fiber of his soul and the warmth of her smile filled his heart with an excess of jubilant glee that drifted over into euphoria.

After a brief bit of extended conversation between the two, Elias found Gywnn to be in full agreement with these life changing plans. He experienced virtually no resistance from his bride-to-be when he convinced her the wedding ceremony should be conducted with a hint of romanticism. The gentle persuasion of her fiance was convincing Gywnn, and she agreed, to have the wedding date set for February, Valentine's Day.

Those plans for matrimony were exciting and all, but the reality of Gywnn's financial situation was now weighing heavily upon her mind.

Gywnn reached out to hold Elias's hand, then softy said, "I believe a strong relationship should be based upon honesty ... don't you, Elias?"

He responded with a concerned reply of, "Yes," then added, "Is something wrong?"

"I haven't been entirely honest with you today ... I'm not really fine at all! The bank's ready to repossess this place ... I thought you were the banker when I answered the door. I fell behind in my mortgage payments after the boarders dried up." With a tear beginning to well in the corner of her eye, Gywnn said, "I'm sorry ... I will never lie, or hide the truth from you again ... I love you ... please forgive me!"

Elias grabbed Gywnn by the neck and pulled her to his chest for a long extended romantic embrace. Gywnn cried while Elias rubbed his fingers through her hair. He reassured the love of his life that, "Everything's gonna be fine ... it's nothing that can't be fixed ... trust me."

Before Elias left for his trip to Chicago, he jokingly told Horatio he might stop by Gywnn's place and give that second proposal a try. Horatio didn't seem overly optimistic, but he did wish his business partner and close friend all the best of luck - if he decided to try.

After Elias returned to Mt. Prospect, he informed his friend of Gywnn's acceptance of the marriage proposal. Horatio seemed to be reserved with his happiness and wasn't overly elated with the favor Elias asked for at the time either. That request was one that would truly test Horatio's patience and the strength of his friendly relationship with Elias.

The truth of the matter was, Elias hadn't been entirely honest with Gwynn either.

Although the *Irwin ~ Cavendish Company* shareholders were reaping an above average return on their investment, Elias and Horatio weren't privileged to that same type of financial benefit. Because he was the President and Treasurer of the Corporation,

Horatio stood firm to believe that type of fiscal policy should be maintained, and he hung on to that line of thinking for at least the first few years while the business flourished.

Elias and his partner weren't living in poverty, but they weren't living high on the hog by no means either. They were both living together in one of Lourse O'Grady's worn-down rental properties in Mt. Prospect. Their office was nothing more than a glorified shack that needed a few coats of paint and a great deal of repair as well.

An explanation of why Lourse O'Grady was so interested in real estate on the distant outskirts of Chicago would be best explained by a brief historical narrative of how Mt. Prospect came to be.

A mass of people from New England and the New York area began to migrate to the upper Midwest in the 1830's. By 1833, a treaty had been signed with the Indian tribe, the Potawatomi. In that treaty, the Potawatomi ceded all the land surrounding Chicago which then made it available for settlers.

When the first American settlers came to what would later become Mt. Prospect, they found a wide-open space covered in prairie grass. Yankees were the first American settlers to the area and the first to clear the land and establish farms. However, around 1850, most of those first settlers left the area. They left for different reasons, some were adventuresome and went further west, others headed for the coasts, either by being drawn by the gold rush in California or finding the west lonely and moving back to New England.

The second group to come to the area were German. A wave of German immigrants came to American in the 1840's along with a major Irish immigration as well. The Germans tended to move further west than the Irish did and those Germans, who were almost entirely Lutheran, were said to be the first to take up residence in Mt. Prospect.

What the German settlers did that the Yankees hadn't, was work to establish a community. Many of them came to the "New World" with the intention of preserving their religious and cultural traditions. Because of that, it was important to the community to establish institutions of which would pass on cultural traditions.

In 1848, a short time after the first Germans arrived, the "Saint John Lutheran Church" was founded. The village went on to be developed as a farming community; then in 1850, the first train rolled into town.

The person who actually decided to build a train station and a town was a man named Ezra Eggleston. He bought most of the land that later became downtown Mt. Prospect in 1874. Eggleston planned to build a train station, lay roads, and then divide the land up into small parcels to sell at a profit. He also gave Mt. Prospect its name. ”Mount” because the land sat on some of the highest land in Cook County, and "Prospect" to proclaim there were great prospects in the area. Ezra meant to make his fortune from that development, however he had poor timing. Three years before Ezra started building, in 1871, the "Chicago Fire" blazed through downtown. People in Chicago were rebuilding when Ezra was trying to sell them new land. As if that wasn't bad enough there was also the Panic of 1873, which was called the "Great Depression" until 1930. Because of those financial factors, there were few who were interested in Eggleston's land speculations.

Although Ezra was not very good at making money, he did give the town its name and built the first train station.   He also laid the roads and divided the village into city blocks. A couple of years after Eggleston sold his interest in the community, other people began to build houses and stores downtown which made Mount Prospect come to life.

Lourse O'Grady was one of the those who finally took notice of Eggleston's speculative adventure, but financial gain wasn't the only reason why the wealthy Chicago businessman had an interest in Mt. Prospect.

It's been said the love of money is the root of all evil and absolute power corrupts men absolutely. Both of those statements could no doubt be construed as a vivid description

of the personalities of Ezra Eggleston and Lourse O'Grady. Although not even a single word from either quote would ever be etched upon either man's tombstone, all those who knew them had the consensus of opinion that both men had a fascination for money. It was their endeavors to acquire that almighty dollar that gave them such a reputation, and their thirst for power. Ezra had big dreams, his being financial. Lourse had lofty goals too, but his were somewhat of a different sort.

Many think money is power. Wealth can provide a sense of security, but large amounts of those green bills can also twist an individual's mind with misapprehension and illusion.

O'Grady purchased most of Ezra Eggleton's interests because he wanted to buy his own town. He envisioned substituting names like "Lourseston" or "O'Gradyville" for what he perceived as an awful tag called Mount Prospect. Once Lourse realized his investment in Mt. Prospect wasn't returning dividends as quickly as anticipated, he gave the matter some more thought. He then later decided to recede on that lofty ambition. He would eventually sell off what property he could and rent the rest.

In reality, O'Grady just wanted to unload some property in Mt. Prospect when Horatio came along. Lourse heard through a mutual friend that the young Cavendish had lofty goals in mind. O'Grady was aware of Horatio's vision of vast fortunes in railroads, but he wasn't so optimistic about the young man's future either. If Lourse could make a few bucks from a deal he would, but the tycoon's financial well-being was always first and foremost above all else. Lourse was a powerful and persuasive man. He thought if he could convince Horatio his business offer was a good financial fit for all involved, he could relieve himself of those run down Mt. Prospect properties he longed to unload.

He would never verbally say so, but Lourse thought Horatio was young and naive. The wealthy businessman was confident he could convince Horatio to accept his offer. Lourse would repeatedly lend his reasoning to the following thoughts: "The railroad runs through town and there's a train station. It won't be hard to convince that young pup to take the deal. Besides, if he fails on the loan I still got the buildings and something called risk-free collateral ... locomotives!"

For quite a while, Elias had been under the impression Lourse O'Grady was looking out for the well-being of himself and none other; Horatio's mind was etched with the same type of perception as well. It was the heart's desire of both those fledgling entrepreneurs to separate themselves from the influence of that dominating Chicago businessman's greed.

That favor Elias requested of his friend was for new terms on the living arrangements they had. Elias wanted to know if Gywnn could live with them for a while. Horatio was totally against the idea at first, but he later gave the matter a great deal more thought and relented on that hard stance he had. He even suggested to Elias that, "If you think you really love Gywnn ... which I'm sure you do ... well ... who am I to stand in the way of happiness?"

Elias assured Horatio that as soon as Gywnn's home sold, and the couple could put together the financial arrangements to buy another place, he and his bride would make their departure.

Gywnn and Elias's wedding plans were carried out with relative ease and were absence of all incident. The couple were married on Valentine's Day, 1882, and they honeymooned in upstate New York at Niagara Falls the following week. But before they left Mt. Prospect, Elias used his savings to bring Gywnn's mortgage payments up-to-date, then he put her home up for sale. Gywnn's De Koven Street home was purchased by an older couple only twenty-one days after it was put on the market for sale. The closing ran smoothly, and at the end of the meeting Gywnn's banker handed her and Elias a tidy some of cash - it was money due them from the equity remaining in the home. Shortly after the banker began to count out bills and lay them down, Elias said, "Wait a minute!"

"Is something wrong?" the banker inquired.

Elias quickly glanced over at Gywnn and gave her a wink. "I got an idea ... trust me!" He suggested.

The energetic newlywed scooped up the bills lying on the table, then handed them back to the banker. With a puzzled look on his face, the banker said, "I don't understand!"

"We wanna use this money for a down payment on a new home!" Elias explained with a great deal of enthusiastic reasoning.

Still bewildered, the banker reluctantly pulled the cash back to his side of the table.

Then he said, "What was it you folks had in mind?"

Elias said, "I got my eye on this nice comer lot in Mt. Prospect, you see!" He then reached over to grab Gywnn's hand, and added, "I know a contractor or two ..." Elias turned his head to stare at Gywnn, then he winked at her while saying, "Sir ... we wanna build a new home!" Gywnn's smile was then quick to become enormous. Elias knew he had gained the approval of his wife so he turned his eyes toward the banker to engage that stern look he had. As he stared the banker in the eye to explain, "The way I see it ..." Elias turned his head to quickly wink at Gywnn once more, then added, "If there is a note, I'll have it paid off in less than five years, guaranteed!"

The banker was truly surprised by this new twist, and that tum of events forced him to make an immediate decision. After he raised his forefinger vertically to position it to his lips, the banker gave the proposal a brief moment of thought, then he reasoned the plan to be a safe one financially. He then lowered his hand to the table and folded his arms over each other. As he nodded his head, the banker informed the couple, "If that's what you'd like to do, I'll draw up the papers next week."

Elias was quick to stare over at Gywnn, but only briefly, then he raised his head to focus his eyes on that concerned stare of the banker. After a brief moment of thought, Elias cleared his throat, then asked, "Does that mean we have a deal?"

As he extended his hand toward Elias, the banker said, "I believe we do!"

A wealth of things was set in motion when both men shook hands that day; it was truly a favorable time that the couple wouldn't soon forget. From that day forward, a tremendous blessing of financial prosperity would begin to build for the Irwins as well.

The 1880's and 90's were decades that exhibited a tremendous amount of growth for the *Irwin ~ Cavendish Company.* The decision to go public with the sale of corporate stock was the best decision Horatio and Elias could have ever made - it gave them the monetary means and provision needed to expand into markets that were only just now being explored. As company stock prices rose, more and more investors were willing to take the risk of coming along for the profitable financial ride.

It was early on, at the threshold of their business adventure, that both partners shared the conviction they should follow what avenues they knew best and were most familiar with. It was the memory of Elias's father, and the thought of his ranching profession, that gave the *Irwin ~ Cavendish Company* inspiration to form their first corporate division. It was the memory of Eli that gave them the determination to venture into a new, yet booming, market as well. That market featured a commodity called BEEF. It didn't take long for the partners to make an assessment the cattle industry was a unique and lucrative business. Once they began to ship the stubborn beasts, the freight contracts seemed to just pour in! Boxcar upon boxcar, filled to capacity with bovine, would eventually make their way from the cattle ranches out West to the slaughterhouses of the Midwest,

East Coast, and Deep South. The residents of Chicago, New York, Philadelphia, and Atlanta could all enjoy the taste of a great steak by now, but *The Irwin ~ Cavendish Company* was enjoying the sweet savory smell of financial gain as well.

In the 1890's, Elias and Horatio switched their focus once again to another market - it would be the most valuable decision they ever made; the importance of which seemed to be beyond their human understanding or sense of measure. Another corporate division was formed from that reasoning, and with that decision came the success all Wall Street analysts are looking for in terms of wealth and social status.

The 19th century was coming to a close, but *The Irwin ~ Cavendish Company* had only just begun to reap the financial benefit of time. The company felt it was necessary to take advantage of the land grant opportunities the government had given railroads, and they used it to their advantage in purchasing the timber rights on large tracts of land in the Pacific Northwest.

The Government wanted to develop the West by offering those generous land grants, but in doing so many companies lined their pockets with the benefit of it. One of those companies was *Irwin ~ Cavendish,* and it wouldn't be until well into the 20th century before Horatio and Elias would cease using such generous congressional rewards.

The housing industry was a ripe market to pluck at the turn of the century and Horatio knew there was an ever-increasing need for homes, so he and his partner began to build an elaborate system of sawmill operations in states like Oregon and Washington to supply lumber for all those families who needed a roof over their heads. Once the trees were felled, they were hauled the short distance to the mill where they were cut into finished lumber. The finished product would then be loaded upon boxcars and shipped to a number of destinations eastward. The idea did indeed give leverage to the truth of "The Supply & Demand Theory," but it was also that concept that made Horatio and Elias rich beyond their wildest dreams!

It was obvious the miraculous power of prosperity was shining its glorious light upon the offspring of those immigrants, the ones who had dared take a life changing chance. It had only been a few short years since Horatio and Elias made that costly voyage with their parents from England, but money and its hypnotizing effects had spellbound them. It lured them in the direction of forgetful reasoning, and the selfish attitudes that come with that line of thought. Those men, who had experienced struggle and tasted the bitter experience of fate, were now too busy to understand the illusory phantom that had a grasp on their hearts. The spiritual blessings that were being rained down upon them was something far beyond their compreh e nsion - a greedy mind will always be clouded from the truth! In spite of their failure to comprehend the origin of all that wealth, and where it really came from, the Irwins good fortune did indeed abound - but God wasn't finished with His delivery of divine gifts quite yet.

The Creator's decision to endow the couple with a bit more blissful happiness was magnified when Gywnn discovered she was pregnant. The pregnancy went well and Gywnn gave birth to a beautiful baby boy on April 3rd, 1888 - the jubilant couple chose to name their bushy, red-haired, son Jessup Lee.

It was evident, to all who knew them, the Irwins were a

happy couple; but Horatio viewed that covenant called marriage in a much different light than his partner did. The idea of being "tied down" in a long-term relationship with a woman was something that Horatio Cavendish could never accept, and he vowed to never marry. Instead, he chose to follow an ancient path that many a man before him had mistakenly trodded with a delusory hope of finding that blissful avenue called content - that happiness Horatio sought would come in the form of a shapely brunette who went by the name Mary. Her last name was a mystery, for she would never reveal it, but her profession was never in question. She was a prostitute.

Horatio met Mary for the first time when the Mt. Prospect Pub opened in 1885. She would become a regular at the tavern and frequent it often. Many of the townsfolk thought Mary was a drifter because she often left Mt. Prospect for short periods of time then eventually return, but it was the consensus for most that this Mary Magdalene was a, "A Loose Woman."

In reality, Horatio was a really lonely man inside. He compensated for that deficiency by working long hours, but he couldn't hide an aching heart from himself.   A solitary life is what Horatio chose, and he hid that spirit of lack rather well among others, but he couldn't escape an atmosphere of loneliness on exhibit in his home; nor could he ignore that cold bed of desolation he must face, then crawl into every night.

Horatio couldn't take the chance, nor did he dare risk, being seen in public with Mary - it would tarnish the prosperous businessman's reputation. Horatio thought Mary was beautiful, and he desired her company, but if anyone found out he was doing such things it would ruin him. So, with that conclusion in mind, the crafty Cavendish devised what he thought was a foolproof plan.

Horatio's plan not only consisted of deceit and deception, it also sought to reward Mary for the pursuit of her less-than-desirable career.

Horatio approached Mary one evening, when he thought no one was watching, to propose an offer. Once Horatio realized he'd gained Mary's interest and confidence, the cunning businessman began to explain his deviate scheme.

The plan called for Mary's cooperation in being Horatio's mistress. She was instructed to visit the businessman's home three times a week, late at night, when no one would notice her entering through the back gate. The task offered payments of seventy-five dollars a month - a sizable amount of money for the time.

It was fall, 1886, and life hadn't been all that kind to Mary that year. She had some difficult decisions to make if she wanted to survive yet another Illinois winter. If she chose to remain in Mt. Prospect, Mary would have to comply with Horatio's wishes; it was either that, or she would have to struggle for life elsewhere. The well-traveled, 28-year-old woman felt she had no choice but to except Horatio's generous offer. Mary's opinion of herself was one of poor self-esteem, and she concluded she could do no better. "I'd like to settle down and become a respectable lady, but I can't see that ever happening soon!" was the reoccurring thought that flooded her mind.

Mary was faithful to pay Horatio a visit every Monday, Wednesday, and Friday each month for the next four years. The lonely businessman was rarely interested in sex when his mistress came to pay a visit though. He and Mary would often sit by the fire to just enjoy a conversation with each other, and the couple did so many a time until the wee morning hours. Then she would leave in the same manner she had arrived only hours before. It wasn't so much of a physical attraction that Horatio sought, it was companionship and someone to talk to that he longed for.

The couple's secret relationship went unnoticed all during that time, but it was then in the summer of '89 that Mary discovered she was pregnant. She was convinced it was Horatio's baby, for she had fallen in love with him months before. Mary's opinion of herself was beginning to change for the better by then, and she had a real heartfelt desire to change what she thought was now a sinful lifestyle. She hoped that if she stopped seeing other men Horatio would consider making their relationship a permanent one and marry her. Mary hadn't been with another man for well over two years, and her excitement was running high.

When Mary first told Horatio she was pregnant with his child the wealthy businessman questioned if it was truly his, but he never got angry though. To be honest he didn't really know quite what to do at the time, but he eventually developed a "wait and see" mentality.

As her pregnant state began to develop, along with the child within her, so did the size of her small bodily frame. Mary began to wear larger, baggier clothing to hide her condition. It was because she had no friends or relatives to notice her physical appearance that Mary was able to go about her business without even a hint of curiosity being stirred upon those good citizens of Mt. Prospect. It wasn't a surprise nobody cared; the townsfolk had chosen to ignore Mary for quite some time. In their eyes, she was an undesirable piece of the community that had no merit or social status.

Mary was just about at full term with her pregnancy when

she began to feel a great deal of pain that particular evening when she was at Horatio's. The wealthy businessman helped her to one of the back bedrooms, then he tried to make her as comfortable as possible in bed. Horatio was afraid his secret would become public so he made the dreadful decision to forego the assistance of a doctor - that would be just one of the many regretful decisions the wealthy businessman would come to make.

Horatio did everything he possibly could to help Mary deliver her baby, but his best efforts simply weren't good enough to save both mother and child. After being in labor for several hours, Mary finally delivered a healthy baby boy - she named her son "Mathius." She had given life to another, but her hope for survival had already begun to fade. Mary lost a lot of blood in the process of giving birth, and it would ultimately lead to her death.

That spring day was a tragic one. Mathius was born on April 1st, 1900, in the wee morning hours. His arrival was a joyous thing, but when someone dies, even if it's on April 1 , it's no joke.

The thought of Mary's death would haunt Horatio for the next twenty years. That self-imposed guilt of his would always drive Horatio to the bottle; the end result was a life littered with heavy drinking. It wouldn't be until 1920, when he was lying on his deathbed, that Horatio would finally tell Mathius something that he'd told no other. It was a dark secret from his tormented past, one which he had managed to keep to himself all this time.

Horatio was a wealthy 61-year-old man, but he knew his time

was short. The liver disease he had was going take his life, and soon. Shortly before his death, Horatio told everyone in his room to depart except for Mathius. After Elias, Gwynn, and the others who were there, had exited the room, Mathius remained to stand beside Horatio's bed.

Horatio instructed Mathius to get a chair and pull it up beside his bed. "I have something I need to tell you!" He asserted.

After Mathius did as he was instructed, he leaned forward in his chair to hold Horatio's hand as he said, "What is it?" but the apathetic businessman would have no part of that sign of affection, so Mathius, being used to Horatio's cold and indifferent nature, just simply slid back in his chair to listen.

"Just sit there and listen ... I got a lot to say" was Horatio's stem reproof.

Mathius replied with a humble, "Okay."

"I did something terrible and I need to bring it out in the open before it's too late."

Once again, Mathius leaned forward in his chair, then asked, "What?"

With another strong rebuke, Horatio said, "Will you just shut-up and listen!"

Again, Mathius slid backward in his chair, then quietly said, "Sorry."

Horatio said, "Good!" then he began to unveil some of those dark secrets he had been hiding for oh so long. "What I've got to tell you is something I've spoken to no one about ... I've been hiding a secret for a long time ... twenty years. I don't know how else to put it ... I'll just be blunt and come to the point. I was secretly having an affair ... she was a whore. I paid her to come to the house ... for almost four years. She got pregnant ... said it was mine."

By now, Mathius's interest was beginning to peak, but he still sat there quietly in respect of Horatio's wishes.

"None of the town's people noticed she was pregnant ... she wore baggy clothes to hide it ... I wasn't really sure if the baby was mine or not." Then closing his eyes as he spoke, Horatio began to explain what happened that night in 1900. "She came to my place that night ... I could tell she was in a lot of pain. I had a pretty good idea the baby was coming."

After a long pause, Horatio proceeded with the continuation of his story. "I did everything I could to save her and the baby ... I was too scared to go get a doctor ... I didn't want anybody to know I was seeing a whore."

After another long pause, Horatio said, "The baby made it," as a tear began to well in the comer of his eye, he then added, "She died ... I buried her in the garden so no one would know."

Mathius leaned forward slightly, then as a show of surprise sat back to place his hand over his mouth.

"She was a drifter at heart ... no one even noticed she was gone ... they probably thought she found a cowboy somewhere." Horatio added, "She named the baby 'Mathius' before she died!"

Mathius was shocked by Horatio's confession - he couldn't believe what he was hearing.

Horatio said, "I told the townspeople I found you abandoned on my doorstep ... I hired a nanny, Ms. Peterman, to look after you." He then reached up to wipe the tear from his eye as he glanced over at Mathius, but his eye contact with his son was for only a brief moment, then Horatio continued to empty out what

had been haunting him for oh so long as he stared at the ceiling.
"Let's face it ... you're a bastard child. I raised you, but let's be
honest ... I don't really know if you're mine or not. I've given
this a lot of thought ... I changed my Will a couple of months
ago ... I wrote you out of it. I'm leaving everything to Elias ...
he's the only true friend I ever had in life."

Horatio closed his eyes once again, then he told Mathius to
leave, and added, "That's all I have to say."

Horatio passed away later that day. It was with the burden of a
heavily troubled heart that Mathius tried to end his life as well that
evening. He tried to hang himself from the rafters of Horatio's
barn, but the suicide attempt failed when the rope broke. After
Mathius fell to the ground he began to give thought of another try,
but he quickly changed his mind once he pulled the suicide note
from his pocket and began to read it over and over again.

It read:

"I can't live knowing what I know!"

People didn't like to talk about suicide in those days, so
Mathius thought it was best to keep the experience to himself
since there were no witnesses - that day, October 31st, was one he
wouldn't soon forget.

Elias felt bad Mathius was written out of Horatio's Will. He
simply couldn't understand why his partner would do such a thing
and not leave at least something for the only son he had. Elias's
repeated attempts to hire Mathius, in hope that he would come
work for the company, would always fail because Horatio's son

was a proud man who refused. Instead, Mathius chose the profession of bartender at the Mt. Prospect Pub.

At the age of 66, Elias decided it was time to retire - the year was 1925. The elderly Irwin left his Presidential post with no regrets; he had been giving the move a great deal of thought for a long time. He decided, with confident conclusion, that it was best for his 37-year-old son, Jessup, to take over. "He's quite able to fulfill those requirements needed for such a tall task." Elias thought.

Unfortunately, Elias wouldn't be able to enjoy an extended retirement - he died from a heart attack in '28.

It was regretful, but Mathius Cavendish lost his life as well on October 31st of the following year. No one actually knew what the contributing factor was in Mathius's death, but many speculated it was from something like cancer; after all, he smoked the equivalent of four packs a day. Some thought Mathius killed himself because of all those lost investments he had when Wall Street crashed on "Black Tuesday," coupled with the stress of the bar closing. Needless to say, it was a sad day for Mathius was just a young man who had no family.

A few days after Mathius was laid to rest, Jessup thought it was best for him to be the one to go through the young Cavendish's belongings. Jessup took a great deal of time to examine each item closely, and after about an hour or so, when he was just about finished with his sifting, he discovered something rather unique - a solid gold spoon. Jessup held the utensil in his hand for quite a while, then he eventually placed it in his pocket for safe keeping once he read what was written on it. He was emotionally taken back by what he read, because engraved on the inside of that solid gold baby spoon were the words: *"I love you, Son!"*[11]

Chapter Four
Extraordinary Stuff

The 1920's were a prosperous time for America. That decade would become best known as *The Roaring Twenties,* but it was also called *The Jazz Age;* some even ventured to describe it as *The Age of Wonderful Nonsense,* but many accused it of being *The Age of Intolerance.*

Tagging a name on someone or something by use of slang isn't anything new, it's probably been around since the invention of that thing called a vocabulary, but one can only speculate as to the reason why some popular jargon can endure the test of time and others won't. For example, if you were a female of low I.Q. in the roaring twenties, you were no doubt called a *Dumb Dora.* On the other hand, if you were *Hard Boiled,* you were considered a strong tough guy. If a gentleman was a ladies' man, he was generally classified as a *Cake Eater,* but if he was *A Drugstore Cowboy,* he often hung around on the street corner to pick up girls, who he hoped were stylish, or the *Cat's Meow.*

The 20's featured things like radios, appliances, automobiles, and something called a suburb to live in. Along with growing mass consumption came a need for mass production as well. America's society was becoming increasingly made up of people living in suburbia who used their automobiles to commute and shop. A whole host of inventions and technologies were now being greatly transformed. Nearly thirty million motor vehicles were on the road by 1929, one for every five residents of the country, and of all those American households, 35% of them were already wired with electricity by 1920.

Thus, the 1920's was a decade that saw the beginning of change in consumer appliances. Items like, sewing machines, washing machines, vacuum cleaners, dishwashers, stoves, mixers, toasters, irons, water heaters, space heaters, and refrigerators were now all being designed to operate on electricity. The United States had become an economy of modern middleclass, but a number of surveys conducted in 1929 showed that the richest 1% of U.S. households held claim to something like 45% of all the nation's wealth.

The Bible makes a bold statement in I Timothy 6:10 when it proclaims, "For the love of money is the root of all evil; which while some coveted after, they have erred from the faith, and pierced themselves through with many sorrows."

Nowhere in the annals of time could such an edifying example of spiritual fact, or enlightening truth, be more evident than in the year 1919. The fall season had arrived and one decade was about to close as another was about to be born. No one dare dream of it, nor could anyone in their right mind imagine it, but "America's National Pastime," baseball, was about to be marred by the tainting stain of corruption - all of which was done by the hands of a choice few.

The 1919 World Series resulted in the most famous scandal in baseball history. Eight players from the Chicago White Sox (later nicknamed the Black Sox) were accused of throwing the Series against the Cincinnati Reds. Details of the scandal and the extent to which each man was involved have always been unclear. It was, however, frontpage news across the country and despite being acquitted of criminal charges the players were banned from professional baseball for life.

Despite their many wins on the field, the White Sox were an

unhappy team. No club played better in 1919, but few were paid so poorly. Many knowledgeable observers believe it was Charles Commiskey, Jessup's longtime friend, and his stinginess that was largely to blame for the Black Sox scandal. If the owner hadn't grossly underpaid his players and treated them so unfairly, they would never have agreed to throw the Series.

Comiskey frequently made promises to his players that he had no intentions of keeping. He once promised his team a big bonus if they won the pennant. When they did win, the bonus turned out to be a case of cheap champagne. Comiskey even charged his players for laundering their uniforms. In protest, for several weeks the players wore the same increasingly dirty uniforms - Comiskey removed the uniforms from their lockers and fined the players.

Although gambling was intertwined with baseball long before the eight White Sox were accused of fixing the Series, the number of gamblers at ballparks had dramatically increased by 1919. Ironically, Comiskey posted signs throughout the park declaring, "No Betting Allowed in This Park." Unfortunately for Comiskey, the signs were not enough.

Player resentment was high and gamblers offers, which were sometimes several times a ballplayer's salary, and they were just too tempting to refuse.

Matched against the Cincinnati Reds, the Chicago White Sox were favored to win the World Series. The 1919 Series looked to be no contest. It was said that people came not to see if the Sox won, but how they won. Early gamblers' odds favored them five to one. The day before the Series opened in Cincinnati, rumors of a fix were everywhere. As quickly as big bills started changing hands, the odds began to shift toward Cincinnati.

Throughout the Series, Hugh Fajjerton, a sports writer for the Chicago Herald and Examiner, had been paying close attention to the rumors of a fix. He hinted about the selling of the Series in his newspaper columns and urged club owners to do something about gamblers' involvement in baseball. Most people didn't believe fixing the World Series was possible.

Chicago did indeed lose the Series that year and in September of 1920, a Cook County, Illinois, Grand Jury convened to look into the allegations and the investigation quickly began to focus on the 1919 World Series and baseball gambling in general. The White Sox were enjoying a good season when the Grand Jury began calling players, owners, managers, writers, and gamblers to testify about what had happened the previous year.

When the Grand Jury finally concluded its investigation, indictments were handed down against eight White Sox players. The trial of the accused White Sox players, who had been suspended for the remainder of the 1920 season, began in June of 1921. The Grand Jury records, however, including confessions, were recorded missing (they turned up four years later in the hands of Comiskey's attorney, George Hudnall, who never explained their reappearance). After a month of hearing testimony, it took the Jury just two hours and forty-seven minutes to acquit all defendants. Lack of evidence and the missing confessions resulted in the not-guilty verdict. In the end, the trial didn't answer many questions. The facts, never clear cut to begin with, continued to be manipulated, distorted, and subject to outright lies.

After the 1920 season, fearing baseball might not survive the gambling scandal, club owners decided to clean up their act. The three-man national commission, headed by Ban Johnson, was replaced by a single, independent commissioner with dictatorial power over baseball. Federal Judge Kenesaw Mountain Landis was appointed commissioner, and he acted quickly to restore the public's faith in baseball.

Immediately after they were acquitted of any criminal charges, Landis banned all eight of those players from the game. Landis said, "Regardless of the verdict of the juries, no player who throws a ball game, no player who undertakes or promises to throw a ball game, no player who sits in confidence with a bunch of crooked players and does not promptly tell his club about it, will ever play professional baseball." True to his word, Landis never allowed any of the eight White Sox to play professional ball again.

1919 was also the year *Prohibition* began. The 18th Amendment made consumption of alcohol, or even its possession, illegal. The general intent of the Amendment was to lower crime and improve the status of life, but the opposite happened, crime increased because people began to rebel when they couldn't get a drink. Gangsters profited well during the roaring twenties by smuggling alcohol and distributing it to different illegal businesses - Al Capone was one of them.

Capone was America's best-known gangster and the single greatest symbol of the collapse of law and order in the United States during the 1920's Prohibition era. Capone had a leading role in the illegal activities that lent Chicago its reputation as a lawless city.

Capone was born on January 17th, 1899, in Brooklyn, New York. He grew up in a rough neighborhood and would eventually become a member of two "kid gangs." Although he was bright, Al quit school in the sixth grade at age fourteen. Capone went on to bigger and more evil things after that when he

executed a couple of men in New York. He had graduated to
murder, thus an early testimony to his willingness to kill. In
accordance with gangland etiquette, no one admitted to hearing
or seeing a thing so Capone was never tried for the murders.

After Capone hospitalized a rival gang member, he went to
Chicago to wait until things cooled off. Capone arrived in
Chicago in 1919, then he moved his family into a house at 7244
South Prairie Avenue.

Once Capone got established in Chicago, he went to work for
John Torrio - a crime boss. Torrio saw Capone's potential, his
combination of physical strength and intelligence, and encouraged
his protege. Soon Capone was helping Torrio manage his
bootlegging business. By mid-1922, Capone ranked as Torrio's
number two man and eventually became a full partner in the
saloons, gambling houses, and brothels.

When Torrio was shot by rival gang members, and
consequently decided to leave Chicago, Capone inherited the
"outfit" and became boss. The outfit's men liked, trusted, and
obeyed Capone, calling him "The Big Fellow." He quickly proved
he was even better at organization than Torrio, syndicating and
expanding the city's vice industry between 1925 and 1930. Capone
controlled speakeasies, bookie joints, gambling houses, brothels,
horse and race tracks, nightclubs, distilleries and breweries at a
reported income of over one-hundred-million dollars a year.

Attempts on Capone's life were never successful. He had an
extensive spy network in Chicago, from newspaper boys to
policemen, so that any plots were quickly discovered.

Capone, on the other hand, was skillful at isolating and killing
his enemies when they became too powerful. A typical Capone

murder consisted of men renting an apartment across the street from the victim's residence and gunning him down when he stepped outside. The operations were quick and complete and Capone always had an alibi.

Because of gangland's traditional refusal to prosecute, Capone was never tried for most of his crimes. He was arrested in 1926 for killing three people, but spent only one night in jail because there was insufficient evidence to connect him with the murders. When Capone finally served his first prison time in May of '29, it was simply for carrying a gun. In 1930, at the peak of his power, Capone headed Chicago's new list of the twenty-eight worst criminals and became the city's "Public Enemy Number One."

The popular belief in the 1920's and 30's was illegal gambling earnings weren't taxable income. However, the 1927 Sullivan ruling claimed illegal profits were in fact taxable.

The government wanted to indict Capone for income tax evasion because he never filed an income tax return, nor did he own anything in his own name, or ever make a declaration of assets or income. Capone did all his business through front men, so he could remain anonymous when it came to income. Frank Wilson, from the IRS's Special Intelligence Unit, was assigned to focus on Capone's activities. Wilson accidentally found a cash receipts ledger that not only showed the operation's net profits for a gambling house, but also contained Capone's name - it was a record of Capone's income. Later, Capone's own tax attorney, Lawrence P. Mattingly, admitted in a letter to the government that Capone had an income. Wilson's ledger, Mattingly's letter, and the coercion of witnesses, were the main evidence used to convict Capone.

In 1931, Capone was indicted for income tax evasion for the years 1925-29. He was also charged with the misdemeanor of failing to file tax returns for the years 1928 and 29. The government charged that Capone owed $215,080.48 in taxes from his gambling profits. A third indictment was added, charging Capone with conspiracy to violate Prohibition laws from 1922 through 31. Capone pleaded guilty to all three charges in the belief he would be able to plea bargain. However, the judge who presided over the case, Judge James H. Wilkerson, would not make any deals, so Capone changed his pleas to not guilty. He was unable to bargain so he then tried to bribe the jury, but Wilkerson changed the jury panel at the last minute. The jury found Capone not guilty on eighteen of the twenty-three counts. Judge Wilkerson sentenced him to a total of ten years in federal prison and one year in the county jail.

In May 1932, Capone was sent to Atlanta, the toughest of the federal prisons, to begin his eleven-year sentence. Even in prison, Capone took control by obtaining special privileges from the authorities such as furnishing his cell with a mirror, typewriter, rugs, and a set of Encyclopedia Britannica. Because word spread that Capone had taken over in Atlanta, he was sent to Alcatraz. The security was so tight there he had no knowledge of the outside world.   He was no longer able to control anyone or anything by buying influence and friends while he was incarcerated at "The Rock."

Capone retired to Florida after his release, and later died from cardiac arrest in '47. Does crime pay? Capone thought so. The gangster even tried to strike up a deal with Jessup once. The mobster's message was forever etched upon the CEO's mind, for it read, "Let's talk, over dinner!" Well aware of Capone's dark reputation, Jessup declined.

The roaring twenties died when 1930 arrived, but unfortunately, Gywnn also perished that year. She passed away in her sleep on March 4th - she was a grand old 77. Although Jessup and his father, Elias, weren't very close, the opposite could be said for Jessup and his mother. There was a vast contrast between Gywnn's treatment of Jessup and Elias's toward his son. Jessup was an only child and that had its advantages and disadvantages.

To say Gywnn spoiled Jessup would be probably an understatement. She felt a need, a longing, to devote her life to that child - especially after she lost her other boy, Edward. Ironically, the opposite could be said of Elias. His demanding work schedule kept him away from home often while little Jessup was growing up. Isolation, in the mind of a child, isn't something a youngster can fully comprehend, nor can those little ones understand the demanding circumstances that surround an adult's life. Elias's absenteeism in his young son's life was something that galvanized Jessup's resentment toward his father. With the passing of time, Jessup allowed his mind to become infected with those bitter thoughts. He was even so bold as to tell his father only days before Elias died, "You were a lousy father! You were never around when I needed you!"

Although Jessup had allowed his mind to be tainted with anger toward his father, Gywnn's passing gave testimony to the healing process of those mental wounds. Shortly before her death, Gywnn told her son to make her a promise. That pledge Gywnn required of her child was one of forgiveness toward Elias. Gywnn was lying in bed that day when she reached over to hold her son's hand, as Jessup sat on the bed next to her. She told him, "He loved both of us, Jessup ... I know it was hard for you to see that, son, but he did. He was always good to me. I still miss him, and those annoying habits of his ... If you don't do anything else in life, son, I want you to forgive your father ... you never knew him like I did. Promise me you'll do that ... okay?" Jessup truly loved his mother, and with a wink and nod of his head it was done.

Soon after his mother's death, Jessup made drastic changes within the company he had inherited. The name *Irwin ~ Cavendish* no longer seemed appropriate, so Jessup changed the legal name of the company to *Irwin Industries*. Jessup was a brilliant man; of his many achievements, he could boast of having a Masters Degree in both Mechanical and Civil Engineering from the University of Chicago. It was his intelligence that convinced him Mt. Prospect wasn't anywhere to be. With that in mind, Jessup moved the headquarters and all of its operations to Chicago. He too had bought into a theory, like so many had before, the allure of that fertile financial oasis called the "Big City" was just too tempting to resist. (His actions were a bold statement of selfish ideology and ones that cared nothing for tradition while sacrificing it)

It didn't take Jessup long to establish himself among Chicago's financially social elite.

He would often brag, "I will never make the same mistakes that other railroad scourge did!" as he laughed and carried on with his wealthy friends, while they enjoyed a glass of brandy and an expensive Cuban cigar at the downtown Gentleman's Club where they met every Thursday afternoon.

That "scourge" was none other than George Pullman - a man Jessup hated. The CEO would often spout off, "Pullman thought he was God!"

In Chicago, the name Pullman had many different meanings: a neighborhood, a railroad car, an industrialist. The story of Pullman started with one man's idea for a luxury railroad car, which eventually led to his dream of a utopian worker community. That dream resulted in one of Chicago's greatest 19th century labor disputes and the end of Pullman's utopia.

George Mortimer Pullman was born in western New York in 1831, where he worked as a county store clerk and a cabinetmaker. With he moved to Chicago in 1859, he coordinated teams of laborers who raised and moved buildings, a service desperately needed by a city built largely on swampland.

Despite this successful career, Pullman had a strong interest in revolutionizing the railway sleeping car. He had once traveled overnight from Buffalo to Westfield in New York and his accommodations were so uncomfortable he spent the entire evening devising a new railcar design.

Pullman envisioned Chicago to be the railway capital of the North, and he soon began to put his ideas in motion. He foresaw the growth of a rail-dominated economy and with it the growing wealth of the professional class.

The Pioneer, Pullman's first attempt at a luxury car, initially failed because it was too wide for railway platforms and bridges and the railroads refused to accommodate it. But after the Pullman car was included as part of President Lincoln's funeral train in May 1865, both Pullman and his car received national publicity and soon became famous for luxury train travel. In 1867, at the age of 36, Pullman established the Chicago-based *Pullman Palace Car Company*.

Pullman Palace Cars featured plush upholstery, ample lighting, and ornately decorated interiors. Other luxuries included freshly prepared gourmet meals, chandeliers, electric lighting, table lamps with silk shades, leather seating, and advanced heating and air conditioning systems. Pullman dining cars allowed for faster cross-country travel because they eliminated the need to stop for meals. Railway networks and cross-country travel increased as well. The desire of passengers to travel in one of those luxury cars grew too - just as Pullman had predicted.

Pullman, like his upper-class colleagues, distrusted labor unions, so when the Chicago rail worker strike of 1877 ended violently with twelve deaths, he sought a solution to the "labor problem." Pullman hoped to improve the relationship between capital and labor by creating a safe, clean, culturally enriching environment for his workers, who would pay him back with loyalty, honesty, and commitment to hard work. He believed a company town would discourage strikes as it increased workers' efficiency and improved residents' moral character.

In 1880, after purchasing 4,000 acres of land near Lake Calumet near Chicago, Pullman began building his model company town. By 1893, the town's population had grown to approximately 12,000, with more than 6,000 of its residents employed in Pullman factories, non-employed family members comprised the remaining population.

The U.S. economy declined in 1893 and 94, causing a nationwide depression. To offset any losses to his investors and himself, Pullman drastically cut productivity in his factory and reduced wages by one-third without reducing rents, utility charges, or store prices. Since he deducted rent (approximately $14.00 per month) before paying wages (approximately $16.00 per month),

workers found themselves taking home scant pay for
their labor, if any at all. After the charges had been deducted from
workers' paychecks, they were often not worth cashing.

Desperate Pullman workers and their families begged the
company, and Pullman himself, to reduce rents during the tight
economic times, but their pleas fell on deaf ears. In the spring of
1894, many Pullman workers turned for help to the American
Railway Union. After Pullman refused to discuss employee
concerns, 90% of his workers went on strike on May 11th, and
ARU called for a national blockade and work stoppage against all
railroads using Pullman cars. Railroad management responded by
firing all ARU members.

Public sentiment was quick to tum against labor. President
Cleveland sent federal troops to Chicago on July 4th to protect the
Pullman factory. Even though the strikers were told to refrain
from violence by the Union, various riots occurred between July
5th and 7th. Although it is unclear who initiated those riots, those
events resulted in hundreds of burned railroad cars, several
wounded soldiers and civilians, and six dead rioters. By July 10th,
federal troops broke the railroad blockade and trains began
moving again - the strike officially ended on July 12, 1894.

Although the strike collapsed, George Pullman's model for
handling the "labor problem" had failed. Pullman had prided
himself on his paternalistic approach with his workers, and he
could not see how his heavy-handed methods had resulted in this
worker rebellion. Criticized and scorned, Pullman died a bitter
man in 1897. To prevent his body from being stolen or desecrated
by angry employees, Pullman had made special provisions for his
burial in Chicago's Graceland Cemetery. His casket consisted of a
lead-lined box covered in one inch of asphalt, and it rested in an

eight-foot-deep concrete-filled pit. Eight steel rails were placed above the casket and a final layer of concrete was poured on top.

Robert T. Lincoln, the son of President Lincoln, became head of the company after Pullman's death and simplified its name to the Pullman Company. The Pullman Company (again renamed to Pullman Incorporated in 1927) continued to produce its famous cars at 111th Street and Cottage Grove Avenue; but with the explosion of automobile ownership, rail passenger traffic went into rapid decline. Pullman Incorporated's future appeared bleak, and indeed it was, for the once lofty dream of George Pullman would come to an end when the doors closed only thirty years later.

Jessup, as he had so boldly prided himself on before, never took a similar path or made the same foolish mistakes that "Other fellow" (Pullman) did. Jessup was no failure. He had a brilliant mind for business; there was no denying that. Jessup had been successful in his efforts, during that eighteen-year span as President, to turn a perceived average company into a corporation that many now considered a "Corporate Transportation Giant." *Irwin Industries* had been transformed into a "Conglomerate" that consisted of a number of subsidiaries and divisions in a wide range of vastly profitable industries that was growing at a steady rate - all of which was fueled by the war effort and an increase in consumer demand.

An Engineering Division was formed in 1940. It boasted of the many road and bridge design projects it was undertaking, but the most profitable areas were the subsidiaries that manufactured building supplies. Although the railroad division had become financially sluggish in recent years, it was now a booming business because of the war. The transportation of troops and the shipment of equipment was quite profitable during World War II.

Jessup was fortunate enough to avoid participation in that conflict, his money, many thought, was a contributing factor, but he couldn't escape the struggles he often created for himself. You see, Jessup loved women. His "Playboy" mentality was leading him into a lifestyle full of obstacles and sinful transgression. His lustful appetite for the company of beautiful women had become a real problem; it was the root cause of all his legal troubles. Although he had been lucky enough to avoid criminal prosecution, Jessup wasn't so fortunate when it came to civil matters. A number of people sought to enrich themselves by suing the wealthy businessman and those lawsuits were spiraling out of control, but a talented team of "well-paid" attorneys always seemed to wipe that slate clean with the promise of minimal financial loss.

Jessup's morality had been on the decline for some time; he had been anything but celibate, nor was he decent or modest about it. His careless attitude and unethical conduct among all those women was a blunder, an error in judgment, for he was placing his health at risk; he found that out when he began to experience symptoms of what he thought was a sexually transmitted disease. Jessup didn't waste any time making an appointment with his doctor once the symptoms grew worse. Jessup's doctor was able to treat the symptoms with medication, but he warned his patient of the grave consequences of living such an immoral lifestyle.

That experience scared Jessup, so he took his doctor's advice and put an end to that "Wild" attitude and lifestyle of his. The year was 1943, and Jessup had a decision to make. What was he to do with his spare time now? He chose to enroll in a couple night classes at the University of Chicago and there, Jessup thought, his time would be best served back in school.

The courses Jessup enrolled in were *Art Appreciation* and *English Lit,* both classes met on Tuesdays. The wealthy businessman thought if he furthered his education, he would hopefully change some of those sinful ways while broadening the horizons of his mind. "Tuesdays will work out fine," he thought, "that won't interfere with my Thursdays at the downtown *Gentleman's Club* either."

Jessup was 55 when he once again registered at Chicago U; needless to say, being an older student, he was the "talk-of-the-campus." Many of the professors knew who Jessup was. For most of the college staff, it was Jessup's money that drew their respect for him. Several still remembered that rich "Redhead" from his earlier college days also.

One instructor didn't share the same admiration for wealth her colleagues did. It was 70-year-old English Professor, Ms. Lake. Jessup couldn't buy a grade from her, although he tried, so he was left with little choice; he would have to participate in class, or fail like all the rest of Ms. Lake's students who didn't try.

Jessup first thought his old crusty English prof should be thrown in the lake of fire herself, but he eventually grew to respect her stand on the issue and those "Chiseled in Stone" principles of hers. One thing did result from Ms. Lake's "iron-will." It forced Jessup to show up for class; something he hadn't always done in the *Art Appreciation* course. In spite of his absences in Art class, Jessup surprisingly received an A from that instructor.

Another fortunate benefit of attending *English Lit* was Jessup got to sit by fellow student, Sarah O'Neil. She was twenty years younger than Jessup, but was still considered an elderly student among her peers on campus. Jessup told himself he wasn't going to get involved with any of those females at Chicago University, at first, but Sarah's personality was something altogether different than what he was accustomed to. Her soft-spoken demeanor was irresistible, as was her classy style, long flowing blonde hair, and blue eyes.

Semesters were roughly eighteen-weeks long back then, and about halfway through Jessup finally asked Sarah to go out on a date. He was of the opinion, "This woman doesn't actually know who I really am."

Sarah knew actually who Jessup was though. She just kept silent about it.

Sarah agreed to go out with Jessup on the following weekend, and they hit it off so well many more dates followed and a steady courtship soon developed. Jessup proposed to Sarah about six months later on Valentine's Day, 1944. Sarah accepted his proposal and the couple were married less than a month later.

Sarah had never been married before and neither had Jessup. Their relationship was a loving and quite comfortable one - all that money helped to insure that. Jessup earned the bread while Sarah gracefully developed into the role of his elegant, fashionable, stately wife. Sarah grew up in one of Chicago's middleclass families; she had to accustom herself to that new lavish lifestyle, and did so relatively quickly. During the week, the Irwins lived in their multi-million-dollar Chicago mansion, the one they so quaintly named "Winterbrook." They often times spent the latter part of the week, the weekend, at their other mansion, the country residence they called "Fairhaven," located several miles from the city. Sarah no longer had to cook, clean, drive, or do anything. She didn't have to lift a finger, if she so desired, that's what the servants were paid to do.

In the spring of 45,' Sarah discovered she was pregnant, she was 37, Jessup was 57, and it would prove to be their only child. Sarah was excited about the news, as was Jessup, and after the pregnancy had run its successful course, little *Nathaniel Everett* arrived at 9:03 on Christmas morning.

Nathaniel was a fortunate child, very fortunate, for he was born into wealth. He was privileged, lucky enough to be raised as the third-generation heir to a financial empire - that was something only a minor fraction of the population could claim.

Very early on, both parents realized Nathaniel was a smart child, very smart! At the age of nine months, Nathaniel was beginning to learn American Sign Language - Helen, the elderly, hard-hearing maid was teaching it to him. Although there was nothing wrong with the baby's hearing, he just couldn't speak yet. Nathaniel found it easy to use hand signals to symbolize the things he wanted, which was mostly food. All of the servants, including Jessup and Sarah, were intrigued by how quickly the baby learned to sign. Instead of being angry, both parents encouraged the maid to continue with her teaching of the lessons.

Nathaniel was indeed an intelligent child. Early testing found that his mental capacity for abstract thought exceeded even beyond what could be termed intellectual. Nathaniel was taught at the best of private schools. Although they were intended to be institutions of higher learning, it wasn't difficult for Nathaniel to soar to the top of the class and did so with relative academic ease.

With an Intelligence Quotient (I.Q.) of 150, Nathaniel was classified as a genius. Although a normal I.Q. ranges from 85 to

115, only 1% of the world's population have one of 135 or above.

Nathaniel was definitely no normal child. Although the vices of alcohol and tobacco never appealed to him, the sharp appearance of a fine suit did - Nathaniel began wearing the fashionable apparel at age 10. He was a high school graduate by age 14. By the time Nathaniel turned 15, he was working part-time for his father while attending college fulltime. A few classmates, the ones he could consider friends, affectionately referred to him as, "Nate," during those days.

Although Nathaniel's future seemed bright and full of promise, he always maintained his childhood was, "Nothing but a blur!"

The absence of Nathaniel's parents in his life was no-doubt the reasoning for that line of unwavering thought. Jessup indulged himself in the business of acquisitions, mergers, and the quest for even more money. Sarah, on the other hand, dove into the pleasures of the world. The Mediterranean sands of the French Riviera, the sidewalk cafes of Paris, and the casinos of Morocco were all an allure for Sarah, and the emptiness which filled her soul.

Jessup was an absentee father most of the time, his many business trips made sure of that. For Sarah, those long cold nights spent all alone meant an existence of solitude - that was something she couldn't accept - it would result in the loss of all interest in her child, and a motherly instinct voided.

Not long after the couple had married, Jessup began to take a lot of long business trips. Sarah grew tired of it fairly quickly and retaliated by doing some wandering of her own.

She never traveled alone; it was always with the assistance of a couple faithful male servants. Sarah hired a full-time Nanny to care for Nathaniel when she was gone, and her taste for "The finer things in life" would mean disaster for the couple's marriage. Sarah was literally nonexistent in Nathaniel's life. She chose to spend her time traveling the world in search of something she could never find - happiness.

Jessup should have placed restrictions on those antics of Sarah's, her heavy drinking and lavish tendencies to spend enormous sums in particular, but he didn't. He thought it was just a phase she was going through, something she would eventually grow out of if she was allowed her freedom. (That decision, made with poor judgment, was an error of fatal proportion - a psychological failure.)

Sarah had affair after affair on Jessup; a fact he wouldn't discover until years later. Eventually, Jessup told his wife she must return home and put an end to her adulteress ways. Sarah responded by indicating, "I want a divorce!"

Jessup granted Sarah her request, and on June 6th, 1957, the divorce decree became official. Thanks to the wealthy businessman's fine fleet of accomplished attorneys, Jessup retained the "Lion Share" of his financial empire. He was granted full custody of his son, but few were surprised when they heard Sarah waived all visitation rights. Sarah's reward for being married to one of Chicago's wealthiest men was somewhat disappointing, she thought, because it was calculated as a one-time payment that equaled 1% of the estate's estimated value - 7.5 million dollars.

Chapter Five
Movin' up

Nathaniel was now an alumni, of the University of Chicago, and he was only 18 - without a doubt, he was one of the youngest to ever graduate from that school. With a host of honors to his credit, and a bachelor of science degree in business under his belt, Nathaniel thought it was best to get his "feet wet" in the real world of business before pursuing that Master's or Doctorate Degree.

When Nathaniel first began to work for his father it was on a part-time basis, as a clerk in the mailroom. Jessup thought it would be best to assign his son to that demeaning position to build character within the lad. The wealthy businessman had a mindset of, "He needs to see how the other half lives!"

Nathaniel resented being placed down there with what he called, "The common folk. The mass of lowly means." His displeasure with the task, and not being paid for it, was evident. Nathaniel was confident his intelligence was too great for such a degrading job as that.

Even though his son's dignity was bruised, and it felt like punishment to the child, Jessup never backed down on his stance and left Nathaniel there to experience what *life was all about* in that dungeon called the mailroom. Although it took a great deal of time, eventually young Nathaniel came to realize the gravity and educational value of his father's decision; but only after he had moved up **and** out of that lowly place of employment.

Nathaniel did indeed experience what many call, "Sweating out a living," while he worked in that basement called *reality*.

Although most of the mailroom employees were respectful of Nathaniel, and a few possibly fearful of him because he was the owner's son, a couple of them weren't.

Edgar Swift and his friend Gerald McKnight both worked in the mailroom at the same time Nathaniel did. Both men had horrible attitudes, and a genuine distaste for supervision and upper management. Both, Edgar and Gerald, decided early on it was their mission to harass, badger, and persistently pester the young Irwin. Swift was a twenty-year veteran of the mailroom; something he wasn't all that proud of. McKnight was a nineteen-year employee himself. He had held several well-paying positions within the company, but his poor attitude eventually drove him to the bottom rung of that ladder called success - a demotion to the mailroom.

Swift and McKnight weren't unlike any other typical bullies that populated the workplace. They loved to pull practical jokes on their fellow employees. Usually, the meeker ones were their projected targets. Most of the time their gestures were an amusingly playful trick, but, more often times than not, those jokes were considered just down right malicious as far as the recipient was concerned. Although everyone in the mailroom had a pretty good idea who was pulling those stunts, the pair of pranksters always seemed to avoid detection and evade being caught in the dubious act.

Not long after Edgar and Gerald heard Nathaniel was the owner's son they set forth to collaborate, then they thought it was best, for the time being, to focus all their spiteful intentions on the young Irwin.

Nathaniel was assigned an employee locker, as everyone else

was, on the first day. Being young, naive and trusting, Nathaniel didn't take the time to *watch his back* at first when he dialed the padlock's combination daily.

Gerald McKnight's locker just so happened to be located directly across from the young Irwin's.

One afternoon, when Nathaniel wasn't looking, McKnight took the liberty to gaze over the young man's shoulder to observe what the combination was on Locker #1.

A couple weeks later, Nathaniel discovered, when he opened the door, someone had defaced the photos that were hanging on the inside of his locker. The pictures of his mother and father were disfigured, someone had drawn black eyes, scars, mustaches and beards on them. Nathaniel was obviously upset and he told his father about it that evening. Jessup didn't think the prank was all that big of a deal, but Nathaniel spread a whole different light on the matter when he said, "How would you like for me to do that to the photos on your desk, Dad?"

Jessup said, "I see your point," and told his son it was best to report the incident to the supervisor.

Nathaniel reported the vandalism the following day, and the supervisor was quick to issue the young Irwin another lock. Although Nathaniel's supervisor had a fairly good idea who the vandals were, it didn't matter because there were no witnesses - hence no punishment could be handed out.

Swift and McKnight were cunning about what they did. They prided themselves in giving each act a great deal of thought before delivering its measured degree of afflicting calamity. They were indeed skillful craftsmen in the art of pulling off a practical joke. Their technique was artfully subtle, shrewd, and sly. They always made sure not to strike again until the *heat* had cooled down and everyone was once again relaxed, unaware of any pending plight that may come.

It had been about three months since the graffiti episode had occurred, and both pranksters were just itchin' to pull something off once more. It was Friday morning and everyone seemed to be preoccupied with their weekend plans, unaware of their coworkers scheme.

Nathaniel was assigned to clean the cabinets that day, and Edgar Swift was quite intrigued with what the young Irwin was doing. Nathaniel would pile the dirty rags on the counter, but he kept a clean polishing rag tucked in the left rear pocket of his pants just in case he found a stubborn spot. When Edgar saw that rag hanging out of Nathaniel's pocket, the deviate jokester couldn't resist the opportunity and moved into position to carry out his plan. As soon as the noon bell rang, signaling it was time for lunch, Swift hid between two large mail bins. He then reached over with a lit cigarette lighter and ignited the rag that hung from Nathaniel's pocket when the young Irwin wasn't looking. After he had accomplished the dirty deed, Swift snuck back over to his work station with a finally honed degree of stealth and blended in with the others who were exiting for the lunchroom.

As the crowd of workers made their way down the hall, away from the mailroom, they heard a scream. Alarmed by what they heard, the employees ran back to the mailroom in curiosity of what had occurred. Among those curious few were none other than McKnight and Swift.

At first, Nathaniel smelled smoke. Then he realized he was on fire, and he yelled as a desperate reaction. Nathaniel's supervisor was still in the mailroom when he heard the young Irwin scream. He reacted quickly and ran over to jerk the rag from Nathaniel's pocket, then he stamped it out on the floor to extinguish the fire. Once his fellow employees arrived at the scene Nathaniel scanned the crowd, then, in a tone of anger, the red-faced youth said, "I don't think that was a bit funny! I could have been seriously hurt!"

The supervisor also scanned the congregated group and then focused his attention on Gerald McKnight and Edgar Swift. He asked them, "I don't suppose you know anything about this … do ya?"

Both shook their heads in silence as to say, "I don't know what you're talking about."

The supervisor turned his attention back to Nathaniel and asked the young employee if he was okay. The young Irwin said he was, then the supervisor glanced over at the crowd and yelled, "Go on! Get out of here!"

After the spectators cleared the room, Nathaniel's supervisor said, "I'm sorry Nathaniel. I'll get to the bottom of it, I promise you that! Why don't ya go get some lunch ... Okay?"

Nathaniel gathered his composure, nodded his head, then left the room.

Nathaniel's supervisor reported the incident to his boss, the chief executive officer of the division, shortly after it occurred.

The divisional manager then called Jessup to suggest, "Sir, I think we need to talk ... It's about your son."

Jessup's response was, "Is he okay?"

"He's fine," was the reply.

Jessup's instruction was, "I'll see you in my office at four o'clock."

The division head made it a point to visit the Human Resources Department before that appointment with the President. The purpose of the trip was to acquire the employee files of Edgar Swift and Gerald McKnight.

The divisional manager arrived at Jessup's office right on time, and when he knocked on the door a voice from within said, "Come in." The corporate officer opened the door and walked inside. Jessup then stood, extended his hand, and said, "It's good to see you, Jim. Have a seat."

Jim Freeman, an employee of some thirty years, executive in charge of internal offices at the corporate level, shook Jessup's hand and said, "Thank you, Sir," then sat down.

With an air of faintheartedness amplified through the tone of his voice, Jessup presumedly asked, "What's my son done now ... complain some more? I'm listening ... let's have it, Jim."

With a slight nervous tone, Freeman said, "Sir, it's about Nathaniel being picked on ... I'm hearing reports from the supervisor in the mailroom."

"Oh?" Jessup responded with a hint of surprise.

Freeman added, "I'm pretty sure I know who's pulling those tricks on him."

"Tricks?" Jessup replied.

Freeman slid the Swift and McKnight files across Jessup's desk. Then he said, "There's two men in the mailroom who like to pull practical jokes. Here's their employee files."

Jessup replied, "I see!"

"Sir, I've been wanting to fire those guys for a long time. Just look at their files." Freeman suggested, "Thcy'rc thick cnough to choke a horse." Freeman expressed his dislike for Swift and McKnight through the raised tone of his voice - it was a clearcut testimony of his agitation with those two.

Jessup leaned back in that high-back leather chair of his, and interlocked his fingers together behind his head.

Freeman then began to talk even more, but this time at greater length. His explanation of the occurrences which involved Nathaniel, however, were falling upon the deaf ears of the President.

Jessup stared out the window at Lake Michigan while Freeman rambled on. It took him several minutes, but Freeman finally realized Jessup wasn't listening to anything he said. The President had been so lost in his own thoughts, he hadn't heard a single word the whole time.

Freeman repeated the word, "Sir," several times before Jessup's attention was once again finally focused upon the matter at hand.

Turning his head to face the division head once more, Jessup said, "I'm sorry ... you were saying."

Puzzled by the President's apparent lack of concern, Freeman posed the question, "Sir, did you hear what I said?"

Jessup leaned forward in his chair, then slowly pushed the employee files back toward the corporate exec. "Jim, you're not gonna fire those guys."

Freeman interrupted by saying, "But, Sir!"

Jessup raised a single forefinger to convey the silent expression of, "Wait!" and Freeman slid back in his seat in disgust.

With a stern look on his face, Jessup said, "I don't want anything done to those men ... just so long as they don't harm Nathaniel."

Freeman's facial expression quickly turned to that which represented a surprised, yet questioning look. "I don't understand, Sir?"

"Keep me informed on Nathaniel's progress, but don't do anything to Swift or McKnight." Jessup explained.

"What am I supposed to tell the mailroom supervisor, Sir?"

"Tell him exactly what I said." After a brief pause, Jessup added, "I'm not going to sit here and explain my reasoning, Jim."

Freeman gathered the employee files, stood, then said, "Alright, Sir ... I just want you to know ... I respectfully disagree."

Jessup's reply was, "So noted."

Then Freeman left the room.

Nathaniel would be the blunt end of many more practical jokes in the coming days, but Swift and McKnight never had to swallow that bitter pill called termination - Jessup saw to that.

Nathaniel's metal lunchbox, smashed flat one day, was added to the pair's growing list of joking conquests.

Nathaniel's sandwich, filled with grease, was a feat of the proud pranksters on yet another day.

Swift and McKnight would get their last lick in, and play a departing trick on the young Irwin, when Nathaniel's college graduation was only a week away.

The young clerk was assigned to the mailroom's repair station that week. All outbound mail that was damaged internally went to the repair station to be fixed before being sent out.

Only the most trusted employees were assigned to that job. Irwin Industries had a policy of placing high standards on *Confidentiality,* and applied those principles with the upmost of precautionary concern. The written expression of any corporate employee, be it matters weighed down with a heavy tone of importance, or simply private conversation, were dealt with in the strictest sense of care when it came time to the repackaging of those letters or boxes.

A medium size package, having slight damage to the comer, was left upon the repair station table that Thursday during lunch. After his quiet and uneventful lunch was over, Nathaniel clocked back in and discovered yet another box had been left for repair. Nathaniel didn't see anything unusual about the package, nor was he suspicious at all.

Swift and McKnight watched the young clerk from a distance, just hoping Nathaniel would open that package up. Nathaniel heard what he thought was scratching from within the package, then he decided to open it quite slowly. Pulling both sides of the lid back slightly with his hands, Nathaniel peered down when he thought there was enough light filtering into the box for a good look. Suddenly, much to his fearful surprise, Nathaniel was startled by what jumped out of that box. Instantly, Nathaniel screamed; it was a loud, shill cry that echoed throughout the mailroom.

Once again, Edgar Swift and Gerald McKnight reacted like they were totally surprised and ran over to Nathaniel to gather an explanation of what had occurred. The experience would forever scar the young Irwin - for the rest of his life, he would have a terrible fear of *rats.*

That experience in the mailroom would prove to be a valuable learning tool for Nathaniel though, especially when it came time to evaluate personnel issues in the future. It didn't hinder his ambitions of successfully climbing the company's corporate ladder either.

Once his son was a college graduate, Jessup gave him the responsibility of heading up an entire division on his own.

Guard-Tech, along with five other smaller manufacturers, made up Irwin Industries smallest manufacturing division. They specialized in producing components for the transportation industry, specifically guardrails and crash barriers for roadways.

It was no secret the division had been performing poorly financially. As a matter of fact, it had posted losses for seven quarters in a row; making it the least productive division in the entire corporation. It had been suspected all along that Guard-Tech was the biggest culprit, for the smaller manufacturers only furnished supplies to them for assembly procedures.

On *Wall Street,* rumors whirled Irwin Industries was entertaining thoughts of selling off Guard-Tech, but that was only publicly. Privately, Jessup had no intentions of selling the division. He promoted Nathaniel to the new assignment for a reason. It would serve as a training device for his son, an experiment so to speak. The President thought to himself, "If Nathaniel's as smart as I think he is, turning that division around shouldn't be a problem. If he can't, that tells me he's lacking leadership skills for business and he should pursue another career … maybe he would be best suited being a scientist or something."

At 18, Nathaniel had become the youngest corporate executive in company history, and possibly that of the country.

Before Jessup gave his son the assignment, he told him, "You are in charge, Nathaniel. I expect you'll dig into the problems ... find out why the division is losing so much money. You report to me. Now ... go show me what you're made of."

 Nathaniel accepted his father's challenge with open arms, and before he left the room the newly appointed young executive thanked his boss and father.

Jessup gave his son a wink, then said, "Go get 'em tiger."

Nathaniel dove into the job with enthusiasm. But a few members of Jessup's upper management team disagreed with the promotion. They thought assigning the inexperienced Nathaniel to such a highly stressful and visible position was a mistake, especially because he was so young.

A couple of the older employees at Guard-Tech were in strong opposition to an 18-year-old running their company as well, especially the Plant Manager. The Plant Manager, Mr. Jones, was an individual who harbored a great deal of resentment. He originally held the job that Nathaniel now filled. His poor performance had left Jessup no choice but to demote Jones down to the position of Guard-Tech's Plant Manager. The Plant Manager, who Jones replaced, was also demoted. That individual resigned when he discovered he couldn't win in an argument over the situation.

Nathaniel didn't waste much time assigning himself a fleet of assistants, he did so with Jessup's approval, then he proceeded on a conquest to unravel the fiscal mysteries that were inherently plaguing the division. Needless to say, Nathaniel was determined to conquer that problem ridden mountain that lay before him. In his mind, failure wasn't an option.

Research found that previous opinions about the division ran true. The vast majority of problems clearly lay upon Guard-Tech's shoulders, not the other smaller manufacturers. After four months of investigative work, Nathaniel had determined the reasons for the division's massive losses were simple ones and easily corrected - in his opinion. Once Nathaniel had concluded his assessment, he presented the evidence to Mr. Jones.

Jones was the type of man who had a tremendous amount of difficulty in swallowing pride.

When he was confronted by the 18-year-old, Jones's temper boiled over to a flashpoint and it got the best of him. The angry Plant Manger gave his two-weeks-notice and eventually settled into early retirement, then died a bitter man.

Lagging sales were attributed to a lack of market share in that highly competitive market. Guard-Tech was being frequently underbid by other competitors on Local, State and Federal highway projects because of their high costs. That was something, Nathaniel said, which had to be corrected, or Guard-Tech would eventually seize to exist.

Employee morale was at an all-time low as well, even though the workers were being paid a far-above-average wage for a non-union facility. The end result was productivity suffered greatly. Guard-Tech's scheduling system was also a problem. In-coming shipments usually arrived late because unrealistic deadlines were placed upon the suppliers by Guard-Tech, and that forced out-going shipments to be rarely on time either. It created a domino effect within the other manufacturers of the group, and customer satisfaction was waning as well, spiraling downward.

In an effort to boost productivity, Nathaniel lowered the employee wages then installed an incentive program that consisted of base pay and production bonuses. Every job upon the Guard-Tech floor was assigned a production quota; anything produced above that daily quota received a bonus based upon pieces produced. Guard-Tech's employees were furious with the wage reductions at first, but soon realized their hard work would be rewarded through those bonuses. Often times, a worker could now earn more in a five day work week than they did in six, and work less of that dreadful overtime. The idea worked well, and productivity began to soar.

Greater productivity helped reduce those high production costs, but so did several other things Nathaniel introduced.

The 18-year-old first consulted with his father, then he proceeded with his executive plan of attack. With his dad's blessings, Nathaniel had free rein over the division and an "open corporate checkbook" to work with.

One of the first things Nathaniel did was purchase several pieces of new innovative equipment - the most extensive was four industrial robots. They were used to perform tasks Nathaniel deemed too stressful or dangerous for humans. The employees were resentful of the machines at first, but eventually warmed up to the idea.

The executive had enacted his new strategy, but he also drew up new policies and procedures for the entire division as well. Across the divisional board, all material costs used in the manufacture of components were sharply analyzed. When material of similar quality could be purchased at a lower cost, it was. At times, that meant the division had to change suppliers and go with the competitor. That was a hard pill to swallow, for some of those suppliers had been faithful to supply the company with parts for years.

Nathaniel felt the shipping and receiving problem was strictly one of poor scheduling. He was also convinced there wasn't sufficient manpower in place at the time to correct it. To solve that dilemma, Nathaniel hired a full-time Divisional Manager to oversee the newly revamped departments he envisioned. Under the guidance of that person, each facility within the group would have a Scheduling Supervisor, as well as a supervisor to handle Shipping and Receiving. That system was something that had been non-existent in the past.

Although it took several months, and a great deal of effort by all involved to complete, Nathaniel had indeed been successful in turning things around. The division began to regain a major portion of the *market share* within the industry. Profits were once again up as sales soared. It could no longer be said that division was one of the poorest performers within Irwin Industries - thanks to a young man who was overflowing with God-given talent and ingenious thought.

Nathaniel's accomplishments may have been overlooked by Wall Street, but they weren't ignored by the Irwin Industries Board of Directors.

Nathaniel had just turned twenty, and the monthly board meeting started out a little different that day. Board members were soaking up an air of celebration and laughter with flair - something quite unusual for the often seriously stuffy white shirts. It was a rare mood for that boardroom indeed. The corporation's quarterly financial reports were in, and stock prices were on the rise. The company was doing tremendously well.

One of the board members thought celebration was in order so he had something brought in. It was beverage of the alcoholic variety. With a few drinks under their belt, someone got caught up in the moment and jokingly said, "If your kid is that smart, Jessup, we should nominate him Vice-President of Operations!"

Jessup laid his drink down on the conference table and became silent after that. The room grew quiet as well. After running the thought around in his mind for a moment or two, the President said, "That's a good idea, Charlie. Since the board's all here ... do I hear a second on that?"

A couple of the board members were puzzled by that. They quickly piped up to say, "A second for what? What are we voting on?"

Jessup chimed in by adding, "Charlie said, if my son is that smart, we should nominate him Vice-President of Operations."

The surprised board member quickly spoke up to say, "I was just kidding, Jessup!"

"I wasn't, Charlie." The President replied.

You could hear a pin drop at that point.

"Do I hear a second?" Jessup insisted. He repeated himself once again after a lack of response by the board members. With a higher tone in his voice, Jessup repeated the plea a third time. "Do I hear a second?'

Although he appeared to be obviously uncomfortable, Charlie was the first to slowly raise his hand. In succession, hands began to slowly rise until the entire Board was in full agreement.

"It's settled then," Jessup said. "Nathaniel is the new Vice-President of Operations for Irwin Industries ... I'll share the good news with him when I get home this evening. If that's it for our business discussions today… Gentlemen … I'll adjourn the meeting.

One of the members said, "I'll second that ... let's go home." The board meeting was then officially closed and the executives began to file out of the room, but with an understandable bit of uncertainty in their walk.

The year was 1965. The United States was involved in war at the time and the country was truly divided over the conflict. Jessup was struggling with division within his mind as well. He was getting up in age, and had some decisions to make. Jessup's mind was entrenched with an array of troubled thought. He needed an answer to those questions of his, but they wouldn't come easy.

The senior Irwin elected to retire the following year. He had been suffering from a number of chronic ailments for a while, and was often in a state of depression. The wealthy businessman was 78, his health was definitely on the decline and he'd had enough.

Jessup knew his days were numbered so he told his attorneys to rewrite his will. The revised legal document would ultimately leave everything to Nathaniel, except for a few personal items given to the servants. Jessup then sat out to pull the purse strings of his Board of Directors. He had been hashing the issue over in his mind for quite a while, but it was Jessup's personal wish to hand over the reins of Presidential control to Nathaniel.

The senior Irwin was confident his 21-year-old son could run the corporation; so confident he nominated Nathaniel to be his replacement. Again, initially, the board members were skeptical about Jessup's decision, but the elderly chief executive used every persuasive trick up his sleeve he could to move them toward favorable agreement.

Eventually, after a bit of heated discussion among the members, Jessup convinced the board it was best to elect his son and the exec prevailed on those urgings. He won the argument because his influence had been paramount.

With the promotion, Nathaniel had once again broken a company record for being the youngest individual to hold that important office. Word spread quickly along corporate lines that Irwin Industries was now under the leadership of a new CEO.

As President, Nathaniel made it one of his first orders of business to call Gerald McKnight and Edgar Swift into his office. Those practical jokers of mailroom terrorism were about to taste a bitter pill of reproof, and sweat a bit, too.

Both men had a pretty good idea they were in trouble when they were summoned upstairs.

Once they got to the top floor, they had to wait in the lobby some thirty minutes before the President would see them. Nathaniel's personal secretary eventually led the pair to his office and knocked upon the door. The command of, "Come in," echoed from inside and the nervous pair walked through the door into the CEO's spacious luxury office.

"Have a seat ... Edgar ... Gerald." Nathaniel insisted.

Both stooges parked their butts in quick manner.

The young executive stood to stare out the window with his back toward the nervous pair.

As the spokesperson, speaking for them both, Swift softly said, "You wanted to see us, Sir?"

Nathaniel gradually turned, then slowly walked over to his desk and sat on the corner of it. Then the CEO crossed his legs and folded his hands over his knee. "Yes ... as a matter of fact ... I did." He replied.

"What about?" was Swift's nervously sheepish inquiry.

With a serious glare in his eye, and a stem tone of certainty in his voice, Nathaniel said, "We can't prove it, but everyone's pretty sure you're the ones who've been pulling all that stuff in the basement."

Swift and McKnight sat silent and motionless, somewhat frightened, and unaware of what was about to be their fate. After a brief moment of hesitation, Nathaniel once again stared out the window, then stood. The Executive had his back toward the pair of jokers when he said, "What we're running here is a business ... not a carnival ... or some amusement show!"

Nathaniel turned back around to face the two men, then he added, "Do you understand me ... Gentlemen?"

Sinking a little lower in their chairs, Swift and McKnight simultaneously replied, "Yes, Sir."

You could hear a pin drop in the room after that.

Nathaniel glided over to his chair, took a seat, and leaned backwards in it. The CEO had the full and undivided attention of his employees by now.

Nathaniel seemed to relax a bit; then he placed his hands behind his head and interlocked his fingers. "To be honest, boys." He said, "My first instinct was to fire the both of you when they gave me this job. But ... then I thought better of it."

Nathaniel said with a slight smile.

Swift and McKnight were so scared of what they thought was the impending axe of punishment, they couldn't muster a word.

Nathaniel got serious once more and leaned forward in the chair to place his elbows upon the desk. Slowly, he tapped the ends of his fingers together while being absorbed in a brief moment of silent thought. The CEO gave the fearful pair an intense stare, then he said, "Here's the deal, men ... either you shape up, or I'm shipping you out! Do we understand each other?"

Both men, once again, simultaneously said, "Yes, Sir!"

"I'll give you six months ... if I don't see dramatic improvement ... you're hitting the bricks. Are we clear?"

Both jokers replied by silently nodding their heads in simultaneous agreement.

"Just to show you I'm a fair guy ... if you can turn those attitudes around ... I'll see what I can do as far as promotions are concerned in light of reward for any hard work." Nathaniel waved his hand and added. "You can go now!"

The executive had shown mercy and given the troublemakers a chance - something they had needed all along. Nathaniel's experiment in the realm of kindness toward humanity worked, and ultimately paid off great dividends. Both men were successful in their efforts to mold themselves into model employees. Gerald McKnight was eventually promoted to the position of Divisional Supervisor over Shipping and Receiving at *Guard Tech.* Edgar Swift also had an opportunity for a taste of success. He went on to become the Mailroom Supervisor, then eventually the Director of Human Resources. Nathaniel had been true to his word. He kept his end of the bargain once he discovered Swift and McKnight had kept theirs.

The happiness of success is a beautiful thing. Irwin Industries was rolling in it under new leadership, but that air of glee would flee in the fall of '67 with the announcement of Jessup's passing away.

Although Nathaniel didn't always agree with his father, he still respected his dad and loved him a great deal. He took his death quite hard. It would turn out to be a great emotional loss for Nathaniel - one he couldn't easily deal with or get over for months.

There stood a unique fountain at the entrance to Irwin Industries Corporate Headquarters. Nathaniel used to resent it and everything it stood for. In the past, he would walk past that piece of art and purposefully look the other way. He hated that thing; he couldn't stand it, for it represented a measure of lofty successful potential he felt he lacked. In Nathaniel's opinion, an extremely high standard was something he could never rise above. But that was then, when he spent his days struggling in the mailroom.

In the days following his father's death, Nathaniel often found himself sitting by that very same fountain. Elias, the grandfather, had it built shortly after his partner and friend, Horatio, died. It was one of the few things Jessup kept when he took control of the company and moved it from Mount Prospect.

The fountain was beautifully lit at night with an assortment of colored lighting. A constant flow of bubbling streams supplied its concrete base with a never-ending source of clear and refreshing water. Flowers decorated the perimeter, and in the center of it all stood two bronze statues. One figure was the likeness of Elias, the other of Horatio.

Both men were posed in final tribute, hand in hand, arms raised.

Nathaniel's sinking emotions finally conquered a turning point when he threw a coin into the water one day. His silent wish was, "That he standout among all the rest!"

Chapter Six
Transparent Elevation

Nathaniel had successfully gained a realm of notoriety in the financial world of *Wall Street,* considering it had only been a relatively short period of time since Jessup's passing.

Corporation profits were soaring far above the expectations of every analyst and stock prices were steadily on the rise per share. The last three quarters had been a consecutive sequence of successive record-breaking financial plateaus. Revenues were shattering an all-time company high with each fiscal report, by hundreds of millions. Successes were an easy maneuver for the young blooded CEO, and the board held an overwhelmingly unanimous opinion of noteworthy praise for Nathaniel's leadership skills as well. His style was unparalleled in corporate history. Nathaniel's direction was peerless and unrivaled. The intellect shown by this CEO was matchless compared to his father's and unequaled by the founding forefathers as well.

The passage of time dwindled slowly by for Nathaniel, with many a day filled with the mental anguish of grief proceeding his father's death. It had been roughly three months since Jessup's passing and an unusual looking envelope now lay upon Nathaniel's desk.

Betty Montgomery, Nathaniel's personal secretary, had been a faithful employee of Irwin Industries for well over thirty years. She'd been Jessup's loyal secretary for almost twenty-five years of that tender. Jessup had a daily routine, and Betty knew it well. One of her responsibilities included opening all the mail addressed to the CEO. Jessup considered himself far too busy to answer each individual letter so he made it Betty's job to screen all of them. She was entrusted with the prioritizing task of placing all letters of vital importance on Jessup's desk first. As time permitted she was to reply to the rest of the correspondence, the ones determined to be of lesser importance, using her years of experience as a guide, air of good judgment, and a hint of logic - as Jessup so put it.

Although Nathaniel's daily regiment of corporate responsibilities were dramatically different than his father's, the young executive saw no need for change concerning his sixty-year-old, silver-haired, secretary's screening routine of the mail.

A legal-size letter was delivered to Betty's desk that particular day. The envelope was dull vanilla in color, slightly tom across one corner, with a suspicious looking dark stain on the back. Betty didn't usually give letters much thought before opening them, but that tattered one caught her eye. After she opened it and began to read, the secretary soon realized what the precious contents truly were. She then resealed it before placing it on Nathaniel's desk.

Nathaniel didn't arrive at the office that particular morning until around ten o'clock.

As he walked in front of Betty, the young executive said, "Good morning," as he would normally do.

The elderly woman uncharacteristically held her head low in silent refrain. She couldn't even bring it upon herself to make eye contact with her boss.

Nathaniel sensed something was troubling his secretary so he asked, "Is there something bothering you, Betty?"

Tears began to well in Betty's eyes. Then she quickly grabbed a tissue from the box on her desk. As she rubbed the gentle comforting touch of the tissue upon her cheeks, Nathaniel couldn't help but be inquisitive about the sudden outbreak of emotion. He was quick to ask, "What's wrong?" When Betty didn't answer immediately, he repeated the question.

After she had regained her composure, the elderly secretary said, "There's a letter on your desk ... I think you should read it first thing." With her head still hung low, Betty added, "I wish I'd never opened it."

Still puzzled, and a bit uneasy about his secretary's behavior, Nathaniel slowly walked past Betty to open the office door. He then gently turned the knob, opened the door, and briefly glanced at the elderly woman before entering his office. Nathaniel shut the door behind himself, then walked over to the desk and took a seat in that large leather imported executive chair of his.

The letter Betty told him about was lying on the center of the desk, in clear view.

Nathaniel examined the exterior of the envelope, but he couldn't understand why Betty was so upset. " It's just a shabby letter, what's the big deal." He thought. Whoever sent it didn't even take the time to write down a return address. It had a postmark stamped on it from Cleveland and the smeared words read, "To: Nathaniel - CEO, Irwin Industries, Chicago, Illinois."

Nathaniel loosened his tie and removed the contents of the envelope. As he began to read, he soon realized who the author was and leaned back in his chair to read the letter in its entirety.

"Dear Nathaniel,

I don't quite know where to start. I've been sitting here for the last hour or so, running my finger around the rim of my coffee cup, trying to think of what to say. It's a nervous habit I've got - I've had it for a long time.

I read in the paper your father died. I'm truly sorry, Nathaniel, he was a good man! For a long time, after the divorce, I tried to justify what I did by throwing the blame on your dad. I realize now, I was wrong. I was not only a poor mother; I was an even worse wife. I've had a lot of time lately to think about the ones I've hurt, and what I've done with my life. I don't like what I see in the mirror!

I ran out on you and your dad before you even got to know me. I can never make up for that. There isn't a day that goes by I don't think about you or what you may look like.

I knew, after the divorce was over, I made a mistake. I can't tell you the number of times my arms ached to hold you, but I realized it was too late after that - the damage had already been done.

I can't tell you how nervous I am writing this letter. I'm sitting here at the kitchen table, in a robe, staring out the window, trying to gain my composure and think of what to say.

Cramming almost thirty years of remorse into a single letter is a difficult task.

I'm staying with my sister, Bess, and her husband Grant at their home in Cleveland. They're both at work today. I have the house to myself, except for that boxer hound of theirs. They call him

'Prince.' I don't think he likes me much. I don't care for him much either.

Bess and her husband were kind enough to take me in when the money ran out and I got ill. They have a lovely home here and they've bent over backwards to help me.

Grant's a mechanic and Bess is a nurse. I've been visiting the doctor twice a week for the past couple of months and both of them have been sharing the responsibility of driving me there. I'm not allowed to drive. They're good people, Nathaniel. I wish you could have met them.

Bess is all I got left now since Mommy and Daddy are gone. She's always been looking out for me. She's been that way ever since we were kids. I remember once when we were walking to school, the walk was over a mile, and it was pretty cold that day. I didn't have a coat so Bess gave me her thin one. I will never forget what she did that day.

Mom and Dad didn't have much money back then. Mom stayed at home while Dad worked two jobs. He worked in a factory at night and sold beer at the "Cubs" games during the day. I don't blame my parents for what I've become. I knew they loved me and Bess. They did the best they could, considering the circumstances.

Daddy worked hard to put Bess and me through college. I don't ever remember him taking a day off or calling in sick. He was a good provider and he loved his wife and kids - what more could one ask for?

College didn't come easy for me, but then I met your father. He was so handsome! At first, I didn't care about all the money he had. I didn't care he was quite a bit older than me either. I was in love!

Eventually, I let the love wane. I have no one to blame for that but myself. Your father was a busy man. I didn't understand much of that back then. I wanted him all for myself. I was quite selfish then and I let the 'lifestyle' get the best of me.

Your father was the type of person who couldn't say he loved you, but he showed it by buying gifts and providing the necessities to make you comfortable. He wasn't the type to hold hands, embrace, or anything like that. I interpreted that as he didn't love me - that was a foolish mistake on my part.

I made substitutions for what I thought was missing in my life. I did it by going on lavish shopping trips around the world, and taking exotic vacations that never seemed to end. In a way, I wish your father would have been more assertive and told me, 'No.'

He said after the divorce, he thought by letting me do such things it would help iron things out - make me happy - give me time to be me.

They sure weren't kidding when they said, 'Money can't buy happiness.' I let the 'lifestyle' go to my head. Back then, I did many things I'm now ashamed of. I took up smoking, there was always booze around of course, and I can't count the number of men.

Bess and her husband keep telling me all about Jesus. They say he can forgive sin, wash me clean. I don't know how he can do that, or why he would bother saving someone like me. They're faithful to go to church every Sunday. They don't pressure me to go, but they invite me to go with them every week. I haven't gotten the courage to go with them so far.

I'm sorry I've made a mess of things, Nathaniel. I can't say I would blame you if you never wanted to speak to me. I'll give the address at the end of the page if you can find it in your heart to forgive a foolish old woman.

I've been a terrible person, I know. An apology may be too little, too late, but I'm asking you to please forgive me.

I know what you're probably thinking, how could a mother do that? I don't have an explanation for it. I know if I say I love you it will probably seem like just a bunch of empty words, but that's all I have left to offer.

Mom

119 Temple - Cleveland."

Nathaniel made it a point to never answer that letter. Instead, he let the combative hue of resentment cast a shadow over his cold heart. Nathaniel stuffed the letter in a drawer somewhere at home and refused to give it a second thought. Days would turn to months, months eventually into years, while his mom's letter drew dust and its words grew faint.

Nathaniel engrossed himself with work to a much greater extent following Jessup's death. He did so in an effort to forget the loss of his father and the dug-up memories of an absent mother's failings revisited all over again.

Nathaniel's day wasn't your typical one for a young bachelor.

He sold both estates when Jessup died and moved into a luxury penthouse apartment on Lake Shore Drive shortly thereafter. The CEO felt he needed to be closer to work and he didn't need all that room at those estates anyway. The memories both houses embodied were also a consideration for Nathaniel before he put them on the auction block.

Most days for the executive consisted of waking at six in the morning. After knocking the alarm clock off the night stand with a brush of his hand, as he normally did, Nathaniel would crawl out of bed. While rubbing his eyes, Nathaniel would sit on the side of the bed then shove his feet into those monogramed slippers of his - the ones that had his initials stitched on them with golden thread.

Often weary eyed from the lack of a good night's sleep, Nathaniel would always begrudgingly make his way toward that mammoth crystal shower of his. The shower was a walk-through structure constructed of the finest imported glass block money could buy. The master bath, one of three in the apartment, was also filled with symbols of the finer things of life. The solid gold faucets, costly marble countertops, imported Italian tile and expensive oil paintings that hung from the walls, boasted of wealth and luxury.

Some would say Nathaniel's apartment was bigger than most homes. He had a housekeeper to care for the place, but Maria didn't usually arrive until sometime after eight. Nathaniel was always long gone before then.

After he had dressed himself, Nathaniel would typically read the morning paper while sitting in his favorite chair at the end of the kitchen table. He usually scanned through the business section of the *Chicago Sun Times* while drinking a cup of hot chocolate. He would often glance at the sports section to see how the "Cubbies" fared, as he enjoyed a dunked piece of toast.

That was just one of the many routine habits he had. After breakfast was finished, the executive would call for his chauffeur to pick him up at 7:30.

Jimmy, Nathaniel's personal chauffeur of nine years, would always knock on the young executive's door when he picked him up. He was always right on time. His arrival never varied more than a minute for two from the designated time. Jimmy had always greeted his employer in that fashion rather than waiting in the car. The executive would have it no other way because Nathaniel enjoyed making small talk with his driver as they walked to the car. It was what Jimmy was long accustomed to.

As Jimmy maneuvered the streets of Chicago, Nathaniel would write notes reminding himself of matters that needed attention that day while he and the driver continued that often pleasant conversation of theirs. Once the Limo reached its destination, Nathaniel would almost always insist on Jimmy opening the door for him. The executive wanted to be let out on the street that ran parallel to the front door of corporate headquarters. The CEO did so because he wanted to experience the feeling of going to work, just like his employees did on a daily basis.

Nathaniel made it a point to take a slow stroll through the front lobby each morning while offering greetings to all those there. As was his usual early morning demeanor, the executive would shake a few hands as well before entering the elevator. Once the CEO reached the top floor, Nathaniel would always say "Good morning" to Betty before getting her input on the day's schedule. It wasn't unusual for Nathaniel to surprise his secretary with an occasional box of chocolates, a card, or small practical gift when he arrived in the morning. The exec would never let a week pass without doing such a deed of kindness at least once.

When one walked into Nathaniel's office, the sheer size of it would often times overwhelm the visitor. The individual could tell they were in the midst of luxury, and the presence there was somewhat of an experience to behold.

This particular office was a masterpiece of architectural design. The large open room was constantly bathed in sunlight, for it was surrounded by walls of tinted glass on three of its five sides. Several rare imported tropical plants lined those transparent walls - an independent horticulture service saw to it, on a weekly basis, that those plants remained as beautiful as they were.

Several expensive antiques decorated the room as well. A black leather couch, once belonging to the famous *Sigmund Freud* himself, stood as a show piece at the heart of the room. When Nathaniel grew bored, he would curl himself on the piece of furniture and cover himself with pillows and a favorite comforter. Often times, the young exec would reach between the cushions to retrieve a small tennis ball he often played with. Nathaniel enjoyed playing pitch and catch with himself while he lay on his back throwing the ball skyward; as his mind wandered.

A saloon bar, dating back to the early 1800's, was also a topic of conversation for all those who entered as well. It sat in one comer of the CEO's office and as legend has it, *Billy the Kid* shot a man at that very bar while arguing about a horse, a whore, and the cheap whiskey. Although, in itself, the bar was an interesting bit of history, Nathaniel never slid anything stronger than a *Royal Crown Cola* across its marred surface. RC was the exec's drink of choice, for he chose to never cloud his thoughts, or the minds of his visitors, with the numbing effects of alcohol.

Two walls of the room were adorned with expensive oil paintings. Some of the art was modem, but most were done by masters of old. Mixed in with the priceless masterpieces were old photographs of Nathaniel's grandfather and his partner Horatio. Several of the photos dated back to the late 1800's and featured the pride and joy of the newborn company. The dream of the founding fathers was on proud display. Their vision of fame and fortune and a railroad empire had become a reality, thanks to that invention called the locomotive - *The Iron Horse.*

Even though corporate headquarters stood tall among Chicago's elite skyline, and Nathaniel's office hovered some forty stories above the picturesque beauty of Lake Shore Drive, Lake Michigan and Navy Pier with all the fine sailing craft docked there, the young executive often times complained of a life plagued with emptiness. He would eventually define the office as being nothing more than "a lonely room." His conclusion was a discovery learned while staring out the window on a frequent basis. An analysis for existence was something the executive would give reason to quite often.

Nathaniel had many days that were busy and sometimes he didn't, but, more times than not, each day was packed with a great deal of stress. A typical workday for the young CEO consisted of time spent with Betty drafting letters, the attendance of numerous meetings, an enormous amount of time spent on the phone, and precious little time for the luxury of self. Nathaniel was rarely lucky enough to eat lunch outside of the office. If he did so, it was only on rare occasions or usually when a generous client would pick up the tab. Most of the time, the young executive would bypass eating all together or he would just have his favorite deli drop a little something off.

Nathaniel very rarely made it home any earlier than eight or nine at night. When he did arrive, there were usually several messages on his answering machine; even though his telephone number was unlisted. Although he had a large console television set, Nathaniel didn't seek the satisfaction of any programming the networks offered. He found most shows of the time either repulsive, boring, or something that lacked humor. The exec always made it a point to grab a snack before bedtime and, in doing so, he would read the interesting facts *The Wall Street Journal* had to convey.

Nathaniel enjoyed a good read and would frequently curl up to a fine novel while lying in bed. He said it would often times help him in the effort of drifting off to sleep. The CEO was usually in bed by midnight. After waking the following morning, he would start his busy routine all over again. He would eventually label it a curse, the dull, distasteful, drudgery of it all running its course six days a week.

In the years that proceeded Jessup's death, Nathaniel made it a contentious point of conscious thought to absorb himself in the educational process and the continuation of his collegiate studies. He successfully acquired a Masters Degree in Business Administration from the University of Chicago, then eventually earned a doctorate degree in business as well. Even though he had experienced great wealth and that *D.B.A* degree of success, Nathaniel still felt impoverished in life. In reality the CEO was an impecunious man, deficient, for logic would suggest what more could one ask for out of life? But, in fact, he was truly a being of poor spirit in those days.

It was going to be just another typical day Nathaniel thought, as he ascended toward all that work awaiting him at the office. He must have ridden that glass elevator a thousand times before, but was it really going to be just another day though. The executive didn't know it, but his life was about to dramatically change.

The elevator was a masterful piece of architectural wonder. Its brightly lit crystal-clear panes and decked out brass trim made it a marvel, something which proudly decorated the corporate headquarters lobby. Its mission was to impress all those who entered with its beauty, then carry its cargo to the destination of choice. That elevator could travel up and down the entire forty-two floors of the building, and it did so just inside the continuous glass front that adorned headquarters. The ride always provided a spectacular view of the Chicago skyline and that particular day was no exception. The weather was a little nippy that day and a few snow flurries were predicted, but the elevator's transparent protection held comfort from the harsh elements outdoors. As the elevator moved upward that morning, Nathaniel enjoyed the luxury of having the ride all to himself. As luck would have it, the elevator came to an abrupt stop somewhere between the 6th and 7th floor. Nathaniel pushed several buttons on the control panel, but it was all to no avail. However, he wasn't panicked though. In the nine years the executive had ridden that particular elevator, he'd never seen it break down more than once or twice. Even when it wasn't in service, the maintenance department usually had it repaired within a matter of no time.

Nathaniel pressed his face closely to the glass, steadied himself on the handrail with his right hand, then glanced down at his watch to find the time. It was 7:45, and the executive was also quick to realize the importance of the day. His watch

displayed the date of November 3rd - it would have been
Jessup's birthday. For Nathaniel, the day was significant indeed
for it was also the eighth anniversary of his father's passing.

The period of time Nathaniel had to wait on the elevator's
repair was relatively short in duration, but it seemed lengthy and
drawn out to him. A crowd was gathering in the lobby below
and their focus of attention was directed solely upon the CEO,
but as the executive took time to reflect he noticed something
unusual among the crowd.

The year was 1975 and Nathaniel was thirty now, but what he
was about to experience was just the beginning act of divine
demonstration in his life. He would later define the encounter as
being, *"The real turning point in my life!"*

Nathaniel saw an individual among the crowd that reminded
him of a special someone from the not-so-distant past. The
executive would recall the experience as vividly as it was
yesterday and the recollection of a handful of days as well.

Nathaniel took notice of a homeless man sitting on the floor
just inside the front door. He was curled up in a ball, trying to
warm himself. No one amongst the crowd noticed the man, but
that green army jacket he was wearing brought back a lot of
memories for the executive - it stood out like a sore thumb in that
tiny sea of humanity. Nathaniel thought to himself, "I can't
understand why security hasn't noticed and escorted that guy from
the building?" Nathaniel clearly remembered encountering a
similar individual of minutia means, or so the executive thought, at
that very same front door in 1969.

The Vietnam War was a full-blown ordeal back then and many
Americans weren't in favor of the conflict. Included in that group

of negative public supporters was none other than Nathaniel Irwin himself. He was one of the fortunate few though, his wealth had saved him from the draft and that horrible experience many a young man had to face.

Nathaniel's mind quickly flashed back to the time when he ran into another man wearing a green army jacket. That day wasn't all that much different than the one he was experiencing. It was cold that particular day and the executive was in a hurry when he opened the front door. Nathaniel had a lot of things on his mind and wasn't quite paying attention to where he was going when he accidentally bumped into someone. That someone was Jeremiah Olson.

When Nathaniel ran into that man the papers in the executive's hand were jarred loose. The young executive then scrambled to retrieve those documents and without ever glancing up to take notice of who he was talking to, he said, "Excuse me. I guess I've got a lot on my mind today."

The stranger's soft reply was, "That's okay. Here ... let me help you with those." After he had handed Nathaniel the few papers he'd recovered, the kind stranger said, "There you go."

Then the finely dressed CEO stood and began to visually size up who he'd been talking to.

The stranger also stood and extended his hand toward Nathaniel. Then he introduced himself. "I'm Jeremiah Olson."

The executive refused to shake the stranger's hand and quickly began to form his lowly opinion of Jeremiah based on the stranger's appearance; then Nathaniel stereotyped his place in society accordingly. With a smug tone of arrogance in his voice, Nathaniel questioned, "Are you a war protester, pothead, or what?"

Jeremiah responded by saying, "Why do you ask that?"

Nathaniel replied, "It's that dirty green jacket you're wearing." Scanning the poor soul up and down, the executive took pride in himself by adding, "I figured that's what you were ... being that you're wearing those grimy tennis shoes and those moth-eaten blue jeans of yours." After a slight pause, Nathaniel added further insult by saying, "Or is it you just no longer desire to work ... that's why you claim to be homeless?"

Taken back by that flurry of insults, Jeremiah was quick to comment, "I apologize for not having an expensive suit like you're wearing." Then the individual of seemingly small stature inquired of the executive, "I don't believe I caught your name, Sir."

The CEO proudly said, "Why ... I'm Nathaniel Irwin ... Chief Executive Officer of the Company's property of which you're trespassing on. Or is it beyond your comprehensive thought process when it comes to the laws against loitering."

Jeremiah remained silent, in spite of Nathaniel's threats and angry response. After a brief moment or two, the meek stranger slid his hand inside his coat pocket and removed a small piece of paper. He handed it to Nathaniel and the executive was quick to ask, "What is this?"

Jeremiah replied, "It's good news."

The angry CEO glanced down at the paper and instantly recognized it to be a religious tract. Nathaniel quickly wadded it up and threw it in a nearby trash can. When Jeremiah recognized he was getting nowhere with this fellow, he slowly walked past the executive and placed another tract in the exterior breast pocket of Nathaniel's overcoat without saying so much as a word. The executive was so overcome by the burning anger within, he became speechless. Although try as he might, Nathaniel couldn't gather as much as a single word to inflict another parting blow - he could only stand and watch in disbelief as the distasteful foe disappeared into the crowd.

Nathaniel remembered all too well how Jeremiah would repeatedly show up on the front steps of corporate headquarters day after day after day. The CEO's second encounter with him was only two or three days after the first. The persistent stranger was dressed pretty much the same way he was before, and Nathaniel was still irritated by his presence, but the executive did give Jeremiah some credit. Under his breath, Nathaniel commented, "At least he's no quitter!"

When the executive noticed Jeremiah for the second time, the young sandy blond stranger was once again passing out those tracts of his to anyone who would except them. Jeremiah didn't know Nathaniel was looking at him, for he had his back turned to the executive. The CEO wanted to confront Jeremiah at first, but he couldn't readily reach him because the sidewalk was becoming clogged with those interested in what the well-spoken Jeremiah had to say. Nathaniel couldn't understand why anyone would bother taking the time to listen like that. After a few minutes of observation, and seeing a clear path had opened, Nathaniel made his move.

Once the executive got to where Jeremiah was, he placed his hand on the stranger's shoulder to get his attention. Jeremiah turned around to notice it was Nathaniel again. To avoid a confrontation, Jeremiah turned away without saying a word.

Nathaniel then grabbed Jeremiah's shoulder once more to slightly turn him. Jeremiah said, "What do you want?"

The executive replied, "At first, I thought you were just an inebriated derelict." When Jeremiah didn't answer, Nathaniel added, "But now ... I get it ... you're one of those fun-lovin' Jesus freaks ... a street preacher or something." When Jeremiah still refused to answer, Nathaniel further added to his stern comments by saying, "I see you're still passing out those *Salvation* pamphlets of yours. If you stop what you're doing and promise to never come around here again, I'll forget about calling the police."

As he did before, Jeremiah slowly walked past the executive and slid a tract in the exterior pocket of Nathaniel's overcoat before once again disappearing into a sea of humanity.

As he reflected back upon that day in '69, Nathaniel thought he had ridded himself of the pesky fellow back then, but he had been sadly mistaken.

The third time the CEO ran into Jeremiah was roughly a week after he had met him the first time. He was still passing out those tracts on the sidewalk in front of corporate headquarters, preaching what he called *The Good News* and being a general nuisance as far as Nathaniel was concerned.

The executive was in good spirits that particular day and his anger with Jeremiah had cooled considerably, so when he approached the lowly street preacher things were noticeably different. Nathaniel once again placed his hand on Jeremiah's shoulder to get his attention and when the young man turned, Jeremiah recognized who it was and said, "Oh ... it's you again."

Nathaniel replied, "I don't want any trouble." Then, in surprising fashion, the executive asked, "Have you had lunch?"

Jeremiah reasoned, "No ... why?"

The CEO would never reveal it, but he read one of Jeremiah's tracts the night before and his curiosity had peaked.

Nathaniel extended his hand toward Jeremiah, then simply said, "Truce!"

Jeremiah wasn't quite sure whether to shake the executive's hand or not, but he did so anyway. Then he said, "I except your offer ... on one condition."

The executive replied, "What's that?"

Jeremiah stipulated, "That you listen with an open mind."

Nathaniel said, "You got it," then both men walked to the executive's favorite Deli to get a bite to eat and engage in a lengthy conversation.

After they'd ordered their food and sat down, Nathaniel began the conversation by saying, "You don't talk a lot ... do you?" When Jeremiah didn't answer, the executive fired another question. This time he asked, "What's your credentials, anyway?" When Jeremiah appeared somewhat unconcerned by the inquiry, Nathaniel rifled, "What's your education?"

"I have a Masters Degree in Religious Studies from Moody Institute." Jeremiah replied.

"Moody?" Nathaniel asked.

In between bites of his sandwich, Jeremiah replied, "Moody Bible Institute. It used to be called the Chicago Evangelization Society. It was renamed in 1900 shortly after the founder died. D. L. Moody. The place is on North LaSalle Boulevard ... you familiar with it?"

"I've heard of it." Nathaniel replied. After a brief pause, the executive added, "I had no idea you were so well educated."

Jeremiah responded by saying, "That's the problem with most people ... they form an opinion without ever taking the time to listen."

Nathaniel nodded his head in silent agreement, then asked, "What do you call yourself?"

Jeremiah's reply was, "Huh?"

"What's your title?"

"I'm just a servant" was Jeremiah's humble decree.

Intrigued by that response, Nathaniel thought to himself, *"I'm the master. I'll never be anybody's slave!"* Then the executive asked of Jeremiah, "Why do you beg like that on the streets ... dress the way you do?"

Jeremiah's response was, "First of all ... I don't beg ... I offer something. It's called the plan of salvation through Jesus Christ ... I dress the way I do because it wouldn't do me much good to witness before the lost in a three-piece suit and tie ... now would it?"

Nathaniel took a bite of his sandwich, swallowed, then interjected the words, "I see," with a dash of pride mixed in.

Jeremiah then asked, "Why are you asking me all these questions ... why'd you bring me here?"

Nathaniel took another bite out of his sandwich and once he'd finished swallowing it, he said, in a smug way, "Just curious."

At that point, Jeremiah had just about enough of the conversation. He laid his uneaten sandwich on the plate and pushed it to the center of the table before saying, "You don't believe in much more than all that money ... do you ... Mr. Irwin?"

Nathaniel's stinging response was, "I pride myself in being an amoral character ... I'm neither moral or immoral. Neutral ... you might say ... Indifferent ... if that's what you're getting at."

Before he walked out of the Deli, and Nathaniel's life forever, Jeremiah's parting words were, "You measure wealth not by the things you have, Mr. Irwin. You measure it by the things you have that money can't buy."

Nathaniel never saw Jeremiah Olson again, but those words from a lowly street preacher were forever etched upon the young executive's mind.

The CEO's daydream of visionary fancy quickly burst when he heard the echoes of commotion reverberating from below. It seemed security had at last discovered the green jacketed intruder and two guards were forcedly trying to throw the struggling homeless man into the street. Nathaniel waved his hands repeatedly in an effort to make the security guards stop, but no one was paying attention to the trapped executive any longer. The focus of the crowd was now upon the impending fate of that less fortunate fellow.

Not long after the guards threw the bum into the street and warned him to never trespass again, they returned to the warm building and the applause of the crowd. The sight of all that made Nathaniel sick to his stomach. Then the miraculous happened.

As he stared out the window, Nathaniel heard a loud audible voice say, ***"Why do thy hide in a glass house? Turn to me!"***

Needless to say, the CEO was startled. He said, "What?" a couple of times, even though he'd heard every word. After looking around several times to see who was speaking, Nathaniel opened a door on the control panel labeled, *Intercom*. There was a note taped on the inside of the door. It read, "We're sorry for the inconvenience, but the Intercom is out of order!"

As soon as Nathaniel read the sign, his mind began to fill with wonder. Then, seemingly as if on cue, the elevator began to move once again.

Chapter Seven
The Crowded Chapel

Eventually, the translucent capsule made its slow descent back downward. As soon as the elevator doors opened, Nathaniel burst out the front door to find that poor soul who had been roughed up and thrown face first in the gutter by those security guards.

Nathaniel walked several blocks before he was able to catch a glimpse of that homeless man. When the executive yelled, "Hey!" the green jacketed fellow bolted like a thoroughbred from the starting gate. The unsightly bum was apparently accustomed to the challenges of pursuit, for he was a skillful dodger of traffic and a knowledgeable master of Chicago's urban terrain and that detestable environment of which he lived; the milieu of which no socialite cares to talk about or dare venture into.

Nathaniel gave chase while yelling, "Wait," but, in the end, the tramp was just too fleet-footed for the young CEO. Nathaniel was able to keep up for a while, running through numerous alleys and across many a street, but he eventually tired and had to stop to catch his breath. Bent over from exhaustion, the executive placed his hands upon his knees then mumbled to himself, "I just wanted to talk to you!"

Nathaniel failed, in what was probably considered a noble effort, but he learned something far more important in the process. The executive, for the first time in his life, was given a vision, a reality check, a peer into the world of the unfortunate few.

The more Nathaniel thought about that homeless man's treatment by his employees, the further enraged he became. The executive slowly made his way back to corporate headquarters, then made it a point to seek out those security guards. The young executive took both men and their supervisor behind "closed doors," then he proceeded to give the trio a tongue lashing.

"If I ever see you brutalize someone like that again, you'll be on the streets yourselves! Do you understand me!" Nathaniel shouted. The three sat in fear and could only nod in silent reply. "If anything like that happens again, you call me directly. Is that understood?" Once again, Nathaniel's stern words gained more thoughtful nods of approval from the trio.

All three men were then instructed to apologize to that homeless man if he ever showed up on the steps of corporate headquarters again. Although the fearful employees were more than willing to say they were sorry, that chance would never come because the long-bearded fellow, adorned in that tattered green army jacket, was never seen again.

The reality of it was, the homeless man had a name - John. He was a Vietnam Vet; the by-product and castoff of an unsavory war. He's a "baby killer," some would say. John was the symbol of deliberate neglect, a distasteful member of society, one ceased to be remembered quite some time ago. John, the recipient of two purple hearts and numerous other medals for bravery shown in the line of duty, was later found froze to death in one of those dark lonely alleys that Chicago has so many of.

John's identify was never truly determined so the death certificate bore the lowly name of "John Doe.[11] No one ever claimed the body, thus his poor soul was laid to rest in a pauper's grave. (All thanks, in part, to the generous taxpayers of the city of Chicago.)

The circumstances of the day had indeed affected Nathaniel. By all indication the events that transpired, although they seemed somewhat less than meaningful at the time, were going to impact the future thought processes of this executive in a profound way.

The CEO eventually made it back upstairs to his office, but then he asked Betty to put a hold on all of his calls for the rest of the day. The inquisitive secretary was quick to inquire, "Are you alright, Sir?"

The CEO simply replied, "I'd rather not be disturbed."

Betty nodded her head with silent understanding, then the young executive slowly closed the door behind himself in an effort to explore that ever shrinking world of solitude he seldom enjoyed and to console those emotions that were now so deeply engrained within him.

To alleviate our memory of the past is a daunting task, somewhat of an impossible creed for even the most disciplined of minds. The search for solace, in light of one's misfortune of previous mistakes rendered, can be a haunting endeavor indeed.

Nathaniel spent the majority of the afternoon staring out the window as he contemplated the deep thoughts which frequented his conscious.

It got to be evening, the sun was sinking fast over the horizon, when a thought quite literally struck the executive. He'd never experienced anything quite like it before, although Nathaniel would only dare describe the ordeal to a choice few, he best described the experience as something of a white blinding force.

Whatever the executive was thinking about at that particular moment was interrupted by temporary blindness. "Everything just went white!" He would later tell a close friend. The CEO would add, "It lasted for only a few seconds, but it felt like an eternity. I couldn't see a thing, but my mind began to flood with the thoughts of a street preacher I met once ... His name was Jeremiah Olson."

After the blinding bright light had vacated the executive, he rushed over to his desk.

Nathaniel remembered saving one of those tracts Jeremiah gave him a few years back. As the executive rummaged through the contents of the desk, he had a sincere hope that little tract would still be there.

Nathaniel found the tract. It was stuffed among other things in one of those infrequently used bottom drawers of his. When the executive pulled the tract out, he began to read it. It's title simply said - *Salvation.*

Tucked away inside the tract was a handwritten note that read:

"There was once a wealthy man who pleaded with God to let him take his money with him when he died. He was so persistent that eventually God agreed to let him bring one sack with him to eternity. The tycoon liquidated all of his assets and purchased gold bars which he kept in a gunnysack at his side at all times.

When he died, the wealthy man stood before Peter with his sack in hand.

When Peter said he couldn't take anything with him through the pearly gates, the tycoon explained he had special permission from God himself. Peter peered into the sack and shook his head in bewilderment at the bars of gold.

*Peter then contacted God for special instructions. 'There's
a man here who says you granted him special permission to
bring one sack with him,' he said. 'But for the life of me, I can't
understand why a man would bring pavement!'"*

A little further on down the page Jeremiah also wrote:

*"It's my sincere prayer that hopefully, someday, you'll
understand what sharing the good news of Jesus Christ is truly
all about. ' What good is it for a man to gain the whole world,
yet forfeit his soul?' (Mark 8:36)*

In the warmest of regards,

Jeremiah Olson."

Nathaniel got a chuckle out of the story, but he had to blink
back the tears when he read Jeremiah's personalized message of
concern. The executive read the latter part of the note several
times before he was able to put it down.

Not too long after that, Nathaniel picked up the phone and
called Moody Bible Institute. After the executive explained
who he was and how he had come to know the young street
preacher, the secretary handed the phone over to the Dean who
was just about ready to leave the office for the night.

A soft, elderly, yet deep sounding, voice on the other end of the
line said, "Hello."

"I'm Nathaniel Irwin ... I was checking on the whereabouts of
one of your graduate students." The executive replied.

"It's nice speaking with you Mr. Irwin. I'm Dean Wilcott. I've read a lot about you in the paper. How can I help you?"

"I'd like to know the whereabouts of a Jeremiah Olson. Do you keep a file on that?" The executive inquired.

The Dean replied, "We don't normally track students after they leave school, but I know which student you're talking about."

"Can you tell me where I might find him."   Nathaniel asked.

There was a long pause on the other end of the line, for the Dean had to gather in his thoughts. "I got to know Jeremiah rather well when he was here, Mr. Irwin. He was a dedicated young man. Someone who believed quite strongly in his faith."

Nathaniel interrupted the Dean to ask, "Why do I get the sense not all is well?"

The Dean once again paused, then said, "Jeremiah was killed by Nicaraguan rebels a little over a year ago. He and the two associates he was with were tortured for quite some time. The three were on a mission of mercy trip there when they were captured. Someone said they were executed when the government wouldn't make a deal with the terrorists."

The executive was shocked and unable to say anything for quite a while. The Dean wondered if the CEO was still on the line when he asked, "Are you still there, Mr. Irwin?"

Softly, Nathaniel replied, "Yes."

"I believe we still have a letter on file from Jeremiah's mother. She sent it to us shortly after Jeremiah died. If you like, I'll try to find it ... see if there's a return address on it. I'm sure you'd like to send your condolences."

Nathaniel replied, "Yes, I would."

The Dean put the CEO on hold and went to find the letter. It was five minutes or so before Dean Wilcott returned, then he gave Nathaniel the address of Jeremiah's mother.

Before hanging up, the Dean said, "We don't normally give out personal information on students ... living or deceased. But ... I think this is not one of those run-of-the-mill circumstances. I can't help but believe this is something far greater than you or I. You wouldn't be calling if it wasn't. I pray you find what it is you're looking for, Mr. Irwin."

The young exec didn't get a wink of sleep that night. His mind was plagued with turmoil.

The chaotic and volatile events of the 60's, which included a noticeable antagonistic American distaste for the repugnance of war and social change, were surely destined to spill over into the 70's. Major trends would include a growing disillusionment with government, an increased influence of the women's movement, a heightened concern for the environment, an escalation of space exploration, and the augmentation for civil rights.

One trend in particular, not related to education at all, heavily impacted the nation's schools and campuses during the Seventies. Social movements, particularly the anti-war movement, were highly visible on college campuses - the Kent State massacre being the most disturbing and devastating of them all.

On May 4th, 1970, Ohio National Guardsmen were called upon in an attempt to stem the anti-war demonstrations that were occurring on the campus of Kent State. In the confusion several Guardsmen opened fire on the thousand or so students protesting that day, killing four of them and injuring eight others. Many colleges around the country were quite literally forced into shutting down in the face of all those demonstrations against the war.

Speaking out against the war and country, shortly after that tragic event, actress Jane Fonda said, ***"It's my fondest wish, that some day, every American will get down on their knees and pray to God that someday they will have the opportunity to live in a Communist Society."***

An even more graphic display of violence would unfold before the eyes of the world just two years later. It was at the 1972 Munich Olympics, that eight Arab terrorists used the medium of television to display a horrific demonstration of just how far hatred can darken the soul. Fear would once again grip the heart of man, as a global audience watched the kidnapping and murder of innocent lives in shocking detail. The terrorists had taken several Israeli athlete hostages and demanded the release of 200 Palestinian prisoners, but when the West German government offered to pay any price for the release of those athletes the extremists responded by saying, ***"We care neither for money nor lives!"***

The Germans offered an airplane as a means of escape for the terrorists, but a firefight ensued at the airport which killed some of the extremists and, unfortunately, all of the hostages. Evil, with all of its schemes of intimidation to dominate and rule, once more rose its ugly head and, in the end, eleven Israelis had been sacrificed in the cause.

The dawn of a new year would bring a glimmer of hope for peace in '73 though. A crease-fire was signed at the end of January that year and all U.S. ground troop involvement in Vietnam came to an end, but the war wouldn't be officially over until April of the following year when South Vietnam's president resigned. The end of the struggle for Vietnam would be highlighted by a mad scramble of U.S. helicopters to evacuate the last of the Americans before the fall of Saigon. The cost of hostility would be an extensive one though, quite steep in claim, for over 45,000 American soldiers paid the ultimate price.

The 70's were a fascinating accumulation of labels. It was called, *The Decade of the Woman* as well as *The Decade of Disco,* but it also had the dubious distinction of being termed *The Me Decade.*

A splendid example of wallowing in that *Me* mentality, along with the unsavory appetite of greed, was the demonstration of transactions done by way of the darker side of doing business during the first half of the decade.

The success story of real-estate giant *U.S. Financial Corporation* could have been fashioned after that magical Cinderella story, but, it too, was just a fairy tale at best. Things started to unravel for the company in '73 when auditors and government agencies began to follow the money trail, often times through the complicated path of subsidiaries or affiliates. The enthusiastic head of the firm, R.H. Walter, vowed "to make housing happen," and he did. But a 900-page confidential report soon burst that bubble and catalogued the alleged sham transactions designed to create millions of dollars of phony profits and inflate earnings per share and the stock price. The approach gained international attention when it was featured in the book, *Unaccountable Accounting: Games Accountants Play,* by Abraham Briloff, a professor of accounting at the City University of New York. Excerpts also appeared in the *Barron's*

Weekly financial newspaper. A shadow of suspicion had been cast upon *USF,* and the company chose to forego a walk in the light of trustworthiness to hide in that dark, secretive, cloud of foreboding apprehension and filed for bankruptcy protection the following year - at the time, it was the largest Chapter 11 bankruptcy case in United States history.

Was 1974 a corruption plagued year? Absolutely, but it also had a striking ring of prosperity about it for an up-start business tycoon who's name the world would come to know. After scoring a perfect 800 on the math portion of the SAT, William Henry Gates, III dropped out of Harvard to write computer software. He called that proud new company of his *Microsoft.*

Organized labor wasn't exempt from their share of trouble either. *The Teamsters* lost their leader, Jimmy Hoffa, on July 10th when he mysteriously disappeared. His efforts to regain control of the union had, at last, been halted. Many said he was buried at sea, but the tabloids would have themselves a field day once the rumors began to whirl Jimmy's remains were inside the concrete support pillars of Giants Stadium.

Life Magazine had ceased its publication a couple years earlier. The lucrative business of "Rock & Roll" was alive and well, becoming a worldwide industry, as it gained a full head of steam in the process. The music industry, as it continues to do, showcased artists who had a dramatic influence on the younger generation of society, and kids would never quite be the same for it. A parade of rock stars, most adequately described as negative role models, would change the way music is viewed and taint many an innocent mind along the way.

The birth of the decade would also demonstrate tragedy of a

somewhat lesser note. A host of fans, many struggling to find their identify, would suffer the despair of a Beatles break-up. The group, only six years after they first came to America, decided to call it quits when all four members went solo. The term, "Rock & Roll" had become nearly meaningless by that time. The decade not only saw the split of the Beatles, but it also ushered in the death of Elvis Presley - robbing rock of its two major influences. Pop music splintered into a multitude of styles: soft rock, hard rock, country rock, folk rock, punk rock and shock rock, just to name a few. But then, everyone was introduced to that dance craze called *Disco!* Needless to say, whatever sub-genre(s) you preferred, music was big business.

America had a growing fascination with fads in the 70's as well. *Pong* began the video game craze. Mood rings, the Rubik cube, smiley face stickers and pet rocks all captured the fancy of the country, but the wildest fad of them all was a stunt called *Streaking!*

Running nude through very public places became the entertainment choice of a daring few.

Fashion of the age was also something to behold. The fashion influence of Sixties hippies was mainstreamed in the seventies, as men sported shoulder length hair and nontraditional clothing became the rage. Knits and denims were the fabrics of choice. Bellbottom pants, hip huggers, platform shoes, clogs, gypsy dresses and leisure suits all became commonplace. Women were fashionable in everything from ankle-length grandma dresses to hot pants or miniskirts.

The 70's were a time of wonder indeed, but no one could dispute the world was becoming a fleeting place - a planet of shriveling proportion. The inception of the decade would unveil a world population hovering somewhere around 3.7 billion; of which over 203 million Americans were attributed. Chicago's population was ballooning as well, the figure was slightly over three million, second only to the City of New York.

The economy in the 70's was anything but a fixture of stability in the minds of most citizens though. The new decade began with humiliating reality, for over four million Americans were standing amongst the ranks of the unemployed. The unemployment rate stood at 5.5%, the highest it had been in over five years. The average annual salary was $7,564; in a time when you could buy a quart of milk for 33 cents, a loaf of bread for 24 cents and a pound of round steak for $1.30. All was not well in *the land of the free and the home of the brave;* for the United States government was in absolute turmoil.

Postal workers ushered in the new decade by going on strike. That motto, *"Neither rain, nor sleet, nor dark of night"* didn't mean much. The Army had to be called in to deliver the mail; that prompted the *1970 Postal Reform Bill,* making the Postal Service a government corporation.

The Environmental Protection Agency was also born in 1970. Within five years, it would be spending over two million dollars a day!

The following year, President Nixon imposed a 90-day freeze on wages and prices in order to combat runaway inflation that was just over 3% annually. The stock market responded enthusiastically to that move, but the celebration would be short-lived.

OPEC cut oil production in '73 and the shortage of gasoline

had an effect on everyone.

Petroleum refineries in the United States couldn't meet the demand. Critics claimed the shortage was contrived by those big oil companies! The following year, in an effort to save fuel and lives, President Nixon signed a bill creating a national speed limit of 55 mph.

In an effort to curve the soaring price of food, President Nixon ordered a freeze on all retail pricing in the summer of 1973. A year later, in light of a Soviet Union that was beginning to crumble, the U.S. agreed to sell the U.S.S.R. eight million tons of wheat and com per year.

A dark cloud of gloom was hovering over the White House in the summer of '74 as well. The administration of President Richard Milhous Nixon would suffer a black-eye of its own. Amongst a growing cloud of suspicion over *Watergate,* the threat of impeachment by Congress, and all those rumors that testified of corruption, President Nixon had no choice but to resign and did so on August 9th. It had only been ten months prior that Nixon's Vice President, Spiro Agnew, made a shocking confession of his own. For he too, had been forced into resigning after he pleaded "No contest" to the charges of income tax evasion. Gerald Ford became the 38th President of the United States when Nixon stepped down. President Ford would then declare, "Our long, national nightmare is over."

Although many thought a bad dream was over, the anxieties that surrounded life weren't quite yet a thing of the past. The National Debt had skyrocketed to well over $382 billion at the inception of the 70's and the economy was now experiencing its worst recession in over forty years - unfortunately, the decade was only half over.

Nathaniel was looking forward to the coming new year - '76. Anything would be better than what the company was experiencing in 1975. Profits were down across the board and every division was posting substantial losses. With Nathaniel at the helm, *Irwin Industries* had previously bragged of everlasting success. But the corporation couldn't lay claim to that gesture of pride any longer - it was now reeling to find some answers. The first three quarters of '75 were all disastrous and Nathaniel couldn't calculate a solution or plan of escape this time. The logical equivalence of such loss would imply stock prices must suffer decline, and they did, dramatically. "The numbers don't lie!" The head of the board would so anxiously, yet fittingly, complain. Because there's not much a corporate executive can do to bolster the economy, Nathaniel, CEO of the third largest fortune 500 company in the world, was really feeling the squeeze of all that national hardship.

Stuffed between all those agonizing thoughts of corporate financial depravity were the anguishing recollections of that "homeless" man, and the unexplainable voice he heard in the elevator.

After tossing and turning for most of the night, Nathaniel decided to get up. The young exec convinced himself a midnight snack, along with a nice warm glass of milk, might do the trick. The reality of it was, divine forces weren't allowing him the rest he so desperately sought - Nathaniel would never enjoy that *salami on rye* he dreamed of.

Nathaniel took a quick peek at the clock before shuffling to his feet. The alarm boldly said 03:30. He then made his way to the bathroom, where he discovered something strikingly different about himself. The young executive filled the sink with warm water and then began to wash his face. After he had dried off with a towel, Nathaniel began to stare at himself in the mirror - he didn't much like what he saw. Talking to himself, Nathaniel shouted, "Not that whiz-kid you thought you were, are you?" That brash abode of confidence the executive once had was about to radically disappear. Disgusted with his own reflection, Nathaniel threw the towel at the mirror and walked out of the room.

Nathaniel then decided to get dressed and go for a walk. It was totally uncharacteristic of the executive to walk the streets of Chicago, especially late at night, but the troubled young man did just that.

Nathaniel didn't give it much thought as to where he should go. He just started walking.

He didn't get far before a police cruiser slowed to give the exec a once over look. Once Nathaniel made eye contact with the cop, the policeman nodded his head and sped off. It's quite possible the law enforcement official did so because Nathaniel was white, or it could have been because the exec was wearing a suit and tie - his attire was a reflection of what the enforced ritual of habit can do.

Observing what it was like for the homeless that night didn't fare well for the emotional trauma the executive was experiencing either. All those images of that piece of society, rarely spoken of, were just too much for Nathaniel to ignore. Many of those poor souls took shelter in cardboard boxes, some were covered only in newspapers. The vast majority of them hadn't bathed for weeks it appeared, and their clothes resembled something out of a rag pile.

Nathaniel wandered aimlessly for hours that night. With utter assurance, it could be said he sought resolve amongst a disturbing quagmire of thought.

As the hint of morn began to unveil itself, the city awoke and Nathaniel found himself standing in front of *The Winchester Arms*. Although the establishment had been renamed years earlier, Nathaniel recognized it to be that old "Gentlemen's Club" his father loved to frequently talk about. A flood of memories absorbed his soul as Nathaniel stood to examine that elegant canopy which stretched forth from the curb to the front door. "Many an important fellow strutted his stuff with swagger under that thing, for sure." Nathaniel thought. How could he forget all those stories Jessup had spun? He found himself standing before a shrine - a bold symbol of power - the structural feat of what money can buy!

A recollection of pride is what Nathaniel remembered most about his father's stories; just how Jessup would brag and carry on about who he associated with. As Nathaniel tried to peer through those stained-glass windows, he couldn't help but notice the *Crests* so proudly etched upon the glass. All those ornaments of pride, *escutcheons,* shields of which all the wealthy Chicago families *Coat of arms* were colorfully depicted.

Nathaniel never had the opportunity to experience the lavish decor of the *Winchester Arms,* nor was he privileged enough to dwell amongst all its royal inhabitants, for Jessup died before the young executive could visit that marvelous place. Nathaniel could only dream of the days when his father drank expensive brandy and smoked imported Cuban cigars with some of the most powerful men in the world. He could only imagine those men toasting themselves with glasses full of pricey champagne while they bragged of their financial exploits.

If Nathaniel thought those memories would give him rest, he was sadly mistaken. He didn't feel the least bit better, even after he'd thoroughly explored the exterior glory of the *Winchester Arms*.

The sun was beginning to peer over the horizon by that time and Nathaniel noticed a bright glare emanating from a building about a block away. Much to the executive's surprise, Nathaniel discovered a small stone chapel wedged between the skyscrapers next door. "That's funny ... why haven't I noticed that church there before?" He thought. The glare he experienced was the sun's reflection off the glass which encased the church's sign. Quite tired, and somewhat exhausted from a lack of sleep, Nathaniel leaned over to read the sign as he placed both hands on top of it to steady himself. The bottom portion of the sign read: "Sunday School begins at 9 am."

The turmoil that raged within Nathaniel's mind was almost too much for him to bear by then. With his hands stretched fourth, Nathaniel closed his eyes and tilted his head back upon his shoulders.

Even though the executive never did relate the experience to being one of a solitary soul in dire need. He also could not imagine a CEO like himself standing before a house of God like he was.

Nathaniel soon turned his head to experience the warm glow of the sun upon his face, then he began to weep when he saw the

orange rays begin to rise. He then said, with a humble heart,
*"God, if you can hear me ... help me ... I feel so all alone.
There must be more to life than this!"*

Chapter Eight
Big City Life

Some considered the 70's an era relative to that of postindustrial order, but many would affectionately come to define the time period as a birthplace of new age. The financial success story and rise of (IBM) International Business Machines, symbolized yet just one example of another shift in the economic scheme of things which emerged from the 1970's. The computer and its capacity to store, manipulate, and communicate vast quantities of data would herald in that new era - *The Information Age.*

Postindustrial era employment in the older manufacturing industries increased only modestly during the 70's. The "smokestack" industries, like steel, surprisingly found themselves more and more depressed economically with the passage of time - it appeared those types of businesses were swiftly becoming a shrinking antiquated relic of the past.

An amazing development of electronic revolution would accelerate in the information age at an extraordinary rate, no doubt the result of driven minds and the unbridled fascination with imagination man has, spawning hundreds of relatively small firms like *Apple, Microsoft* and *Intel* to name a few.

The invention of the floppy disc had occurred at the inception of the decade and in '71 Intel introduced something called a microprocessor, the "computer on a chip," but it would be another five years before Steven Worniak and Steven Jobs could develop their Apple I computer. Both men finished the dream in the Jobs garage on April Fool's Day - 1976. No one could have known, or possibly joked about how serious the invention truly was, it would be a revolutionary change of life. The initial retail price projected per unit was $666.66 - a bargain for 8 bytes of RAM some would claim.

The computer was going to revolutionize life as it was known, but so were those incredible state of the art electronics being developed. Atari's first low-priced integrated circuit TV games and the (VCR) videocassette recorder, would have a hand in changing home entertainment forever.

The Seventies was the decade of big comeback for the movies. After years of box office erosion caused by the popularity of television, a combination of blockbuster movies and new technologies such as Panavision and Dolby Sound brought the masses back to the movies. The sci-fi adventure and spectacular special effects of George Lucas's *Star Wars* made it one of the biggest grossing films ever. Other memorable movies were the disaster films, *Towering Inferno, Earthquake, Poseidon Adventure,* and *Airport.* Sylvester Stallone's *Rocky* reaffirmed the American dream and gave people a hero with a "little guy comes out on top" plot.

Hollywood was cashing in on America's rapidly growing insatiable thirst for entertainment, but so were network moguls like Ted Turner. Turner changed the face of television forever when he launched a satellite in 1976. His strategy was a brilliant one; for he ushered in nationwide programming and an ever-increasing horde of channels would follow - all available twenty-four hours a day.

Barbara Walters became the highest paid woman on television the following year, but the literary works of Chicago author Saul

Bellow didn't go unnoticed either. He won the coveted *Nobel Prize* in '76 for literature - his accomplishments had finally been recognized for all that memorable work.

Many a critic argued it was evolutionary in the late seventies, but it's an unmistakable fact television programming began to lean toward the dark side once *Saturday Night Live* burst on the scene. It satirized people and a number of topics once thought to be off limits. Such things as religion and sex were no longer considered sacred - a few choice network executives saw to that.

In '78, Nathaniel's favorite newspaper, *The Chicago Daily News,* the city's last afternoon paper, ceased its publication.

Earlier that same year, the executive read a small article in the *Daily News* about an unusual partnership formed in Burlington, Vermont. Childhood friends, Ben Cohen and Jerry Greenfield, renovated a gas station there and changed the lives of Ice Cream lovers forever. Nathaniel loved the taste of a cool cone on a hot summer day, his favorite flavor being vanilla, but the exec and everyone else wouldn't have to wait long before they could bask in the pleasurable savor of *Ben and Jerry's* ice cream.

Also in the headlines was the development of medical advances in the area of ultrasound and diagnostic technique. Amidst a storm of moral controversy, scientists had successfully given birth to the first test tube baby as well. They had accomplished the unthinkable; created a child by artificially inseminating an egg, then implanted it in the mother's womb. The sites of DNA production on genes had also been discovered, but the fledging research in genetic engineering had to be halted - pending development of safer techniques.

While scientists were laboring in earnest to create life in the laboratory, the U.S. government was diligently putting forth an effort to destroy it. *The Neutron Bomb*, a powerful weapon used to kill living beings but leave buildings intact, had been successfully perfected according to the praise of the Pentagon.

Death and destruction grabbed the headlines, taking centerstage in the fall of that year. On November 19th, 1978, cult leader Jim Jones and nine hundred of his temple followers committed mass suicide in Jonestown, Guyana. Nathaniel was surprised to learn Jones had previously been a pastor in Indianapolis. A distasteful feeling of loathing overcame the executive when he read about the atrocity. Nathaniel was so repulsed by the article, he verbally professed, "Where was God when that was going on? If religion drives people to do things like that, who needs it?"

The United States went through severe changes in the Seventies. The nation had been bruised by a flurry of corruption stemming from the White House, followed by a Presidential resignation. America's trust had been strangled, its faith in politicians impeded, and uncertainty about government prevailed.

Nevertheless, public confidence wasn't the only thing in deterioration. The largest erosion was occurring at home. The divine invention of family life was disintegrating, crumbling in a manner of which God never intended. Divorce rates had doubled since '65, but before long, one out of every two marriages would fail. Seven times more kids would be affected by divorce than at the turn of the century. The oddity of children commuting between separated parents was becoming commonplace. Traditional families were not only falling apart at an alarming rate, but they were increasingly slow to form in the first place.

U. S. economic instability was climbing to new heights at the top of the problematic list of concerns as well. The value of the dollar had been severely weakened. People were startled regularly in the supermarket to first see sugar soaring from nineteen cents a pound to well over a dollar, then coffee tripled in price, followed by gasoline prices that left many scratching their heads and the empty feeling of a much thinner wallet. Fuel was becoming hard to get, and long lines at the gas pump were common.

1979 was a significant year for the United States financially. Interest rates began to sky-rocket. The prime lending rate reached 21% and the thirty-year bond reached 15%. (The citizenry of the nation was, understandably, in panic mode)

The pleasantries normally littered about the *Irwin Industries* boardroom were now a relic of the past, a fleeting fancy which waned long ago. Patience was a scarce commodity that particular day - it being the final boardroom session convened for conclusion of a wanting decade. The demeanor of the members gave claim to hopeless devastation. Facial expressions said it all. Their reaction to the reading of *Wall Street's* ticker tape told the tale. The manly resolve of intestinal fortitude had been swept under the rug by this bunch.

The atmosphere of the room was heavy laden with a mood of accusatory blame. The boardroom was a dreary, depressing place at best. A bleak future, filled with economic ruin, was the dominating thought for most. Nerves were frayed and emotions were running on edge. Financial barrenness had been the norm for too long and the board wanted some answers for this daunting dilemma - Nathaniel had few.

All corporate plans related to Capital Improvement projects came to a screeching halt that day, and employee layoffs lurked in the shadows with the realistic appearance of being profoundly eminent. Contention in the boardroom had become so thick you could cut it with a knife.

Opposition now separated all sides of the table. Directional views for the corporation were fragmented, split by a number of opinions. Strife was laying waste to the meeting. Things were getting out of control. It was a struggle to get a word in edge wise by now. Every point was met with controversial dispute, each thought contended with seemingly endless heated debate. Tempers were beginning to flare and loud arguments amongst the board members were bordering on eruption. The boardroom was rapidly plagued with conflict and rivalry.

An outburst of, "You stupid S ... 0 ... B!" could be heard above it all and then it happened - a fist fight. It was brief, for other board members broke the two combatants apart. But, nevertheless, in spite of Nathaniel's best effort to intervene and mediate the proceedings, things got dramatically out of hand.

Angered by what he was a witness to, Nathaniel slammed the palm of his hand on the table. That got the attention of the feuding board members. The CEO was so disgusted with his board's behavior by now his face was beet red and the protrusion of veins were predominantly on display upon his forehead and neck. After he had given each individual board member a prolonged glaring stare of condemnation, Nathaniel gathered up his papers. Then he placed the documents in his briefcase and made for the door. As he was walking away, someone had the nerve to ask, "Are we done?"

With a disdained feeling of tarnished confidence, Nathaniel replied, "Gentleman ... you can adjourn on your own!" Then the executive walked out of the boardroom.

Still enraged by the childish behavior of the board, Nathaniel slammed the boardroom door behind himself and swept past his secretary. Betty could tell something was terribly wrong, the disturbances echoing from within the boardroom laid witness to that.

"Are you all right ... Sir?" Betty inquired with a great deal of curiosity and concern.

Nathaniel was making his way to the elevator when he heard the elderly receptionist's interrogative pry.

The executive pushed the *Down* button on the control panel adjacent to the elevator door, then Nathaniel waited briefly before he distastefully threw his hands up in the air.

The CEO wasn't prone to such displays of negative behavior - to the contrary, he was generally optimistic about everything. Betty was unaccustomed to reactions she was witnessing from her boss. Nathaniel was usually a calm, even-tempered fellow. He would never ignore the inquiries of his secretary, let alone turn his back on her in silent refrain, but today was the exception.

When the elevator door opened, Nathaniel quickly stepped inside. The executive turned to make his floor selection, then briefly glanced at Betty. He hung his head slightly, then said with quiet resolve, "Cancel all my appointments for this afternoon." Soon after he uttered those words, the elevator door closed.

As the elevator was enroute to its destination of the front lobby, the executive's mind began to flood with that of a single thought. "I just want to get as far away from this place as possible." Nathaniel had his coat in hand and quickly adorned the garishly fine dark leather garment once the door slid wide.

The lobby was like a literal gauntlet of verbal and personal intrusion for the executive. Nathaniel just wanted to leave, but he was greeted by many a friendly "Hello" and several handshakes by those who populated that crowded lobby. The CEO donned his political "game-face" of joyous glee so he could make short work of every approach - all of it was just a clever ruse. Nathaniel wasn't the least bit interested in the well-being of his employees that day. His concern was a superficial illusion. The deceptive technique he displayed was applied with every effort in mind to exit the building as quickly as possible.

Once his mission, geared toward swift departure, had been cleverly accomplished, Nathaniel exited the crystal-clear revolving doors of Irwin Industries to find himself once again amongst a crowd; the hustle and bustle of a busy sidewalk along one of Chicago's main thoroughfares.

The air was quite brisk that December day. The temperature had fallen considerably since Nathaniel's arrival at work earlier. The second half of the Seventies hadn't been good for business, but you couldn't tell among all the colorful displays of Christmas decor. The facade of corporate headquarters was brightly decorated with an estimated quarter million lights. Many a neighboring storefront was adorned in like fashion with Christmas cheer. Giant yuletide ornaments hung from every lamppost in sight. They reminded the executive of many a memory, previous decorations, and visions of Christmas long past.

Christ's birthday was only about a week away, but the CEO's attention was only slightly affixed upon that. His hope grasped for *a better tomorrow* come 1980. The books were about to close on '79 and Nathaniel quite frankly couldn't wait.

The temperature was hovering around twenty and the executive thought it best to break out his gloves and don that

strange looking hat he recently purchased. Tiny snowflakes
were adrift upon the wind and Nathaniel wrapped his favorite
scarf, the stylish one his father gave him for Christmas some
years ago when he was a teen, around his neck.

The wind was stiff, but blocked somewhat by all the
surrounding buildings - the ones so tall it hurt your neck to look
up at them for a prolonged period of time.

Nathaniel's stomach was telling him it was dinnertime, so he
made his way toward his favorite deli. Along the way, the
executive let many a depressing thought enter in. He whispered
to himself, in repeated disgust, "Welcome to the hassle of Big
City Life!"

Dooley's was the delicatessen Nathaniel loved to frequent.
The deli was tucked away, conveniently, on one of Chicago's
busier side streets. The store's owner, Amos Doolittle, opened the
business in 1950 and was about to celebrate thirty years of
successful operation at the same location.

Amos knew Nathaniel well. Doolittle, a small but pleasantly
outspoken person, made it a point to memorize the names and
occupations of all his regular customers. Jessup, Nathaniel's
father, had also been a regular customer of Amos and Doolittle
knew the Irwin family quite well.

Nathaniel ordered the usual that day - Roast Turkey and
Swiss on Rye with a slice of pickle. The executive ordered the
sandwich and quietly shuffled over to one of the dark secluded
corners in the deli.

Amos watched with a curious eye as the executive took a seat.
Nathaniel didn't touch his meal for the longest time, and the
concerned deli owner took notice. Amos rubbed his hands on the
apron he was wearing, untied it, then instructed a female

employee to take over for him.

Nathaniel was staring out the window, seemingly lost in a cloud of conflicting emotions, when Amos approached him.

Doolittle said, "Hello," several times before Nathaniel snapped out of that daydreaming state of mind he was in.

Once the executive realized he was being spoken to, he said, "Oh ... Hi Amos."

The curious deli owner gently pulled a chair away from the table, with a bit of insightful intrigue, and sat down directly across from Nathaniel, then asked, **"What's** wrong, Nate?"

Amos was like a therapist, of sorts. Although Nathaniel wasn't tempted or prone to drink, Doolittle had a similar relationship with his valued customers much like that of a bartender and his clients. Amos was a good listener, and many abided by the wise words he spoke.

Only a relatively small hand full of people were allowed to address Nathaniel by his first name. He almost always insisted on being called Mr. Irwin. Only a select few were allowed to call him "Nate" - a nickname his father tagged him with when he was a boy. Nathaniel considered Amos a close personal friend, thus allowing him to freely address him as "Nate."

Nathaniel's reply to the Amos inquiry was, "Oh ... nothing."

"Do I look stupid to you, Nate?"

The executive shook his head gently from side to side to give a symbolic, "No."

With a bit of bold flair, Amos inserted, "You got my undivided attention, my friend."

"How is it you can read me like that?" Nathaniel inquired.

"I don't know ... I guess it's a God-given talent ... or it's probably because I've known you since you were a boy. I'm almost seventy you know."

Nathaniel began to wrinkle his face; for he was driven by a nervous, yet unconscious, impulse. He wasn't aware he was, but nevertheless he was. When emotions began to stir within the executive, and he felt he would lose his composure, Nathaniel would unintentionally fight back the tears by wrinkling his nose, mouth, and cheeks.

"There ... you're doing it!"

"Doing what?" The executive asked.

"Nate ... I know you about as well as anybody else. I know something's bothering you. When you don't want anybody to share your pain, you fight back the emotions by making that funny face like you do."

Nathaniel glanced out the window briefly, then commented, "You can read me like a book ... for the life of me ... I can't figure out how you do that!"

"Trouble at the office ... right?" Amos asked.

With a concentrated look of concern on his face, Nathaniel said, "Amos ... for once in my life I don't know who or what to believe. I've always prided myself in knowing what to do and delivering the solution. But ... you're right ... things aren't going well at the office. I'm surrounded by a bunch of angry board members who'd like nothing better than to tear the company apart. Quite frankly ... I'm torn in a number of directions. I simply don't know who to trust or who to confide in."

Amos then added, "The economy isn't always going to be this way ... you know? Go with your gut ... that's what your dad would do!"

Nathaniel asked, "My father used to discuss his business with you?"

"Of course, he did! When something's bothering you, it's best to get it off your chest ... besides … what do you think friends are for?" Amos reasoned.

Nathaniel's reply was, "I guess I didn't realize you and my father were that close."

"Closer than you might think." Amos added. "Your dad told me … on more than one occasion … he appreciated the long talks ... after your mom left. He never told you about that? Or the times I closed shop and we talked for hours."

"No ... he didn't" was Nathaniel's response.

"Your dad may have seemed like a hard man, Nate, but he wasn't like that at all around me. It tore him apart when your mom left, but he let very few people know it. We talked many a night ... about a lot of things ... after I closed up and all."

Nathaniel said, "I had no idea!"

Amos leaned forward slightly, then said, "These things shall pass. There's always a bit of truth in everything, Nate. You'll find it ... if you seek it."

Nathaniel replied, with a half-hearted smile, "You've been talking to that priest of yours again ... haven't you?"

Amos rose, tucked the chair he was sitting in back under the table, then said, "You feel any better?"

Nathaniel nodded his head "Yes" in silent reply.

Amos patted the executive on the back, then said, "I better get back to work ... besides … your dinner's gettin' cold." As he turned to walk away, another thought struck Doolittle. He bent over slightly to whisper something in the executive's ear. With a gentle squeeze of his hand upon Nathaniel's shoulder, Amos whispered, "I attend mass every week ... and yes ... I confess my sins to a priest when need be."

Nathaniel was inclined to take a stroll along Lake Shore Drive after he finished his meal. The executive remembered taking a similar leisurely walk of inclinational wander back in the summer. Navy Pier was littered with boats back then, but it now exhibited the dreary gloom of desolation. The beach adjacent to Lake Michigan was swarming with people then. It now boasted of vacancy and disconsolation as the executive tracked the way of frozen sand. The multitude of bathers congregating that day were mostly children; as Nathaniel recalled, numerous tiny faces filled with pure joy.

But Mother Nature had faithfully substituted a bone-chilling cold with winter's throw and it was getting late. The grayish blue skies were turning orange and Nathaniel thought it best to make his way toward home. The executive thought the time spent to himself had been well worth the effort.

Nathaniel passed a small outdoor garden he hadn't noticed before on his way back home. The CEO relented to his fascinated mind and stopped to examine the various concrete fountains and bronze statues scattered about that beautiful place. In doing so, the executive would be taken back by a flood of thoughts that would eventually refine him.

The north side of the garden proudly displayed several bronze statues. The abstracts reminded Nathaniel of the fountain in front of corporate headquarters - the one he so terribly hated for all too long - that tribute to his grandfather and partner Horatio.

Each statue had a commemorative plaque attached to it that boasted of life's accomplishments for that particular individual. One of the bronze marvels was a likeness of none other than George Mortimer Pullman himself.   His tablet read, among other things, "Inventor and railroad car designer. 1831 -1897."

Nathaniel could still vividly recall those yams his father would spin about Pullman when he was a boy. The executive's unwavering opinion of George Pullman was much like that of his father's. Nathaniel's mindset was, "Pullman was a man everyone loved to hate."

A bronze likeness of Lourse O'Grady was there as well. Nathaniel's opinion of the real estate tycoon wasn't any loftier than that of Pullman. Jessup had instilled that distasteful view in his son many years ago, as did Elias with his boy. Perception is often times guarded as truth, but the opinion one holds shouldn't be absorbed from an ancient line of hostility.

Nathaniel thought to himself, "Is that what I'll be when I die? Something the pigeons sit on."

The executive soon came to realize the southern portion of the garden was decorated with concrete fountains that were also a resemblance of figures past.

One fountain, in particular, caught Nathaniel's eye. Its plaque read: "Dedicated this day, June 12th, 1978, by the city of Chicago. In recognition of: Father Timothy Hutton. A respected community leader and advocate of the poor."

Nathaniel was more than a little repulsed by the appearance of that statue. The refreshing pools had been drained of life months before. The outstretched arms were full of pigeons and all of the fingers on both hands, except one, were broken off.

The executive gazed upon the foolish looking birds for quite a while before saying, "I bet you think we're the stupid ones ... don't you?"

As the CEO exited the outdoor memorial garden, he couldn't help but dwell upon the wonderous realm of reality that lay before him. The executive would ponder these thought-provoking words of his for quite a while. "Wealth buys you bronze, but a dedicated life gets you some sand, cement, and a little stone."

On the way back Nathaniel noticed a familiar site, *The Winchester Arms* and that tiny church nestled next door - the very same chapel that had aroused his curiosity some years earlier. The executive walked right past the Gentlemen's Club and made his way toward the chapel. As he stood in front of the tiny church, Nathaniel could hear the loud echo of wonderful songs bellowing from inside. Before long, his curiosity won the struggle over logical reason and he convinced himself to walk through those inviting doors. Once inside, Nathaniel sat on the back row and began to soak in the evening's event; it being the tail end of a Wednesday night service.

The pastor eventually concluded the service with a prayer and as heads were bowed, Nathaniel took that as his liberty to leave.

The remainder of the workweek was a hectic one for the CEO, but he just couldn't get that tiny little chapel off his mind.

When Saturday night arrived, Nathaniel told himself he was going to bed at a decent hour. He planned on getting up bright and early the following morning, then eat a hardy breakfast. His intentions were to visit that "Crowded Chapel," as he called it, to see what they were all about and had to offer. As the executive recalled, the activities began at nine.

Chapter Nine
The Sermon

Nathaniel's tiny Timex alarm faithfully erupted with that annoying buzz at the chosen time early Sunday morn. The sound was jolting and a startling interruption of restful bliss for the executive. The wake-up call wasn't all that welcome, but as it is for most, to arise, partaking of what life has to bring, is the acceptance of reality. Nevertheless, the day was going to be a historic one for the CEO, for it would be Nathaniel's first adventure to Sunday school.

As routine would so often generously dictate, Nathaniel slightly tilted his face on the side of the pillow and visually checked the soft orange glow of the numbers revealed. The executive then aimlessly reached for the "snooze" button and slowly slid himself to the side of the bed once the extinguishing deed had been done. Physically dropping his lead-filled legs to the floor, Nathaniel then adorned those fancy slippers of his - the ones strategically aligned beside the antique marble nightstand.

As the alluring thoughts of the day ahead filled his inquisitive mind with anticipation, Nathaniel rubbed his sleep-riddled weary eyes.

After a brief moment or two, the executive adjusted the alarm to the *off'* position and arose to trudge that dreaded path toward the bathroom.

Nathaniel had just finished washing his face when he heard a soft murmuring sound corning from what he thought was the bedroom. The executive's investigative instincts were then aroused. Nathaniel would surely contemplate and justify, with a reasonable amount of certainty, "I could have sworn I turned off that alarm!" But, the disturbance was also a bit puzzling for the executive. The *Cooing* being emitted wasn't characteristic or familiar to the CEO at all.

With a burst of anticipation, followed by surprise, Nathaniel swung the bedroom door open wide. The executive's slightly inclined assumption was it wasn't the alarm making that relaxing noise.

Nathaniel then began to search the apartment with an intriguing hope of discovering what was initiating the dilemma.

The executive's penthouse apartment was unquestionably a showpiece of beauty, an eye-catching astonishment to behold. For all those who entered its hallowed walls, the sacred domain gave credence to the spectacular wonder of luxurious architectural design that was symbolic of no sacrificial expense. The living room boasted of nothing but the best in furnishings and basked itself in the constant rays of sun during the day. The living room was, by far, the most spectacular room of them all because it was orchestrated so. It was a defining point for the architects who'd dreamed it - the centerpiece of man's clever hand. The room was a masterpiece of design. The idea had come from the minds of several of the best architectural minds in Chicago, and unquestionably the most expensive indeed.

Nathaniel had quickly shifted his focus of investigative prowess to the living room, for the sounds appeared to be emanating from there. By now, those "Cooing" sounds were driving the executive into an agitated fit of frenzy.

A search of the room's interior was unsuccessful. Nathaniel

then thought it might be a long-shot, but he decided it was worth it to look behind those Asian silk drapes covering the living room windows. Three quarters of the room was encircled by glass and the drapes were many; numbering ninety-three. In the scheme of things, the lead architect had reasoned opening and closing so many drapes would be a monumental task so he specified remote control closure devices for all twelve window sections.

Nathaniel bent over to pick up the remote lying on the coffee table, then he clicked the "Open All" button. The drapes began to slowly open and, after the rising morning sun had revealed it, Nathaniel realized who the culprit was making those annoying sounds.

Perched on a tiny ledge, where nary a pigeon would go, was a dove bobbing its way back and forth on the narrow lip. Nathaniel thought a dove forty stories up was an unusual sight, though a fascinating one. The executive bent down on one knee to closely examine the curious fowl. Once the creature caught a glimpse of Nathaniel, it began to extend its neck up and down with a tilting motion of the head. The executive's fascination with the bird grew with steady intrigue as he stared through the pane. Nathaniel would have opened the window, but the building's design made that quite impossible; for the windows were made of solid plate glass and were affixed in a stationary position. The artificially controlled environment within the structure was revolutionary, but made an individual's access to fresh air improbable.

Nathaniel slowly raised his hand to the window and gently pressed his palm against the cool pane. When the executive did

so, the dove began to "Coo" a little more and peck at the glass.
The bird's response held Nathaniel's attention with a firm grip of
fascinating wonder. He thought, "Why in the world is that thing
trying to peck at my hand?" The executive then began to softy
speak to the dove; as if he wanted the fowl to understand his
reasoning plea of concern. "It's the dead of winter. We're forty
stories up. Why aren't you off somewhere trying to stay warm
with some other birds?"

After a brief moment of silence, the "Cooing" fowl spread its
wings upon the glass with a gentle rubbing motion, then it
dropped from the ledge to soar off upon an uplifting current of
wind.

Nathaniel thought the bird's behavior was more than a little
unusual. He'd never witnessed anything quite like that before, and
imagined he probably wouldn't again.

To say the executive was a bit taken back by the dove's strange
behavioral display would have been an accurate assessment, but
Nathaniel was now absorbed in other things that were
preoccupying his mind.

After the executive closed the drapes, he made quick work of a
shower. Since it was his first official visit to a Sunday service,
Nathaniel reasoned it best to adorn himself with one of those
expensive three-piece suits of his. The selection, being one of
his favorites, was a gray Italian blend. The tie he chose had a
slash of bluish-gray in it that matched the vest. Never of concern
to the executive was the trivial matter of wrinkled shirts, for they
were always dry-cleaned and pressed by his favorite cleaner -
Classic Express.

Nathaniel slipped stylish polished wingtips on, then shined

them with a bit of pride once he gazed upon his stunning reflection in the mirror. The executive was, without question, confident he was ready to go - once he'd indulged himself in a gratifying breakfast of course.

The CEO prepared himself a ham and cheese omelet, two sausage patties, a couple pieces of toast burned to a crisp as usual then scraped before buttered, a cup of black instant coffee and a tall cool glass of orange juice.

Nathaniel saw no reason to disturb his driver on Sunday, so he elected to forgo a limousine ride for the pleasurable experience of a brisk morning stroll.

The CEO arrived at the church somewhere around twenty till nine. Catching a glimpse of *The Crowded Chapel's* front sign brought back a gaggle of memories for the executive; all from years prior. In a futile effort to frame the words, Nathaniel struggled to vocalize, in a low tone of uttered evaporating articulation, the reasons upon which he pinned those frivolous excuses for embracing the failure of not being a churchgoer.

The executive briefly stopped, then stood on the sidewalk to read the information displayed upon the sign.

The placard read:

*"Welcome to the First Baptist Church of Chicago. Today's sermon - **'Put yourself in God's shoes!'** The bottom of the* sign also revealed: *"Established in 1862. The very Reverend Daniel J. Matthews presiding."*

Troubled slightly by the display's wording, Nathaniel's mind raced with the thought of, "The very Reverend? ... What's with that?" With an ever-so-slight flutter of those agitated eyelids, and a brisk shake of the head while demonstrating that menacing undertowed curled lip of his, the CEO concluded, "It's probably just a joke or something."

Nathaniel quickly concluded the observation, then turned to approach the church. A bright array of sunshine revealed a few things the executive hadn't noticed before; that which appealed to the senses and swayed him by way of intrigued fascination.

The executive experienced a mixture of emotions while strolling toward the front door. His entangled thoughts were not only adrift upon that spectacular exterior decor of the building, but the lingering question of, "Who's waiting on the front steps?" was also a daunting concern.

The church bells were ringing with harmonious song that morning, but it wasn't an overly familiar tune for the executive. Those large dark oak front doors were quite impressive to the CEO and drew his fanciful attention rather quickly. Nathaniel estimated them to be about eight feet tall and then again that wide. The doors were definitely a showpiece. They were proudly original, crafted in Europe by those of an era long gone. The weight of the doors, both tipping the scale at roughly five hundred pounds each, was only dwarfed by their amazing exhibition of elegant detail. The craftsmanship demonstrated on the doors and their frame was a work of art - something refined by their creator. It was obvious to Nathaniel the craftsman had once appreciated the finer things of life; that he had the up-most respect for it and worshipped its graces.

The exterior design of the church testified of European

architecture as well, almost castle-like in appearance and strikingly picturesque with a hint of magnificent splendor. The copper roof had turned antiquely green with the passage of time, a bit of streaked stone bore testimony of it being so. The what-appeared-to-be original wooden rain troughs hanging from the eaves were obviously a dated feature. It seemed modern gutters were definitely out of the question. Historical value had clear-cut meaning and no doubt meant something.

A concrete wheelchair ramp, specifically designed for the elderly and handicapped, justified into being by mandated law, had been recently constructed at the side entrance. It was an added feature that looked somehow out of place in the orchestrated scheme of things. The ramp was unquestionably a modern convenience affixed to benefit those suffering, yet, it had been opaque in the minds of many and foolishly ignored for a long time.

A dual set of towering steeples rose far above the church roof on the north end and each proudly displayed a large brass cross. Rumor had it they were original as well. The stained-glass windows were quite impressive in their own right. They individually bore the likenesses of previous saints - possibly John, Peter, or Paul. But there was intention and defined reason given to the placement of the largest stained pane of them all. Positioned directly above the front door was a stained-glass window bearing the likeness of Jesus.

The image was a depiction of Christ kneeling before a large rock, praying with folded hands. It was a masterpiece, bathed in the glory of colored glass, no doubt a work of art as well, but Nathaniel's intrigue was focused upon that shaft of light beaming upon the Savior's face in the pane.

A gentle coaxing prod, used by the polite one waiting upon the front steps, eventually snapped the executive's concentration.

"Is it your first time here?" The kind stranger asked.

Nathaniel replied, "I've passed by a few times in recent years."

The dubious and hesitant fellow gave his head a nod in ponder then questionably uttered the word, "Huh." Then, with a quick pat of the executive's back, the jovial stranger said, "I'm Pastor Matthews ... I appreciate you taking the time to visit with us today."

Tucked away in the cellarage depths of his mind, Nathaniel had stored a clever saying his father coined years prior - *The measure of a man is in his grip.* Dredging up that memory of Jessup's impressionable wisdom, in an effort to test its merit, the CEO extended his hand toward Pastor Matthews. The minister's grip was anything but firm. His handshake was only a shade or two away from being limp-wristed. Consequently, Nathaniel's first impression of the clergyman was less than favorable, yet it grew dimly worse, for the minister's skin was uncomfortably cold and clammy to the touch as well.

The weather was cool out, slightly bordering just above freezing, yet the minister's temples were notably adorned with tiny groups of beaded sweat.

Pastor Matthews was a heavy man. His appearance that morning, for some reason, reminded Nathaniel of a modern-day *Friar Tuck* - one of Robin Hood's merry men. The famed character was quite possibly the most celebrated criminal of them all, for the legendary English outlaw of the 12th century was infamously known to "steal from the rich and give to the poor." Nathaniel

may have possibly had a delusion or two the good Reverend was
going to pick his pockets dry, but that ceremonial garb Pastor
Matthews wore was definitely the kindling that fueled the CEO's
stereotyped driven opinion.

Pastor Dan, as he was often fondly referred to, battled, like the
majority of the population did, an expanding waistline, no doubt
due to one-too-many fried chicken dinners on Sunday afternoon,
the executive reasoned with unkindly thought. The good
Reverend had a shiny forehead as well; it bore of a hairline in
recession. The clergyman's thick spectacles boasted of middle
age, even though the poor fellow was only fifty two.

Nathaniel never vocalized any of those rude thoughts of his.
He kept every one of them to himself. But, that "Friar Tuck
clone" wasn't dumb. Pastor Matthews had an acute sense of
perception when it came to understanding body language. He
had an uncanny ability, in a weird way, to read people. It was
like he could tell what they were thinking.

The perceptive Reverend glanced the CEO over, slightly
raised an eyebrow, then mentally twirled an assumption around
in his head about the executive. But Pastor Dan quickly laid that
cognition to rest. After a flash of hesitation, Pastor Matthews
said, "Glad to have you with us today!"

The minister had a death-grip on that Bible of his when he
spoke. Perhaps involuntary or out of nervous habit, the good
Reverend raised that tattered King James Version he held
toward his heart when he verbalized those orchestrated courteous
words of his.

Conversely, and in the absence of withstanding logical
reason, the Reverend's voice now seemed stem and looming to

the executive - in a strange, odd, sort of way.

In Nathaniel's arsenal of personal savvy for business lay a striking niche for reading people as well. He had little trouble distinguishing brazen boldness when he saw it, especially in those branded with confidence. The CEO assessed, in relatively short order, Pastor Matthews was gifted with such a characteristic. What the minister may have lacked in some areas he made up for with fervent firmness and vigorous attitude.

Pastor Dan knew God's Word, that was a given. But he also had a way with people - a simplistic manner of bringing out the best in the least. He had a unique personality, one capable of soaking into your veins. Encapsulating a fiber of trust was Reverend Matthews's specialty. Once you were around Pastor Dan for a while, you couldn't help but fall in love with his passion; foremost was his longing for the things of Christ, coupled with a true spiritual compassion for God's people. (Nathaniel, as a sinner, had no idea he was being divinely ensnared.)

Nathaniel's response to the Reverend's greeting was one of a generic, "Thank you." The CEO realized others were approaching Pastor Dan, wanting to shake the minister's hand, so Nathaniel made his way up the stone steps and through those massive doors. He was a bit more ambitious this time, for the executive took a seat in the third row from the rear. It was an advancement of only a couple rows compared to his previous visit, but it held symbolic meaning nonetheless. His actions were clad in curiosity, yet exhibited a slight hint of courage nevertheless; for Nathaniel chose to no longer occupy, dwell, or justifiably hide, amidst the isolated social seclusion of the back row.

Once he made himself comfortable, Nathaniel began to read the church bulletin the friendly usher had given him; the kind fellow handed it to the CEO as he awaited the crowd's arrival, just inside the front door. The executive took mental note of the usher's neat appearance, his kind personality, and helpful attitude. Nathaniel had acknowledged the polite mannerisms of the friendly gentleman by invoking a verbal courtesy of his own. "Thank you, John," was the executive's reply. For the CEO had observed the usher's bright gold, black lettered, name tag that was on proud display, pinned to the elderly man's chest. The colorful identification badge read: "John Leonard - Head Usher."

As the executive leafed through the bulletin, he couldn't help but notice all the numerous, yet diversified, activities the church had to offer. The ladies had recently established a group called, *God's Gals.* The bulletin stated they were actively seeking new members and that they would meet every Tuesday evening at 7 o'clock at a different lady's home. The men also had a group. It consisted of any guy eighteen and up. They had a catchy name too - *Guys of Faith.* They met for breakfast every other Saturday morning at 8 o'clock. Nathaniel noticed the children and teenagers were included as well, and had groups of their own. The kids, twelve and under, had various activities scheduled off and on throughout the month, but Nathaniel was most intrigued with what the church had to offer the young adults.

On Friday nights, between seven and eleven, The First Baptist Church of Chicago opened its doors to all teens throughout the community. The church sponsored what they called *Rockin' for Jesus* on those nights. In an effort to keep kids off the streets, the church converted the basement into a "teen hang-out." The boys and girls could eat to their heart's content, play some pool, indulge themselves in a wholesome video game or two, dance to Christian music, or just experience the friendly fellowship of friends.

Nathaniel thought the idea was an ingenious one. There were though, on any given Friday night, over twenty adult volunteers monitoring those activities.

Once Nathaniel had intellectually digested the bulletin, he began to observe those who made up the congregation. The crowd consisted of men and women, the young, as well as the old. The executive estimated the number of those in attendance to be around a thousand.

A few men were wearing stylishly fine suits that morning. A couple older guys wore suits suspiciously considered outdated classics. Quite a few ladies were wearing dresses and one elderly gal caught Nathaniel's eye. She had fashionably adorned herself with a bright blue Sunday bonnet and long, elbow length, white lacy gloves.

There were, of course, those who stood out like a sore thumb to the CEO. A handful of kids wore faded jeans and T-shirts, but so did a number of adults. One middle-aged guy had the "brazen nerve" to wear a Cubs shirt to church, the executive thought.

Nathaniel was appalled, to the point of scorn, that, apparently, rules for apparel were forsaken. "What ... no Dress Code?" The executive thought. "There must not be one here." One of the CEO's disdainfully contemptuous feelings were, "The attendant at the Winchester Arms next door wouldn't let someone dressed so ridiculously like that step a foot inside the door."

Nathaniel's focus soon shifted to the front of the sanctuary once he heard the pipe organ begin to play. He noticed an elderly woman perched upon a bench in front of the massive instrument. Her fingers were now whirling about the keyboard as she belted out the whimsically spiritual tune. The executive had never seen, nor heard, anything quite like that before. The pipes arising above the instrument varied in length, but also followed the slanted curvature of the wall. The magnificent musical piece was a visual wonder, but not lost in the immenseness of importance was its sound. The almost hallow sounding air driven notes it produced were captivating to say the least. They were reverberating throughout the sanctuary.

To begin the service, the choir, some fifty strong, sang several hymns, but a couple of those were most intriguing to the CEO. Nathaniel wasn't familiar with the songs listed on pages 43 and 92 of the hymnal, so he followed along by reading the printed lyrics. The executive didn't sing at all that day, but he did listen carefully as the choir sung *Amazing Grace* and *Just A Closer Walk With Thee*.

Once the choir had finished offering those worshipful resonations of divine praise, its robed members exited the stage. Nathaniel thought it odd every single man and woman making up the choir wore the garnishee of a smile. When they left the platform, that's when the executive realized it was time for the sermon because Pastor Matthews now stood upon the elevated pulpit.

The good Reverend began the sermon by telling his congregation, "I'm not going to give a typical Christmas message today. I won't bore you with the type of sermon that routinely lends itself to the historical values of the Christmas story. We all know what Christmas represents." Gazing upon the congregation, Pastor Matthews further reasoned, "Don't we?" Several heads in the crowd nodded in silent agreement. "We sang about it some this morning in song. Everyone's familiar with the tale of a babe in the manger ... even the children are." With that said, a few of the little ones in the crowd shook their heads up and down with a display of excitement.

The minister cleared his throat, then added, "If you would, please turn with me to the book of John ... I'm sure most of you will recognize this verse ... it's one of my favorites ... John 3:16."

The rustle of turning pages could be heard all across the sanctuary. Nathaniel felt somewhat embarrassed though, for he had no Bible. An observant elderly lady, sitting next to the executive, realized he couldn't read along. So, with a gentle nudge of her elbow, the senior citizen silently offered her opened Bible to the CEO. Nathaniel thought it was odd she wanted to share her book with a perfect stranger. The executive was polite, but declined the tiny gray-haired lady's generous offer.

The Pastor began to read. Then a hush fell upon the crowd. "Jesus tells us in this passage. For God so loved the world ... that he gave his only begotten Son ... that whosoever believeth in him should not perish ... but have everlasting life." The minister cleared his throat once again, then went on to say, "I know you've probably heard that verse many a time throughout the course of your life ... maybe even numbed yourself to it ... I'm sorry to say, I did." The minister briefly looked down at his notes, chewed on his lip a bit, then raised his head and went on to say, "You know something. I love a lot of things ... football for one. But, there for a while, I got caught up in things that weren't really important. I was too busy for my own good, you might say. Of all things … it took a fan to wake me up ... I was watching a Bears game just the other day. They had just scored on the opening drive. Then they panned the camera on the end zone." The minister hesitated briefly. He was notably stirred with emotion by then. Pastor Dan blinked back the tears, then went on to say, "The camera was focused on a guy in the crowd. He was holding a big sign. It said, John 3:16. To be honest ... when I saw that … I lost it ... I couldn't stop crying ... After that … I shut the game off." Pastor Dan hesitated a moment, then he added, "I want you all to understand the deep spiritual roots of that verse … especially this week ... let its meaning soak in … won't you?"

The Pastor closed his Bible and briefly glanced at his notes. He then began to slowly point out individuals in the crowd. While pointing at a gentleman, sitting on the end of the first row pew, the minister said, "Jim, you have just one child ... Right?" The distinguished stocky fellow nodded his head to agree. "Could you sacrifice your son ... give him up to an angry mob ... a sinful bunch who were just itchin' to kill him?"

Jim could do no better than hang his head low in response to that piercing question.

The minister then pointed at a couple sitting directly in front of Nathaniel that were only three or four rows away. To acknowledge them, the pastor said, "Bill ... Sue." Then with a gentle wave of his hand, went on to say, "I've known this couple for a lot of years. They too are parents of a single child ... a boy ... his name's Jacob." In an effort to reiterate the point, Pastor Dan said, "Could you love a corrupt world? Bill ... Sue. A world so sinful ... you wish you hadn't created it at all? How about throwing your boy to the wolves ... to those who hate him, and everything he stands for ... Could you do that? Could you hand Jacob over ... knowing he was going to die ... for a bunch of strangers? Strangers who know nothing of you, or your son ... ones totally unworthy of love."

Nathaniel couldn't help but notice the impact Pastor Dan's words were having upon the crowd. The sanctuary air was heavy-laden with the stir of stark reality - dead silence.

A few amongst the congregation were beginning to weep, others stared downward at the floor, some chose to glare at the ceiling or walls, the blank expressions exhibited upon the many faces of the crowd pretty much summed u p the feelings of them all.

The CEO watched from behind, as Bill tilted his head slightly toward Sue. Then the loving husband stretched forth a hand to hold his wife's shoulder. She, in tum, laid her head upon the comfort of his shoulder.

After he had assessed the response of the audience, Pastor Dan proclaimed, "I've entitled this message, *Put yourself in God's shoes.*" After clearing his throat, yet again, the minister asked an usher for a glass of water. He then went on to add, "We all know Jesus was born in Bethlehem ... We all know the story about the three wise men ... That Jesus was born of virgin birth ... and ... that he was the Son of God. But, why did He, who was perfect, sinless, have to die? That's a good question ... it brings me to my next point. Why was Jesus crucified on a cross ... at that place called Calvary?"

After the good Reverend had looked around, to study the many faces amongst the crowd, he asked with stern resolve, "Who killed Christ?" After a long pause, Pastor Dan said, "We all did!"

A hush settled over the crowd and after a moment or two, the minister continued. "Some think the Romans had a hand in Jesus's death ... maybe they did. But whether we understand it or not, Christ's death was all in God's plan. Those Roman soldiers carried out only what the father allowed."

After a brief pause, Pastor Matthews interjected, "Christ was a sacrifice for the sin of man ... we all had a hand in killing him! I know that sounds harsh ... but it's the truth."

As soon as he finished that statement, the minister looked down at his notes and surprised the audience further by saying, "You know something?" There were many a blank look upon the faces of the crowd by now. "We're all Morons!"

The audience didn't respond in kind fashion to that comment. There were quite a few "Huhs" that arose from the crowd, and a few "Hummmms" of dissatisfaction. One man in the back of the sanctuary even yelled, "Hey!" Another gentleman toward the front commented, rather loudly, "Come on!" Nathaniel found himself, along with others, questioning the minister's reasoning.

Almost immediately, a baby began to cry rather loudly as well. Only after several minutes, and a directed glare of apprehension from the minister, did the mother finally decide to remove the infant from the sanctuary.

An elderly lady, sitting to Nathaniel's left, leaned over to the executive and whispered something in his ear while the baby was crying. With a bony hand cupped over the comer of her mouth the small gray-haired senior said, "I wish she'd take that kid out of here ... it's disturbing me!"

Nathaniel chose to keep his thoughts to himself, although the executive had already formed quite a few opinions of his own about that little old lady. The executive couldn't help but notice that moth-eaten dress she wore. Nathaniel wondered if she even noticed it was that way when she dressed herself that morning. It was hard to look upon that gal.

She appeared to be a skeleton with skin stretched over it. Quite possibly, Nathaniel reasoned, it was the smell of anticipated death she was trying to mask because he thought, "This lady reeks of stale perfume!" Her smile had an ominously blackish tint about it too. The woman's teeth hadn't been kept and their appearance was eerie. The executive's mind filled with many a thing about that old gal. She probably suffered from dementia. Who knows, he finally reasoned, "Maybe she's just poor!"

Once the mother removed the child from the sanctuary, that same elderly lady leaned over to Nathaniel again. With a cup of the hand over the comer of her mouth, once more, she said, "It's about time!"

Nathaniel thought, "She needs a mint!" For the woman's breath was nauseously appalling, expressively pungent, and offensively revolting. But the executive didn't dare tell her that. He didn't want to risk the chance of insulting her, and the possibility of her making a spectacle out of it. Nathaniel was so repulsed by the woman he scooted a little to his right to avoid her. When the executive did that, the elderly lady reacted by nudging a little closer toward him.

The good Reverend sensed his last comment didn't go over well with the crowd, so he went on to say, "Please ... hear me out ... A Moron's defined as one who lacks wisdom." Pastor Dan went on to explain, "It's amazing to me ... We can recite the Christmas story by heart ... but, we fail to understand why we're really here ... Christ paid an ultimate price ... He paid it for you and I!"

The minister's eyes began to redden, then the tears began to flow. After he had regained his composure, Pastor Dan went on to say, "I, myself, have been a Moron for quite a few years. As you all know, I haven't been feeling well for a while. I've had a lot of time to think about my own wisdom lately ... why I'm here ... especially now ... at Christmas time and all. Don't get me wrong. There's nothing wrong with Christmas cheer, and all that which comes with it ... I just think we lose focus sometimes."

The minister waited a moment, then said, "I've been asking myself a lot of questions lately. What's the real reason for the season, for one ... Another being, what's important to God. In my own little way, I've been trying to put myself in God's shoes this week."

The good Reverend looked down at his wife, who was sitting directly in front of him on the front row, and gave her a wink. He added, "I told my wife I didn't want to open presents this year. You might say I've gained a little knowledge in light of the hard times we're all facing ... a better understanding of what life's really all about, I might add!"

After appearing to be lost in a moment of thought, Pastor Dan went on to say, "Instead of giving each other presents this year, my wife and I are going to do something a little different. We plan on buying as many gifts as we can, then write, *From Jesus,* on every label. We're gonna load 'em up in the car on Christmas day, then pay a visit to the homeless shelter. We plan on taking a few bags of food along too. Maybe a gallon or two of hot chocolate as well ... make a day out of it!"

Pastor Dan hesitated once again, then added, "I'm ashamed to admit it, but it's been all about *US* in the Matthews household for too long ... those days are over. My wife and I have a better understanding of things now ... we've gained a little more of that refined wisdom you might say. We finally got the big picture. What the Holy Spirit has laid upon our hearts to do on Christmas Day ... well ... I'm sure it'll put a smile upon God's face ... Matthew 19:30 has taken on a whole new meaning for us." Pastor Dan leafed through his Bible to that verse, then he began to read. "'But many that are first ... shall be last; and the last ... shall be first.' "

A humble calm soon drifted over the crowd. The congregation could sense a sincere echoing from the pulpit - the Pastor's cracking voice revealed it to be so.

"If you would, I'd like for you to turn with me in your Bibles to a couple verses. We'll start with Second Timothy, chapter three, verses one through five. Then we'll tum to Second Thessalonians, chapter two, verse three."

The rustle of pages being turned could be heard all across the sanctuary, and soon the minister began to read. "'Know this also, that in the last days perilous times shall come.' We're there folks." The good Reverend added. "'For men shall be lovers of their own selves, covetous, boasters, proud, blasphemers, disobedient to parents, unthankful, unholy, without natural affection, trucebreakers, false accusers, incontinent, fierce, despisers of those that are good, traitors, heady, high-minded, lovers of pleasures more than lovers of God; having a form of godliness, but denying the power thereof: From such tum away.'" The minister gazed down upon the crowd and said, "Let that soak in for a minute ... now, if you would, let's turn to that second verse."

After a brief pause, Pastor Dan began to read again. "'Let no man deceive you by any means: For that day shall not come, except there come a falling away first, and that man of sin be revealed, the son of perdition.'" What Paul's trying to tell us in this passage is simply this … Don't be deceived. In other words … don't get caught up in all the things of the world, some of it isn't what it appears to be ... Most of it isn't spiritually healthy anyhow. The day Paul's referring to in this verse is Christ's return. He points out that Christ's return won't happen until a falling away from the faith ... morals ... occur first. I'd say we're already there ... wouldn't you? The man of sin he speaks of is Satan. The son of perdition ... damnation."

The good Reverend paused a moment, then continued on with the message. "I've come to realize there are a multitude of believers, but I'm convinced many are Christian in name only." A little nervous and unsure of how the crowd might react to that last statement, Pastor Dan added, "With that said, Let's move on!"

The Pastor looked down at his notes, then took a drink of water from the glass an usher had provided. He briefly glanced up at the ceiling, then began to change the subject slightly.

By now, Nathaniel was becoming quite interested in what the good Reverend had to say. The executive, on more than one occasion, caught himself verbally saying, "Go on ... Go on!"

"Rome did thousands of crucifixions." The good Reverend added. "It wasn't something new. It was their way of keeping order ... They'd line the roads with people hanging on crosses to get their point across. In other words, if you didn't bow to Caesar ... if you got out of line ... that's what your fate would be. I'm sure it was an effective deterrent ... barbaric ... but psychologically effective.

So why was Jesus's crucifixion any different than the rest? In many of today's Christian circles, that's much too deep a thought to probe. It's far easier to just block out that mental image of pain and suffering. I guess they don't really understand who Christ was or why He had to die ... why he came to save a lost world. It's quite possible ... the commitment many believers once had toward Him has since waxed cold with the passage of time ... they loved Christ once, but now, they're not so sure. Maybe our busy lifestyles have something to do with that, I don't know."

With that said, Pastor Dan looked down at the crowd and began to visually scan the congregation. He recognized many a familiar face out there. The minister winked at a few he knew, and at others he just simply nodded.

"I see we have a couple professional ball players in attendance today. Ernie's a centerfielder for the White Sox ... Blair's a shortstop for the Cubs ... it's good to

see that you're in the house of the Lord today guys." An
applause arose from the crowd with that announcement;
when it died down, the minister continued. "We also
have with us today, a few distinguished attorneys ... I
counted four councilmen and we're glad to have the
Honorable Judge Lewis J. Rankin with us. It's nice to
see you in the house of the Lord today ... Your Honor."
Again, an applause erupted from the crowd - it wasn't
nearly as loud as before though.

"I appreciate everyone being here today. I thank you for
gracing us with your presence. But I'd like to emphasize
something far more important than Home Runs or RBI's ...
something far more important than winning that big case ... or
what kind of social justice you've championed lately."

Pastor Matthews then found Nathaniel in the crowd and
began to stare at him. It wasn't a long-sustained glare, but,
nevertheless, it made the CEO feel a little uncomfortable. The
minister then glanced down at his notes to say, "It doesn't really
matter how much money you have either!"

"Why is he looking at me?" The executive thought. "Until
today, I've never met that preacher before! That's eerie!"

Nathaniel didn't realize it, but Pastor Matthews recognized
who the CEO was the moment he laid eyes on him. The minister
knew exactly who Nathaniel was. The good Reverend
recognized the CEO from various newspaper and magazine
articles he'd read; the ones that proudly displayed photos of the
executive.

The minister was quick to interject, "Life's short ... ladies and
gentleman. What we do with it ... what type of shoes we fill ...

what humble paths we dare take ... well ... that's what's important
to God ... the creator of our soul."

After the pastor spoke, Nathaniel began to reason with
himself, "I've foolishly jumped to conclusions about that man."
He thought, "Those words he speaks are not only moving and
powerful, but they're piercing too. I think I've carelessly
misjudged him. He's a lot wiser than I gave him credit."

Nathaniel was ashamed to admit it, but he knew nothing of
this Gospel the minister was proclaiming. You might say the
accomplished business exec, someone who was literally a
genius, one who excelled in just about everything he did, was
ignorant. He was illiterate when it came to a grasping
knowledge of God's word. For Nathaniel had never read a
Bible, let alone cracked one open, although he recalled hearing
the many stories about his great-grandparents and their found
faith.

"I'm a dolt!" The executive thought.

As things began to stir within his soul, the CEO began to look
around the sanctuary. He noticed a few interesting things about
the congregation; the most disturbing of which was the lack of
concentration by a choice few. Nathaniel noticed a handful of
men who had fallen asleep. A couple of women weren't exempt
from that urge to slumber either. A few of the spouses nudged
their partners, but others just simply ignored their behavior and let
them doze.

In spite of the noticeable waning interest of a select few, and
the obviously careful examination of many an individual who
sported a wristwatch, the minister boldly waded on with the
sermon. "I'd like to share with you a dream I had a couple weeks

ago." He said, "The dream had two parts. In the first part, my wife and I took a taxi to a large church. It looked like a big sports arena ... it was that large! We were greeted at the door by a bunch of nice folks. They shook my hand and gave my wife a hug. They said they were glad to see us. We walked into the building, but there was nothing there ... it was totally bare! A lot of people were walking around acting as if something was going on, but there wasn't! There was even a guy cooking hamburgers … he asked us if we wanted one ... we said no. My wife and I explored that entire place. It was completely empty ... nothing but bare walls ... but a large number of people there acted as if something was happening.

In the second part of the dream, I was invited to speak out West. When I got there, I discovered I was being locked away in a room with several others. In that room, the master of ceremony was dictating to us what to say. He told us ... I assume the others in the room were ministers as well ... to not mention the name of Jesus too often in the services or do anything that would seem controversial. In the dream, I stood up to say, No! I said, we're not ashamed of the Lord ... we'll do no such thing! Two or three others in the crowd stood up to agree. I then told who was running the show we wanted to go. He then made arrangements to take us to the airport. As we were leaving, I noticed the building we were in was completely vacant ... it looked like an abandoned warehouse. The signs on the outside of the building said it was a church, but there was nothing inside. As the driver drove our van away, I was staring out the window. I then noticed a small ... what appeared to be a car wash ... next door. When I asked the driver what that was, he said it wasn't important. When

I pressed him, he said it was a tiny church. Car upon car was in line to be washed up there. I thought to myself, they must be doing something right! Obviously, God's moving over there ... look at the souls being cleaned!"

The good Reverend paused a moment, then went on to say, "First of all, I'd like to point out that Acts 2:17 says, 'And it shall come to pass in the last days, saith God, I will pour out of my Spirit upon all flesh and your sons and your daughters shall prophesy, and your young men shall see visions, and your old men shall dream dreams.'"

In an effort to break the tension a bit, the minister jokingly said, "I'd like to think that dream of mine was actually a vision ... being that I haven't applied for a senior citizen's discount card yet." Several in the crowd got the joke, some didn't. Needless to say, the ice-breaker tactic worked and quite a few chuckles could be heard all across the sanctuary.

"But seriously folks!" The pastor added. "That dream has a lot of meaning. God was telling me the churches of America are getting larger, but there's nothing there. Nothing there because His spirit's absent. There's quite a few people who go ... there's a lot to do ... But the one and only isn't there! The God of my existence ... my all and all ... doesn't grace their doorstep. That's truly sad ... for I feel we've sold out to things that aren't really important to Him. We've become too preoccupied with entertainment ... too self-absorbed in ourselves to see the light. I think it's time to throw away those selfish shoes we've worn and try His on for a while!"

For the first time during the service, people began to slowly stand and applaud. Pastor Dan slightly hung his head, in part to regain composure and choke back the tears, but to also gaze upon his notes. He placed both hands on either side of the pulpit he was preaching from, then said nothing for several minutes while more and more individuals in the congregation began to arise.

Their applause got louder and louder, as hands began to rise up in praise, and the shouts of "Amen" could be heard.

After things calmed down, the minister began once again. "Christ was 33 when he died. His ministry lasted roughly three years ... not long. In light of all the religions in the world, what makes His teachings any different from all the rest?

It's my understanding that the Sanhedrin ... the ruling Jewish council during the time ... was appointed by Rome. They were in Rome's back pocket ... so to speak. It's a safe bet to say the high priest ... Caiaphas ... could have cared less if Jesus died. Especially when he made that bold statement ... he was the Son of God. I can hear him now! Who in the world do you think you are, Jesus? Coming in here like that saying you're the Son of God ... How dare you! It wouldn't be hard to imagine how mad he was. After all, they never believed ... not for a second ... that Christ was the Savior ... their Messiah ... the deliverer of Israel ... let alone the world!"

The minister quickly glanced down at his notes once more, then added, "Jesus tells us in John 14:6, 'I am the way, the truth, and the life; no man cometh unto the Father, but by me.' ... He's the real deal, folks! God sent a Savior all right, but He had more than just the country of Israel in mind. He sent his only begotten Son, Jesus, to save an entire planet of its sins ... and the Sanhedrin never caught on!"

The good Reverend cleared his throat again and took a short

sip of water before interjecting, "I'm sure many of you probably aren't aware of this, but Pontius Pilate converted to Christianity seven years after Christ died. When Rome found out about it, they executed him ... that's the honest facts, folks! ... But why would Pilate do something like that, especially when he knew, going into it, that Rome might kill him for it? It's because Jesus really was who he said he was! Our Savior ... the Son of God! Too bad you never read about that in the history books."

In an effort to conclude, the minister said, "I'd like everyone to please bow your head and close your eyes ... I don't want anyone looking around."

Those who made up the crowd hung their heads and closed their eyes in silent respect of the pastor's instructions, that included Nathaniel as well, for they knew the good Reverend was about to pray.

The minister's prayer was, "Father ... we stand before you today with a humble heart. It's you Lord ... and only you ... that's important. Speak to our hearts ... show us the way you would have us go. It's your will we seek ... your shoes we choose to fill. Help us this day to better know you ... in Jesus's Holy name we pray ... and everybody said!"

With that, the crowd ushered forth a robust "Amen!"

Many were of the impression Pastor Dan was done, so they began to gather their belongings with the intention of leaving. The good Reverend shouted, "Hold on! We're not done. I haven't given an altar call yet!"

Once everyone was back in their seats, with heads bowed, the minister began once again. "I won't dismiss this service until I've given everyone here an opportunity to accept Christ. Now ... here comes the serious part! I don't want anyone looking around or being disruptive."

There was a long silent lull before the minister spoke once more, and that's when things began to stir within the CEO's soul.

"If you're here ... and you're a sinner ... I don't have to tell you where you'll spend eternity ... I believe you already know. When Jesus died ... he dealt Satan a losing hand. The reason He died is that we might live. Christ holds the trump card ... it's called ... *Salvation!* Only Jesus can forgive us of our sins ... the essence of it is ... when Christ died on the cross, God said ... Devil ... you lose!"

After a long pause, Pastor Dan added, "I can't help but feel there's those here who have the best of material things in life ... you may even be rich ... but I ask you this ... Do you feel fulfilled? Maybe you can't share that feeling that there's something missing ... that there's more to life than just this ... well ... the answer you seek is Jesus Christ ... He's the final piece of that puzzle you've been trying to put together."

After another long pause, the good Reverend said, "I know what I'm about to ask of you is hard. I'm not trying to embarrass anyone, but if you know your heart's not right with Christ ... I'd like for you to raise your hand ... don't think about it ... follow your heart."

When Pastor Dan asked for a show of hands, Nathaniel's was one of the first to shoot up - the executive couldn't understand quite why either.

"I see those hands." The minister said. "Now I'm going to ask those who raised their hands to take a step of courage. I know it'll be difficult, but I want you to come down here to the front ... so I can pray with you. I guarantee you ... your decision to accept Christ into your life will bring dramatic results ... your life will never be the same again … I guarantee it! ... I usually count to three when I give altar calls, but I'm not going to do that today ... I'll ask those who raised their hands to come forward now!"

Nathaniel hesitated for a second, then decided it was best to go forward. When he tried to move past that little old lady, sitting to his left, she reached up to grab his arm. The executive looked down at her with a great deal of questioning concern. Nathaniel thought the scary little gal was a lot stronger than she looked. She had a death grip on the CEO's forearm. The woman didn't say a word, but it was like she didn't want the executive to go forward. That wasn't going to detour Nathaniel though. He jerked his arm away from the lady and stepped out into the aisle. Once Nathaniel had made his way toward the front, being only steps away from what he was about to commit to, he decided to look over his shoulder and give that mean old lady a stem glare. When the executive did so, the little old lady wasn't there. It was as if she'd vanished! (The experience haunted Nathaniel for a while, for he didn't know quite what to make of it)

Once the executive made it to the front, several others were standing there as well.

Pastor Dan grouped them all together and told them to recite a prayer with him. "Salvation isn't a complicated thing." The good Reverend added. "Romans 10:9 says, 'That if you confess with your mouth, Jesus is Lord, and believe in your heart that God raised him from the dead, you will be saved.'"

He said, "It's that simple!"

As he looked down at the eager group of wanna-be believers, the minister said, "Now ... repeat after me."

Those seeking salvation recited the words, but so did several other members of the congregation as well. It's a safe bet to say those in the congregation, reciting the prayer, were trying to make that life-changing decision a little more comfortable on those standing down there by repeating the words with them. Or it might be they did something similar before.

The Pastor's prayer was, "Lord ... I'm a sinner ... I need you! I believe you died on the cross for my sins, and that you arose on the third day. I truly believe you're the Son of God ... a deliverer ... my Savior. I ask that you wash me clean ... make me new! It's my desire to make you the Lord of my life. I claim it in your Holy name ... Amen!"

Nathaniel raised his head, and then opened his eyes. Pastor Dan glanced over at him and gave the executive a wink. Nathaniel felt like a huge burden had been lifted from his shoulders - a tiny comparison to the weight of the world, one could propose. He felt a lot better as he reached up to wipe away the tears. The CEO thought, "That was easy enough!"

Nathaniel left the service that day truly changed; for he was now experiencing life in a Christian perspective. The executive had made the best decision he ever could - it was just like the minister had claimed.

The CEO took Pastor Dan's advice. At the conclusion of the service the minister suggested Nathaniel should spend some time alone that afternoon ... reflect on what's happened ... and pray a little as well. The executive did just that. He wound up back at that outdoor memorial garden; the one he thought so peaceful. The CEO spent the rest of the day sitting on the steps of Father Hutton's fountain. He fed a lot of pigeons there, and Nathaniel did his best to figure out what life was truly all about.

Chapter Ten
A Never-Ending Circle

It didn't take long for that steamroller called time to move on by. The wheels of progress are always turning. This rollercoaster called life was inviting Nathaniel on for a little spin. The *Eighties* had officially arrived.

The decade was probably best known as *The Amazing 80's.* Many would affectionately label the period *The Decade Of Excitement,* a few even lovingly tagged it as being *The Happy Decade.* Ten years of colorful appeal wouldn't exactly be its ultimate distinction however, for the decade was marred with dubious corporate behavior, many an executive's avarice desire, a rapacious appetite for the hoarding of wealth that was highlighted by unsurpassed greed, then a falling of foolish folly - something divinely defined as **Covetousness.**

That ancient adage, "The rich get richer and the poor get poorer," was still a very real perception and mindset of many. For those who lacked around the world it wasn't just a saying, it was a proverbial reality. Poverty's a stark fact that needs no interpretation. It's a maxim called truth for all who dare gaze. Need portrays itself as a cruel circle, often times deadly at that, and a cycle rarely broken.

The planet was indeed becoming smaller, an ever-increasing conduit for further populace, yet a shrinking realm for which humanity could roam, and with each passing year, the world was inching toward becoming yet another sliver of what it once was. The 80's rung in with a global population of nearly four and a half billion souls, the U.S. accounted for nearly 227 million of that.

Nathaniel's hometown, Chicago, boasted it had over three million now, second only to New York City, but Los Angeles was challenging "The Windy City" for that distinction. "The City of Angels" was growing at a rapid pace and its destiny would soon dictate a surge past Chicago into the runner-up spot.

The burden of debt upon Americans swelled as well. During that time, many economists were defining debt as a tool. Conversely, others warned of credit's disastrous consequences yet the vast majority couldn't resist that temptation to have more. The increasing popularity of credit would eventually take its toll on many who wallowed in it. Those who suffered under the curse of debt would ultimately have to endure its lasting effects for years. Only a humorist could jest, "Installments are easy payments." Debt would, in the long run, reveal itself to be the true misfortune it can be. The term debt, disguised in all those colorful forms called credit, would ultimately be a haunting reality for many. For debt is: *Something easy to get, yet far more difficult to lose!*

At the threshold of the decade, the National Debt was a little over nine hundred billion dollars. Within five short years, that liability would soar to well over two trillion. The average annual salary for a U.S. citizen was roughly $15,500 back then. The future looked bright for most Americans, but a lot of them were living far beyond their means in that quest for financial success. Working for minimum wage in those days, as it is today, was a daunting task for many a poor soul as well. You might say it was a challenging exercise in the game of survival for more than a few. It wasn't easy scratching out a living on minimum wage in those days - the compensation was a mere $3.10 an hour.

Society still had a love for the movies though.   Paying customers were standing in the box office lines to spend those hard-earned dollars of theirs like never before. Well over twenty million were flocking to the movie theaters every week.

It would appear divorce made for a more popular script than love however. Couples were falling out of love at an alarming rate; for the dawn of a new decade gave witness to over a million couples saying, "I don't!" Many a married pair were no longer willing to commit to, "I do." They were more eager to separate, happy to dissolve it all by declaring something more along the line of, "I won't!"

The Eighties was indeed the dawn of a new era. Sweeping changes were lunging forth to swallow all. An American obsession for entertainment was in overdrive, longing to shift into high gear. *CNN* was the first to introduce a 24-hour news channel in 1980. That same year, Sony developed a *Walkman* tape player. A fad had been given birth and the electronics age was ushered in. The following year, *IBM* acquainted us all with something called a personal computer.

The field of medicine was making great strides as well. Smallpox had been successfully eradicated in '80. Scientists identified the *AIDS* virus the following year. Soon afterward, the first permanent artificial heart was transplanted.

The institution of Government wasn't exempt from modification either, for the United States had acquired itself a new President, Ronald Wilson Reagan, the 40th head of state in the nation's two-hundred and some year history. A conservative, Reagan would serve two terms from '81 to '89. He would become best known for his radical economic policies. *Reaganomics* was here and was a fiscal version of the supply-side theory.

President Reagan, a man of faith, was generally either loved or hated, but no one could dispute the validity of his administration or the sweeping reform it brought. In '83, the President called the Soviet Union an "Evil Empire." Those were strong words back then, not very diplomatic in nature, but they rang true. Eventually, the U.S.S.R would collapse and so would *The Iron Curtain* communists built a few years earlier. One could faithfully reason Ronald Reagan had an instrumental hand in the scheme of those things.

Oddly enough, *OPEC* agreed to cut crude oil prices that year as well - something they hadn't done in their twenty-three-year long history. The following year, yet another Middle Eastern country agreed to free-trade terms with the United States. That agreement was signed in cooperation with Israel.

Back home, Nathaniel read all about Harold Washington's successful bid to become Chicago's first African-American mayor. '83 saw the birth of the cellular phone networks as well, but anxiety arose in the CEO to an unsettling level when he read of the Government's crackdown on AT&T that year. One of Nathaniel's favorite newspapers, *The Wall Street Journal,* had articulated a thought-provoking frontpage story which outlined how the administration had successfully presented its case in eliminating that AT&T corporate monopoly. That was something of which the executive was most disconcerted to learn; for he had a considerable amount of money invested in that company, several thousand shares to be precise. AT&T had been forced to break up their holdings. In the process, the government gave birth to seven baby *Bells.*

The good news was, business was starting to pick up again at *Irwin Industries.* (Something Nathaniel was all too relieved to see) It was probably a clear sign the economy had begun to tum around.

Nathaniel marveled at all the new intentions that were coming of age too. '84 introduced the arrival of a *Portable Compact Disc Player.* Something called a *Camcorder,* a camera with tape deck combined, had been developed as well. And now, of all things, one could boast of wearing a television set on your wrist.

The 80's, a decade of stable prices, unprecedented low unemployment, and the longest sustained economic expansion in history, was also one of the lowest, greediest, most corrupt periods in modem American economic history. Hostile takeovers, mergers, and corporate buyouts were gaining prevalence in America - dishonesty was rapidly becoming a norm.

There will always be a hint of demonic influence in the conspiratorial heart of man when it involves monetary gain - it appears to be a fixture of the age.

American corporations were becoming inefficient, run indulgently in favor of incumbent management, and immune to shareholder pressure. Executives should have been pruning their companies into more profitable shape, but few were. The real forte for most was corporate politics. CEO's were especially good at narcotizing their boards of directors with "goodies" dipped from the company's bountiful cash flow.

1980 and '81 were witness to recession, and were particularly calamitous for the Savings & Loan industry (S & L's), the most inefficient, undercapitalized sector of the American financial system and also the part closest to the voting public ... but then came Ronald Reagan.

His administration used tight credit to crush inflation in the Eighties, an action which had the incidental effect of depressing stock prices and thereby trashing Wall Street. The climate of the time became quite conductive for corporate mergers and takeovers.

Many felt the villains of the age were Reagan's administration itself, with its often noted fiscal recklessness, and those wizards, capitalists of junk bonds who were accused of having leveraged and pillaged our economy into calamitous hypertrophy.

Several alleged financial malefactors of the 80's were shysters, high-flyers, and pyramid-scheme artists who flocked for the kill. It must be noted that most of the S & L operators who helped fuel that junk-bond market were players in an overprotected industry kept alive by a special-interest-conscious Congress as well.

Reagan approved deregulation of the financial industry back then, and Congress in turn moved to free up the desperate S & L's to invest, for the first time, in high-risk enterprises, including junk bonds.

In the 70's, a junk bond was a downgraded security, a promissory note, deemed unworthy of its promise. A junk bond had the lowly distinction of being a corporate bond with a low rating and high yield, often involving a great deal of risk.

A man named Michael Milken pioneered the use of junk bonds in leveraged buyouts. A *leveraged buyout* has the dubious distinction of being the purchase of a company with borrowed money. Using the company's assets as collateral, the debt's discharged and the realization of profit is made by liquidating the company.

Milken's famed discovery, as a student at the Wharton School of Business, was that the actual risk of default on a non-investment-grade security was considerably less than the assigned risk; as reflected in the high interest rate that the junk bond issuer had to pay. In the very beginning, there were socioeconomic implications to Milken's crusade. He spent the early 70's promoting his notion, and in the process created a populist rationale for his business: *Supply-side debt.* The aim of bond traders, like him, was to fleece unwary customers, make millions, then eventually take their shares back to the stock market for big profits. The fees generated for deal-makers and investment bankers with such activity expanded tremendously. The sheer volume of money running through the financial markets in the Eighties brought forth a distortion of judgment, a lust to wallow in the spectacular thrill of it all.

Milken wasn't the first to issue so-called junk bonds, the firm Shearson-Lehman could claim that honor. But once Milken's application of the idea caught on, everyone wanted to jump in. At times, capitalism takes on a destructive tone; a dynamic refined by the dark driving forces of *greed.* Gradually Milken's idea caught on all-the-more when the inflation rate soared and investors had to cast further afield for attractive rates of return.

Nathaniel never forgot the quote he once read by one of his favorite artists. The painter Edgar Degas, born to a banking family, wisely said, "Some forms of success are indistinguishable from panic."

Outside rarefied financial circles, few people have ever understood what really goes on in the securities markets anyway.

Dishonest intent by S & L operators no doubt gave incentive for junk bond dealers to peddle more and more exotic forms of high-risk paper in a market that had little choice but to demand it. The wickedness of the day would eventually lead to debacle, and a government bailout of the failed savings and loan industry to the tune of $300 billion.

According to economists, who thought the S & L's were in need of a shakeup, it wasn't a bad thing that many of those institutions were facing bankruptcy. But those economists didn't reckon on the political clout of an industry whose principal product was money. Congress would eventually approve a doubling of the federal deposit insurance (FDIC) guarantee, from $50,000 to $100,000, ostentatiously to protect small investors but by the same token lure more money back to the S & L's.

Milken's greed would in turn birth a host of problems; all stemming from the fact he tried, with notable success, to control the market. The same government that bailed out the S & L's also brought charges against Michael Milken - 98 counts in all. The king of junk debt would, with the guide of attorneys, eventually except a plea agreement and plead guilty to six counts of felony stock fraud and tax evasion. He faced a fine of 60 million and a jail term of up to 28 years. But the judge sentenced Milken to only two years in prison. The convicted would eventually serve out his debt to society after only a year. The reaction of many in the "enlightened" quarters was Milken hadn't been punished nearly enough because he'd swindled the public out of millions, maybe billions, and been rewarded for the effort.

Nathaniel's temper boiled as he read the daily headlines of that

Chicago newspaper.

The executive, no longer lying relaxed upon his Italian sofa, wadded the paper then threw it across the coffee table. The frontpage news was a smeary portrayal; a summary of Milken's white-collar crimes and the light-hearted gesture of a judge in rendering sentencing.

The CEO met Milken once, in New York. Nathaniel thought he was a self-centered slob, one who had lofty opinions of self-glory, an individual who had a personality like sandpaper, someone who was full of himself and personified the embodiment of being devilishly slick.

A number of loud shouts echoed throughout the executive's penthouse that night. It was a good thing Nathaniel's apartment occupied the entire top floor, for his vocal outbursts would have been a disruption for quite a few annoyed neighbors.

"I told that idiot! ... I told him! ... He wouldn't listen though ... Oh God … that was the best thing I ever did was getting rid of that creep!" The print Nathaniel read was no doubt disheartening, for his disgust was now verbally evident. That "creep," the executive referred to, was former Irwin Industries CFO Harold Lusk.

Nathaniel fired the Chief Financial Officer a few months back. It took a while to find a suitable replacement for Lusk, but Nathaniel had no regrets in making the decision.

Lusk and the CEO were often times at odds with each other. Nathaniel was, more times than not, conservative in his views of the financial horizon. Lusk's opinions were just the opposite. You might say he was a Michael Milken wanna-be.

Lusk reveled in the festivities of high-risk maneuver for he was absolutely obsessed with those theories behind supply-side debt. Lusk's mindset would eventually become his demise though; for he rarely sought approval from Nathaniel on anything, especially when it involved something risky. He even went so far as to go over the CEO's head a couple times in hopes of persuading a few board members to see things more his way.

The first time Lusk approached a board member outside the hallowed corporate walls, Nathaniel found out about it and warned the CFO. The second time Lusk pulled that stunt, his boss fired him.

After venting his frustration, Nathaniel arose from the couch to gather up that wadded newsprint from off the floor. The executive pondered leaving it for the maid, but once his fit of anger had subsided he decided otherwise - his habitually orderly personality forbid the presence of the rubbish's appearance.

Nathaniel threw the wadded ball in the trashcan, then elected to take a shower, in light of a long hard day. Once he'd finished his bathing, the executive emerged from the crystal shower to adorn himself in a favorite set of silk pajamas. The CEO then began to lather his face with shaving cream. He was only a few strokes into the process of shaving when the mirror became steamed over. Nathaniel grabbed a towel and wiped a pass or two over the glass to reveal his image. Before he could strike another pass of the razor over his face, Nathaniel's mind began to ponder as he stood to stare at his reflection.

The executive began to slowly observe his image from the head down. He had a full head of wavy brown hair, something he'd inherited from his mother no doubt. The trait of his father's fiery orange glow hairline had obviously passed him by.

Nathaniel's eyes were a captivating baby blue, which was another characteristic passed on by his mother. His nose was sharp and slightly pointed, as was his dented chin, a trait shared by all Irwin men, he was told.

The middle-aged executive was built fairly well. His six two, one-hundred-eighty-pound frame was finely toned; for Nathaniel worshiped a bit of fitness. The executive worked out often, usually three or four days a week in his private gym adjacent to the living room.

Nathaniel barked out a surly gruff once he'd analyzed the mirrored reflection. "What are you looking at?" was the stern rebuke of himself.

After finishing the shave, the executive began to settle in for the evening. Nathaniel made himself a tuna fish sandwich and a glass of milk before retreating to the den that night. The den doubled as a library, for Nathaniel's love of reading was eminent. His collection of systematically categorized books numbered in the thousands. Once in the room, Nathaniel sat down at an antique oak roll-top desk. It was originally purchased by his great-grandfather. Oddly enough, the 19th century piece had survived because it had been well cared for. It was a bit of history, a wonderful piece of furniture indeed, for it had been passed down through the generations; that desk being the first fixture brought by Eli when the company was founded.

Nathaniel leaned back in the matching antique chair and began to enjoy his meal. Once he took a bite, the executive noticed a couple of books lying on top of the desk. He'd purchased them at the bookstore days earlier. The leather-bound specimens were *King James* and *NIV* (New International Version) Bibles.

The executive bemoaned a regretful, "Hummm," then reached over to obtain the NIV copy. With a quick flip through, the Bible fell open to **Ecclesiastes 5:10.** Nathaniel was intrigued to read, "Whoever loves money never has money enough; whoever loves wealth is never satisfied with his income. This too is meaningless."

The executive was fascinated by verse eleven as well. It revealed, "As goods increase, so do those who consume them. And what benefit are they to the owner except to feast his eyes on them?"

Scurrying through the desk drawer, Nathaniel tried to find a pencil and pad to record the verses. Instead, he came across an aged letter from his mother. It was the one he'd stuffed away, forgotten about, and neglected to answer years earlier.

The executive's curiosity got the best of him and thus he opened the letter to refresh his memory of its contents.

Nathaniel's reactions to his mother's correspondence were different this time. His anger of her memory had long since fleeted. Overcome by the emotional experience of reading her very words struck a cord within the executive's soul. He finally found a pen and notepad, then Nathaniel began to concentrate on a genuine heart-felt reply:

"Dear Mom,

The date is August 26th, 1984. I know this letter's been a long time in coming. I owe you an apology for that. I let my anger get the best of me. I once felt you cheated me out of something - my childhood. I held malice against you for that, but I was wrong back then. I was wrong to not forgive. A person by the name of Jesus Christ helped me to understand that. I've changed my line of thought in recent years on the subject of forgiveness. Please forgive me for all of my shortcomings, Mom, I'm truly sorry. I forgive you as well for the wrongs you laid before me.

I'm sending this letter to your last known address. When it arrives, I pray you will read it and allow me to finally become part of your life - as I now long to!

I've spent the last four years trying to find myself as a Christian, but I'm ashamed to say I've told only a rare few about my conversion. Nor am I proud that I sparingly go to church. That's going to change in the coming days however. I bought into the lie I was too busy to attend services. I'm well aware I sold myself out for the love of money, Mom.

I felt it best to answer your letter with a short note. I'd like to get together. You name the place and time - Okay?

I'll close for now. I'm enclosing a tract on salvation with this. I think it will help you, Mother - I know it did me. I've been saving that tract for a long time, now I'm passing it on to you. An old friend, a street preacher, handed it to me once.

With love,

Your once foolish son, Nathaniel."

The executive wisely turned in a little earlier than normal that evening for he had to catch a flight to Indianapolis the following day.

Nathaniel's driver dropped him off at Chicago's *O'Hare* Airport around 6:15 that bright sunny morn. The flight lifted off the runway at 7:09 and touched down in "The Circle City" less than an hour later. Waiting in line for the executive, much like a black dotted speck amongst a sea of yellow taxis, was another limo at *Indianapolis International* when Nathaniel's flight landed.

The executive had a business meeting scheduled that morning with the CEO of ***Global Technologies International*** and its Board of Directors. The exec was told a limousine would be awaiting when he arrived. When Nathaniel walked out of the terminal, he soon noticed a chauffeur standing next to the curb, outside of his car, with a sign in hand. The cardboard plaque simply read, "Irwin Industries CEO." Nathaniel approached the driver, then said, "That would be me my good man."

The chauffeur asked for some I.D. and Nathaniel willingly complied. Once he'd checked the CEO's identification, the driver handed it back, shook Nathaniel's hand, then he opened the rear door for the executive. The driver said, "Welcome to Indianapolis, Sir. My name's Herald."

Nathaniel cheerfully said, "Thank you, Herald," then got in.

Herald was a curious fellow, Nathaniel thought, for he tried to occasionally stir in a little small talk with his quest, an effort to break the ice one would suppose, while enroute from the city's west side to downtown where ***GTI's*** corporate headquarters were. The chauffeur was a wise one indeed, for he was overly experienced in the area of hospitality and would be tipped quite well by Nathaniel for the effort.

Herald was a skilled gentleman, but he was an outstanding driver also because he found a prime parking spot only a few yards away from the Global Technologies building.

After he'd parked the stretch limo, the jovial chauffeur made his way to the rear of the vehicle to open Nathaniel's door. As soon as the CEO cleared the curb, Herald shut the door and opened the trunk to grab Nathaniel's briefcase and a small handbag. The driver shook the executive's hand, wished him a good day, then the pair parted ways.

After the limousine drove away, Nathaniel crossed the street and made his way through a massive set of mahogany doors which graced *GTI's* lobby. He didn't have to wait there long, for Nathaniel was escorted upstairs by a lovely young receptionist to where the company's Board of Directors and Chief Executive Officer were awaiting his arrival.

Inside that spacious boardroom, standing at the head of a long table, was Les McGree, *GTI's* Chief Executive Officer. Sitting on both sides of the table, on McGree's end, was a group of eight men, mostly elderly gents, *GTI's* Board of Directors. The CEO greeted Nathaniel, then said, with a slight wave of the hand, "Have a seat, Mr. Irwin ... Can we get you something? Coffee? A soft drink maybe?"

Nathaniel's response was, "A glass of ice water would be fine."

McGree told the receptionist to retrieve the refreshment for their guest. During her brief departure, the CEO introduced his Board of Directors to Nathaniel one at a time. When the receptionist returned, she handed Nathaniel the drink along with a napkin - he in tum, thanked her. She then asked of her boss, "Will there be anything else?"

McGree replied, "No ... I believe that will be all, Linda."

As soon as the receptionist closed the door, McGree turned on an overhead projector and began to weave something that had a resemblance to, and all the markings of, a lengthy sales pitch. The presentation was a general outline of *GTI's* fiscal strengths. It was no doubt intended to be a professional ploy of persuasion. McGree used a number of illustrated bar charts, graphs, and statistics, displayed on transparencies, to drive home his point. The menacing images were projected upon the wall as McGree narrated the spill.

Nathaniel sat through the presentation for roughly thirty minutes before his patience began to wear thin. After he'd cleared his throat, Nathaniel was successful enough to gain a glance from everyone in the room, including McGree.

"Gentlemen ... Gentlemen!" Nathaniel interjected. "What does this have to do with the acquisition of an escalator division?"

Appearing to be somewhat annoyed by the interruption, McGree asked of Nathaniel, "A moment ... please." Then, the CEO went right back to his presentation.

McGree rambled on for a while longer, then Nathaniel's fortitude quickly disappeared.

"That's enough ... Gentlemen ... I don't see that this has any bearing or importance upon matters lying before us!"

Notably irritated by the interruption, McGree stopped what he was doing to ask, "Is there a problem ... Mr. Irwin?"

Nathaniel responded by pointing his finger at the wall, then said, "I don't quite understand what you're trying to accomplish, but I've seen all that I care to of that!"

All eyes in the boardroom were now affixed upon Nathaniel. McGree and the Board of Directors had quickly exhibited bold facial expressions denoting their feelings of offense in light of the executive's appalling behavior. One of the board members chimed in to express, "I think you should shut that thing off, Les. I don't think Mr. Irwin cares to ponder the presentation any longer."

The CEO, with a good deal of repugnance revealed, turned the projector off and took a seat at the head of the table.

Nathaniel then stated: "Gentlemen ... I'm a busy man. Let's cut to the chase, shall we? My company's prepared to offer seventy million for that escalator division of yours. I understand it consists of five factories, two warehouses, and an engineering subsidiary. I'm here to formalize a written proposal ... take it back to my board for final approval ... then we can move to close the deal."

McGree paused a moment, glanced at his Board of Directors, then spoke up. "We expected you to indulge us with your interest a bit more this morning, Mr. Irwin. We obviously haven't been able to accomplish that."

One of the board members, sitting directly to McGree's right, interjected, "Les ... if I may?"

With a stiff wave of the hand, the CEO replied, "Certainly, Paul."

The board member leaned forward in his chair slightly, clutched both hands to each other, then said, "We had somewhat of a different agenda in mind for today ... Mr. Irwin. We apologize for drawing you here under false pretense. However, it's our intent to propose a friendly buy-out of your company."

Shocked, and dreadfully appalled that they would even make such a suggestion, Nathaniel lashed back by saying, "First of all … Gentlemen … I don't appreciate being lied to. Secondly … Irwin Industries isn't for sale ... not at any price. The company was founded by my great-grandfather and a good friend of his over a hundred years ago."

As he stared at the CEO, Nathaniel gave him a strong scolding. "I'm insulted by such beguiling deceit, Sir ... the suggestion is out of the question!"

Nathaniel began to gather his belongings at the onset of a reddened face. The effort was a rapid one, for he wasted little precious time stuffing papers his briefcase - anger was quick to get the best of him.

As he prepared to leave, another board member bluntly added, "It's not a suggestion, Mr. Irwin!"

Nathaniel finished gathering his belongings, closed his briefcase, locked it, then stood to retrieve his jacket from where he'd placed it on the back of the chair. As he slipped that part of his suit on, Nathaniel said, "This meeting's over, Gentlemen!"

One of the other board members spoke up, to conclude, "I assure you, Mr. Irwin, we're prepared to initiate a Hostile Takeover if need be ... it's certainly not out of reach ... nor is it beyond us ... we usually get what we want!"

Nathaniel walked, with a brisk pace, toward the door and grabbed the handle. He opened the door, then promptly added, "You can damn well try a stunt like that ... Men ... You can damn well try!" Then, in short order, the executive departed their building.

Nathaniel had a reservation at a four-star hotel just down the
street. He'd planned on spending the evening there, then catch a
flight back to Chicago early the following day. The luxurious
high-rise inn was located only a few blocks due north of the
Global Technologies building. The executive had every intention
of going back to his room so he could lay down for a while,
hopefully cool off some, for he was still hot under the collar.

Contrarily though, as he walked farther the executive's face
became less inflamed. Nathaniel then stumbled across something
wonderful. The locals called it *Monument Circle* - "The Heart of
Downtown." The executive was quite impressed for it was a
masterful work of spectacular architectural splendor.

At the center of it all was a 284' tall stone monument.
Nathaniel couldn't help but marvel at the craftsmanship and
soon found a description of the monolith on a plaque. It was
called the "Soldiers and Sailors Monument." Constructed in
1902, it was the first of its kind at the time and was dedicated to
the common soldier. There were bubbling fountains at the base
of the statue, a large circular concrete walkway all about, and it
was encompassed by a circuitously round street lined in brick
pavers. Nathaniel estimated the thoroughfare to be roughly four
or five hundred yards long.

The day was warm and Nathaniel chose to amble with jacket
in hand. The executive passed several trash cans along the way
before deciding to stop by one. With a half hearted smile now
upon his face, the CEO rolled up his sleeves, removed his tie,
then discarded it along with the jacket. Nathaniel would
spend the rest of the day perched upon a set of steps, in
observation of humanity, only a few yards from there.

It wasn't long after Nathaniel took a seat upon the cement treads that he noticed, from the corner of his eye, something a little out of place in approach from the right. The executive soon recognized the phenomenon. It was a "Bag Lady" - a homeless person. The smallish, frail woman was quite dirty, her face dreadfully blotchy black. It was hard to estimate her age for her lifestyle forewarned an elderly appearance. Her less than decorous bearing was no indication of her actual years; for although she was only twenty-nine, she could have easily been mistaken for someone sixty.

Nathaniel couldn't help but notice the passing stares the woman got when people walked by. Sadly enough, no one offered to help the down-and-out lady. It was as if nobody cared. Aside from the ugly stares, only a scare few even paid attention. Nathaniel was surprised she wasn't begging. Not once did she ask for a handout from anyone. She just pushed along that old broken-down shopping cart, loaded with rubbish. When the Bag Lady came to that trashcan Nathaniel had stood at moments before, she discovered some small treasure. Her excitement of the glorious find was evident, because a slight smile broke out upon her face when she reached down to retrieve Nathaniel's cast away jacket and tie. The executive soon became lost in a mix of thoughts as he watched the poor woman eventually disappear around a corner.

Nathaniel then longed to spend his entire afternoon studying the mannerisms of people.

It was close to noon and the hotdog vendors were beginning to arrive. They would eventually litter the sidewalk with their stainless-steel carts. Quite humorous to the executive were those daredevil pigeons - the ones that swooped through traffic to grab the delicious crumbs. Like the Bag Lady, no one apparently cared about the birds either - they were generally ignored.

Nathaniel made it a point to greet everyone who passed him by. Only a slim few responded; most looked glum and never looked up at all. Many who ate lunch wore suits like Nathaniel. Cops were also in abundance that day. Many patrolled the beat while pounding their sticks in hand, humming a tune.

For the first time, Nathaniel noticed just now noisy city life can truly be. Jackhammers were beating the pavement and sirens blared, but no one seemed to care.

Nathaniel got a kick out of a foreign couple, Asian he thought, who were asking for directions. No one paid them much attention either, for their English was awful. They weren't the only ones lost though. The executive watched a delivery truck driver circle him about forty times before the "Hack" found what he was looking for.

The CEO thought it best to record the observations in a journal, something he'd never done before. Once Nathaniel found a pen and pad in his briefcase, he began to write. His final entry at day's end read:

"I feel like I'm on a merry-go-round. I try to grab that brass ring, but the happiness it represents seems to always pass by. It's much like a *Never-Ending-Circle,* a path run, similar to the loop I gaze upon now."

Chapter Eleven
Painted Mountain

The flow of calendar pages was a less-than-memorable whirl for Nathaniel. It was a symbolic gyration of time; for the summer of 89' had arrived.

A few more years had slipped past since he'd ventured a throw of a wrench in the gears to that proverbially rotating never-ending-circle. A recent entry to his journal read:

"It's been ten years as a Christian. What have I done with my life?"

The takeover boom of the 1980's challenged entrenched corporate management, who since the thirties held the reins of corporate decision-making often at the expense of shareholder interests. The effect was to transfer control over vast corporate resources to smaller more focused, and in many cases, private companies and individuals, who returned huge amounts of equity to shareholders. It would accomplish the freeing of resources long trapped in mature industries and those of uneconomic conglomerates.

Times had vastly changed on the business horizon since Irwin Industries first opened its doors over a hundred years before. Nathaniel's pride and joy, his destiny, the consuming fire of life, the company, was one of those mature industries and he was a determinedly entrenched fellow. No one could have possibly disputed the nineteenth century was more simplistic, but the world was a constantly changing place and time stood still for no one; not even for a staunch guy like Nathaniel.

The fastest-growing employment opportunities were now in the service sector, notably information processing, medical care, communications, teaching, merchandising, and finance.

Growing especially lustily was government, which, despite cutbacks, employed about one in seven working Americans. The number of state and local government employees more than tripled. White-collar workers constituted some eighty percent of the U.S. workforce. They proved far less inclined to join labor unions than their blue-collar cousins. Only about sixteen percent of workers were unionized, down from a high point of nearly thirty-five percent in the 1950's.

Computers utterly transformed age-old business practices like billing and inventory control and opened new frontiers in areas like airline scheduling, high-speed printing, telecommunications, and space navigation. High-tech industries like aerospace, biological engineering, and especially electronics defined the business frontier.

Rocketry had advanced to place astronauts on the moon in the 60's, produce a reusable space shuttle in the 80's, and inspired talk of a manned Mars landing, but the breakthroughs had also equipped the United States and the Soviet Union with bristling arsenals of intercontinental nuclear weapons.

Critics claimed life was becoming more stressful; in part due to a fast-paced lifestyle which helped fuel the collapse of a traditional family structure. The cause was much deeper than poverty or any shortcomings in the economic or political system. Child rearing, the family's foremost function, was

being increasingly assigned to "parent substitutes" at day-care
centers, schools, or to the television, a modern age "electronic
babysitter." Estimates were that the average child by age
sixteen had watched up to fifteen thousand hours of TV - more
time than was spent in the classroom. Alarmingly enough, in
1960, five percent of all births were to unmarried women, but
by the end of the decade one out of six white babies, one out of
three Hispanic babies, and an astounding two out of three
African-American babies were being born to single mothers. It
was sadly real every fourth child in American was growing up
in a household lacking dual parents.

The *Cable Shopping Networks* had invaded the airwaves and
many a set, but shock would be fall all who gazed upon the tube
back then to witness the Space Shuttle "Challenger" explode only
74 seconds after lift-off.

Two years prior, IBM introduced something called a CD-Rom
drive for computers.

About a year earlier, *Wrigley Field,* home of major league
baseball's Chicago Cubs, hosted its first night game which was
rained out in the fourth. That same year, the highly controversial
film, "The Last Temptation of Christ," directed by Martin
Scorsese, opened despite demonstrations and protests from
religious groups.

Nathaniel read of Clarance Page's accomplishments as the '89
Pulitzer Prize winner. Page, being a columnist for the Chicago
Tribune, was the first African-American journalist to receive the
cherished award. The headlines that summer bragged that after
28 years of keeping Eastern Germany from freedom, the Berlin
Wall was coming down and the fall of Communism was in full tilt

they thought. But Communism hadn't been entirely expunged from the globe just yet. China's army had opened fire on a crowd of young demonstrators that year, killing several, in what began as a student demonstration on behalf of democracy.

The times were indeed bathed in an array of definition. However, a curtain call was about to fall upon the decade. Those who rolled in the phosphorus lap of luxury no doubt thought things couldn't be better, that the loaded money tree of fortune was ripe for the plucking, but Nathaniel no longer worshipped those views. Contrary to a long-standing conviction, money was now beginning to lose meaning for the executive. One might say he was growing a little tired of it all.

The 80's were defined by greed, and an inaugurating grasp of interpretation was now embarking upon the CEO's soul. History would eventually reveal the truth of perception, for greed has a way of avowing its ugly hand.

Shockingly enough, the chairman of the New York Stock Exchange himself would have to step aside in time, the symbolic consequence of sin. It would seem, he too, the most trusted of them all, couldn't keep his hand out of the proverbial cookie jar either. Amidst accusations of corrupt practice, the chairman would ultimately step down, but not before lavishing himself with millions.

Showering one's executive self with monetary orgies, equivalent to nothing more than lewd gluttony, was becoming increasingly attractive and popular for most; for it boasted of a rousing thrill with licentiously immoral zeal. Indulgence of sinister revelry always has a toll however; all in a time when mailroom clerks were struggling to make six or seven bucks an hour as their CEO's were wallowing in the flounder of millions. Few in charge could resist the temptation though, the urge to lather themselves with corruptness.

Nathaniel's mind was now becoming frequently flooded with what he'd read, the words of Paul and his warning outlined in 1 Timothy 6:10. "For the love of money is a root of all kinds of evil. Some people, eager for money, have wandered from the faith and pierced themselves with many a grief."

Nathaniel had several colleagues who were immersed in the interpretation of that verse. A bright light of conviction now reigned upon him as well, a divinely stroked masterpiece of previously selfish tendencies revealed.

In time, the rise of public outcry would lead to governmental intervention. CEO's were called to testify before interrogative Congressional Committees and would have to give account of their company's actions, and thus fidget for answers upon that Capital Hill "hot seat." Stockholders, and in some cases, employees, would lose it all. But, as someone once foretold, "The truth always comes out." Unfortunately, the dark truth would reveal a loss of public confidence and the fact that billions of dollars in hard earned savings were gone. With the lowly deed, "Corporate America" had ruptured countless lives as well.

Something called *Corporate Scandal* was abounding amidst the temptations of Wall Street expectation. "It's nothing more than a fancy word for embezzlement, a genteel way of describing theft." The exec thought.

Tired and wary of reading those trashy headlines, the dirt on it all, Nathaniel gave the paper he read a good toss then thought it best to take in a church service for the evening, something he hadn't done in a while. The executive was hopeful his spirits would gain a boost before a flight to New York the following day.

Because of the lateness of it all, Nathaniel gave Jimmy a call. The executive told his driver, "I'll like to attend a church service tonight, Jimmy. Swing by in about a half an hour. I'll take a quick shower ... be ready when you arrive."

The chauffeur's reply was, ""Very good, Sir."

As usual, Nathaniel's personal chauffeur and long-time friend arrived right on time. Jimmy conducted himself, as he would, in a gentleman-like manner. He knocked on the CEO's door and escorted Nathaniel to the limo. Jimmy opened the rear passenger side door for the executive and waited until Nathaniel was comfortably seated inside before he closed it.

That Wednesday evening was a little unusual, for Nathaniel's behavior was a bit out of the ordinary. The executive didn't talk hardly at all. The trip was a relatively short one, but uneventful and boring at best. The only words spoken were by Jimmy. "Is everything all right tonight, Sir?" was the chauffeur's inquiring concern upon arrival.

Nathaniel mulled the question over for a moment, then he replied, "Yes ... I'll be fine, Jimmy. I apologize for not being myself tonight ... I guess I have a lot on my mind."

The driver pulled up to the curb in front of the church, put the vehicle in park, and then reached for the door handle. Nathaniel interrupted his driver's actions by saying, "Jimmy ... would you care to attend the service with me this evening?"

The chauffeur was a bit surprised to hear his employer say that and replied, "I've never been to church before, Sir. How does one act or dress for a service?"

"I felt the same way my first time, Jimmy ... a bit apprehensive." After a brief pause, Nathaniel instructed his driver to pull the vehicle around to the parking lot at the rear of the building. "I could use some company this evening." The executive suggested. "We'll walk in together."

Jimmy's nervous reply was, "Very well, Sir."

As soon as the chauffeur parked the limo, Nathaniel grabbed his Bible and opened the door himself. Once Jimmy reached the rear of the vehicle, he realized his employer hadn't waited for assistance. "I could have gotten that door for you, Sir." The driver replied.

"I know ... we better hurry ... I hate to be late." Nathaniel added.

With a nod of his head, Jimmy gave his silent acceptance.

As the two walked toward the front door, the CEO placed his hand upon Jimmy's shoulder to say, "You've been a good friend, Jimmy ... I appreciate what you do for me ... I want you to know that."

The chauffeur was becoming a bit suspicious of Nathaniel's behavior by then. "You pay me well, Sir ... it's not necessary to thank me ... it's my job!"

Nathaniel plunged his fingers into Jimmy's shoulder a little tighter, then added, "Call me Nathaniel from now on."

"I can't do that, Sir ... that would be totally out of line ... disrespectful ... that's something I could never do."

The executive smiled at the driver, then said, "I'm telling you to!"

Jimmy replied, "Yes, Sir!"

Nathaniel's smile grew a bit larger, for he knew his old friend couldn't commit to a request such as that. The CEO gave Jimmy a final silent pat on the back, then ended their brief conversation because another old friend, Pastor Matthews, came into view.

Nathaniel noticed something different about the good Reverend as he and Jimmy approached the church while walking up that long narrow concrete walk. Pastor Matthews was no longer a "Friar Tuck" look-a-like, he'd lost a considerable amount of weight. As Nathaniel drew closer to the minister, surprise began to heighten within him and that foolish old opinion he once held of the good Reverend began to fade; no doubt administered by the shredding fate of God's conviction.

With a good long scan of the now skinny minister, Nathaniel shook Dan's hand then commented, "Oh ... Wow ... You look great, Pastor! How much have you lost?"

"It's been a while, Nathaniel. I've been missing you." With an extended hand, the good Reverend gave the CEO a slight pat on the back to say, "Don't be such a stranger from now on ... okay?" A slight grin was now exposed upon that notably slender face of Pastor Dan as he extended a hand toward the executive's driver to ask, "Who's your friend, Nathaniel?"

As the minister shook the chauffeur's hand, Nathaniel replied, "This is Jimmy ... an old friend of mine."

Somewhat puzzled by his employer's simplistic yet unavailing introduction, Jimmy could only slowly nod his head vertically a time or two in silent wonder as he gave his boss a glare laced with aroused intrigue.

With a jovial smile, Pastor Dan greeted the visitor with a, "Glad to have you with us tonight, Jimmy. I hope you enjoy the service." Focusing his attention back on the executive, the minister conveyed, with a big grin from ear to ear, "I've lost over a hundred pounds, Nathaniel."

Nathaniel was genuinely happy for the good Reverend, and out of character gave him a quick shoulder hug. Pastor Dan was a little surprised by that, and so was Jimmy. In all the years he'd served Nathaniel, Jimmy had never seen the executive display even a hint of emotion like that. To say Jimmy wasn't becoming a bit unnerved by his employer's unsettling actions would be a fleet from truth.

With a strategically placed hand upon the executive's back, the minister ushered the way up the front steps with a symbolic sweeping motion of the other hand. "We better get inside." The clergyman said with gentle persuasion.

Nathaniel and Jimmy knew the service would start soon so they made their way through the lobby, as they entertained the customary handshake greetings given all visitors at the front door, to ultimately seek out a seat upon the back row of the sanctuary.

Pastor Matthews did something a little unusual that evening. He gave an altar call at the beginning of the sermon. Nathaniel gave Jimmy a stealthy glance, once in a while, to observe the driver's reactions to the good Reverend's words. It was all done in an effort to mask the CEO's intrigue and camouflage the true reason for him inviting the chauffeur there. The executive was a bit disappointed to witness Jimmy's decline when the invitation for salvation arose from the pulpit. Nathaniel whispered in his

friend's ear, "I'll go down there with you … if you like." But
Jimmy gave no indication he was interested, so the executive let
the matter go.

The sermon was titled, *A Time to Die*, and dealt with the
killing of selfish desires within one's heart for the sake of others.
Nathaniel got a lot out of the message. He wasn't so sure Jimmy
did, although the driver was attentive and respectful of everything
that was going on during the service.

The sermon lasted roughly two hours and ended around nine.
Nathaniel and his chauffeur were talking to other congregation
members in the front lobby after the conclusion of the service
when, much to everyone's surprise, a drunk staggered through
the front door.

Nathaniel kept a curious eye on the intoxicated fellow, as did
Jimmy and several others.

When one of the ushers stepped forward to ask, "May I help
you?" the inebriated jerk threw him to the side like he was a rag
doll. Another gentleman, who Nathaniel recognized as a
Chicago Bears football player, stepped forward to say, "Hey!"
When he said that, the drunken man hauled off and slugged the
all-pro punter; knocking the athlete to the floor where he now
lay unconscious.

A few ladies were beginning to scream while others cried. The
drunk, now enraged, caught site of Nathaniel and began walking
toward him. In fear for his own safety, the executive stepped
back a few steps and with that unknowingly backed himself into
a comer.

The drunken fool kept shouting, "I know you … I know
you!" to Nathaniel as he pointed a finger of accusation at the

executive.

Nathaniel's reply was, "I've never met you before!"

The inebriated gent was in Nathaniel's face in the blink of an eye, but before he could touch the executive Jimmy stepped between the two.

Jimmy wasn't a small man by any means. He stood roughly six foot four and weighed well over two hundred, but he was no match for the enraged drunk. Before Jimmy could react, the intoxicated ruffian landed a hard right-hand jab to the chauffeur's chin followed by a quick upper cut and another right. Nathaniel could only watch in horror as his friend fell to the floor.

Fear now had a piercing hold on the executive's soul.

Once the brute realized Jimmy was out cold, he quickly shifted his focus off the damage he'd done to the chauffeur to turn his wrath upon Nathaniel. Confident Jimmy was no longer a threat, the drunk glanced up at the executive and shoved his face into Nathaniel's while grabbing the CEO's throat.

Many a thought raced through the executive's mind, but foremost was the perception, "I'm gonna die!"

Nathaniel was scared, and the bully knew it. The drunk clenched Nathaniel's throat a little tighter, then slowly raised the executive up the wall with one hand to say, "You're sweating ... Oh ... You're afraid!"

The man was strangling Nathaniel, hell bent upon choking the life right out of him.

Nathaniel, for the life of him, couldn't figure out where the man's strength was coming from. He looked to be about five two and no more than a hundred and twenty pounds, but he had incredible strength! How could someone so drunk, do the things he was doing?

Nathaniel began to fight back, throwing blows to his attacker's face and kicks to the drunk's legs, but it was to no avail. The enraged man was slowly stealing Nathaniel's life.

His eyes were pure evil, almost unbearable for Nathaniel to look at, hellishly black in appearance they were. With each disgustedly foul taunt and every smearing obscene word, the assailant's face would distort even more.

He was saying things like, "Famine, starvation, want, hunger, misery are my charge! I know who you are! I've been sent to end that divine relation of yours!"

Nathaniel could hardly usher forth the words, but said, "I don't know what you're talking about!"

Just as the executive thought his life was about to end, Pastor Dan stepped between Nathaniel and the attacker. Turning the man's shoulder slightly, the minister said, "Drop him! In the name of Jesus Christ ... I said ... drop him!"

The man shook his head a couple times, but didn't immediately stop the attack.

The fearless Reverend grabbed the man's face and said, "I command you ... you foul thing ... to drop him in the name of Jesus!"

With that said, the man released his hold on Nathaniel's throat and the executive slid down the wall.

The drunk then tried to run for the door, but several men tackled him before he could escape. As they were subduing the assailant, Pastor Matthews said, "Drive him to his knees!"

Nathaniel marveled that it took eight or nine men to overpower the attacker. He also noticed Jimmy and the football player were now starting to come around, all while he rubbed his sore throat in an effort to regain his breath.

Those men did indeed drive the aggressor to his knees and when they did, the brave Reverend grabbed the drunken man's face and said, "Look at me!" When he refused, Pastor Dan slapped him as hard as he could across the face. He repeated, "Look at me!" once more and when the attacker refused, only to look away, the minister slapped him several times more.

Several stood by to watch with shocking expressions of revealing surprise in light of what the good Reverend had done. How could he do such a thing? He's a man of the cloth many thought.

When the man did finally look up at the minister, he began to speak. But his voice deepened and began to change.

Pastor Dan demanded, "By the powerful name of Jesus Christ, I command you foul demons to leave this man!" The drunk was now starting to sober up, and when he would look away Pastor Matthews would grab his face with both hands and stare into those evil eyes.

One by one, the bold Reverend began to cast those demons out which possessed that poor soul. A lady standing in witness of the event, would later claim she saw a black mist escape out of the man's lips every time a demon left the man's body.

Nathaniel was in shock and disbelief as he sat against the base of the wall to watch the horror of the whole exorcism unfold.

Pastor Dan cast all of the demons out except for the last one, but when it came time to cast that one out its stubbornly scary reply was, "Come and get me!" It took some doing, but eventually the last of those evil spirits were gone from the man.

The drunken man didn't realize what had happened, but he was now totally sober. Not even a trace of alcohol could be detected upon his breath. The good Reverend told everyone to let the man up, and when he stood Pastor Dan asked him if he'd like to accept Christ into his life - make his life anew. The man, now calling himself Jerald, accepted the minister's invitation for salvation and the good Reverend led him in a short prayer.

After they'd finished their prayer, someone yelled, "Look!"

Behind the minister and the small prayer group was now a spinning black cloud, a twisting vile whirlwind about the size of a child.

Pastor Matthews told everyone to step back while he approached it. With a stern voice, he commanded the sinister presence to, "Leave this house ... in the name of Jesus ... I command you to depart ... go back to the pit where you came from ... Do it now!"

As soon as the minister ushered forth those words, the evil thing disappeared.

A moment or so after it left, the sound of breaking glass could be heard. But upon inspection, none of the church windows showed any signs of damage. Pastor Dan told everyone to get a hold upon themselves and reassured all, "It's left!"

Rest assured, that wasn't something everyone present would soon forget.

Jerald, a previous drug addict and alcoholic, but now born-again believer, started coming to Sunday school almost immediately. Pastor Dan would give him an opportunity to testify of the experience a week or so later, but when he was called upon to speak Jerald Lamp could only cry. After the good

Reverend said, "He's speechless" before the crowd, the humble
man fell to his knees, tilted his head back, and raised his hands
in praise.

Pastor Matthews would add, "This man's spent most of his life
trying to paint a picture of happiness with drugs and booze."
After a brief pause, the good Reverend looked down at Mr. Lamp
to ask of him, "Those beer commercials ... you know ... the ones
with the good-looking women and all ... they're just a whole lot of
fraud ... aren't they Jerald?"

The weeping man was only able to nod his head with silent
agreement.

Pastor Dan then bent down to hug Jerald and after a brief
moment of embrace, the minister stood to conclude, while
pointing to the crowd, "Jerald spent a lifetime painting landscapes
for failure, folks … but then he threw himself upon the canvas of
the Master ... Hallelujah! ... Somebody give the Lord a great big
hand clap of praise!"

Nathaniel and his driver left the service that evening feeling a
little scared; a little empty. As both men were walking through the
parking lot to the limo, Nathaniel asked his chauffeur, "What did
you think of all that back there?"

Jimmy waited to give a reply until he opened the rear door for
his employer. "Sir … I've never seen anything like that before."

With that said, Nathaniel gave his driver a half hearted smile,
climbed into the vehicle, and Jimmy closed the door.

Jimmy then made his way around to the driver's side, opened
the door and took a seat. He removed the keys from his pants
pocket and inserted the ignition key to start the vehicle. But
before he turned the key, the chauffeur appeared to be lost in a

moment of deep thought. Nathaniel noticed the pause and inquired, "Is something wrong, Jimmy?"

The now troubled driver turned around in his seat and placed his right arm over the backrest to ask, "Sir?"

Nathaniel knew something was bothering his employee. "What is it, Jimmy ... what's on your mind?" the curious CEO inquired.

"Sir ... can I be honest with you?"

"Absolutely!"

"Sir ... It takes a lot to get me scared, but what went on in that church tonight really freaked me out!"

Nathaniel slid back in his seat a little to add, "Yeah ... me too!"

Jimmy's tone then got a bit more serious. "Sir ... I know you wanted me to go up front with you when they gave the altar call. I apologize if I let you down ... I'm just not ready for that Jesus thing. I know what the pastor was saying was right. My grandma went to church every Sunday. She said she prayed for me all the time." Jimmy realized he was about to lose his composure so he turned back around and placed his hand upon the key while saying, "God rest her soul."

Before Jimmy could start the vehicle, Nathaniel leaned forward to place a hand upon his driver's shoulder. "Jimmy ... you have nothing to apologize for. I should be the one handing out apologies." Then the executive slid back in his seat.

Jimmy reached up to adjust the rear-view mirror, caught site of his employer in the reflection, and then asked, "Sir ... what do you need to be sorry for?"

Nathaniel hung his head slightly, then with a regretful tone expressed, "I've been ashamed to admit, to anyone, that I'm a

Christian, Jimmy. God's word says we're to be the laborers. I haven't done anything but help myself for the last ten years." Nathaniel became so embroiled in those thoughts he began to break down emotionally. Jimmy watched in the rear-view mirror as his employer began to weep.

When Nathaniel reached in his pocket to retrieve a handkerchief, Jimmy started the car, then asked, "Home, Sir?"

Nathaniel just nodded his head in silent reply.

The trip to the CEO's apartment was a silent one for both men. When Jimmy arrived at his employer's building Nathaniel asked to be dropped off on the street, at the building's front door. After Jimmy parked and walked around to the rear of the vehicle to let his employer out, Nathaniel shook his friend's hand, and then added. "You're a good man, Jimmy ... an even better friend."

The honored driver replied, "Thank you, Sir."

"Pick me up at seven in the morning. I've got to catch a flight to New York tomorrow. I'll be meeting with a new advertising agency ... they'll be pitching a new promotional program for the company."

Jimmy's response was, "Very good, Sir."

Nathaniel stared his employee in the eye for a brief moment, then asked, "You're not going to call me Nathaniel ... are you?" Jimmy hesitated for a while, then succumbed to a, "No ... Sir."

Nathaniel then gave his driver a quick embrace, something he'd never done before, and then walked away.

A little shocked and stunned, Jimmy stood on the sidewalk in observation of his Employer's approach to the front of the apartment building for a while before eventually driving away.

As always, Jimmy arrived right on time the following morning

and drove Nathaniel to the O'Hare airport. The executive thanked
the driver and told him he'd see him in a couple days, then both
men parted ways.

When Nathaniel arrived at the terminal, he was a little disturbed
by the assigned flight number, but shook it off as nothing rather
quickly. Besides, "It's just a number." He thought. " It's
insignificant that the flight number's *666.*"

In the end, the evil of the number for the flight was just
something out of Nathaniel's imagination, a thought running wild
on him, for the trip went well. The plane touched down at New
York's LaGuardia airport on time, without incident, and a limo
was waiting for Nathaniel when he arrived.

The executive was driven to the *Waldorf Astoria* hotel, where
he was later called upon by a representative of the advertising
agency. The representative said she would pick Nathaniel up
around one, take him to lunch, then they would head over to the
agency's corporate headquarters.

Before Nathaniel hung up the phone, he thanked the kind
woman and said, "I'm looking forward to it."

The executive knew he had a little time to kill so he left his
room, made his way down the stairs and through the hotel lobby
to the street. He'd ventured a few blocks when he saw
something a little unusual, an artist painting a landscape amongst
the busy crowd.

The painter was composing a scene upon a medium size
canvas. He'd set up a small table in front of a coffee shop and
was stroking the brush over his masterpiece as Nathaniel walked
by.

Several were looking over the artist's shoulder at his work

when Nathaniel decided to gaze upon his craft as well. The small crowd eventually thinned out and the CEO was the only one who remained. Intrigued by the work, and the artist's choice of location, Nathaniel asked, "I see you're creating your painting from a photo. May I ask where that photo was taken. What mountain is that? Where's it located?"

The artist replied, "All I know is it's somewhere in Wyoming ... I believe it's near a place called *Circle J Ranch* .... That's about all I know ... I got a friend who's a professional photographer ... she took it."

As the painter continued to stroke the picturesque work with his brush, Nathaniel responded with a curious reply. "Huh ... Wyoming's the least populated state in the nation ... Did you know that?"

With a fleeting tone of interest, the artist said, "Can't say I did ... why you askin'?"

In a devised effort to change the subject, Nathaniel asked, "Is that picture you're painting for sale?"

The artist's reply was "Everything's for sale ... for a price!"

Nathaniel was taken back a bit by that response and pondered in hesitation of the artist's meaning before he offered ten thousand for the work.

The artist was surprised and more-than-a-little skeptical of Nathaniel's genuineness.

The painter laid down his brush, stood from where he was sitting, tilted his straw hat back a bit, then said, "You're going to give me ten thousand dollars for that?" as he pointed to the unfinished canvas resting upon the table.

"That's right." Nathaniel replied.

The artist took a seat back at the table and resumed what he was doing, and then in a joking tone said, "Yeah ... right!"

When the artist said that, Nathaniel knew he didn't believe him. The executive then reached down in his rear pocket to retrieve his wallet. He removed a couple thousand in cash from his billfold, all hundreds, then threw them on the table in front of the artist.

The artist looked down at the cash, stopped what he was doing, pushed himself away from the table and stood before Nathaniel to say, "You're serious ... aren't you?"

Nathaniel replied, "Yes ... I am."

"Mister," the artist raved, "I've never gotten more than a few hundred bucks for my stuff ... I have to be honest with you ... what I do ... well ... it's not that good!"

Nathaniel ignored all that and reached down to grab the money, then folded the bills and stuffed them in the artist's shirt pocket. "I'm staying at the Waldorf ... room 347 ... drop it off tomorrow night and I'll give you the balance." After a brief pause, Nathaniel said, "Drop off the photo too ... write what you know about that place on the back of the snapshot ... I'd appreciate it."

The artist was still in a bit of shock, unable to even give a decent reply, so Nathaniel extended his hand to say, "Do we have a deal?"

The dumb-founded painter extended his hand to shake on it, as the exec nodded his head in silent agreement.

Nathaniel glanced at the painting once more, then stared at it for a while before commenting, "It's all just a painted mountain ... isn't it?"

The artist's puzzled response was, "What?"

The CEO said, "Life!"

As Nathaniel began to walk away, the artist said, "Thanks Mister ... I'll finish it up in about an hour ... I'll deliver it myself around nine tomorrow night."

Nathaniel shook his head slightly, then turned to leave. When the exec turned his back and began to walk away, the artist yelled, "Would that be okay?"

Nathaniel never turned around, but did throw his hand up in the air to signify it would be.

The artist kept his promise and delivered the painting to Nathaniel the following evening. In tum, the executive kept his by paying the balance of eight thousand.

The CEO cherished that painting, and when he arrived back in Chicago he asked his head-of-staff to do some research on that place where the photo was taken.

Nathaniel mandated everything his employee did was to be kept secret and held in strict conference. No one else was to be informed of it or the chief-of-staff would be fired, according to the executive.

Nathaniel even went as far as to have his employee sign a binding legal document stating so.

The employee's research found that the mountain was indeed located in Wyoming. It's near a place called *Muddy Gap* and is elevated some 6,250 feet above sea level. It's one of the Buttes along the Green Mountain Range, not far from the Antelope Foothills.

There was also a place called *Circle J* there. It was a 90,000-acre ranch that was vacant and for sale. The property was vast and stretched across three counties, Carbon, Fremont and Sweetwater. The Sweetwater River ran through the property as well. Highway 220 was to the east and 287 was to the west, but dirt secondary roads were the more prevalent thoroughfares.

That mountain Nathaniel was so interested in was located on the southern corner of the ranch, but the CEO was more intrigued with an abandoned cabin near a secluded body of water along the north slope - a place called *Lost Lake*.

It's quite possible the ranch remained tenantless for so long because the asking price was so high. The price tag was in the millions, but that didn't matter to Nathaniel. He had the money and wanted the place. He was determined to purchase that property at any price, and did. In the end, Nathaniel made up his mind it didn't really matter when he found out the land was near a town called, *Turmoil*.

Chapter Twelve
Sell, or be Sold

It'd been a short-lived transitional slippage of time endured since that business trip to New York. Over the last few weeks Nathaniel had experienced difficulty sleeping. He speculated the trouble began after his return from "The Big Apple." The CEO felt his lack of sleep was borderline insomnia, and he pondered whether or not to see a doctor about the condition. The executive led a complicated life, there was no negating that, but it had become an existence full of increasingly clouded, self-induced complexity and thought provoked dilemma that just wouldn't subside. Nathaniel had a brilliant mind, but his logic failed to recognize the burden as one divinely guided.

It was a Friday night and although the executive had nothing planned for the following day, except to sleep in, he still had a hard time dozing off. His best efforts to grasp some slumber were in vain, for the executive tossed and turned until the wee morning hours.

As the night wore on, Nathaniel's struggle to embrace contentment appeared to be just a demonstration of futility. Feeling the urge to rise, the executive looked over at the alarm clock and became disheartened when he read the displayed numbers of 3 AM.

Nathaniel thought, "What's the use!" got up, put his robe on, then made his way toward the bathroom.

The executive had every intention of relieving himself, but his curiosity soon circumvented the urge. For Nathaniel distinctly heard a low pitch humming sound coming from somewhere inside the apartment. After a brief scan of every room, Nathaniel concluded the noise was coming from his computer in the den. The executive then reasoned to himself, "I turned that thing off!" When Nathaniel approached the machine, he noticed something odd. Written in small print across the screen were the words, *Sell - or be Sold!*

Bewildered and perplexed by the text, Nathaniel thought, "I didn't write that!" As he reached for the keyboard to press the delete key, that primal urge to urinate became too great for the executive and he had to flee the room.

When Nathaniel returned to the den a couple minutes later, he became all-the-more puzzled because the words were not only erased from the screen, but the machine was off as well.

A revelation of the strange encounter, true mental meaning of it all, wasn't in Nathaniel's immediate grasp then. Yet, in time, the CEO would recognize the phenomenon as divine and eventually come to understand its crucial message and deep spiritual intent.

Nathaniel's amazement with what had occurred drove him to stare at that blank computer screen for a good hour. As he glared at the dark void of the monitor, Nathaniel's mind began to play tricks on him. The executive was beginning to believe, if he sat there long enough, the machine would tum itself back on - to his disappointment, it didn't.

Eventually, the executive grew tired of staring at the machine and glanced up to catch sight of a Bible. Unable to sleep, Nathaniel thought he might read some for a while.

As the executive flipped through the pages, his attention fell upon the book of Isaiah, the 48th chapter in particular, verses 17 and 18.

The text read: *"This is what the Lord says - your Redeemer, the Holy One of Israel: 'I am the Lord your God, who teaches you what is best for you, who directs you in the way you should go. If only you had paid attention to my commands, your peace would have been like a river, your righteousness like the waves of the sea.' "*

Nathaniel was intrigued by that passage, but grew even more fascinated when his Bible appeared to just fall open to a few more. Two additional verses caught the executive's attentive eye as well. Their meaning registered loud and clear with the executive. The words were bold and piercing, seemingly jumping off the page into Nathaniel's soul.

Proverbs 3:6 was the first to shed light upon the CEO's probing mind. It avowed, *"In all your ways acknowledge Him, and He will make your paths straight."*

Psalms 25:12 was the other. It revealed, *"Who, then, is the man that fears the Lord? He will instruct him in the way chosen for him."*

The executive would spend a great deal of time analyzing those verses, reading them over and over again that night, before the recognition of a promise made took center stage.

Nathaniel recalled having an article Pastor Matthews gave him three weeks prior. The good Reverend handed it to the executive on a Sunday morning. The minister said he found it in one of those Christian Newsletters he subscribes to. Nathaniel remembered tucking it away in the desk drawer, and he was now in search of it. Pastor Dan suggested Nathaniel might find the article interesting, but he'd forgotten all about it until now.

After a moment or two, the executive found what he was looking for. He then pulled it from the drawer, unfolded the clipping, and began to read.

The article was titled, ***Wall Street Thievery.***

"Hundreds of corporations, some notable, are being deliberately bankrupted.

Responsible authorities are closing their eyes while multitudes throughout several states are blatantly robbed and swindled out of their life savings. It's theft of your money!

During economic prosperity, thieves sell untold bogus certificates. Why do corporations allow thieves to control their securities?

The scam is rather simple: The sale of counterfeit certificates to naive citizenry while illegally manipulating prices below the natural balance of public supply and demand. Thus, lowering price below the value established by a variety of factors entices a continual supply of 'suckers' buying those certificates - run off on printing presses by the market operators. Meanwhile, assets represented by bogus paper must be severely damaged and perhaps maliciously bankrupted to artificially destroy the value of both the legitimate and 'watered-down' receipts to complete the vile robbery of their myriad victims.

Note: **The thieves get your money up front.**

Destruction may be delayed until years later but it surely comes. The thieves are not about to buy back counterfeit ... at

least not at higher prices. Conversely, the prices of certain legitimate items are artificially raised above the value determined unwarranted advantages over others.

Yes, many agents serving the thieves are in the employ of government being paid as public servants but, in reality, are agents serving despicable people. Many agents, of course, don't even realize who they truly serve but simply do the bidding of their bosses to keep their jobs, get promotions and raises. The laws are meaningless as the thieves and their agents are protected.

Modem scams involve: Securities representing ownership, Bonds representing loans, Partnership Shares representing profit sharing, Commodities representing articles of commerce, Bullion representing precious metals, etc.

Even in ancient times merchant thieves operated in the temples, selling items representing a variety of offerings.

I the Lord do not change. So you, 0 descendants of Jacob, are not destroyed Ever since the time of your forefathers you have turned away from my decrees and have not kept them. Return to me and I will return to you, says the Lord Almighty.

But you ask, 'How are we to return?'

Will a man rob God? Yet you rob me.

But you ask, 'How do we rob you?'

In tithes and offerings. You are under a curse - the whole nation of you because you are robbing me. Bring the whole tithe into the storehouse, that there may be food in my house. Test me in this, says the Lord Almighty, and see if I will not throw open the floodgates of heaven and pour out so much blessing that you will not have room enough for it. (Malachi 3:6-10)

People would take their donations to the Temple; however, few were aware that those same offerings were being sold over and over and over again as thieves pocketed the lion's share, gave the high priest a cut, and the Temple Treasury got only a fraction of what was due. Thus, the temples were dens of thieves just as are today's Wall Streets of the world.

When it was almost time for the Jewish Passover, Jesus went up to Jerusalem. In the temple courts he found men selling cattle, sheep and doves, and others sitting at tables exchanging money. So, he made a whip out of cords, and drove all from the temple area, both sheep and cattle; he scattered the coins of the money changers and overturned their tables. To those who sold doves he said, 'Get these out of here! How dare you turn my Father's house into a market!' (John 2:13-16)

Awake, people are being robbed blind!

When the thieves are ready, **retirement** funds and investment plans are depleted, jobs are lost, seniority gone, economic turmoil arises, homes are lost, 'Nest eggs' are wiped out, bankruptcies are deliberately manipulated, along with artificially depressed prices.

People have lived in poverty while others lived 'High off the hog' while generation after generation is robbed.

Oh, yes, burdensome laws, corporate secrets, crooked judges and lawyers all prevail today.

In addition to the vast sales of bogus certificates, the thieves' games involve, falsifying reported data, rejection of blame, liability, **and the** protection of wrongdoers.

It's sad, but the tentacles even stretch throughout this

nation and around the world as corrupt brokerage houses
pedal both legitimate and bogus certificates to naive
citizenry with impunity.

Yes, the Executive Branch, the U.S. Congress, the
Judiciary, especially the bankruptcy courts, the Justice
Department, the Treasury Department, the Securities and
Exchange Commission, the Internal Revenue Service, the
FBI, even the Defense Department, all work for, service,
and protect those stealing your money.

The Scriptures speak of those events as the sin they are.

*My mountain in the land and your wealth and all your
treasures I will give away as plunder, together with your high
places, because of sin throughout your country.*

*Through your own fault you will lose the inheritance I gave
you. I will enslave you to your enemies in a land you do not
know, for you have kindled my anger, and it will burn forever.
This is what the Lord says: 'Cursed is the one who trusts in
man, who depends on flesh for his strength and whose heart
turns away from the Lord He will be like a bush in the
wastelands; he will not see prosperity when it comes. He will
dwell in the parched places of the desert, in a salt land where
no one lives. But blessed is the man who trusts in the Lord,
whose confidence is in him. He will be like a tree planted by
the water that sends out its roots by the stream. It does not fear
when heat comes; its leaves are always green. It has no
worries in a year of drought and never fails to bear fruit.*

*The heart is deceitful above all things and beyond cure. Who
can understand it? I the Lord search the heart and examine the
mind, to reward a man according to his conduct, according to*

what his deeds deserve. Like a partridge that hatches eggs it did not lay is the man who gains riches by unjust means. When his life is half gone, they will desert him, and in the end he will prove to be a fool.' (Jeremiah 17:3-11)

Will not all of them taunt him with ridicule and scorn, saying, Woe to him who piles up stolen goods and makes himself wealthy by extortion. How long must this go on?

Will not your debtors suddenly arise? Will they not wake up and make you tremble?

Then you will become their victim. Because you have plundered many nations, the peoples who are left will plunder you. For you have shed man's blood; you have destroyed lands and cities and everyone in them. Woe to him who builds his realm by unjust gain to set his nest on high, to escape the clutches of ruin! You have plotted the ruin of many peoples, shaming your own house and forfeiting your life. (Habakkuk 2:6- 10)

Elementary logic dictates that an entity would have to have an endless supply of cash to always sell at lower prices while purportedly insuring a steady flow, smoothing out price changes - conversely, to always buy at higher prices to insure the reverse. Neither is true when it comes to the operations of national markets throughout the world. Thus, the true operations of those markets are founded on selling bogus receipts through fraud, deceit, larceny and illegal price manipulation.

Everyone, including investors and corporate management, should know and understand what's going on.

When the New York Stock Exchange first got their initial

computerized system on line in 1964, their programmers did a
poor job of concealing the fact that the Dow Jones Industrial
Average, for example, was artificially generated.

The Securities and Exchange Commission still continues
as a watchdog for the thieves and not for citizens.

Price manipulation, up or down, is child's play for those
given illegal license to ignore the laws, to sell scam, to steal
vast sums from people - their invested wealth. All while
protected by agents on the government payroll.

The whole game is very similar to that of ancient times
when people tithed via offerings to thieves in the temples.
The thieves took it all and God got little or nothing. Oh, the
high priest and a few others got a cut of the swag too;
otherwise the thieves would have been cut off.

Yet, the people did not object or were ignored since the
government and the priesthood were protectors of the
vileness. So, history reveals that eventually God destroyed
each of the corrupted temples and the people were cast into
an unrighteous world.

*Who will rise up for me against the wicked? Who will take a
stand for me against evildoers?* (Psalms 94:16)

Everyone should know and understand what's going on.
Remember, everyone except the thieves get hurt when the
markets are dumped and trillions in buying power are
maliciously removed from the economy.

Blow the trumpet!"

Nathaniel milled around the apartment a bit more after that, then
he tried to catch a few winks of shut eye after saying a lengthy
prayer. For the first time, in a long time, the executive was able to

fall asleep, slept in, and awoke around two the following afternoon.

When the CEO checked the Saturday mail, he got a rude awakening though. That letter he sent his mother a few years earlier had been returned. The envelope was weathered, been torn, opened, and then resealed with tape. Nathaniel couldn't remember exactly when he wrote the correspondence, but the original postal mark read: September 12th, 1984 - the letter had been written five years prior. The executive opened the envelope to discover his letter was intact, just as it was when he sent it. There was nothing else enclosed with the letter, nor was anything written upon the page in response to Nathaniel's words. It was no different except for the word *Deceased* was transcribed on the face of the envelope.

As Nathaniel sat at the kitchen table, he stared at that letter with his head hung low. He braced himself with his left hand upon a knee, and with his right palm he rubbed his forehead while a mind full of stirring thoughts did race.

A flood of imposing questions gripped the executive's soul. "Is my mother really dead? If she's gone, when did she die? How'd she die? What did she die of? I wonder if it was from natural causes or fatal disease? Who wrote the word 'Deceased' on the envelope?

Was it mom's sister, her brother-in-law, who wrote that message on the envelope and sent it back? Why wasn't I told anything? It's been five years without so much as a phone call or simple note … why? Where's she buried? When was the funeral?"

Disappointment boiled within the executive. Nathaniel finally vented his frustration by balking out a scream of, "God! ... That's all I get ... Deceased!"

As it was with Nathaniel and the unveiling word of his mother's possible death, things aren't always absolute or fully revealed. Life isn't always delivered with a complete explanation; it's seldom fair nor just in that regard. Although the CEO longed for the truth about his mom, some answers to those probing questions of his, most of the future queries concerning the mother he never really knew went unanswered. In spite of a heartfelt longing to know more about the woman who gave him life, Nathaniel would find little solace in what he learned about her over the span of his remaining years.

The executive spent the next four hours reading nothing but that letter. Over and over, Nathaniel would read his handwriting in an effort to conclude something other than the original intended meaning. But no matter how hard he tried to reason his words as something else, Nathaniel couldn't distinguish any difference between what he felt then compared to now.

Nathaniel thought he was a *money grubber* five years ago, someone preoccupied with making dough, but now all doubts were removed. The executive wasn't content back then, nor was he now. Nathaniel was a billionaire who lacked for nothing - except there was something more valuable than gold he didn't own, a fortune called happiness.

The executive knew if he lay around the apartment that evening, he'd get more depressed than he already was. With that in mind, Nathaniel got dressed and made his way over to the local bookstore. *The Book Nook* was the CEO's favorite bookstore. Its owner, Jonathan Lane, was a close friend of Nathaniel's. The executive frequented the shop often because it was convenient, only four blocks away, and his friend stocked all of the new releases - Lane's inventory of used books was diverse and sizeable as well.

When Nathaniel walked through the front door, Lane caught sight of him and greeted the executive with a warm hello. "It's good to see you, Nathaniel!" The merchant added, as he stepped out from behind the counter to shake his friend's hand.

"Good seeing you too, John." The CEO added.

Giving Nathaniel a quick glance over, the inquisitive shopkeeper probed. "You been feelin' alright?"

"Yeah ... why?" Nathaniel pondered.

"Oh ... nothing ... I didn't mean to be nosy ... It's just that you look a little tired to me ... I didn't mean nothing by it."

"You're not prying ... good friends care ... don't they?" With a pat on the merchant's back, Nathaniel added, "Thanks for asking ... I wish I was sleeping a little better though."

"Anything I can do? ... Short of calling a doctor." The joking merchant asked with a grin.

The CEO said, "No."

Lane placed his hand on the executive's shoulder, then said, "I tell you what. You've been a good customer of mine for a long time. I consider you one of my closest friends ... I'd like to bless ya with a little something."

"What's that?" Nathaniel replied.

"When you get ready to leave, look me up. The books you pick out today are on the house ... Okay?"

"You don't have to do that, John ... I appreciate the gesture though." Nathaniel added.

"I know I don't have to ... I want to!" With a slap of the executive's back, Lane said, "Now ... Go on!" then he pointed to the *New Release* section. "I won't have it any other way. I just got *Beyond Good and Evil* in ... check it out, I think you may like that one." After a brief hesitation, Lane told his friend, "Look me up when you're done shopping."

Lane's generous offer gave his friend a much-needed boost in morale. Nathaniel wasn't accustomed to people blessing him like that. Money wasn't a problem for the exec, but Nathaniel knew it had been for Lane in the past. Yet, John was willing to bless his friend even though Nathaniel hadn't offered to help anyone who was in need before. The thought of, "I've got all I ever want ... he's been struggling to make ends meet ... and he goes and does something like that!" raced over and over again in the executive's mind.

Nathaniel took his friend's advice and soon wandered over to the "New Release" section. There he found what John was referring to.

The book wasn't really new at all. It was another version of the original. It was originally released in 1966 by Random House, but the new addition was printed by Vintage Books. The title actually read: *"Beyond Good and Evil: Prelude to A Philosophy of The Future!"*

As Nathaniel flipped through the pages, he came across the Author Bio, then jokingly said, "Humm ... Born 1844. Died 1900. Boy ... it sure took him a long time to get published."

The book was written by Fiedrich Nietzsche. Nathaniel thought the author made a few good points from what he read, but one particular statement stood out in the executive's mind.

Nietzsche stated, "In individuals, insanity is rare, but in groups, parties, nations and epochs it's the rule."

Once Nathaniel pondered what he'd read, he voiced under his breath: "I'm beginning to think I'm the exception."

Nathaniel wandered over to the *Used Book* section once he'd peered through a few more of the New Releases. None of those books seemed to interest the executive, but an older title called, *Ronald Reagan: In God I Trust,* did. Published in '84, the book was written by Reagan and coauthored by David Shepherd.

Nathaniel was a staunch Republican, a supporter of Reagan, and a firm believer of *Reaganomics.* The executive had been a beneficiary of the President's fiscal policies for the last eight years. Nathaniel loved Ronald Reagan, for his dual terms in the White House had indeed been "user friendly" for the business sector.

Reagan, the 40th President of the United States, had been defined by a number of things. He was born in Dixon, Illinois, a town due west of Chicago along Interstate 88, a fact Nathaniel never knew.

Before becoming President, Reagan was an accomplished actor and served two terms as California's governor. In 1980, he accepted the highest office in the land and became the oldest president to be elected to that position. He would also become the oldest president to have lived on record before his eventual passing at age 93. The cause of death would officially be contributed to Pneumonia, a complication of Alzheimer's - a disease of which he suffered with for over ten years.

When Reagan took office, he inherited double digit inflation and interest rates that were so bad a *Misery Index* was developed to measure the suffering. In spite of the relentless pressures associated with the presidency, Reagan always seemed to shine with that quick-wit of his.

Ronald Reagan was never reserved with his spiritual beliefs either. He was a vocal believer, a man of strong principals and integrity, someone who cried out to God in prayer often.

The 80's would eventually be defined as a decade of greed, thanks to Reagan, some thought. He would go down in history as a president known for tax cuts, deficit spending, a man who had a sweet tooth, a lover of jelly beans, but more so a figure who was instrumental in promoting global democracy. No matter whether you cared for Reagan or not, he quite literally changed the world for he found an end to *The Cold War.*

Nathaniel found the Reagan book interesting, but he soon laid that one down and began scanning another. The executive began leafing through a book by Stanley Frodsham. It was printed by the Gospel Publishing House in '93 and was titled *Smith Wigglesworth: Apostle of Faith.*

Nathaniel had never heard of Smith Wigglesworth before, but the more he read that paperback the more intrigued he became with his life.

Smith Wigglesworth was born in Menston, Yorkshire England, in 1859. Smith, a simple man, grew up picking turnips then eventually became a successful plumber. He was illiterate throughout early life, only learning to read and write after reaching adulthood. Wigglesworth was led to Christ at the tender age of eight, by his grandmother, but didn't receive the Baptism of the Holy Spirit until he was forty-eight. His life would dramatically change after that. From that date in 1907 until his death in 1947, Smith would evangelize scores on an unprecedented scale over a span of some four decades.

Wigglesworth was not only noted for his powerful sermons, but amazing healings occurred in his services as well. Many of them were nothing short of miraculous. More than a dozen people were raised from the dead, as confirmed and testified to by a host of witnesses, when Wigglesworth prayed over the corpses. He was, without question, one of the greatest evangelists to ever come from England.

The more Nathaniel read about Smith Wigglesworth, the more fascinated he became with how God used that man. Before closing the book Nathaniel convinced himself, "I've got to have this!"

A flood of probing thoughts began to fill the executive's mind and there was no escaping their spiritual stir. Nathaniel hadn't distinguished what sort of voices, those frequenting his head, truly were. The revelation of their origin hadn't come to his intellect just yet; for they were intrusions designed by divine intervention.

"Look at what God did through Smith Wigglesworth ... My, my... a simple plumber from England!" Nathaniel thought. "He was illiterate ... and the *I Am* used him in a mighty way! Boy ... I've got all those degrees ... money." With a slight tear beginning to well in the corner of one eye, the executive verbalized, under his breath, "I wish God would use me in a great way!"

No sooner than he'd expressed that opinion, Nathaniel's mind began to race with the thought of, "You aren't going to take it with you ... Money will burn!"

Nathaniel hadn't figured out, so far, what that "*Still Small Voice*," as some call it, was just yet. He reasoned it to be something along the lines of consciousness or intuition, but nothing more. He failed to link it as a "tug" of the *Holy Spirit* upon himself. But, in due time, the executive would come to know that personality of the *Trinity* and accept that fold of the *Godhead* into his own life.

After checking out a few more titles, Nathaniel tucked the Wigglesworth book under his arm and headed for the checkout counter. There were three or four customers in line in front of the executive when he got there and Nathaniel noticed that his friend was working the cash register. When Jonathan caught sight of his friend, he instructed one of his employees to take over for him. With a silent motion of his hand, Lane waved at Nathaniel as to say, "Follow me," then pointed to his office.

When Nathaniel reached the office door, his friend was just sitting down at his desk.

Lane asked, "What'd you pick?"

Nathaniel replied, "Have you ever heard of a man by the name of Smith Wigglesworth?"

After pondering the question for a moment, the shop owner in turn said, "Can't say I have ... Why? ... That sure is a funny name!"

Nathaniel stepped forward through the door, and handed the Wigglesworth book to Jonathan.

Lane glanced at the book, then added, "Is that it?"

Nathaniel nodded his head in silent reply.

The curious shopkeeper asked, "That's all you want?"

Again, Nathaniel nodded with silent reply.

As he flipped through the pages, Lane's comments of examination were: "This thing's worn out ... four bucks ... surely, there's more in the store you want." As he stared up at his friend,

Jonathan asked, "Right?"

In an effort to change the subject, Nathaniel quickly said, "That'll do," then asked, "You stock Bibles, don't you?"

Jonathan replied, "Some ... Why?"

While the proverbial gears were a spin in Nathaniel's head, Lane waited a moment or two then again asked, "Why?"

"Well ... a missionary visited our church the other day. He was asking for Bibles. I didn't give it much thought at the time ... I guess I should have."

After a brief pause, Nathaniel recalled still having the missionary's card. "I think, I still may have his card." The executive told his friend. "The man's African ... I think." Nathaniel added, as he reached in his pants pocket to retrieve his wallet.

As the executive handed the missionary's card to his friend, he said, I want you to send him a couple thousand Bibles ... the nicest ones you can get your hands on. Special order them if you have to."

"Two thousand?" Jonathan replied, with a bit of alarm.

"Yes ... Why? ... Is that a problem?" Nathaniel asked with a hint of concern.

With a small lump in his throat, Lane said, with a shake of his head, "No ... What color though? ... What language? ... What version?"

"I recall him asking for two hundred Bibles ... written in English." With a broad smile now upon his face, Nathaniel said, "Well ... I'll leave the rest of that up to you. Send it by air though ... It'll get there quicker."

As he prepared to leave, Nathaniel added, "Let my secretary

know how much it is and I'll have someone drop off a check ...
How's that?"

Lane was a bit dumbfounded for he'd never witnessed such a
bold act of kindness out of his friend before, but, in turn, he
quickly shared an enthusiastic, "Sure!" in reply.

Once again, the proverbial gears were spinning in Nathaniel's
brain and Lane had to soon interrupt the executive's train of
thought for the shopkeeper realized the CEO had been
daydreaming for a brief time. "You haven't heard a word I've been
saying ... have you? Jonathan pried.

With his focus now trained upon his friend once again,
Nathaniel said, "I'm sorry ... you were saying?"

A bit annoyed by his friend's mental wandering, Jonathan
added, "Oh ... never mind!"

"You still do business with *Capital Mortgage* on this
place?" Nathaniel asked.

The shopkeeper said, "Yeah ... Why?"

"Oh ... just wondering." Nathaniel said.
In less than a week, the executive pulled a few strings and
found out what John's balance was on the mortgage for the store.

A courier soon delivered a sealed envelope to the *Book Nook*
after that and Jonathan opened it - he about fell over when he did.
Along with the check for the Bibles was a certified cashier's check.
It was for ninety-seven thousand dollars, made out to the mortgage
company. Written on the memo line of the check were the words,
"Payment in full for loan #11387-69."

The envelope also contained a note, which read: "Thanks for
teaching me a little something about what *Sell, or be Sold* means.
Your friend, Nathaniel."

The shopkeeper had no idea what the executive was referring to, but, nevertheless, he was truly grateful to Nathaniel and would become a lifelong friend till the end of his life.

By no means was Nathaniel lazy. As of late though, he found himself being lost in nothing more than blank thought while staring out the office window for hours at a time over the course of a given week. Friday came and the employees of lrwin Industries prepared to depart, for it was late in the day and each had high hopes of an enjoyable weekend in mind.

Nathaniel, however, was more concerned with other matters and the weight of serious intent drove him to dial the phone; that device of which he'd been staring at, in anticipation, for a good while. (The executive didn't have a clue what he was about to do was a play into the Creator's hand, when he dialed the number for *Global Technologies)*

The CEO held the majority of stock in *Irwin Industries* and had for a long time. With a share total of roughly 59%, Nathaniel was in a position to sell the corporation - if he was so inclined.

During an ensuing telephone conversation, Nathaniel told Les McGree, the longstanding CEO of Global Technologies, that if *GTI* were still financially prepared to do so, he was willing to sell Irwin Industries for fair market value.

Surprisingly, McGree wasn't the least bit curious as to why Nathaniel was receptive to a *Buy-out* now, and willing to sell low on top of that. Oddly enough, the subject never once came up in the discussion. Surely there was a simple explanation though, an underlying factor, for one might possibly reason there was a lean toward unwavering greed.

"I'm speaking on behalf of Global Technologies when I say

this." McGree added. "I'll have an independent accounting firm ... one other than our own ... formulate a final figure. Then we'll put a formal offer on the table." In a jokingly subtle pitch, McGree jested, "I trust there's no lingering hard feelings. That hostile takeover threat a few years ago was just a bluff ... strictly business of course."

Nathaniel was no fool. He knew McGree was lying through his teeth. If "McGreed," as the executive so negatively referred, and his board could have pulled it off back then, they would have forced the young Irwin out of business and took it all.

Nathaniel knew he didn't dare vocalize his true thoughts. So before hanging up the phone, he said, "I'll have our law firm send over all statements of net worth ... and anything else you need ... look them over … have your lawyers draw up the paperwork ... and I'll have our attorneys do the same ... If all's in order … we'll move forward and finalize."

With that said, the divine will of God was swept into play and the tides of great change were set into motion.

Apart from the small core of corporate attorneys on retainer, those paid to assure secrecy, Nathaniel sought to confide in only his VP of Operations, George Willis, a faithful friend of many years. In a private discussion held with the Vice President in Nathaniel's office a week later, the CEO imparted what his true intentions were. Willis was astonished his employer would even contemplate such a move. "I'm leaning toward selling it all." He told his trusted friend.

"It's probably just some mid-life crisis I'd imagine." Willis reasoned. "You're probably just lonely ... that's all ... How about I fix you up with my wife's friend? ... You know ... The one I was telling you about the other day ... If you want my opinion ... I think you need a woman, Nate."

(Only a select few would be able to get away with talking to the executive like that, especially calling him anything other than "Sir.")

Nathaniel pushed himself away from the desk, then stood. Turning his back to the subordinate, Nathaniel stared out the window at the gloom of a dark dreary day. With a wedge of extended intentional silence applied, the CEO shirked the implication by adding, "You mean one like my mother."

Nathaniel wasn't the least bit interested in heeding the advice of a subordinate. A cloud of subversive thought laid waste to such counsel.

The following day the CEO took it upon himself to rent a vehicle, then he told his secretary he'd be out of touch for a couple days. Although she was a bit concerned and curious, the secretary never questioned her employer's motives. She knew her boss hadn't been himself lately and reasoned he just needed a little space.

The burdens associated with such a hectic lifestyle were growing heavy upon Nathaniel's shoulders. Sacrificing it all wasn't something he took lightly and would be a colossal move on his part. Relinquishing a successful company, one his family built over a century before, would no doubt constitute a ripple of consequence in the lives of many. The agonizing thoughts of actually going through with something like that had anguished the executive's mind for a while; torturous probes they were, disguised as reason.

Nathaniel left the city that day with no specific agenda in

mind. That was a bit out of the ordinary for the exec. He just drove with no particular sense of direction, but eventually decided upon a destination of Burnt Plain.

Upon arrival there, Nathaniel found a town consisting of four homes and an aged church adorned by a towering white steeple topped with a cross - that which remained was only a glimmer of what the historic village once was.

A graveyard lay directly in front of the house of worship. Nathaniel's loved ones were buried there. The picturesque chapel wore a plaque above the front door, it bore a faded date of 1881. The executive was quick to adopt the perception, "That house of God stands ritually symbolic, guardian over the saintly inhabitants of that cemetery."

As Nathaniel entered the resting-place of his relatives he couldn't help but ponder, "This place is in the middle of nowhere." An old iron arch, bearing the name "Burnt Plain Cemetery," covered the unassuming entrance. The lane dividing the graveyard was obviously used to a lesser extent, compared to the adjacent road. The guided way past many a headstone was riddled with imperfection, its need of repair and a layer of gravel was obvious. Potholes were abundant, washed deep by several storms no doubt, and the lane's center was nothing more than a vague stripe of grass.

The executive parked his vehicle and began to search for the place where his loved ones rested. Many of the tomb stones were so old the words etched upon them were now unreadable, and the support beneath some were crumbling.

Because the graveyard was small, Nathaniel found Jessup's marker in relative short order. Beside the single grave of his father lay the headstones of Nathaniel's grandparents and great-grandparents, both couples sharing the gravestone of each other. All three sites were void of flowers. No visible sign of visitation was present, for the tombstones were badly overgrown by weeds - it was as if no one cared.

Nathaniel fell to his knees and began to weep as he plucked the weeds from around their graves. After he'd finished the task, Nathaniel stood to wipe away the telltale signs of remorse. Then the executive drove to a neighboring town to purchase flowers; in doing so, he bought a carload totaling over a thousand dollars.

When the executive returned to the cemetery, he proceeded to decorate those lonely graves in which his relatives lay. As Nathaniel placed the last grouping of flowers around his Great-grandparents grave, he noticed a bold phrase etched upon the face of their stone. It read: *"They loved God and each other deeply."*

Nathaniel knew little about his Great-grandparents except for the few stories Jessup spun. They were devout in their faith - Nathaniel remembered that quite well. "How fitting they should perish together, dying in each other's arms during that awful winter storm." He thought.

As the executive began to weep once more, he reasoned himself to be neglectful and selfish too. Over a span of many years, Nathaniel had only visited that particular graveyard twice. The first occasion occurred with the death of his father. "Why had he never ventured there before?" He thought. "Why … am I here today?" The executive justified it as a longing to trace his roots. Possibly, it may have just been the pressures of the day.

Nathaniel ambled to the back of the cemetery after that and stood by a broken-down fence. The aged rails had definitely seen better days, but several still stood to separate the vast rolling fields from the adjacent burial lot. The executive also saw an old water pump, it too was overtaken by weeds, not far off. When he approached it, the curious CEO had little luck making it work. It appeared to be rusted shut, for the handle wouldn't move.

As Nathaniel gazed upon those fields, his mind began to fill with a sustaining sense of peace. The crops were a wave, rippling in the wind, a vast sea of green they appeared to be. The executive's imagination was now adrift, lost in the tranquil vision of his surroundings. He could envision in his mind's eye that very place, a quiet plot during the 1800's, and those horse-drawn funeral processions concluded there.

That cemetery visit made a profound impact on the executive - the winds of change were beginning to swirl.

When Nathaniel returned to Chicago he brought back some added baggage, the complexity of troubled thought. The exec had convinced himself of a few things, but one forged perception stood head and shoulders above the rest. Nathaniel reasoned he'd be entwined with a horde of wealth when the end came ... but ... his tombstone would probably mark a lonely grave after death.

A mental image of empty legacy, stark demise, now lay sear upon the executive's mind. It bore strikingly similar the cold granite sentinels shadowing that weed infested burial ground of his relatives. Remaining transfixed to the present path, the whims of self-indulgent pleasure, was no longer appealing to the CEO. With a hint of reticent, yet resolute certainly, Nathaniel concluded, "It's '89, late summer at that, time to move on!"

Chapter Thirteen
Provision

Nathaniel was accustomed to making tough decisions; his career bore familiarization with such mandates. However, throwing away the family inheritance was unprecedented and any directive he'd given before paled in comparison - the stature of what he intended would be paramount for many. Although the executive had a formalized plan, it wasn't void of dilemma. Nathaniel was convinced he was making the right move though; the most important one of his life.

A lot of hard work went into building *Irwin Industries,* making it the successful company it truly was. Nevertheless, before long, the efforts of three generations and a century of sweat would all be in vain. There was a number of contributing factors leading Nathaniel to finally forego it all. Foremost was the combination of a wife and kids missing from his life, followed by the absence of any known living relative. There was no mistaking the executive's creed however. Nathaniel arrived at the decision with reservation, it wasn't one he dwelled upon lightly.

The CEO thought his resignation would probably trigger skepticism amongst the financial circles, especially those of *Wall Street.* Nathaniel reasoned the markets might possibly view his decision as a departing failure, but it was something he must hold himself to - thus, the executive didn't embrace haste. He moved quickly to implement that defined will of his by calling a meeting of the board. Those who would be affected directly by the decision were invited as well.

Friday had rolled around, and it was depressingly chilly that morning. The weather forecasters had successfully predicted those cool temperatures and the accompanying rain which fell all week. It was the end of the workweek. Early fall had also arrived. A day's dagger of precipitation was beyond escape for the skies were churning with a darkened gloom. Heavy drizzle fell upon Chicago that day, dampening the city with a discouraging persistence. However, Nathaniel's determination hadn't been the least bit detoured, nor clouded, so he called the meeting to order.

"Gentlemen!" The executive declared as the members meandered about the wet bar, gorging themselves on the numerous cocktails they'd fashioned. "Please ... have a seat ... I'll try to make things brief."

Leonard Rush, an old family friend and long-standing board member, one of the wealthiest newspaper men in the Midwest, questioned the imperative nature of Nathaniel's hortative mood by slurring out something like, "Oh ... what's the rush?"

Already inebriated by the time he'd arrived, the elderly Rush poured himself another Gin and Tonic and downed it as Nathaniel glared at him with arms folded.

In silence, with an opened hand pointing to a vacant chair, the CEO invited the intoxicated man to sit. Rush took a seat at the table, but only after he'd poured himself another drink and downed that one first.

Nathaniel was anxious to convey that life-changing decision he'd made to the board, but a distaste for their behavior took brief precedence for a moment.

The CEO fumed, then vented under his breath, "Souses! ... I

should have tom that stupid bar out long ago!"

Nathaniel's derogatory candor grasped the vigilance of no one.
The choice few occupying the room were too busy with a dialogue
of their own.

One of the junior board members said, "What's so important
that you're dragging us out on a Friday? ... Afternoon no
less?"

That thin line of patience had been crossed with the CEO
and Nathaniel slammed an open hand upon the table.

Silence fell upon the room almost immediately, then all eyes
became transfixed upon the executive. "I have some urgent
business to bring to your attention!" Nathaniel blurted out.

In a sheepish tone, the drunken Rush added, "Well ... you don't
have to act like that about it!"

With an incredulous glare, Nathaniel snapped his head in
disgust, then barked, "Leonard ... Shut up! Either sit there
and be quiet, or I'll have security throw you out!"

The elderly Rush grew a bit sober with that piercing jab -
thus a hush now hovered over the group of men.

Nathaniel then took a moment to compose himself, in an
effort to let that simmering temper wane, as he gathered his
thoughts and apprehensively gazed about the room.

Those occupying the room were now all too aware that the
atmosphere had become soaked with concern. Nathaniel made it a
point to peer upon each individual member. Several maintained
eye contact with the executive, a couple had to glance away, but
the pride-ridden Leonard Rush chose to stare at that ice-filled
glass he had a death grip on.

Also in the room, sitting along the wall to Nathaniel's right, were George Willis, the Vice President of Operations, and Clarence Conn, the Irwin family's long time personal attorney, along with a couple legal cronies from his law firm.

Nathaniel didn't bother introducing the trio of lawyers to the board. He, instead, slid slowly backward from the forward stooping position he'd acquired. The executive gracefully straightened his back while raking his palms in a reverse motion across the table. And before taking a seat in his expensive high-back chair the CEO took the time to straighten his suit with an air of disgust.

Once he'd taken a seat, Nathaniel interlocked his fingers and slowly raised the clutch to his mouth. As he pressed the closest knuckle to his lips, the CEO entertained a deeply probing thought while demonstrating a somewhat relaxed moment of hesitation to scan the room.

With a hint of smugness, Nathaniel piped up to ask, "Does anyone know what Proverbs 29:23 says?"

The CEO was greeted with many a blank stare.

"It proclaims a man's pride will bring him low, but a man of lowly spirit will gain honor."

One of the board members was quick to ask, "What's this all about, Nathaniel?"

The executive in turn raised a finger to signal patience, then added, "Who knows what Jesus had to say in Matthew 19:23?"

Again, the room was filled with a horde of blank stares and an errant silence.

"He said it's hard for a rich man to enter the kingdom of heaven ... easier for a camel to go through the eye of a needle." Nathaniel explained.

Someone said, "What's going on?"

But the executive interrupted to further add, "Let not the wise man boast of his wisdom, or the strong man boast of his strength ... nor the rich of his riches. But let him who boasts boast that he understands and knows the Lord, the One who exercises kindness, justice and righteousness on earth, for in that the Lord delights."

The executive was quick to ascertain, "It's a safe bet none of you knew that was in Jeremiah, Chapter 9."

Earnest Creel, a grouch with a mean disposition and board member of some forty years, chimed in with a contemptuous slur of, "Got religion on us, huh?"

Nathaniel ignored the remark, then continued on with the point he was trying to make. "1 Timothy 6:17 -19 states, Command those who are rich in this present world not to be arrogant, nor to put their hope in wealth which is uncertain, but put that hope in God, who richly provides us with everything. Command them to do good ... to be rich in good deeds, it says ... be generous and willing to share. That way they will lay up treasure for themselves, a firm foundation for the coming age, so that they may take hold of the life that is truly life."

By then, Creel had pretty much had enough so he countered with a line of sarcastic taunts. "That's nice ... real nice." He said. "If we wanted a lecture on morals ... a sermon! ... we'd ask. Stop with the preachin' crap and get on with it! Now ... tell us ... what's so important that you had to drag us up here this afternoon?" With a quick glance around the room, Creel reasoned, "I'm sure we all need be on our way ... soon! Besides, I'd like to get out of here sometime today, myself."

It wasn't easy for the CEO to ignore those derogatory slabs, but Nathaniel knew he must reach down a bit further to gain an added edge of humble composure.

With a glance toward his secretary, Nathaniel interjected the remark, "That'll be all for today."

The surprised stenographer replied, "But ... Sir?"

Nathaniel then gently nodded his head, as to signal his approval.

"What about the dictation?" was her inquisitive pry.

The executive got out of his chair and walked over to his faithful confidant to place a gentle hand upon her shoulder. He reassured her it was okay. Then he added, "Your husband needs you ... more than we do."

The secretary's response was a blank silent stare toward her employer.

"You didn't think I knew he'd had a heart attack ... did you? Now ... get out of here." Nathaniel urged quietly.

With a tear or two beginning to well, the secretary gathered her things and made a quick exit toward the door.

Nathaniel, in turn, slowly strolled over to the window. After staring for a moment at the day's dark rolling clouds, he announced, with his back toward the board, "I'm stepping down. I've decided to liquidate assets ... to *Global Technologies.*"

The board members were understandably stunned, but they chose to listen in silent surprise.

With a casual gaze at his old friend, the VP of Operations, the CEO concluded, "George can handle the loose ends from here." Then with a nod at Willis, he added, "I'll initiate a *Power of Attorney.*"

Nathaniel then gave the family attorney, Clarence Conn, a

stern glare and said, "See to it that it gets done."

Subsequently, the gravity of the moment had made a problematic stir of things. There wasn't a single board member in the room who hadn't had the brew of consequential thought run around in his head.

With a hint of sarcasm to his voice, one of the panel members chimed in to ask, "Is this a Howard Hughes thing?"

Nathaniel replied, "No ... I'm afraid not." After a brief moment of absorbing thought, the executive added, "You wouldn't understand ... even if I gave clarification."

In a display of unity, every individual who comprised that advisory board began to grasp for reason by countering with the phrase of, "Try us!" One after another would egg a fellow member on by saying, "Yeah ... Try us!"

When Nathaniel didn't answer immediately, continuing to gaze out the window, an air of concern, mixed with frustration, began to settle upon those occupying the room.

One of the curious ones probed the CEO by asking him if he'd seen a psychiatrist about the matter.

The executive's sharp reply was one of a firm, "No!"

Not all were taken back by that brashly verbal lash, but some were. Then after a brief moment of silence, Nathaniel went on to add, "I've only informed one person of my impending intentions ... but ... I swore that individual to secrecy."

Nathaniel made his way back to his seat at the head of the table. He then casually leaned forward in his chair, with the pressing of interlocked fingers against his lips, to give every member a silent stare - the wheels of thought were spinning.

With a jeer, and an occasional brush of his pant leg, Nathaniel scoffed at their notion by reasoning, "I question Christians need a psychiatrist anyway."

With a bit of surprise etched in their voice, a couple men on the panel said, "What?"

The CEO hung his head slightly, as his constituents looked on, then confessed, "I've been living a lie for quite some time." As the curious board members listened with intrigue, Nathaniel went on to explain, "I've been ashamed of my faith. I haven't told anyone in this room ... few for that matter."

One of those who grew impatient blurted out, "Get to the point!"

The executive overlooked that verbal jab by adding, "I'm a Christian ... and I'm no longer ashamed to say so. Jesus Christ is my Savior ... that's something I'm now quite proud of."

Nathaniel's pretentious implication of self was met with an occasional sneer; the face of a contemptuous few displayed that reflective scorn.

An unsteady silence held the room for a moment, but that hush soon waned when Lawrence Penn spoke. Penn was an extremely wealthy eighty-year-old, a tycoon who'd made fortunes in shipping. He'd held a position on the Irwin Industries Board longer than anyone, but, more so, when the elderly statesman said something people usually took notice; for Penn was a highly respected individual in and about the Midwest.

"I was friends with your father for quite a few memorable years, Nathaniel." Penn announced with wavering words. "I've watched you grow into a fine young man." After clearing his throat, the stately gentleman added, "I don't condemn you, son ... as a matter of fact ... I applaud your belief."

All eyes were affixed on the elderly man by now, and acute ears were now attuned to his forthcoming insight. "My doctor tells me I've got cancer ... I've got six months at best."

A humbly reverent stir deepened with each ensuing word, for Penn tastefully joked, "I've been able to control any circumstance that presented itself ... until now." With a half-hearted smile, Lawrence insisted, "I took pride in my ability to buy a way out of any fix."

After an extended bit of hesitation, Penn confessed, "I've been giving death a lot of thought lately ... went to church … for the first time last week." The elderly gent then lowered his head to reflect with an enduring sullied shame.

Nathaniel seized the opportunity to console his friend by pushing himself away from the table. And then as he stood behind the elderly statesman, the executive carefully placed a hand upon the base of Penn's neck and adjacent shoulder as he uttered a simplistic, yet emotional phrase of, "I'm sorry, Lawrence." Nathaniel then added, "I'll be diligent in asking the Lord to give you peace."

Penn's response was, "God bless you, son ... you're a bigger man than I."

In light of that sad announcement, and respect for an old friend, Nathaniel decided it was best to adjourn the meeting shortly thereafter.

The young Irwin would later toil all night, that night, with the thought of just walking away from it all. That Friday night was a sleepless one for Nathaniel, because the executive grew weary as he fought through a gauntlet of emotions over the impending decision which lay heavy upon his heart.

Eventually, come dawn, Nathaniel decided upon leaving Chicago that weekend.

He was about to embark on a new venture, one that would change his life, and the world, forever. His rationale, the CEO thought, was apparently void of any reasonable explanation. Nevertheless, *The Call* was building in Nathaniel's bones and it was driven by a divine pull to sell it all, then move to a place where no forwarding address need apply.

The executive had a few loose ends to tie, and proceeded to do so first thing Saturday morning by paying Pastor Dan an unanticipated visit. With an absence of fanfare, Nathaniel signed the deed to his Pen House and building over to the church. He then instructed the good Reverend to sell it and use the proceeds as he saw fit. Surprisingly enough, the kind minister never questioned Nathaniel's motives; instead, he chose to wish the young man luck with a firm hug and a humble "Goodbye."

With a stop at the bank, Nathaniel withdrew a large amount of cash and then transferred the balance of his remaining assets to a Swiss account - one that had been established weeks prior.

The exec, in turn, made several purchases that day; all in preparation for a forthcoming trip. He paid one last visit to his favorite bookstore as well, to say farewell to a close friend. Nathaniel eventually left with a pair of books. One was titled, *Fortunes and Torments of the Christian Martyrs.* The other a biography on John Newton - the author of the classic hymn *Amazing Grace.*

Nathaniel also bought a rather expensive phone that afternoon.

It was an Inmarsat, the best in global mobile satellite communication. The phone was a bulky one, roughly the size of a small suitcase.

Nathaniel purchased a new computer too. It was a *NEC UltraLite*, the latest technology, for it was the first of its kind, a notebook style laptop. It weighed just under five pounds, a feather compared to other computers of the time. The machine featured a stylus with handwriting recognition and a modem that could talk to other computers. It had a full-sized screen and keyboard, but no disk drives or moving parts. However, an optional external floppy drive was available and Nathaniel purchased one. 1 or 2MB of data could be stored in memory, backed up by a battery.

The battery also served as a silicon disk, one that could hold a charge for a whopping two hours. With 64 K of Ram, the $5,500 UltraLite was "the classiest machine of its day."

Nathaniel's last destination was a car lot. "Will you be long, Sir?" His driver, and long-time companion, asked.

"I'm relieving you of your duties." Nathaniel said.

"Sir?" w a s his driver's puzzled reply.

"I don't expect you to understand ... just know this ... you've been a good friend."

The driver then asked, "What's wrong, Sir?"

As the exec reached for the door, his chauffeur made an effort to exit the vehicle to offer assistance. With a touch of the driver's shoulder, He said, "Never mind ... I've stepped down from the Company ... I'll see you around."

Once Nathaniel climbed out of the limo, he stood beside it for a moment. Because the chauffeur didn't drive off immediately, Nathaniel motioned toward him with a sweep of his hand then yelled, "Go!"

The bewildered driver obeyed his employer's command, but did so reluctantly slow.

Nathaniel's final purchase was a big one, a brand new 4-wheel drive *Range Rover* sport utility vehicle. The SUV's sticker price was forty-three thousand dollars, yet the salesman glorified a deal by implying a bargain of some three thousand off. A spendthrift Irwin agreed, paying cash for the British machine.

Nathaniel's determined focus had been affixed on solitude for quite some time, his resourceful preparation for seclusion was now engaged, so he was of no mind to tarry or make waste of the afternoon.

A tugging on Nathaniel's heart was reality, one that had fought every fiber of logic. It was God who **initiated** his *Call,* and a mapping of destiny which lay ahead. The Creator knew who Nathaniel Irwin would be **before he** was even conceived, and the potential greatness of his mind and soul. A divine hand was being swept over this man's life - it was a foreshadow of things to come - something of earth-shaking magnitude.

Nathaniel's motivation for privacy was geared primarily toward self-gratification, or so he thought. Nathaniel hadn't been privileged to the *Revelation* just yet, however, it wouldn't elude him for long though. Although Nathaniel was being guided by spiritual forces, ones that evaded his recognition, it would take the passage of time to shed light on that realization.

Shortly after climbing into those new wheels, Nathaniel made his way to the Penthouse to retrieve a few belongings he reasoned he'd need. Nathaniel eventually left the city with over a hundred thousand in cash - all under the cover of evening - his contentious conviction was to never look back.

The Executive's flee didn't evade notice for long though. A blanket of red flags spouted a signaling flare of panic a few hours later. Speculation began to whirl throughout a news-starved media. The airwaves soon filled with rumors and an assortment of stories comprised primarily of half-baked truth. There was an added ornament of noteworthy journalism though; that was an accompaniment.

Nathaniel's derived voyeuristic route of escape was a composition of foreboding thought comprising solidarity highway - its label bore the tale-tell markings of l-80.

The exec was compellingly determined to distance himself from that which he left behind. Only stopping out of necessity, for occasional nutriment or a much-needed restroom break, Nathaniel racked up quite a few miles prior to the proceeding nightfall. He'd been on the road a little over twelve hours, roughly ten of which was behind the wheel, before deciding upon a night's rest in a two-star motel somewhere near Hastings in Nebraska. The seven-hundred-mile trek wasn't void of mind-plaguing second-guessing either. Reasoning gave birth to an occasional stir in Nathaniel's analytical conscious indeed.

Nathaniel made little haste of check-in; his determination was steadfast in that regard.

He paid cash for a night's stay, a real bargain, or so he thought, at $49.50.

The clerk's grumpy instructions were, "No smoking in the rooms." With an imposing glare, she added, "Check-out's tomorrow ... by noon!" Nathaniel was much too tired to complain about the young lady's less-than-professional attitude.

He, instead, grabbed the room key from off the counter and glanced away with disdain, in light of her rotten mood, before proceeding to the room.

The Stuffed Bun, a burger joint adjacent to the motel, looked all too inviting to the weary traveler as he unloaded his belongings from the Range Rover. The smoky smell of roasted beef, emanating from the diner's exhaust hoods mounted on the restaurant wall, was too much of a tempting lure on Nathaniel's tired senses. After a chuck of his luggage on the bed, the tired and hungry one ventured across the street to satisfy an urge.

He placed an order to go, one representative of his vigorous craving. Three deluxe cheeseburgers, a double order of fries, and a large vanilla shake, rang up to a shade under eight dollars.

Nathaniel enjoyed the meal in the quiet solitude of his room, shortly before taking a relaxing shower in preparation for a restful evening. After he'd emerged from the bathroom, the exec changed into his silky PJ's and proceeded to curl up in the bed sheets. The impulse to watch a glimpse of the nightly news, a habit he'd developed over the years, soon won out over sleep and Nathaniel sat up in bed to click on the remote. He was surprised to see the motel had cable. It had been something the front desk failed to mention.

A surfing of the channels soon revealed a WGN broadcast, it was none other than Chicago's Channel 9. Much of what the anchors had to say bore no interest to the executive, but that soon changed when the words, "Alert - Billionaire missing!" began to scroll along the bottom of the screen. Nathaniel had missed an earlier clip on his disappearance. However, he was intelligent enough to surmise, with conjecture, the panic of those he'd left behind. With a faint thought before dozing off, Nathaniel concluded, "That didn't take long!"

The Irwin's attorney, a worried Clarence Conn, would pursue, with desperate effort, all avenues he could think of to contact the runaway exec in the coming days. His investigative toils, many occurring in the proceeding weeks, all met with failed results.

The Global Technologies Board and its CEO would, in turn, take an aggressively offensive position on closing the deal, and did so when they were made aware of Nathaniel's disappearance. They would go on the prowl, positioning themselves much like that of a congregating gaggle of buzzards.

With pressure building upon Conn and his firm, he would have little choice but to show his cards - a hand forced. Yet, nevertheless, the wily attorney would have a few tricks of his own up his sleeve. He would move forward with the transaction, but with a few added conditions. Foremost was a waiver, consisting of a *Buy-back* clause. The duration of the waiver would be eighteen months, including accrued interest of course, and it would be attached to the terms of sale for the company's assets.

Conn would add the clause without Nathaniel's permission or consent, but would do so for the following reason: If the billionaire did reappear, with a change of heart, a window of opportunity would be affixed.

The Global Technologies Board wouldn't be warm to the revised contract at first, but their persuading CEO would eventually prevail with that itchy pen of greedy execution.

Surprisingly enough, Nathaniel had a good night's sleep for

once. He was up and dressed, had breakfast, checked out, and back on the road by eight the following morn. The exec had always been an early riser; it was an instinctive tendency, one not easily broken.

It was early fall '89, and for once in his life Nathaniel had nothing but time. There were no longer any appointments to keep or schedules to maintain. It was a freedom most of us can only dream of. He was a man with much to contemplate as the mile markers clicked by. For a change, Nathaniel had no titles or worries - it felt odd, yet liberating. Nathaniel began to feel like a part of himself was beginning to turn, or die off in a way, much like the passing landscape he observed.

Oddly enough, Nathaniel never once gave consideration to turning on the Range Rover's stereo during the whole trip; even though it was an AM / FM. The power door locks, power windows and power brakes, were state of the art at the time, but Nathaniel paid little attention to them. The air conditioning and cruise control were added features as well, yet they were never used. The SUV had a 3.9 Liter, 178 horsepower, 8-cylinder engine with 4 speed automatic transmission, but that didn't matter much to Nathaniel either. It was painted a navy metal flake blue, had black leather bucket seats, a power sunroof, rear windshield wiper, defroster, fog lights, and power steering, but none of that really mattered to Nathaniel. In his mind's eye, the Rover had lost its value, it was no longer a "fine" ride. It was just another four-door as far as he was concerned - for Nathaniel's mind was now adrift, no longer moored to the dock of material gain.

The road seemed like a long one because it took Nathaniel a

little more than three days to reach that stake in Wyoming.

He spent the first couple of days there in visual assessment of the land, all 90,000 acres. At the heart of the spread was a somewhat run-down cabin. Nathaniel figured it would do just fine.

Bordering the cabin, a short distance to the north, was a crystal-clear lake. The body of water measured roughly 30 acres in size. Nathaniel thought its clarity came from the water shed of the nearby mountain. A small handful of area outdoorsmen knew of its location - they called it *Lost Lake.*

The closest town was *Buffalo Ridge,* located some 70 miles to the southeast, and it boasted of a population of 213.

On the third day, Nathaniel made a list of supplies he thought he might need then he made his way to town.

Buffalo Ridge was a sleepy town, so to speak. Everyone knew each other by name and most things a stir in the rumor mill.

The burg was comprised of a few rustic homes, all appearing to have been built around the turn of the century, and a combination of four small businesses. There was a small cafe, *The Last Brew,* that opened its doors from 8 till noon daily. The town also had a small bank, *The Third National;* it too had limited hours. Then there was a 1950's era filling station, *Jim's.* It too lacked a steady flow of customers, seeing little gas pumped anymore. But Nathaniel wasn't interested in getting to know the town folk, or the like. He was solely focused upon that list and the General Store that might have those items on hand.

Nathaniel garnished a slight grin and uttered a muffled chuckle when he caught a glimpse of the establishment's name

crudely painted upon the front window pane. It was fittingly
named, *Calamity Jane's,* for its name bore resemblance to the
Western décor inside.

Mounted above the interior of the front door was an old-
fashioned bell. It rang out when Nathaniel entered, signaling a
customer's presence.

A middle-aged female employee emerged from the back room
within moments, as Nathaniel began to look around.

Her cheerful greeting was that of, "Howdy!"

Nathaniel's response was one of a gentle nod.

"Not from around here ... are ya?" She asked.

With a meekly sheepish grin, Nathaniel stared at a stack of
shovels and hoes and said, "No."

The inquisitive clerk soon realized her customer wasn't
interested, nor quite in the mood, for small talk. With that in mind,
she went about the task of stocking a bit of merchandise which had
just come in.

Nathaniel, at first, thought he'd get a three, or four, week supply
of essentials. After contemplating on the notion for a while, he
decided it was best to stock up for several months. In the back of
his mind, Nathaniel began to reason, "Why not a year?"

With a jot of determination to his step, Nathaniel began to
systematically scan every shelf and every isle of the store for the
supplies he concluded he'd need. With each armload, Nathaniel
would cross that item, or items, off the list while laying them
upon the cashier's check-out counter.

Nathaniel's purchases consisted of some rope, a shovel, and a
couple other tools. He bought all the bottled water they had and
cleared the shelves of all their vacuum-packed dry goods,

including some K-rations he saw. Nathaniel emptied the food isle
of almost all the canned goods as well, his favorite being com and
green beans, yet he thought he'd try some of those pork-n-beans
for the first time.

Nathaniel had his eye upon a new fishing pole upon the wall
too. He took it down, gave it a quick glance-over, then laid it
upon the counter with the other items. Nathaniel had never been
fishing in his life, however, he figured, "Now's a good time to
learn."

The clerk couldn't help but notice the large pile of
merchandise. She told Nathaniel she's ring it up, then bag it for
him while he shopped.

He thought that was a curious deed.

Matches, candles, toilet paper, and other miscellaneous
articles were amidst Nathaniel's hefty purchase. The gathering
of those forethought necessities took a little over an hour. As
the clerk was ringing up the remaining items she commented,
"This is goin' be a big tab!"

Nathaniel's reply was a shadowy, "I know."

When all was said and done, the clerk said, "The bill totals
over two thousand!"

Nathaniel said, "That's fine," much to the clerk's surprise.

As the stranger dug for his wallet, the clerk stuck out her
hand, in grateful gesture, to add, "My name's Johnnie."

With a curious look upon his face, Nathaniel looked up to ask.
"Did you say Johnny?"

"Yeah."

"Do you spell that J-o-h-n-n-y?" Nathaniel wondered.

"It's spelled with an i - e." She countered.

Nathaniel uttered the word, "Interesting," as he shook the clerk's hand and visually scanned her appearance. As he counted out the cash, through unconscious impulse, he sized her up to be a "Rube." A Rube being an unsophisticated person.

His mental instinct was to label her a "Hick," for her bearing was quite lacking and her smile was in drastic need of a good dentist.

The judgmental one began to have second thoughts when he observed a cross hanging from her neck.

Nathaniel then posed the question, "May I ask where you worship?"

"I'm a member of the First Baptist in Ripley ... it's a real nice church ... forty minutes from here." The clerk replied.

With a nod, Nathaniel said, "Hummm," then began to load those things he'd purchased in the SUV after payment was made.

There were quite a few bags to load, and because she wasn't that busy, the clerk volunteered to help Nathaniel with the task - that which he appreciated.

As Johnnie handed Nathaniel the last bag, she offered her hand to say, "Thank ya!"

Nathaniel quickly shook her extended palm, then said, "You're welcome."

The clerk went back into the store while Nathaniel tried to close the Rover's back hatch. The vehicle's door wouldn't close because a couple bags were in the way. When Nathaniel pushed on one of the bags it broke open, spilling the contents. He discovered he had three towels, not two like he'd originally planned to purchase. Nathaniel realized the clerk had made a mistake after he examined the receipt - she'd only charged for two.

Nathaniel then went back into the store to point out the error. Johnnie was embarrassed, but more so, she was surprised by the stranger's honesty.

"How much do I owe you for the towel?" He asked.

She thanked Nathaniel for pointing out the mistake, then added, "Folks now days don't rightly do such things!"

That analytical mind of Nathaniel's began to spin, for he couldn't understand the full meaning and seemed a little puzzled by the statement.

After she'd given it a brief thought, Johnnie said, "I'll pay for that there towel," as she reached for her purse. "It was my mistake," she concluded, "Not yours." "I'll make it right." She added.

As Johnnie inserted the four dollars into the drawer, Nathaniel became intrigued.

He surmised the candor of her heart to far exceed his. With that in mind, Nathaniel went to the back of the store. He then removed a few bills from his pocket and placed them in a blank envelope he had. He sealed it, then walked back toward the front of the store. Nathaniel slid the envelope across the counter, then said, "Here ... drop that in the offering plate Sunday."

Without giving it much thought, Johnnie folded the envelope and shoved it in her pocket. She said, "Thank ya." Then added, "I best be gettin' busy."

Like most women, Johnnie had also formed an opinion of this guy. She thought Nathaniel to be one of those "Big City Dudes." The clerk pondered a bit on that as she watched the kind stranger depart, then two more customers entered the store. She was busy with them for a while, then things thinned out once more.

It would be roughly two hours later before Johnnie gave thought to reaching down into her pocket for a bit of change. It was only then she discovered the envelope; the one she had forgotten all about. She opened it, examined the contents, then fell to the floor - She'd fainted. Her loss of consciousness was solely attributed to surprise, for ten one-thousand-dollar bills were stuffed inside.

It was a first for Nathaniel for he had unknowingly done something he'd never given consideration to before, that being following the divinely guided principles of *Tithing*.

Chapter Fourteen
Illumination of the Insightful

An **ardent** enthusiasm grew with each passing mile, Nathaniel was anxious to get back to the cabin. Yet, harmoniously, an indignant grin began to radiate from the reflection in the rear view mirror every time Nathaniel took notice of his image. He was pretentious with flashy distinction, silently boastful of that seemingly generous deed he'd done in town. It was a refined habit he had called *Pride,* a vile consuming characteristic indeed, one he'd long held dear. For now, Nathaniel was blind to its plaguing affliction, however, in time, it would become purged - thanks to the redemptive powers of the Divine.

The winding way began with that paved two-lane departing Buffalo Ridge. County Road 9 stretched some fifteen miles before asphalt turned to stone. The trip back consisted of another twenty-five miles from there. It was a route full of twists and turns, one anchored by a handful of gravel roads, but a majority were nothing more than dirt thoroughfares.

Masked by a long grove of pines, at the outskirts of Nathaniel's property, was the grassy lane which **led** to Lost Lake and Nathaniel's future home. If one wasn't aware of the way, you'd drive right past - it was camouflaged that well. The trees and undergrowth at the beginning of the lane hadn't been maintained for a good number of years. The lane itself was in poor shape as well, neglect had taken an obviously visible toll. However, its lay appeared to have been done with an effort to evade detection, done so with a hint of stealth in mind.

The lane itself covered many miles, maneuvering in and out
of several tree lines, up and down many hills, over a large peak,
around a few ridges, across three valleys, and through a couple
dry creek beds, before it reached Lost Lake.

At first Nathaniel thought it was a little odd the Atlas would
say, in bold red print, "Inquire locally for current conditions before
driving on unimproved roads shown on this map."

The term "unimproved" was foreign to Nathaniel, for Illinois
had no such roads. As far as he was concerned, all the roads in his
state were well developed and either graveled or paved. Once in
Wyoming though, Nathaniel came to realize the need for the
disclaimer and a good four-wheel drive.

The lane was a long rough one, nothing more than a grassy
path in most spots, for it took a hint of skill and some patience to
negotiate.

As Nathaniel crested the hill, to conquer that incline in exit of
the first valley, he saw someone walking along the road in the
distance.

When he approached the stranger from behind, Nathaniel's
mind began to fill with numerous thoughts. "Why would
anyone be out here?" He questioned in wonder. With his
dandruff now a stir, he then reasoned, "This is private property!"
But as he got closer, Nathaniel began to ponder, "Should I tell
them to leave, or offer them a lift?"

At about a hundred yards or so out, Nathaniel reasoned the
drifter to be a man. But, at the same time, he became truly
bewildered with the thought of, "That guy's acting really odd!"

The drifter's behavior was strange for he moved off to the
side when hearing the vehicle draw near; yet he never once

turned to look back.

Whoever it was, they looked like a bum. Age was a hard thing to determine for he wore old clothes, and, of all things, had a trash bag draped over each shoulder.

When Nathaniel drove alongside the stranger, he took a quick glance out the passenger window, then, with caution, drove on past. He didn't get far though, only a few yards, before that clever mind of his began to deliberate.

Nathaniel's fleeting impression of the drifter, an assumption he'd made of who he was, led him to assess he was a man. A quick glimpse of the stranger's torso slammed the door on speculation.

As it is with any genius, logic almost always prevails in the overall scope of things. Yet, this time, curiosity won out as the predominantly conductive guide.

A compulsory urge to brake began to flood Nathaniel's soul. The thought, "Stop!" danced around in his head several times with intensifying persuasion. Although Nathaniel wasn't quite aware of God's various modes of communication just yet, needless-to-say, he didn't resist the prod.

Nathaniel eased on the brakes ever-so-slightly and eventually rolled to a stop, but did so with a twitch of reservation before applying pressure to the pedal. He thought it was best to wait on the stranger, a leading of a few yards, then Nathaniel reached upward to give the rear view mirror a slight adjustment.

As he watched the image of the stranger close in, an added measure of apprehension began to boil.

The day was a bright sunny one, a clear sky absent a

single cloud, but Nathaniel couldn't see the drifter's face. It was broad daylight, the sun bearing down, but the stranger's face was shaded. Although he was looking right at Nathaniel, his facial features were masked in shades of gray. Nathaniel thought that was a little odd, to the point of being weird, but, at the same time, a dagger of worry had been thrust, with a lean in the direction of uneasiness.

The peculiar feel of it all gained momentum when the radio came on all by itself. A blare of, "Feed my children," was all the fearful Irwin heard before he shut it off to peer over his shoulder through the back window.

The stranger was still coming. Nathaniel was getting scared by now, for he didn't know what the drifter was going to do. With that in mind, Nathaniel reached for his wallet. He then removed a few bills, with the thought of throwing them, and rolled down the passenger side window. Nathaniel leaned over to heave the cash out the window, then he yelled, "Take the money ... then leave!"

Nathaniel leaned back over in his seat to gain an upright position, then he threw the vehicle in "Drive." But before he could speed off, the stranger had surprisingly stuck his head inside the passenger window.

Nathaniel would later wonder, for many days, how that drifter could have made up so much ground in such a short span of time.

Within an instant, the moment Nathaniel turned to look at the stranger, the Rover's cab was engulfed in brilliant light. The beam was so intense it blinded Nathaniel for a second. Needless-to-say, it freaked him out bad enough he mashed the accelerator to the floor.

After he'd retrieved his bearings, and gained a little distance between himself and the macabre, Nathaniel glanced up to look in the rearview mirror. He was shocked by what he saw, so-much-so he slammed on the brakes and got out of the vehicle to look around for the mysterious drifter was gone - he'd vanished into thin air.

Nathaniel wandered the vicinity for a while. He was no doubt shaken. The man was a bundle of nerves by then. Perplexed by the episode, driven to the edge of bewilderment, Nathaniel's wits invoked a leap to the depths of the unhinged. He'd never experienced anything like that before, that which bore the definition of bizarre. A cool sweat of fear had gripped him. His mind was an entangled mess, rattled by a scare of confusion.

He sat on the hood of the Rover for a time, with head in hands. Once he'd gotten a grip, Nathaniel elected to continue on and climbed back into the vehicle. With the slide of a jittery hand, Nathaniel slowly retrieved the key from his pants pocket. He started the vehicle, then pressed his face to the steering wheel for some time. It was a concerted effort to slow down that reeling mind of his, a ploy to regain some bearing of rational.

After a bit, Nathaniel leaned back in his seat, took a long deep breath, then adjusted the rearview mirror. Before engaging the brake to shift the thing into drive, Nathaniel took a quick glance at the dash. The hair on his neck then stood erect. He recalled exiting the SUV at 10:00 AM. The clock now flashed a new set of numbers though, numerals a glow with an aura of disturbing sensation, *for the time was now ... 9:31.*

Over the course of ensuing weeks, Nathaniel would give embrace to the solitude of that cabin, his soul bent, forever changed by the encounter.

He would, in turn, devote a great deal of time to the study of nature. It was Nathaniel's way of exercising aspiration toward a closeness with the Creator. The seasons being amidst change, he soaked in the beauty of it all.

Nathaniel even tried his hand at photography on occasion. But, he found it more enjoyable to dabble a paint brush across a canvas of expression though.

Fascinated with the thirst-quenching gift of a morning dew, the breathtaking view of that rainbow of change amongst the leaves on the trees, and a host of other things man could never forge, Nathaniel was becoming an apprentice, fathomed or not, to a divine insightfulness only few gain - an experience often neglected.

A quest for enlightenment, a probe into the invisible forces behind that of a guided wind, grasped Nathaniel's intrigue one day while reading in the shade of a nearby Elm. The rustle of limbs among a stretch of neighboring pines, the swaying ripple, a roar, across a sea of tossed grass, bore witness to God's presence indeed. Although the senses bear their inherit limitations, restrictively human by design, Nathaniel was beginning to conceive a soul purged focus of who *The Great I Am* truly is. He would, in time, relate it to an intensifying fervor for wisdom, an unexplained pull, a longing for the comprehension of a pure truth, to the fullness there of, like never before.

A written entry, etched upon the inaugural pages of

Nathaniel's journal that night, read:

"I gained a foothold amidst some depravity today. It was a shed of light upon that chasm of gray.

While on bent knees this afternoon, a washing of my tears occurred. I believe there's passion in the rain. I could hear a reoccurring theme of, 'I'll never leave nor forsake.'

It's poetic, for there was a voice in it all. I wrote on a piece of bark, 'There's a rustling all about me. The wind has swept over me. A sensation of His presence brought me to my knees. I can honestly say, for the first time, I felt a gentle breeze ... that invisible hand upon my cheek.'

I discovered the treasure of Amos 4:13 tonight as well:

'He who forms the mountains, creates the wind, and reveals His thoughts to man, He who turns dawn to darkness, and treads the high places of the earth - the Lord God Almighty is his name.'

I recall a poem I once read. Its title was, 'Think on This.' I believe it went something like this:

'A day of worry seems like an eternity. A day of happiness goes so quickly. Like the morning sun, it seems to vanish before we've enjoyed it enough. But, with night, we have the memories.

What a difference one short day can make, when we think how five minutes can change the whole course of life.

We need the faith to think the day will bring the very best.

On our insisting, do we really give our attention to new beginning?

I choose to lean my arms upon the window sill of heaven, and gaze upon my Lord. With that vision in my heart, I turn strong to meet the day.'

(I must admit, Lord, you're like the friend I never had.)

I've been having a reoccurring dream of which I must note. In the vision I'm surrounded by a wildfire. Oddly enough, I show no facial features that would represent alarm. With no other options at my disposal, I dive into the lake. The water's quite comfortable. Strange, in a sense, because Lost Lake, from my experience in the short time I've been here, has always had frigid water temperatures in spite of the warm degree of the air. When I surface, I can see a raging fire consuming everything in its path and the blaze is headed straight for the cabin.

As I'm dog paddling to stay afloat in the water, I detect a sudden shift in the wind. The fire then appears to be guided toward the lake. One would think all that heat and smoke would suffocate me, but I endure the entire ordeal with no visible signs of harm.

In the secondary part of the dream, I awake from my bed to discover the structure has been spared. As I'm dressing, I find it striking that there's no trace of smoke in the air.

After stepping outside I discover a burnt plain indeed, but there's beautiful wildflowers popping up everywhere amongst the ash. Everything's beginning anew in the morning sun.

As I ponder its implied meaning, of which I'm convinced it surely boasts, several things speak to me:

I'm surrounded by an all-consuming fire. I dare conclude it's related to the glory of God.

I'm not alarmed in the least by what's ahead of me. Are

these things to come?

Freely, I dive in. I've never really liked the water, much less the deep part. The act points to an impartation toward the flee of fear.

The water was comfortable; compatible to a cleansing degree.

There eventually came a shift in the air. I can't help but think the winds of change will surely come, that which I await.

No harm befell me. It was protection by One higher than I.

I awoke safe and sound, then I ventured through that opened door.

Flowers and beauty arose from the ashes. A revelation of Isaiah 61:3 - I take."

With a gentle close of the Journal, Nathaniel ran a feathered caress of fingertips over the cover's leathery bound engrain. Then he opened it, once more, to dissect what he'd written.

He soon uttered, with a measure of begrudged scrutiny, "I'm rambling," when an ensuing close of the chronicle came. After he'd closed it, Nathaniel pushed the book away. He then leaned back in that cane chair he was sitting in. His intent was to relax some as he placed a dual set of cupped hands with enter-locked fingers behind his head. With a slight close of the eyes, the curtain was lifted ushering in a brief daydream of Nathaniel's past.

Still etched upon the ole gray matter was Miss Marts, Nathaniel's English Lit prof from Chicago U, and her perceptive thoughts. Her editorial plea, the first week, had stuck. Those nuggets of wisdom she'd lent hadn't faded from that insightful mind just yet.

Nathaniel recalled, like it was yesterday, "Lean back, loosen that tie a bit, Mr. Irwin!

Structure's nice, but it's what flows from the heart, not the mind, that'll change the world. *Life's not a file cabinet, my friend.* Be spontaneous, that'll reach a soul."

Nathaniel's journal entry had been a bit of adducent brainstorming, one in need of a good buffing or a dab of polish. Miss Marts would have been proud though. Strangely enough, she only taught a semester.

His thoughts, a reflection, a spill upon the page, marred with a stain or two of imperfection, were all too human - perfect.

The cabin was dark that night, yet calmingly quiet. The thought of "bedtime" crossed Nathaniel's mind. But, as he leaned forward to blow out the candles, his mind began to reel, then he hesitated.

As he sat, soaking in the dim light, Nathaniel became studious. The actions of the few candles he'd lit began to intrigue him.

One candle, a big one, burnt quite fast. In fact, the wax melted so quickly Nathaniel had to place a pan under the candle's base in order to catch that which fell.

Some of the smaller candles bore flames that flickered, others didn't. Yet, there was no breeze to be felt.

A couple of those candles were tall, burning fairly fast as well, only to lean upon their foundation and then fall.

A sustained mindset, refreshed and born anew, would soon follow. Nathaniel's reasoning would give compare to the choices made in life. It was a lesson learned from something as simple as a candle.

Some of us, he gathered, *are fat and well off, but we burn out quickly - leaving nothing useful.*

Others are tall and important, yet they lean, possibly fall, when the signs of trouble arrive.

Some, seeming small in statute, have a flame that will endure - leaving little or no waste afterward.

Nathaniel would, in turn, equate his past to that of the tall and fat. Yet, now, his vision of himself lay in a cast of the short.

As he watched the flames dance, and the shadows upon the wall, a hint of fear struck a cord in Nathaniel's soul. The garnished thought of, *Satan's always in the shadows, trying to snuff out the light,* filled Nathaniel's mind.

A flame is usually yellow at the top and blue at the center, the hottest portion. In comparison, Nathaniel's logic did reason, *Love is at the center of it all, that foothold of light called Christ.*

Nathaniel thought a little reading after that, before turning in, would help him to doze off. When he opened his Bible, he came across the wonder of Matthew 5:14-16:

"You are the light of the world." The scripture said. *"A city that is set upon a hill cannot be hid."* It added. *"Neither do men light a candle, and put it under a bushel, but on a candlestick; and it gives light onto all that are in the house."* The words that remained, which Jesus shared, seemed to jump off the page and lodge their way into Nathaniel's rummaged heart, with emphasis. *"Let your light so shine before men, that they may see your good works, and glorify your Father which is in heaven."*

While on bent knees, finishing a prayer before bed that night, Nathaniel began to take notice of those clasped hands before his nose. As he slowly opened both palms, his curiosity heightened. Nathaniel then began a close examination of his fingertips, fascinated with the fact that no two sets of prints are alike.

As he pondered the creativity of it all, Nathaniel recalled someone once said, "Thoughts disentangle themselves when they pass through the fingertips."

An all-consuming thought of, *"I knew you before you were born,"* then began to flood Nathaniel's mind. He stood at the gate of understanding God's ways, yet Nathaniel's destination was far from complete. That divine communication had quickly saturated his soul and was in reference to Jeremiah 1:5, something Nathaniel would later discover.

The proceeding feeling of, *"You're mine,"* occupied his thoughts for some time before he fell asleep - Nathaniel broke down and wept with that.

The following morning was a rainy one and Nathaniel chose to read a while. He began by reading excerpts from that John Newton biography he purchased back in Chicago. Nathaniel would come to view Newton as a common man who later gained great insight, a pillar of glorious wisdom.

Newton was widely known and recognized for the classic hymn *Amazing Grace* of which he penned. Behind its simple lyrics and expressive melody, stood the dramatic real-life story of a man miraculously changed by God's mercy. He was saved from a life of depravity and slave trading. Newton never forgot the depths from which he was pulled, by God's incomprehensible grace.

"How sweet the sound that saved a wretch like me. I once was lost, but now am found; was blind, but now I see." It was that particular lyrical line that brought a welling of tears to Nathaniel's eyes.

Newton was born in London, 1725. At the age of eleven he went to sea with his father, a shipmaster on the Mediterranean. Disregarding his mother's prayer that he enter the ministry, he engaged in the lucrative yet brutal African slave trade for a number of years. After his conversion he served in the Church of England as a pastor and later at St. Mary's in London.

Newton was a prolific songwriter and in addition to the words of *Amazing Grace,* he penned other hymns such as *Glorious Things of Thee Are Spoken* and *How Sweet The Name Of Jesus Sounds.* He lived to be 82.

As Nathaniel examined this great man's life, with the turn of each page, a couple of those lesser-known thoughts of Newton's seemed to jump out.

"A man always in society is one always on the spend. On the other hand, a mere solitary is, at his best, but a candle in an empty room."

Nathaniel pondered on that probing quote for quite a while.

Newton was also quoted as to say, "Professors who own the doctrines of free grace often act inconsistently with their own principles when they are angry at the defects of others. A company of travelers fall into a pit, and one of them gets a passenger to draw him out. Now he should not be angry with the rest for falling in nor because they are not yet out as he is. He did not pull himself out. Therefore, instead of reproaching them, he should show them pity. He should avoid, at any rate, going down upon their ground again and show how much better and happier he is upon his own. We should take care that we do not make our profession of religion a receipt in full of all other obligations. A man truly *illuminated* will no more despise others than Bartimaeus, after his own eyes were opened would take a stick and beat every blind man he met."

Nathaniel chose to reflect on that statement for quite some time as well.

He was experiencing a daily instance of apprehension into the nature of things, an intuitive understanding, a penetrating vision of discernment through the perception of motives behind the behavior associated with thought, a honing of the definition of *insight.*

With the passing of each day, God began doing rather unusual things to reach Nathaniel. One of which was speaking to him while he slept. Nathaniel wouldn't be dreaming at the time, but he could hear the Creator's voice quite clearly and remember every word when he awoke. The cleverness of that method, its ingenious approach, puzzled Nathaniel for a time, but then he realized God is spirit and He was simply trying to communicate with that spirit instilled within him.

The promise of, "*The path I taketh thee is trusted to few,*" was given to Nathaniel one such night and he held it close, never doubting that implication of a glorious future.

Nathaniel would question, however, the existence of so many ministries and why the need always outweighs the supply.

In a dream, not too long after that, Nathaniel was given a revelation. Each of us has a plate, he saw, an agenda, one which we fill. Most of us take on *self-imposed* things that weigh us down, till the plate is overflowing so to speak. Then when a need arises, the pile is too great and it falls to the floor to be discarded, so burdened down by it all we can't help anyone if we wanted to. Nathaniel's quest for wealth was a prime example.

Nathaniel also pondered the nature of those whose only desire is to help themselves.

Jesus, on the other hand, was a shining example of someone who wasn't burdened by agenda, or absorbed in self.

In the coming weeks, with the aid of his satellite phone and laptop, Nathaniel carried out a devised experiment, one of which he gave great thought to. Through a series of emails, Nathaniel began to write all the "Big name" ministries throughout the United States. His request of them was a simple one, food. He invented the name *Hear the Call Ministries* and posed as a minister to gain their favor. Much to his surprise, it gained a reply of rejection every time.

Answers like, "We don't know you," or, "We're stretched so thin we turn everyone away," were frequent. A troublesome reply of, "What comes here stays here," really bothered Nathaniel. And a throw-away statement of, "We can't help you, but here's the addresses of others that may," left Nathaniel wondering. (Several weren't even curious enough to reply at all)

Nathaniel hashed the dilemma over in his mind for days before giving a final reply to those returned emails. He accessed, "I will probably never meet any of those poor people, the ones I choose to help and love, but that won't stop me from doing so!"

As a last-ditch plea for assistance, Nathaniel sent the

following email to all concerned: "With in mind that people are dying overseas, begging for food, I ask of you something as simple as a dollar a week - it will make a dent in the need." Oddly enough, the request never drew a single reply.

In light of such apathy, Nathaniel made it a point to be further absorbed with scripture after that. A discipline of at least half a dozen chapters read per setting was his venture.

He reasoned those writings of his should take more precedence as well, and Nathaniel leaned toward that goal with each passing day.

So moved by Jesus's words in Matthew 6:19 - 26, later to be a favorite passage, Nathaniel inscribed the words, "*God takes care of his own*," on one of the interior walls of the cabin.

Chapter Fifteen
Withered

Autumn was in surrender of its splendor, and '89 would soon fade with the impartation of a new decade.

The evenings now grew cool with the departure of the sun, the observance of your breath was becoming a routine event, and the trees had since shed their withered leaves. "A stroll was akin to walking on a crunchy carpet," or so Nathaniel thought. It was a delightful experience indeed; one he would have never experienced amidst that concrete habitat of Chicago.

Nathaniel was spending the better part of his days in preparation for the coming winter. He concluded the anticipated wintry season would be long and rough, but he was confident that fortitude of his would prevail.

Solitude had become a comforting rhythm to Nathaniel. He classified it as a welcome embrace, his reassuring peace, a cordial friend.

Nathaniel had built a small fire that evening to slice the chill. The dance of the blaze drew reflection, recollection of the day, and another John Newton recitation.   Newton once admirably said, "Satan will seldom come to a Christian with a gross temptation. A green log and a candle may be safely left together, but bring a few shavings, then some small sticks, and then larger, and you may soon bring the green log to ashes."

Nathaniel had, for the better part of three months, worked hard to build a sizable reserve of firewood. He knew he'd need those cords, every rick, to sustain himself through a harsh winter.

Nathaniel's hands had been smooth and soft, somewhat allergic to manual labor in the past, but the roughness of necessity would bear change. He had become accustomed, all too-familiar, with a routine of *early to bed and early to rise* by now. Of late, Nathaniel's grip bore a closer resemblance to sandpaper and the remanent of a cut, or the black and blue of a bruise, inhabited both palms and just about every finger or knuckle. Nathaniel had often surmised he was physically fit, but the time spent in the Wyoming wilderness would most surely test that theory.

The chainsaw Nathaniel purchased back in Buffalo Ridge made the task of cutting wood somewhat easier. The saw was a 16" Stihl, a good one, but he thought, at times, while slicing thick pieces, the bar should have been a bit longer. Hauling the wood from over a mile away wasn't simple either, but splitting it, with the ax he brought along with the saw, was the most physical chore of all.

The wood pile had become a massive one indeed, stacked in rows down both sides of the cabin, some in back, and a ready portion spread along the wall of the front porch.

Nathaniel used an area, under the shade of a large oak, in the front yard, to split all that which was too big to bum. He spent many an hour there and lost an untold amount of sweat in the process.

One of Nathaniel's favorite pleasures was the enjoyment of sitting on the porch after a hard day's work - his rocker was always a comfortable companion.

The cabin had a beautiful view of the lake. That gentle mist adrift above the tranquil waters stirred an instilling peace. A hand full of ancient forests stood majestically tall, hovering with sentinel prowess over the surrounding plain. A ripple of calming wave atop the fields gave foundation to it all. A magnificent background brimming with mountain bore a stroke of serenity upon the canvas of imagination, those snow-capped peaks in ascent upon the heavens.

A sunrise and sunset often resembled a matching pair of bookends, with a beautiful orange cast, accompanied by a gentle spread of purple clouds, each were a thing to behold.

Nathaniel would often attest, "Only God could orchestrate such wonder."

The cabin, built, in Nathaniel's estimation, sometime around the turn of the century, had a modestly impoverished feel to it. Yet, Nathaniel grew even more fond of its paltry existence with the passage of each wonderful day.

The heavy timbers used to construct the walls bore a sense of unflinching ruggedness though. Great care had been taken to carve out those miters, those resembling a double wedge, the fit was a good one, for it was interlocking and joined the comers together.

The evidence of some skilled and honed craftsmanship, many a day swinging an ax with a proceeding dressing, the proficient use of a wood plane, were all-to-apparent.

The furrows separating each member were filled with a substance to keep the elements out; it was one Nathaniel wasn't familiar with. The material was tan in color, quite hard, yet it didn't appear to be mud. Mud's something that could be chipped away, or so Nathaniel thought. It wasn't mortar either, but it had a funny granular feel about it.

The rafters, in support of the roof, appeared to be split limbs - beams of average size.

The smooth portion of the rafters were installed facing upward, and the planks which looked to be about a foot or so wide and less than an inch thick were affixed atop that.

The roof had been built with a measured degree of expertise. It was well constructed, Nathaniel thought, for it was still intact and didn't leak. Its make-up of thick and curled cedar shakes showed the progressed signs of age. The moss growing along the wooden rain troughs, stretching the length of both sides, gave testimony to that.

The cabin's interior decor wasn't all that different than the exterior. The timbered walls were pretty much identical on both sides. Its architecture resembled the surroundings, that flavored with a quality of nature and tangible jaggedness.

The windows, three in all, were a single pane of glass mounted in a wooden sash that wouldn't open. The front door, surprisingly enough, was a solid piece of pine some four inches thick; it was a heavy one, held in place by three large hinges made of beaten wrought iron.

Someone had, in years gone by, taken great care in creating the fireplace Nathaniel so enjoyed, the one affixed to the end wall. It was made of field stone, had a hearth which extended into the room a couple feet, and rose through the roof.

The mantel appeared to be the simple carving of a beam, just wide enough to hang any wet clothes one may care to dry. An old iron hook mounted just inside the firebox swung from side to side, and could accommodate a pot or jug if so desired.

Nathaniel spent a lot of time sitting in front of that fireplace, as he did on the porch.

The front porch was relatively open so to speak, as was the ceiling of the cabin, for you could see the rafters, the roof planks, and the underside of the cedar shakes.

Nathaniel, at times, wondered if the warmth generated inside would be any benefit in the elimination of snow and the weight placed upon the structure in the winter.

The planks of the porch and the flooring inside were similar. The lumber appeared to be a thick reddish oak, stained with the fade of age. They were hard to keep clean and seemed to be dusty all the time.

There was an old cook stove that had been left there. It was a vintage cast iron version that could hold the glow of an amber for quite a while. It sat along one of the longer walls, jutting out a foot or so to accommodate the flue pipe which made exit through the roof overhead. Its finish was flat black. The legs were trimmed in chrome. The cooking surface had four round removable plates, two large ones positioned in the rear and two smaller ones in front, each nestled in a circular recess. A slot on the side of each plate enabled its removal when inserting a handle.

The belly of the *Beast,* as Nathaniel so fondly called it, could hold half a dozen medium sized chunks of wood - Nathaniel would often marvel at its relative ease of use and commentary efficiency.

The apparatus lent a distinction of veiled intrusiveness, for a scenic view could always be enjoyed through the window only inches away.

Nathaniel's desire for furnishings was scarce however;

decoration was now, oddly enough, unimportant to him. The
walls were cold and bare. Only a few rusty nails, serving as
hooks, could be seen.

Some crude furniture, made primarily of split rails, occupied
the rest of the space. Nathaniel's small bunk bed sat against the
wall in the comer. A pillow, sheet, and two wool blankets were
just the ticket for a good night's rest. A square table, of average
size, was in the center of the room. It was accompanied by a pair
of matching chairs. The table had seen better days though. It
appeared to be a little weak under the pressure of some weight,
but it was still usable in Nathaniel's opinion. He often found
himself in study of the carvings upon the table's surface, done
with a knife one lonely night no doubt. They were mostly initials
with dates, some dating back to the thirties.

The privy, basically nothing more than a disgusting shack out
back, had a lot of graffiti brandishing its walls too; all hand-
carved masterpieces indeed.

Nathaniel retrieved all the water he'd need from the lake.
He couldn't have found a clearer H2O anywhere; one that was
suitable for a number of purposes, yet clean enough to drink.
He had a ready supply of plastic containers to hold all that
water as well, ten in total. They held roughly five gallons each,
and his stock would last a good week.

That particular afternoon, Nathaniel thought it'd be a good
idea to relax and enjoy some fishing. Once he'd finished up a
hard morning's work of splitting wood.

A few nights before, after a good day's rain, Nathaniel thought
he'd try his hand at catching some bait. His prey would be a few
dozen nightcrawlers - some good ole' earthworms. "You can't

catch anything without bait." He so reasoned.

Nathaniel knew the creatures rose to the surface after dark, especially after a cool rain, yet he'd never had to stoop so low. Gathering bait was a virgin venture. Concisely, it was a chore that made Nathaniel shudder.

A foregone conclusion of, "It's an undignified act, scooping up those slimy things," was Nathaniel's solicit jeer. It was with a pledge of humbleness pushed aside, that Nathaniel scoffed, "I'm still an *Irwin* for crying out loud!" (Reason has a way of surrendering itself to the pry of necessity though)

Nathaniel previously buried a container in the cool soil to keep his anticipated catch alive. He hoped they would live long enough to entice a hungry trout and had planned for hours prior, in light of accomplishing the feat.

The first hour or so of Nathaniel's stalk was rather comical. He searched about, with a rather powerful flashlight, in search of the slimy prey. Often times when the light hit the wigglers, a nickname they were commonly called in that part of the country, they would immediately recede back into the burrow from which they came. Nathaniel soon learned it was better to shine the beam to the side while attempting the capture. Even by doing that, the creatures were still quite elusive.

Nathaniel made a dignified stab at catching the worms, in the beginning, by slowly reaching down to pluck them up. That proved to be daunting. Their evasive nature quickly became a challenge to Nathaniel and he soon found himself pouncing on them with the prowess of a cat.

At first, using the tip of his index finger and thumb, Nathaniel would grasp the creature and give it a quick jerk.

They were generally never far from a cleft of safety though. A
hard pull would prove to be premature however, for the slimy
things would stiffen and constrict making it difficult to pull
them out of the ground. (Thus, the hunt required a bit of
patience for even a worm doesn't relent easily)

Nathaniel had a nice spot picked out on the north end of the
lake where he thought the fish may be biting - it was a favorite.
The afternoon was a relatively warm one for that time of year.
Nathaniel took a thin jacket with him, but never felt the necessity
to don it.

The bank slowly tapered into the water there. It was an ideal
place to relax and enjoy throwing a few casts. Some cattails
graced the shore, but those large rocks hugging the bank on
either side were the most majestic of all. Almost cliff-like in
appearance, those rock formations helped block the wind from
every direction accept the south.

Nathaniel had little reason to wear a watch and he had no idea
how long he'd been there, but the passage of time had seemingly
dragged on.

Although he tried everything, a worm carefully threaded on a
hook dangling under a bobber with the adjustment of various
depths, a nightcrawler thrown on the bottom and at times pulled
along, even an artificial lure or two, but nothing would entice a
fish to bite.

Nathaniel soon grew bored and eventually accepted the
realization, "These fish aren't hungry."

Not long after he'd reeled his pole in and laid it down,
Nathaniel sat and leaned back on his hands. He eventually lay
on his back, with hands folded under his head, to stare at that

beautiful blue sky.

It wasn't long before Nathaniel caught himself on the verge of dozing off. Yet, the glimpse of an eagle soaring high above gathered his full attention. He watched it for a good while before he realized it was a bald eagle. In a fairly loud audible voice, Nathaniel said, "Now that's the definition of freedom!" At the end of a long-sustained pause, with the palm of his right hand used to shade his eyes, Nathaniel added, "That's a magnificent creature you've created, Lord."

"Boy ... some fresh fish for lunch sure would be nice," was his delayed comment, vocalized out of a trailing thought.

Shortly after that, the huge bird banked sharply a couple times, as if a gust of wind had hit it, then it glided in to eventually perch atop a tall tree not far away.

For the longest time, Nathaniel studied the creature - he was most impressed. "Uncle Sam's own bird ... perhaps the noblest-looking creature that ever flew." He pondered.

No doubt its nesting ground was somewhere up the mountain, in a rock ledge somewhere under a cliff.

Nathaniel once read a bald eagle could live a hundred years.

As Nathaniel gazed upon the kingly bird of prey, that snowy white head, great hooked bill and taloned feet, those fierce yellow piercing eyes below those bold brows, its wingspread of some six to eight feet, he remembered reading about the Romans and later Europeans and how impressed they were with the bird. The eagle was an emblem of more than one European empire; it was also the symbol of nobility, a badge of orders. The standards of Roman legions bore the image of an imperial eagle as well.

"What a bird!" He gathered. "A national ornament for the U.S."

Then, suddenly, Nathaniel eyes became enlarged for the eagle flapped its wings several times to gain lift then began to swoop over the water. With its claws extended, the eagle grabbed a fish swimming close to the surface. It then veered upward, heading straight for Nathaniel.

The fish was a large one, and Nathaniel could see the bird was having a difficult time holding its grip. As the eagle was trying to gain attitude, it flew only yards above Nathaniel's head - needless to say, he was fascinated.

Within moments, the bird lost its grip upon the fish and it fell to the ground not far from where Nathaniel sat. The creature was obviously angry at failure, for it blurted out a loud screech and then flew away.

As the bird flew off, Nathaniel waved to say, "We're clumsy fishermen, my friend."

Oddly enough, his prayer had been answered. Nathaniel didn't know the species of the fish, but he surmised it was a salmon or trout - weighing well over twenty pounds.

As the fish flopped upon the ground, Nathaniel said, "Thanks Lord!" Then he waited for his meal to expire.

Within the hour, Nathaniel was enjoying every mouth-watering morsel of that heavenly surprise dropped from above. He'd never claimed to be a world-class cook, but what he had prepared wasn't too darn bad. One of the large fillets, surrounded by a few sliced potatoes, a bit of diced red onion, covered with a shake or so of salt, pepper, and a dash of butter, would be more than enough to fill him up. In letting the offering brown for a while in a big iron skillet, well, the smell would drive any hungry soul wild.

Nathaniel wasn't sweating the little stuff much anymore. "The heck with the details!" He thought. It didn't make any difference what kind of fish it was. What held importance was it was a blessing and a godsend, added, it was a great tasting one. Nathaniel was enjoying that tasty lunch from the front porch too much, and not a whole lot mattered as he gently swayed back and forth in that ole' rocker.

Once he'd finished, Nathaniel laid his plate to the side and began to soak in the view while letting his food digest for a while.

A spider had recently spun a small web above the handrail, next to the comer post where he sat. Nathaniel hadn't noticed it until now, but it was fascinating to him for it demonstrated nature's beauty and some spectacular triangular designs made of silk.

In short order, a fly became snared in the web and the spider wasted little time sliding down to encase its future dinner with a deadly wrap.

Nathaniel watched in wonder as the predatory arachnid finished its prey off, then to wait nearby as it seemingly celebrated by repeatedly bouncing up and down in quick fashion.

That awe of haughty celebration ended quickly however for a black wasp landed on the spider, stringing it several times and eventually to death. When it was sure of its conquest, the wasp picked the arachnid up and flew away.

Although nature's chain of fury can be cruel, Nathaniel was

still dumbfounded by the astonishing sight. He would, later that night, wisely pen a journal entry of, *"No matter how condescendingly superior you think you may be, you're not above being the prey of an enemy who just lays in wait."*

The notion of taking a nap after lunch sounded pretty good to Nathaniel, so he did so for a while. It wasn't long after he dosed off that a loud boom abruptly woke him. When Nathaniel peered out the door, he saw nothing that would raise suspicion.

Then he heard it again; a deafening clap of thunder with a proceeding rumble. As Nathaniel stared upon the sky, he thought things were strikingly odd. The sun was on the verge of hugging the horizon, yet there wasn't a cloud in the sky except for a small lonely dark one hovered above the base of the mountain, near the north end of the lake.

As Nathaniel watched, with a hint of amazement, he began to realize there was no wind. The birds weren't singing either. It was eerie, for all was dead silent.

Then, without warning, lighting hit. It hit so close, Nathaniel's ears rang for a bit. He was temporary blinded for a few seconds as well.

Within a manner of moments, Nathaniel could smell smoke. The grass was ablaze, but the wind mysteriously picked up to quickly extinguish it. Nathaniel's mind began to reflect back on that dream he'd had only a few nights before. The one where he jumped into the water to escape the flames, yet the wind saved him and his abode.

Soon after, that solitary cloud vanished. Nathaniel then decided to set out and investigate that which burnt, once he'd gathered his senses.

It took him a minute or two to get over there, but when Nathaniel reached the north end of the lake he discovered what had occurred. Lighting had indeed hit, striking that tree which the eagle had earlier landed on. The heat must have been so intense it ignited the surrounding grass. Nathaniel knew a million volts contained within a lightning bolt could have that type of devastating possibility.

There was a curious spiral groove that ran from the top of the tree to its base as well. Nathaniel was fascinated with the damage, especially how that three or four inch groove wrapped around the trunk and fractured the wood beneath the bark. The wood appeared to have been dried out under that tremendous surge of heat, leaving hundreds of tiny stress fractures behind. The bark was peeled from the tree, much like a banana - Nathaniel found it quite easy to pull off.

Nathaniel also noticed something else that was a little odd. There was a large branch hanging over the water and steam was escaping from its outer tips. No doubt, the sap, its lifeblood, had been cooked. It looked relatively healthy at first, but within a matter of moments the branch withered to nothing before Nathaniel's eyes.

Nathaniel was amazed by what he'd witnessed, but then, for some reason, he was distracted by his reflection in the water. He wasted no time in taking notice of his likeness, for his mind began to fill with thoughts that were probing.

As he stared upon that rippled appearance, Nathaniel recalled reading Proverbs 27:19 some two nights prior.

The truth of, *"As water reflects a face, so a man's heart reflects the man,"* was now etched upon that curious mind of his.

As only He could, God was bartering with Nathaniel. In a far-reaching way, the Creator was confounding the wise. The great *I Am* was beginning to have a crumbling effect on Nathaniel's amassed fortune of pride. It appeared an abashing of self was the Lord's goal with Nathaniel. Pride was an unsavory possession, of which Nathaniel had held dear for a long time.

With the witness of that tree being hit by lightning and the astonishment he felt by how quickly the branch withered, Nathaniel later in the evening took a peek at the concordance hidden away in the back of his Bible. By doing so, he aspired to gain some added insight while reflecting upon the day.

There were five passages that stood **head** and shoulders above the rest. They held Nathaniel's interest, for they were absorbing with intrigue.

The first verse was Psalms 1:1-3:

"Blessed is the man who does not walk in the counsel of the wicked or stand in the way of sinners or sit in the seat of mockers. But his delight is in the law of the Lord, and on His law he meditates day and night. He is like a tree planted by streams of water, which yields its fruit in season and whose leaf does not wither."

The second passage was from James 1:2 - 12:

"Consider it pure joy, my brothers, whenever you face trials of many kinds, because you know that the testing of your faith develops perseverance. Perseverance must finish its work so that you may be mature and complete, not lacking anything. If any of you lacks wisdom, he should ask God, who gives generously to all without finding fault, and it will be given to

*him. But when he asks, he must believe and not doubt, because
he who doubts is like a wave of the sea, blown and tossed by the
wind. That man should not think he will receive anything from
the Lord; he is a double-minded man, unstable in all he does.
The brother in humble circumstances ought to take pride in his
high position. But the one who is rich should take pride in his
low position, because he will pass away like a wild flower. For
the sun rises with scorching heat and withers the plant; its
blossom falls and its beauty is destroyed. In the same way, the
rich man will fade away even while he goes about his business.
Blessed is the man who perseveres under trial, because when he
has stood the test, he will receive the crown of life that God has
promised to those who love him.”*

The third verse was John 15:5 & 6 - Jesus' own words:

*"I am the vine; you are the branches. If a man remains in
me and I in him, he will bear much fruit; apart from me you can
do nothing. If anyone does not remain in me, he is like a branch
that is thrown away and withers; such branches are picked up,
thrown into the fire and burned."*

The fourth passage involved Christ and a fig tree:

*“Early in the morning, as he was on his way back to the city,
he was hungry. Seeing a fig tree by the road, he went up to it
but found nothing on it except leaves. Then he said to it, ‘May
you never bear fruit again!’ Immediately the tree withered.
When the disciples saw this, they were amazed. ‘How did the
fig tree wither so quickly?’ they asked. Jesus replied, ‘I tell
you the truth, if you have faith and do not doubt, not only can
you do what was done to the fig tree, but also you can say to this
mountain, go, throw yourself into the sea, and it will be done.*

If you believe, you will receive whatever you ask for in prayer.'" (Matthew 21:18 - 22)

The fifth was a short story found in Luke 6:6 -10:

"On another Sabbath he went into the synagogue and was teaching, and a man was there whose right hand was shriveled. The Pharisees and the teachers of the law were looking for a reason to accuse Jesus, so they watched him closely to see if he would heal on the Sabbath. But Jesus knew what they were thinking and said to the man with the shriveled hand, 'Get up and stand in front of everyone.' So he got up and stood there. Then Jesus said to them, 'I ask you, which is lawful on the Sabbath; to do good or to do evil, to save life or to destroy it?' He looked around at them all, and then said to the man, 'Stretch out your hand.' He did so, and his hand was completely restored. But they were furious and began to discuss with one another what they might do to Jesus."

"The greatest things in life aren't really things at all." Nathaniel later wrote. **"Meaning is more important than gold. A single day in fear of God is better than a wealthy life loaded with headaches."** He concluded the entry by saying, **"My pride withers - joy renewed. I had much to live on in the past, yet nothing to truly live for until now."**

Chapter Sixteen
Odyssey

The calendar tacked upon the wall garnished the dreg of a lone page. An *X* filled most of the squares by now. It was Nathaniel's stamp to signify the lapse of every passing day.

A few light snows had fallen already, one briefly that morning, but none ushered forth any accumulation. In reality, they were little more than an introduction, a gentle offering upon a threshold, an overture in prelude to winter's impending grip.

With the stroke of a pen Nathaniel eradicated the space representative of the previous day, for there was a new dawn in the making. Nathaniel had scarce reason to pay attention in the past, yet, the day, December 21st, was officially the beginning of winter. 1990 would be upon the world in a shade over a week, Christmas was just around the comer, and the calendar so proclaimed a season of change.

Nathaniel's reflection soon leaned upon a not-so-distance memory as he gave brief consideration of the climactic page. He recollected being moved by one of Pastor Dan's previous sermons. Its theme dealt with stinginess, man's selfish, yet, all-too-characteristic nature. It struck a cord, for it spoke of the reluctance of most to dive into that muddy pool called humanity. Nathaniel knew then, as now, the charges of transgression had risen within his soul and he'd been found guilty. Fittingly, the lesson bore the name, "Time is the currency of the world."

Celebration was a lonely experience and scarce anymore. Nathaniel's pleasures were simple and few. Foremost, his merriment from taking a warm bath once a week was the biggest thrill. Frolicking in a galvanized wash tub, filled with water boiled upon the stove, was Nathaniel's way of kicking up his heels on a Saturday night. It was a far cry from a daily shower, those scented soaps, that expensive imported shampoo, a lavish lifestyle once led. Yet, ironically, he was content with this existence.

Nathaniel would probably spend Christmas in front of the fireplace this year, a little decorating, strings of popcorn threaded about the mantel, a snack popped over an open fire, some carols sung off key that no one can hear, or a part of the evening spent playing in that accommodating tub, were his visions of enjoying the coming holiday.

Nathaniel wouldn't be lavished with presents from others this time. The only gift exchange occurring this season would be between him and God, or so he thought. The best he could possibly convey was an impartation of praise, Nathaniel reasoned. (Ushering forth a heart-felt thanks, in celebration of the birth of God's only son, was worth more than precious gold)

Necessity has a way of triggering habit indeed, and Nathaniel's routine of setting the alarm for 3 AM was an intriguing example. Awakening to discover the room is a frigid temperature isn't the most pleasant experience. Seeing your breath in the morning is quite a shock as is your bare feet striking a cold floor. After the fire went out the first couple of times, two nights prior included, Nathaniel forced himself to rise during the night to stoke the coals.

There was no lack of warmth in the cabin that morning though. The fire cracked several times as it roared with a fresh fury. Nathaniel now respected the importance of a good fire and the comfort it bred while preparing breakfast that mom.

After he sat, and in the midst of that indulgence of some tasty scrambled eggs, Nathaniel thought a little reading might be in order while enjoying the meal. He reached for that John Newton biography and began to flip through the pages, then to the back, and began to soak in some of those famous quotes.

"Candor will always allow much for inexperience." Newton wrote. "I have been years forming my views, and in the course of this time some of my hills have been sinking, and some of my valleys have risen; but how unreasonable would it be to expect all this should take place in another person, and that in the course of a year or two!"

Before reading any further, Nathaniel pondered for a moment then pushed his plate away. A thought had pierced his soul, leading Nathaniel to grab a pen and jot it down in his journal.

"In many ways I've given birth to a defeatist attitude." He scribbled. *"Always wanting more! My life's been one of plenty, bathed in glory of self. I'm repulsed now by those wasted years. I had so much, yet done so little.*

I once read Mozart was penniless, sick and unable to find work, losing his children to starvation. Yet, he wrote some of the most beautiful music ever created. What am I to do with my Odyssey?"

After he'd purged himself of a bit of self-inflicted guilt,

Nathaniel continued in study of Newton's writings.

Newton all-too-cleverly observed. "Sometimes I compare the troubles which we have to undergo in the course of the year to a great bundle of sticks, far too large for us to lift. But God does not require us to carry the whole at once; He mercifully unties the bundle and gives us first one which we are to carry today, and then another which we are to carry tomorrow, and so on. This we might easily manage if we could only take the burden appointed for us each day; but we choose to increase our troubles by carrying yesterday's stick over again today and adding tomorrow's burden to our load before we are required to bear it."

Newton was wise to add, "The word *temperance* in the New Testament signifies self-possession. It is a disposition suitable to one who has a race to run and therefore will not load his pockets with lead."

The day had all the makings of being a lazy one. Henceforth, it didn't take much of a prod for Nathaniel to be succumbed by the allure of a nap by mid-afternoon.

With the expectation of obtaining some restful bliss, Nathaniel curled himself beneath those cozy blankets. He wrapped them about himself and tucked a fluffed pillow under his head to doze off. His aim was to catch a quick forty winks, ever-so-mindful there was firewood to be carried in, but Nathaniel's intent would be soon detoured. His effort was indeed a successful one for he slept through the entire afternoon; so deeply in fact, it wasn't until almost dusk before he awoke.

When Nathaniel did begin to wake, something peculiar filtered into his groggy eyes. What appeared before his

fluttering eyelids was something best described as, *a
dance of shadows;* it captured his attention while lingering in
transition to consciousness.

When he opened his eyes, Nathaniel noticed a shaft of
sunlight streaming upon the bed. He laid there for a long
while, intrigued by what he saw and the thoughts
encompassing his mind.

A float in the illumination were air-born particles of dust.
They're an invisible host often times, yet the intensity of the light
revealed their presence. The tiny specks were mesmerizing,
with a lean toward magical, appearing boastful as they danced
upon the revealing air. A reflection of green, yellow, or blue
highlighted their existence.

Nathaniel would later write, ***"They're always there - like God
- sometimes revealed. We breathe them in, yet, they do no
harm."***

With the forthcoming departure of the sun, Nathaniel lit the
sole candle resting upon the table. He then stoked the fire with a
couple pieces of wood and dragged the comfortable rocker over
to enjoy the warmth of the flame.

He leaned backward in the chair for a while, then rocked it
ever-so-slowly a few times before **leaving** the comfort of his seat
to retrieve the book lying upon the mantel. When he sat back
down, Nathaniel began to absorb himself in the thought of the
day and the contents of the book.

By the light of the blaze, he read, "If I cannot take pleasure in
infirmities, I can sometimes feel the profit of them. I can
conceive a king to pardon a rebel and take him into his family,
and then say, 'I appoint you for a season to wear a fetter. At a

certain season I will send a messenger to knock it off. In the meantime this fetter will serve to remind you of your state. It may humble you and restrain you from rambling.'" It was but yet another morsel of Newton wisdom.

It was still early in the evening and Nathaniel thought he'd hit the sack a little earlier than usual for he envisioned the benefits of taking a moderate hike up the mountain come morning.

Before turning in, Nathaniel thumbed through a few verses then came across Deuteronomy 28:47. It read, *"Because you did not serve the Lord your God joyfully and gladly in the time of prosperity, therefore in hunger and thirst, in nakedness and dire poverty, you will serve the enemies the Lord sends against you. He will put an iron yoke on your neck until he has destroyed you."*

Nathaniel softly muttered the phase, "How repugnantly strong?" However, he reasoned the words to be representative though for they were alluding to the condition of an unappreciative soul. It was a light of definition indeed, one shed upon thanklessness.

The pages then seemingly fell to the writings of Paul. Nathaniel would gain added enlightenment from his instructions as well.

"And we urge you, brothers, warn those who are idle, encourage the timid, help the weak, be patient with everyone. Make sure that nobody pays back wrong for wrong, but always try to be kind to each other and to everyone else. Be joyful always; pray continually; give thanks in all circumstances, for this is God's will for you in Christ Jesus. Do not put out the Spirit's fire; do not treat prophecies with contempt. Test

everything. Hold on to the good. Avoid every kind of evil. May God himself, the God of peace, sanctify you through and through. May your whole spirit, soul and body be kept blameless at the coming of our Lord Jesus Christ. The one who calls you is faithful and he will do it. " (1 Thessalonians 5:14 - 24)

After he'd pondered that for a while, Nathaniel closed his Bible then made preparation for bed. But before hitting the sack, Nathaniel penned a few thoughts in his journal.

"Thanksgiving has come and gone, celebrated over a can of tuna." He wrote. ***"I need to acquire an attitude of gratitude. I was handed everything my entire life. The nature of thanksgiving is a gift from God - a mindset longed for. I'm happier now, with nothing, more so, than ever before. I've been an ingrate, blinded by the glamour of riches. Forgive me for my depraved ways! A thankless heart grieves the Holy Spirit - I'm sure. I've been a spoiled brat since birth. Although logic has its own stance, it's by no means a stretch to consider a wealth of self-reliance a curse. The Lord's keelhauling this misguided ship."***

When he'd finished his final entry Nathaniel rose from the chair, cupped his hand over the candle on the table and blew it out. The faint light generated by the fire was sufficient enough to see the way, and Nathaniel climbed into bed. He hadn't laid there long before he got back up. He'd forgotten to pray. A bedtime prayer was something he was accustomed to each night now.

Tonight was a little different however. He didn't hesitate before saying the words. It wasn't one of those stiff prayers, a routine benediction, one rehearsed that you might find in a book, being that there may be one bound somewhere.

The words seemed to flow from Nathaniel's lips with fluidity. His prayer sounded more like a conversation, one that was heartfelt and sincere.

As he knelt beside his bunk, Nathaniel had a groundbreaking experience. He'd never felt anything quite like that before. He described the sensation as an electrifying touch, and later elaborated on that journaled definition.

The Holy Spirit decinded upon him that evening. So moved, he would later describe the encounter as *the hand of God upon my shoulder*.

"Lord." He spoke with a whisper. "I no longer want a one-dimensional experience."

With open palms stretched forth, Nathaniel added, "Ritual is just that ... one dimensional ... an exercise lacking the true you. I long for a higher plain, a three dimensional one bordering upon the spiritual realm ... Moses saw your glory and was forever changed ... transformed ... I long for the same. I understand the spiritual realm is invisible often times to the mortal senses ... yet ... I know it exists. My thoughts are no longer mine. My intellectual capacity is nothing compared to yours ... I fully comprehend what I ask ... If we were privileged to it all ... that of the spiritual side ... it would scare us to death ... I'm sure. Demons ... that of the underworld ... running amuck."

Nathaniel paused for a good while. Then, with the gathering of a few more thoughts, he proceeded with that divine conversation.

"Show me a part, Lord ...let me experience a touch ... for I long for this journey to speak of your majesty ... and little of me. My life has never been my own ... I know that!"

Nathaniel began to cry with that line. Overcome by emotion, he blurted out, "I now see ... like never before," as his arms and back began to pulsate, quiver, as he wept with conviction.

"I've been deficient ... unwilling to dive in ... only to exploit things for selfish gain ... I've groveled at the feet of greed ... I've been foolish, Lord!"

Nathaniel soon crumpled. In a sitting position, draped upon the side of the bed, he sobbed for what would eventually be hours. The blankets were, in turn, literally soaked by the flow of tears. An intermission of staring at that faint shadow of his struck upon the wall, was a brief, yet periodic, rest from the inner stir. His voice was now choked by inarticulate grief. The expressionism of a soul had been cast, the stance of a silent creed forecast, paramount for it stood witness to the carnage of the spoken word.

Nathaniel did eventually drift to sleep once he'd climbed into bed, but only as a result of laborious travail. The anguish he felt, the emotional toil of exertion displayed, did no doubt impede something quicker.

There were times, of late, that Nathaniel didn't sleep well at all; rarely, there were nights that he did. That particular night was an exception though, for he fell into a deep sleep and began to dream.

As his mind began to process the vision, Nathaniel could hear these words out of the tranquil darkness, "Be it granted ... that of which thee ask."

Nathaniel could see himself standing beside the fireplace in the dream. Through the eyes of that individual standing before the fire, Nathaniel could see himself once more asleep upon the bed.

Nathaniel soon felt the presence of a gentle breeze upon his face, it seemed to fill the room. As he gazed upon the sleeping one, a large transparent hand extended downward through the roof. It curled, then cupped itself around the bed and swooped that individual up - himself. Curiously enough, the one lying upon the bed never gained consciousness during the process. In astonishing fashion, that divine hand hoisted the spirit from that person's body. The silhouette of its brightly lit existence was breathtaking; then, in the blink of an eye, it was whisked skyward.

In the next segment of the dream Nathaniel was no longer standing by the fire. Instead, he was standing in an empty room. It was like nothing he recognized, nor was it the least bit familiar. However, there was a peace about that place one couldn't deny.

With the experience of a gentle nudge in the back, Nathaniel glanced behind. It would seem an invisible force was guiding him, for he noticed nothing there. He then reasoned he was being persuaded to walk through an open door, one that lay before him. The door appeared to be a common one, yet, its frame was illuminated. (A provocation to enter in was all-too-apparent)

Nathaniel eventually mustered the courage to pass through that door of invitation, but did so somewhat reluctantly.

The door appeared to be locked, for Nathaniel's attempt to turn the knob failed. With surprise, he soon discovered a single finger will pass through the wood. Nathaniel then proceeded with caution, for its beyond anything he could fathom.

He found that the fingers of his right hand will pass through the door quite easily. That's intriguing so he pulled his hand back, then, contemplates a second try. This time he pushed all ten fingers through the wood. Ever so slowly, Nathaniel creeped forward. His hands passed through, then his forearms, his elbows followed, then he was face to face with the door. With a lump in his throat, Nathaniel couldn't help but imagine what's beyond that door as he admired, of all things, the grain of the wood - it's colorful and striking, beautiful, yet, like nothing he had ever seen before.

With a shove of fortitude Nathaniel leaned through the door, falling to the floor of another room on the other side.

As he rose, Nathaniel noticed the carpet beneath him. He observed a table before him and the decorations upon the walls. The room appeared to be a dining room for the table was garnished with a fine tablecloth, a beautiful centerpiece, plates, and silverware. He could see that the setting was for four.

There was a patio door on the far wall. It appeared to lead to a deck, then the ocean, for Nathaniel could see waves breaking upon the sand in the distance.

The home seemed to be a moderately priced one, in Nathaniel's opinion. Its furnishings were nice, but modest.

As Nathaniel gazed upon the surroundings, a woman entered the room. He was startled when she walked in. He then became fascinated, because the woman can't see him.

Although he didn't recognize her, Nathaniel was enchanted by the woman's beauty.

She had an oven mitt on each hand, cradling a pan full of what appeared to be warm homemade bread.

With the placement of the bread upon the table she left the room, but only to return with more food. She soon yelled, "It's time to eat!"

From other parts of the house Nathaniel could hear a reply of, "Okay," from more than one person.

Two teens, or they would appear to be by their age, a boy and a girl, entered the room and took a seat at the table. It was not long till the two began to scuffle with each other. The hurling of words at each other, name calling and the like, were their feuding weapons.

Nathaniel stood in the comer - the kids couldn't see him either. He watched the drama unfold, observing, with a grin. "Typical teenagers." He jested.

When the woman entered the room, the teens snapped into their best behavior mode.

Once more, Nathaniel grinned. "Typical teenagers." He reasoned.

"Where's your father?" The mother asked the children. They shrugged their shoulders in silence, with lackadaisical regard.

From another part of the home Nathaniel could hear someone faintly say, "Coming!"

"It's getting cold!" The woman replied.

There was a bit of momentary silence at the table, then, to Nathaniel's astonishment, he saw himself walk in. He was older though, maybe late fifties or early sixties, it would appear at first glance.

Nathaniel observed his older self, take a seat, then lead the family in prayer. The woman appeared enthusiastic, nodding her head on occasion, however, the children seemed less so. The prayer wasn't anything flowery or lengthy; it was just a simple one, yet, honest, and moving.

With the conclusion of the prayer everyone began to take a portion of the food being passed around the table.

As they ate, the ceiling above the older Nathaniel began to swirl. The one observing it was taken back by that, but then he saw that large hand from before. It slowly extended downward through the ceiling again.

It was the hand of God, no doubt, and had Nathaniel's spirit still cradled in its palm. As soon as the hand made contact with the floor, its prized possession leaped into that older body.

In an instant, the one observing from the comer was no longer standing there. He was now, somehow, looking through the eyes of the older one.

Nathaniel couldn't believe what was happening.

He soon became absorbed with the examination of his hands, and of all things, his clothes. He was wearing a T-shirt and blue jeans. *"I would never wear rags like that!"* He reasoned with a linger of wonderment.

The backs of his hands were ladened with wrinkles - a testament of age. Seemingly more fragmentary was the sight of a wedding ring.

The woman voiced her concern when she asked, "Are you alright, Sweetheart?"

"Everything's splendid ... Becky." Nathaniel replied.

"How did I know her name?" He wondered.

She was obviously puzzled by Nathaniel's words for she countered with a phrase of, "Splendid?" as a retort. She followed with, "Are you sure you're okay ... You're acting a little funny, Honey."

Nathaniel thought it was best to offer a simple nod of his head to reassure all was well.

His mind was now reeling, yet, oddly enough, most of those thoughts were not his. He couldn't hold his tongue for long though, for he blurted out, "Andy ... Kim ... have you finished your homework?"

The countenance of the children had changed somewhat with Nathaniel's question.

Andy's reply was, "I'm sweatin' it on some math. Can you help me?"

Kim made the comment of, "I could use some with Biology."

Nathaniel thought it was prudent to again forego any words and just nod as to agree.

"How do I know the names of these children? That I'm married to a woman named Becky? That I live on the ocean in California? That I've retired and love to fish in the surf. My ... is the past nothing more than a blur?" Those, and an assortment of other questions probed Nathaniel's soul.

When they had finished the meal, Becky threw a proposal Nathaniel's way. "I'll take care of the dishes if you help the kids with their homework ... how's that sound?" She asked.

Nathaniel nodded his head once more in agreement.

Becky was still puzzled by Nathaniel's behavior and followed with a pry of, "Are you sure you're okay?"

Nathaniel nodded his head, yes.

Becky was not quite convinced of the validity of that, and uttered a muttered "Huh" in disbelief as she cleared the table.

Nathaniel then followed the kids to their separate rooms. He assisted them with their studies. *"It's a snap!"* He thought.

Through subtle interaction with the children, Nathaniel learned he was their stepfather and that Becky was married once before for twelve years. She was married to a man named John and he died of cancer - it was obvious the kids missed him. He learned, in short, Andy was 17, a jock, and thought little of school. The sole focus of his attention was upon girls and that college football scholarship he thought he had all but wrapped up.

Kim, on the other hand, was 16, loved school, and played in the marching band. It was clear she found little time for "creeps." - her tag for guys.

The teens thought Nathaniel was acting a little strange as well, asking all those mindless questions of them.

Nathaniel exited Kim's room last. He then entered the adjacent living room. He found Becky relaxing upon the couch there. Reading a book. As he scanned the room, a rather large stack of letters upon a desk, tucked away in the comer, caught Nathaniel's eye.

Nathaniel walked across the room and made his way to the desk. Then he sat down to examine what lay upon the surface. Becky paid little attention. Nathaniel began to sort through the pile and soon realized the letters were from various places around the globe.

With his back toward Becky, Nathaniel said, with surprise, "These letters are addressed to me ... they're from around the world!"

Becky's reply was a simple one. "You're the salt of the earth,

Dear."

In the blink of an eye, Nathaniel was whisked from there and transplanted back in time to that cabin by Lost Lake.

He was now standing by the fire again, observing himself asleep only a few feet away. The hand of God appeared once more. It's cradling a spirit - his.

The dream concluded there and Nathaniel began to wake. As he does, he found it odd that the sheets, and the blankets, were gently falling about him. It was like everything was happening in slow motion; as if his soul had been lowered upon the bed.

Nathaniel awoke with a stir, to vocalize many a thought that now raced through his mind.

He first got dressed. Mumbling all the while, he whipped up a bit of breakfast. It wasn't until he was in the midst of the indulgence that he realized he hadn't offered a prayer over the food. When he did, the only words that came to mind were, "That was some dream … Lord!"

That dream was significant, but it would take the passage of time before Nathaniel could discover a pertaining wisdom that would apply. While studying scripture one evening, Nathaniel found explanation to the vision amongst the pages of Isaiah.

The prophet was inspired to write, *"Remember the former things, those of long ago; I am God, and there is no other, I am God, and there is none like me. I make known the end from the beginning, from ancient times, what is still to come. I say: My purpose will stand, and I will do all that I please."*

Nathaniel found solace in those verses, nine and ten of the 46th chapter. His conclusion was: ***"God's revealing what will be, before it comes."***

Chapter Seventeen
In Search of a Soul

"February 10th, 1990.

I've often heard the expression 'Dead of Winter.'

Is that which surrounds truly dead? - many cast that contrary shade.

There's definability between bereft of sensation, defunct, or that of deprived life, and the dull or inactive, inanimate, stagnant, or stale. (The latter of which I could attest self-guilt)

Is it my plight to remain here? My spirit is at rest in this place. In contrast, how can I make a difference in seclusion?

How do I benefit mankind, enrich the good of all, by remaining dormant? Like that which sleeps beneath a blanket of snow.

'The ground will be plowed before long.' I hear those words echo throughout my being.

Is my time here that of spiritual introspection, a sabbatical?

God speaks the clearest in the midst of silence - that I'm convinced. One could reason I'm at war with self. I feel I'm in search of a soul."

Anticipation was a brew within Nathaniel. Aroused was the sensation of something new and forthcoming, and he could feel it. His forged thoughts of the day bore witness of it.

The conditions outside were a stir as well. Nathaniel glanced upon the frosted window panes as he placed the final touches on his writings, the flakes were beating the glass without end, then reflection was born.

The snow was deep and blowing about with intensity.
Nathaniel was curious to know its depth and measured a couple
days prior. It was a little under 33" at the time. That bright white
blanket was beautiful, but it was drifting. One drift in particular,
to the side of the cabin, had gained enough height to boast of
touching the roof's eve.

"Mother Nature's harsh in these parts," people would often
say when Nathaniel obtained supplies in town.

Venturing far from the cabin, especially this time of year,
bore risk. There were a few reasons why Nathaniel must
though. The retrieval of water from the lake was by far the
biggest necessity - it represented the greatest challenge however.
The gathering of firewood was essential too, just not as
hazardous. Then there were the frequent trips to the privy that
required the bearing of elements also.

Often times it was a task to clear a path around the wood
pile, or the privy, but the carving of a way to the lake was far
more work. When the temperature dropped to dangerous levels,
or the wind made the task of shoveling an unwise endeavor,
Nathaniel used a pair of snowshoes to maneuver the trodden
way. He paced the distance off once. It was a little over a
hundred yards to the water's edge.

Be it through trial and error, Nathaniel discovered the tool of
choice was an auger for the retrieval of water. He used the tool to
bore holes through the ice, for the ice could be a foot thick or
more, and with the aid of the tool he accomplished the task with
relative speed. Nathaniel found it best to lower a hose down the
hole then siphon the water into a storage container; it became
standard procedure.

Reflection would soon surrender to inquisitive examination though, for with the turning of pages Nathaniel flipped backward through his journal entries until he ventured upon one dated December 31st.

He read the Bible till dawn that New Year's Eve, welcoming the New Year in amidst the tranquil bliss of that cabin, yet the following day was slept away. Nathaniel had recollection of that.

"It would be a difficult task for a camel to pass through the eye of a needle." Nathaniel wrote. ***"In correlation, a rich man entering the kingdom of heaven would be a similar feat - nothing could speak more loudly to me."*** His entry was a throw of commentary, more so, it was the aftermath of an inward probe, reflection upon Matthew 19:16 through 21. It states: *"No one can serve two masters. Either he will hate the one and love the other, or he will be devoted to the one and despise the other. You cannot serve both God and Money."*

"My long-standing choice was that of money, and it appears it was a foolhardy one. The service of it doth wane.

Once immersed in 1 Samuel 8:1-9, I determined I too have rejected a king - that of which I'm ashamed - no more, that I plead.

As I read Luke 12:16-21, I couldn't detour from the last verse. Rich toward God ... Rich toward God ... I ponder the fullness of its meaning, pray that His purpose may be revealed."

Matthew 6:19-21 says: *"Do not store up for yourselves treasures on earth, where moth and rust destroy, and where thieves break in and steal. But store up for yourselves treasures in heaven, where moth and rust do not destroy, and where thieves do not break in and steal.''*

"The treasures of the past no longer appeal to me. They are but a trampling of dust. A renewed vision awaits; that of which I'm convinced.

I was puzzled, yet humbled, when I read Luke 16:19-31. Chasm ... There could be no greater punishment inflicted than to spend eternity in Hades, yet, an added degree of torment will be suffered by all who fall. Sinners, having the capacity to view paradise from the bowels of Hell, seeing all who populate heaven, but unable to partake of any of it is more than I can fathom."

Nathaniel's ensuing thoughts were so singular in complexity they each took shelter upon a solidarity page.

"WORLDLY POSSESSIONS"

"But thou shalt remember the Lord thy God: for it is he that giveth thee power to get wealth, that he may establish his covenant which he sware onto thy fathers, as it is this day." (Deuteronomy 8:18)

"I never thought of what I had as wealth, Lord. Instead I worshipped falsehood, a plateau of power. Ironically, it was never enough! To buy out a corporation bore the despicable - depravity.

Yet, you gave enough to fulfill. You cared for me every day of my life. I haven't appreciated enough how you've taken care of me or the way you have kept me through those times.

Thank you for the spiritual and financial wealth

you've given. I desire to use it for Your glory. Show me how to spend it."

"UNCERTAIN RICHES"

"Command those who are rich in this present world not to be arrogant nor to put their hope in wealth, which is so uncertain, but to put their hope in God, who richly provides us with everything for our enjoyment." (1 Timothy 6:17)
"Heavenly Father, compared to the rest of the world, I'm rich and living well. I have an abundance of funds, and my basic needs are always met. Keep me mindful of those blessings, no matter how much or how little I have. Encourage me to use what I have in a way that brings glory upon you. Riches can fade in the blink of an eye - I'm aware - only You remain forever."

"TAKING MATTERS INTO ONE'S OWN HANDS"

"A faithful man shall abound with blessings: but he that maketh haste to be rich shall not be innocent." (Proverbs 28:20)
"Father, you give richly. Everything I need to live a fulfilling life is mine for the asking, be it in your time, nevertheless, not mine. There were times when I grew weary of waiting, thinking that if I could only have a little more, I might be happier. I took matters into my own hands often, the deed of casting divine direction to the side routine. I worked long hours, yet, for what? I hid from those who were

in need, ignoring a multitude in want. I attest, the past hardening of a heart, walking over many in the scheme of doing business.

Help me categorize the priorities, Lord. Trusting that you will provide for the need, when it's needed."

"STEWARDSHIP"

"The Lord shall open unto thee his good treasure, the heaven to give the rain unto thy land in his season, and to bless all the work of thine hand." (Deuteronomy 18:12)

Father, the world abounds with your blessings: fertile soil, nourishing rain, the warmth of the sun, that cooling breeze. Everything I need is a gift. I comprehend that as never before, I'm free to use it all.

You've given me stewardship of the planet, but I've often failed in my responsibilities.

I've depleted the soil, fouled the rivers and seas, polluted the air, and exterminated your creatures in my haste to make myself wealthy. Forgive me those trespasses against your creation, Father. Show me my wrongs. Teach me how to correct my selfish acts and live in harmony with your precious earth. When I do, that will be the true measure of my success."

"A SAVIOR"

"Better is the poor that walketh in his uprightness, than he that is perverse in his ways, though he be rich." (Proverbs

28:6)

"Father, I tend to listen to the advice of the successful, not the poor. No one would think of going to a poor man for financial advice - he has no power. If he did, he would be rich, wouldn't he?

You sent your son as a humble man; one without power or wealth as the world deems them. Help me see the wisdom of that act, remind me that your son spent most of his life amongst the powerless, suffering the death of a criminal for my sake."

"PEACE"

"The sleep of a labouring man is sweet, whether he eat little or much: but the abundance of the rich will not suffer him to sleep. There is a sore evil which I have seen under the sun, namely, riches kept for the owners thereof to their hurt. But those riches perish by evil travail: and he begetteth a son, and there is nothing in his hand." (Ecclesiastes 5:12-14)

"If more money will make me miserable, Lord, I'd rather forego it. I'd prefer your peace to anxiety.

You've said money will make me self-centered and selfish, focused upon how much I have. I don't want to be that sort of gent. Make me generous to the core. I need trust in your provision, Father. Be the executor of all I have, that I pray, a keeper of the books, the accountant of my life."

"Search the scriptures; for in them ye think ye have eternal life: and they are they which testify of me." (John 5:39)

"For the word of God is quick, and powerful, and sharper than any two-edged sword, piercing even to the dividing as under of soul and spirit, and of the joints and marrow, and is a discerner of the thoughts and intents of the heart."
(Hebrews 4:12)

Nathaniel realized he stood at that crossroad labeled *Purpose.* We all travel there at some point, be it a solitary trip or for the need of multiple visits.

The signs were in plain view, on display for his acquaintance. The road had been a paved one for Nathaniel, nary a bump in sight, yet, he considered a stroll down that long dusty one that many face.

As he read his notes, Nathaniel pondered, then he pondered some more. He was ready to step off that merry-go-round he had long rode. That brass ring representing another ride no longer looked attractive. His life was no longer his own. That he understood, because God had risen to select the pleasure of life's meaning and Nathaniel welcomed that.

"God doesn't visit physically each day," Nathaniel wrote, ***"but He does make His presence known."***

"For since the creation of the world God's invisible qualities - his eternal power and divine nature - have been clearly seen, being understood from what has been made, so that men are without excuse." (Romans 1:20)

"For the earth will be filled with the knowledge of the glory of the Lord, as the waters cover the sea." (Habakkuk 2:14)

Nathaniel's pen gave analogy to, further credence of:

"Our age is one filled with anxiety, which someone

once wrote, 'It's the anxiety of meaninglessness.'

Life is a cascade of choices indeed. We are a continuing expression of those short and long term decisions we make.

Strength, I'm convinced, won't transcend from great accomplishment, rather, it's defined by how we rise above when we stumble along the way.

Each of us choose a background hue for self-portrait. I choose to paint something inspiring new.

Strikingly enough, although I don't believe in fortune-telling or the foolhardy notions of the zodiac, the last fortune cookie I consumed contained a label that read: '*Man is what he believes.'*

Lord, I need to make things right. I've been destitute of You far too long. I succumb to the realization there's no big - little You!"

As Nathaniel read the numerous entries he'd made that night, on the eve of anticipation, he marveled with awe how the spillage of a soul could be scribed upon a page.

"I recall a radio program from the 70's." He wrote. *"It was called Animal Stories. It was broadcast across the AM dial, from the Chicago station WLS. The names of the DJ duo were Uncle Lar and Little Tommy - I'm sure that wasn't their true identify. Before they began the bit, Uncle Lar would ask Little Tommy a question that pertained to animal trivia. If Little Tommy could answer the question correctly, he would win a new shiny dime, that being the redeeming reward given by his partner.*

Unfortunately, Little Tommy never won a coin. I correlate a measure of that upon myself. For years, I speculated the poor were just that, for they chose to be. I'm chiseling away at that rock hard surface, the one layered in callousness.

Little Tommy would always leap to obtain the prize, yet, systematically, he met defeat without end.

I conclude, so it is for the majority of the world's less fortunate, it's determination they grasp, but those of us who hold the prize contribute to that elusion of victory."

The swirl of expressive thought was nary foreign by regard. An evident flow was adrift upon the pages, for Nathaniel further added, *"I unequivocally admire the thoughts of John Newton. I'm sure, as he lived, Newton would have never contemplated a comparison of self and the wisdom he held to that of King Solomon. Yet, I'm convinced God gave him a measure of wisdom as he did Solomon. For Newton's words are statuesque in meaning, displaying a lure of gravitation, that being the sentiment that stirs within me.*

Newton once wrote, 'The heir of a great estate, while a child, thinks more of money in his pocket than of his inheritance. So, a Christian is often more elated by some frame of heart than by his title to glory.'

He added, 'I can conceive a living man without an arm or a leg, but not without a head or a heart; so, there are some truths essential to vital religion and that all awakened souls are taught.'

'When a Christian goes into the world,' Newton so foretold, 'because he sees it is his call, yet, while he feels it is also his cross, it will not hurt him.'

I ponder what may lay forth, be it a beckoning Call one would attest."

Determination surged intensely throughout Nathaniel's veins that night, a by-product of the tossing and turning of an uneasy sleep. Before that final drifting off had been achieved, Nathaniel became resolute, with certainty, that he'd initiate a devised plan, one given birth to days prior, with the rising sun come morn.

It was at dawn that Nathaniel awoke, be it so without the assist of the alarm. He scooted out of bed, gathered his clothes and slowly put them on. He, then out of routine, made himself a pot of coffee. A craving for flapjacks was the allure that filled his mind and Nathaniel prepared himself a moderate helping of those. The enticing smell was irresistible and Nathaniel sat at the table to smother the pile with some good ole' maple syrup, as he watched the dab of butter begin to melt then slide over the side of the stack.

When he was finished with the meal Nathaniel cleared the table, then he cleaned the dishes in a wash pan filled with a bit of water he'd boiled on the stove. Once he'd completed the task, Nathaniel sat back down to gather his thoughts.

Upon the table rest the satellite phone and laptop computer he'd purchased back in Chicago - Nathaniel stared at the pair for a good while.

Fortune would have it that the batteries on both still held a charge when Nathaniel checked.

With a closing of his eyes, and a brief silent prayer, Nathaniel set out to enact that plan he had so devised.

He first connected the phone to the computer by use of a data support cable. Then Nathaniel dialed the number to the Swiss bank which held the funds he'd transferred before leaving town. He then began the electronic transfer of everything in that account to a bank in Chicago. A bit of uneasiness held Nathaniel for a time, but it subsided soon after he'd cleared all those security hurdles. Then, with the last crunch of the numbers, it was done.

Upon completion of the transaction, Nathaniel elected to phone an old friend. It was as the phone rang on the other end that anticipation began to grow within.

"Hello." A voice soon said.

"Pastor Dan?" Nathaniel asked.

"Yes."

"It's Nathaniel."

With a tone of elevated excitement to his voice, the minister said, "Oh … my lord!

"Nathaniel! Are you alright?"

"I'm well," was the reply.

"My god, Nathaniel! The FBI's been here ... asking questions. Where are you?" The good Reverend probed.

"I'd rather not convey that."

The Pastor said, "I need to know you're OK!"

"I'm fine ... you might say I'm working on searing the stigma of a soul."

The good Reverend didn't quite know what to make of that, but was quick to point out, "One of the richest men in the world doesn't just drop off the face of the planet without somebody taking notice ... asking questions and such."

"Not to worry." Nathaniel replied, with jest that was calm and unwavering.

"Your disappearance was headline news, Nathaniel! That's

not something you should take lightly." The minister conveyed with concern. "The story ran on the nightly news for weeks ... it was plastered on the front page of every paper imaginable."

"I phoned to say there's been some funds transferred to the church's account." Nathaniel interjected.

The Minister said, "What?" then tried to calm himself.

"It's a little over seven hundred."

Pastor Dan's curious reply was that of, "Seven hundred?"

Responsive, but with a slight hint of sarcasm, Nathaniel said, "Seven hundred million!"

It was a fight to keep his composure, but Dan's reply was, "I don't know what to say."

"Say you'll put it to good use." Nathaniel added. "Feed the poor."

The good Reverend could sense Nathaniel wasn't in the mood for lengthy conversation and so then said, "I had a dream about you the other night, Nathaniel."

"Tell me."

"At the beginning of the dream you were dishing out food to strangers standing in a soup line." The minister did describe. "In the second part of the dream you were driving a semi. You were the lead of a convoy of trucks that stretched for miles ... all of them were full of food."

Pastor Dan had no way of knowing, nor did he realize it, but Nathaniel was beginning to show the tale-tell signs of choking up.

Nathaniel said, "Better go," as a stir of emotion began to surface.

There was a brief silence that filled the air, then Dan said,

"You take care my friend ... I can't say thanks enough."

Nathaniel sat and stared at the fire for the remainder of the day, never leaving the confines of solace walls.

The following day, along with many others that ensued, gave birth to an unusual warming trend - considering the time of year.

The thought of giving a fortune away was beginning to soak in. The diminishment of all, no doubt, gave Nathaniel reason to ponder his future. Yet, he felt a warmth of peace beyond explanation. It was something mere words could never quite possibly describe.

The temperature outside began to rise that week, hovering in the fifties for a couple more. The surroundings had been in thaw for days, and thus, a sense of adventure began to gnaw at Nathaniel's bones.

A majority of the snow had already melted away. A shift in the landscape had a residual effect upon Nathaniel. It was a boost, of sorts, for his confidence. The thought of *Spring is a time of new beginnings* began to flood his mind daily; the ascension of a spirit, it surely was.

Nathaniel seized the opportunity to take advantage of the unseasonable weather whenever he could. He found many occasions to wet a line by day. The fish, often times, were reluctant and not in the mood for any such offerings though. The evenings were a calming lure, peaceful beyond imagination, for Nathaniel saw many sunsets. A description of beauty, only a master could capture upon canvas, was that orange glow amidst a layering of purple clouds, embraced by the backdrop of a picturesque mountain towering over the surrounding plain.

Twilight drew near that particular evening. The air was warm and refreshing. Nathaniel thought building a small fire to observe a few stars might be nice, and he did so atop one of the cliffs hugging the north end of the lake.

An abundance of dry sticks was readily at hand and Nathaniel had a book of matches in his pocket; which left little struggle to constructing a fire. All was quiet. The stars were now out in ample glory, the fire raged, and Nathaniel was soaking in the tranquil beauty of it all.

However, the fire drew down rather quickly. The small branches used to start it were consumed by the fire in short order, which meant Nathaniel had to gather some more, preferably larger ones, to keep the flames from dying out. He did so, then threw many more upon the burning pile.

The evening was indeed relaxing, but things were about to change.

An uneasiness soon gripped Nathaniel, for he could hear the rustle of brittle leaves behind him. He felt a cold chill, then the hair on his neck began to stand erect. As he moved to tum slowly, Nathaniel could hear the nearby panting of an animal breathing and then a growl.

When he turned to face the uncertain, Nathaniel's fear deepened. Standing only a few feet away was a wolf. The beast appeared quite angry; with fangs protruded, it displayed its teeth and growled at Nathaniel intensely.

Before long three more wolves arrived, no doubt the remaining members of the pack.

Nathaniel was all too aware wild animals could sense fear in a man, and it was a fierce struggle for him to mask that fight.

Then, out of the darkness, a man approached from behind the wolves. He was dressed strangely, adorned in ragged clothes. Oddly enough, the wolves weren't alarmed by his presence. The beasts didn't seem concerned with whom stood behind them, only to stare at Nathaniel with vicious disdain.

The man began to pet the creatures, one by one.

Then Nathaniel asked, "Are those yours?"

"The world is mine." He replied, with an air of boldness.

Nathaniel couldn't get a good look at the stranger's face, for he never glanced up. The stranger looked down when speaking, stroking the head of each beast while doing so.

The stare down by the creatures was beginning to take its toll upon Nathaniel, challenging that once held notion of fearlessness he thought he had.

"What can I do for you?" Nathaniel asked, out of the birth of nervousness.

With that said, the stranger lifted his head to gaze upon Nathaniel. Fear had given way to reason long ago, choking it so without mercy. Terror now had a firm hold, for the stranger's eyes were jet black, pure evil by nature, for there were no whites in those eyes.

"Who ... who are you?" Nathaniel pleaded.

The stranger responded by saying, "I have many names."

The thought of, *"Greater is He that's within me than he that's in the world,"* began to stir within Nathaniel's soul.

The wolves' growls didn't lessen, nor did the man's defiant nature.

Nathaniel then blurted out, "You're Beelzebub!"

With a retort, the evil one said, "You're very perceptive,

Nathaniel."

"How do you know my name?"

Satan then added, "I know all about you. Serve me. I'll give you more than you can possibly dream."

That sense of fear began to quickly subside, then a surge of fortitude began to flow through Nathaniel's veins. He then shouted out, "God of heaven ... help me!"

Without tarry the wind began to blow, be it that there was none evident before, then it intensified. The wolves, in turn, began to circle Nathaniel.   He had no doubt they were about to attack. Then the wind began to swirl about Nathaniel, picking up the fire with it. A wall of fire, gaining height and strength, began to spin, encircling Nathaniel as if to protect him. He felt empowered that God would answer that lone cry.

The wolves began to whimper and then back away, and the evil one shielded his face from the seemingly intense heat, yet, Nathaniel didn't feel a thing from the flames. It was as if he was standing in the eye of a tornado, one churning with a consuming fire, but he was suffering no harm.

The evil one guarded his face, then yelled, for the fire's roar was immense, "Kneel before me and I'll give you the White House!"

Nathaniel refused to answer, and not long after the wolves began to separate and run away. With a taste of defeat certain, Satan followed the pack of four into the darkness and then disappeared.

Within a matter of minutes, the wind began to die down as did the encompassing fire. Left standing alone, the light of the moon now the lone guide of illumination, Nathaniel could only mouth, "Wow!"

That fateful statement which John Newton penned, the one Nathaniel read just days prior, now echoed in his head. "Many have puzzled themselves about the origin of evil." Newton did write. "I observe there is evil, and that there is a way to escape it, and with that I begin and end."

Chapter Eighteen
Glorious Promise

A scarce few could boast of experiencing a wage of spiritual warfare, an intervention of the divine, or the gird of satanic espionage for that matter, yet, Nathaniel had undergone a lifetime's worth in the grasp of days.

He was now, more so than ever, conscious of the supernatural and aware factions were partaking in active hostility all about him. His consensus was great things were in store, an image of that lay upon the horizon, for Satan was no doubt privilege to those facts and the stakes were high.   Besides, Nathaniel foresaw, Beelzebub would never waste his time on those he owns - that was a given.

Nathaniel had never been one to sit idly by, wait upon others or the world to roll past.

Although he would never acclaim the time spent at Lost Lake to be frivolous, he was indeed growing restless inside.

 With the progression of time came those distinctive warming days of May and Nathaniel had scribbled the word *Beginnings* through the dates across the calendar. Toward the bottom of the page he also wrote, ***"Don't be in distress if the majority of the journey lies yet ahead.   Even the tallest of trees in the forest began as a small seed."***

It was evening and a bit cool, yet, it wasn't something a modest jacket couldn't accommodate.

Nathaniel had finished his supper then decided to spend some time soaking in the tranquil night. He enjoyed spending time in observation of God's wonder from that old rocking chair. Many a thought came to him there, often numerous ones, for he gave comparison of that worn rocker and unassuming porch to that of a loving ear of an old friend.

The night sky was clear at first, full of stars. Some of them were a glow so bright only imagination could apprize. They felt as near and remarkable as the heart. With a wave you could almost grab a fist full. Before long, however, a disturbance began afar.

Nathaniel had been called a thinker throughout life, and, by self-admission, he'd accepted that brand. He often thought it a plague though, for he analyzed just about everything and pondered upon things that many would overlook.

The wheels of thought were now a spin in that mind of his and a bit of reason gave calculation.

"The eve was a humbling wonder." He thought. For like God, and the heavens above, it all seems distant at first but they're closer than one can possibly imagine.

It wasn't long before a heavenly light show began to occur upon the horizon. It was a spectacular vision of God's hand cradling the plain. Expanse was but a guess, yet, something was a stir amongst the glorious off to the West.

There was a curious ease to it all though, a slight smell of rain upon the breeze. A silent spectacle of the miraculous was taking stage for Nathaniel's pleasure.

Although the distance was too great to hear a clash of thunder, it was the backdrop of clouds now erupting with a ration of bright light that gave every indication there was a squall ablow afar.

The apparent separation of the tranquil captured Nathaniel's fascination. A slight blue mist held the rippled washboard of thin purple clouds to; it was a forerunner of the storm. The display was a distinctive divide to those puffy clouds a roar with activity. A cascade of glory had been strewn across the sky.

With the instruments of expression in hand, he rocked. Nathaniel gazed for a while upon the wrath afar - that which words could hardly explain. Then he rocked to the rhythm of a few thoughts.

"I feel like a man with no money in his pockets." He chronicled. *"But is allowed to draw upon all he wants from one who is infinitely rich."*

The vacancy of the page had a tendency to mesmerize, but Nathaniel wasn't spellbound for long. For he then added, *"I am, therefore, at once, a begger and a rich man."*

He would later pen: *"That's a statement all too suitable to my circumstance, another foreboding thought of Newton's indeed, one mirroring my soul."*

The continuation of thought didn't end with that for Nathaniel began to document, in that stuffed journal of his, that which was spilling over from within.

"I've been contemplating a return to Chicago." He wrote. *"It's been close to a year now - one of seclusion. I can't disperse an urge to tread upon new beginnings. I feel compelled, swayed, by the divine no doubt, to hear those who cry out. It's a call to mend the fabric of humanity with the thread of compassion."*

Nathaniel wasn't one to talk to himself, only rarely in the past he did, yet, it was becoming a frequent practice of his.

He gave conclusion to his writings then closed the book. Once he'd laid it to the side Nathaniel rocked. Then he affixed his eyes upon the heavens. He stared at the horizon for a good while, then began to have dialogue with himself and the host of it all.

"I've been a real bore ... disappointment ... haven't I … Lord? I compare myself to those cardboard cut-outs I see in the department stores ... The ones that resemble celebrities ... You know. They look real ... yet ... they're just some doctored-up fake ... paper thin in substance. I don't want to be like that anymore ... someone that's in garnishment of self ... Stretch forth Your hand ... visualize Your will for me ... That's all I care about anyway."

A brief duration of silence spent gazing upon the commotion afar followed. Nathaniel's mind began to drift thither, to eventually mull upon what's referred to as *The Great Commission*. It was something he'd read just days before.

"Then the eleven disciples went to Galilee, to the mountain where Jesus had told them to go. When they saw him, they worshiped him; but some doubted. Then Jesus came to them and said, 'All authority in heaven and on earth has been given to me. Therefore go and make disciples of all nations, baptizing them in the name of the Father and of the Son and of the Holy Spirit, and teaching them to obey everything I have commanded you. And surely I am with you always, to the very end of the age.'" (Matthew 28:16-20)

Nathaniel did then divulge, "I've never been baptized, Lord."

With a stir of introspect, he then in turn fashioned an

inquisitive query; it was a notion indeed, one laced in
fascination. Nathaniel was in search of answers.

"Would it be a fallacy to conceive ... act upon the possibility
of immersing myself in the lake?" He quizzed of the thin air.
"An eventual reply on that one would be nice."

Baptism is symbolic. He thought. It's death to the old life,
giving way to the announcement of a new one in Christ.

Nathaniel's thoughts had dwelled little upon such things
before. With a shove of mental gist, he ventured the importance
there of wouldn't be forsaken long.

Nathaniel's mind began to drift once more and with a lean of
his outstretched hand he scooped up the Journal from where it
lay.

He wrote, ***"I can't get the ponder of a reoccurring pry out of
my head.***

***No matter what I say, what I believe, or what I do, I'm
bankrupt without love. I've been contemplating upon that for
days! I went as far as to write it upon one of the walls. Then,
one day, I found some reassurance."***

*"If I give all I possess to the poor and surrender my body
that I may boast, but have not love, I gain nothing."*
1 Corinthians 13:3 states it best."

A jest of conversation bestowed upon self, yet spoken with
boldness before the heavens, made Nathaniel a bit thirsty. He
said, "Thanks for listening Lord ... and ... of course ... the
splendid light show."

Nathaniel then arose from his chair and turned to retrieve
the lantern resting upon the window sill, the one he'd used to
illuminate his writing, and went inside.

Nathaniel's destiny, he perceived, would surely set the stage of change for a minority, his hope was for many however, possibly, a number of the world.

Though of late, Nathaniel was experiencing a reoccurring dream - be it that of blessing or weigh, a benevolent befalling it was. The "mosaic," as he called it, was coming in greater frequency now and was always the same, beginning in like fashion and consistently ending with similar resolve.

Nathaniel began to shiver a little not long after he'd removed his jacket. The thought of a small fire knocking off the chill crossed his mind and he built one. It didn't take long for the blaze to accomplish its task. Nathaniel hadn't been sleepy in the least so he dragged the rocker inside, positioning it in front of the fireplace.

He rocked some, staring at the dancing flames, then Nathaniel began to reflect upon that dream he kept having.

Nathaniel was always alone at the start. The dream begins with a walk down a lonely road. It appears to be a worn country road. A single lane thoroughfare that's in dire need of paving.

Nathaniel doesn't recognize the location at all, nor is he privilege to the destination of which he's traveling toward.

He encounters several chuckholes along the way, yet, the light of a full moon illuminates their hazardous presence that he may avoid them.

Nathaniel walks, for what seems like a long time, before he realizes someone or something is watching him from the bushes that line the way. He can hear a deep breathing, and a sense of fear begins to stir within him. His pace quickens, but the haunt of that breathing won't leave.

It isn't long before he sees the candescent glow of a pair of reddened eyes watching from the shadows. Nathaniel is starting to get really scared by that time, but then something in the distance begins to instill a sense of peace.

Many a dream are opaque, less distinguished, fuzzy at best, diminishing quickly with time, then fading from memory. But this one was much different, it made an indelible impact and seared itself upon the mind's sequestered vision.

From a quickened pace Nathaniel begins to trot, then break out into a run. He runs several yards till he reaches the base of a small knoll. Emanating from the top of the knoll is a lucid display, a soft cast of light, it's luminous, yet limpid at once, calming. Nathaniel soon realizes there's an absence of heavy breathing. When he turns to look around, those noticeable eyes are no longer peering upon him. That sense of fear is now gone, worry and distress have left, and an incredible feeling of peace has arrived.

Curiosity is almost too much for him to bear, so Nathaniel begins a trek up the hill. Surprisingly enough, he's no longer out of breath and reaches the top of the knoll rather quickly.

At the top are many gardens, streams, and fields a glow with a bloom of wonder. It's beauty beyond fathom. Strange. It's no longer night, but now day.

Off to the right, Nathaniel notices something else. Cascading down a series of shallow, steplike, rocky ledges are three waterfalls, all descending into a single pool. The water is clear and in abundant flow. It's blissful indeed.

Nathaniel sees a faint mist hovering over the bank at the opposite end of the pool. With his curiosity heightened he takes a stroll through the mist, which now appears to turn into a thickening fog.

That sense of peace remains surprisingly true, clad all about him, but the haze soon dissipates to reveal that which leaves Nathaniel speechless - well, somewhat.

Before long Nathaniel blurted out, "Where am I?"

A permeating voice does then say, "Are thou ready, my child?"

Nathaniel's a little startled by that and snaps back with a retort of, "Ready ... ready for what?" as he glances about to find who's there.

That voice, which seems to echo from everywhere, asks the same question of Nathaniel again.

Nathaniel then asks, "Who are you ... where are you?"

"I am that I am ... the Alpha and Omega ... the beginning and the end."

At once Nathaniel realizes he's in the presence of God and falls to his knees - weeping. "Forgive me, Lord." He states.

God claims, "All is forgiven." Then He commands Nathaniel to: "Arise!"

Nathaniel is then instructed to step upon that which lay before him. He recognizes it to be a path, but it's like nothing he's ever seen. It measures roughly five feet or so wide, and is paved with transparent brick. Under those bricks are an endless number of stars, planets, and galaxies, stretching to infinitely.

God asks, "Are thou ready?"

A bit of hesitation rears itself, and Nathaniel wonders, "What is this?"

With a consoling tone, as only God can provide, He replies: "A Celestial Life Tour."

Walking upon the stars is a little unnerving for Nathaniel at first. Yet, he's quick to surmise that's, no doubt, what faith's all about. With that, he takes a step, then another, and another. In a moment, all that present fear has disappeared and he begins to amble down the path. In doing so, Nathaniel embraces an admiration for the astonishing beauty of it all.

Forthwith, Nathaniel sees an obstruction just ahead. As he draws near, it appears to be that old boardroom at the office - the path runs directly through it.

Oddly enough, there appear to be no walls. If there are any, they're transparent for Nathaniel waves his arm in front of himself to check for their existence.

There are several men sitting at a large table. The chair on the end, the one Nathaniel was assigned to at one time, is unoccupied. The men appear to be arguing, but the gist of the conversation is hard for Nathaniel to make out.

As he's observing that apparent board meeting, that voice from above urges Nathaniel to move on.

"What am I seeing, Lord? Is this a vision of the past?" For a moment, God says nothing. Then Nathaniel persists.

The answer given is: "It is what thou hath experienced in life."

"How can I continue?" He asks. Then with a slight sweep of the hand, Nathaniel adds, "These people are in the way!"

God states, "They are but an image, my child."

Nathaniel's delayed reply is: "I get it ... apparitions."

That voice from above then says, "Thou must go."

The table straddled the path and as Nathaniel inched forward he moved through the piece of furniture. As soon as he'd made it through, he turned to look at those still sitting at the table. They

were still apparently arguing with each other, unaware of
Nathaniel's presence in the least.

Nathaniel left there and did again begin a stroll. The path
had now begun to parallel a beach. He recalled visiting such a
place as this. He found an occasion once to visit a beach, when
he had a rare moment of leisure time, during a business trip to
California.

He remembered removing his shoes, the wind blowing
about his hair, how the sand felt between his toes, watching a
child build a sandcastle at water's edge, then how the tide
wiped it out, the many just swimming care free, and how happy
he was - be it all for a short while. "Oh ... the smell of the
ocean." Nathaniel pondered.

The path did a bit of winding after that, eventually leading to
the infield of a stadium.

Nathaniel recognized it to be Wrigley Field. Home of the
Chicago Cubs.

A game was going on. Surprisingly so, the stands were
full of fans. It looked to be a sold-out crowd. The noise was
immense, as was the apparent excitement. It was a day game;
one being played against the Cincinnati Reds. As he stood
near second base, to stare at the scoreboard, Nathaniel said to
himself, "I remember that game!"

It was the bottom of the ninth and the Cubs were ahead.
Rarely, were they in the lead at the end of any game that year
for Nathaniel recalled the team had a losing record that
season.

Nathaniel could see concern in the eyes of that Cubs pitcher
when he turned to step off the mound between throws, because

the bases were loaded with opposing runners.

With two outs registered, Nathaniel knew a play at the plate to end the game was forthcoming rather soon. He made his way past the pitcher, walked toward home plate, then Nathaniel positioned himself between the catcher and the umpire.

The batter at the plate was the best hitter the Reds had in their line-up. Nathaniel knew the pitcher would throw a steady diet of fastballs to this guy. Yet he still flinched a couple times when the ball struck the catcher's glove with a loud thud.

He thought, "One cannot imagine the velocity of a pitch from there in the stands."

The fifth pitch thrown to the batter was a fastball down the middle and he drove it deep, off the wall in right field. The crowd roared as the outfielder grabbed the ball on the bounce, then stood to cheer when he threw it toward home.

A couple runs had scored and the third was about to cross the plate when the catcher caught the ball and turned to tag the runner. The runner slid to avoid the tag, but missed the plate with an outstretched hand. When the runner slid past, the catcher dove at him to make the tag. When he did, the game was over for the Cubs were victorious 6 to 5.

As Nathaniel stood behind home plate, he got lost in a bit of inner thought while observing the display of emotions by all in attendance. The umpires wasted little time exiting the field, their faces exhibited a lack of expression, as the Cub players gave embrace to each other in front of the pitcher's mound. The crowd was loud and stood to applaud for quite a while. Several Reds players hung their heads while clearing the visitor dugout.

Nathaniel said, "That was a great game, Lord!" Then his mind began to reflect upon why he went.

Irwin Industries held season tickets, a couple box seats located on the first row between third and home, and Nathaniel took a potential client to that particular game. The client really enjoyed himself, or so it would have appeared, for Nathaniel was successful in his endeavor to land that account.

Nathaniel was lucky if he made a game in a given year. He was always much too busy to excuse himself from work and gave the tickets away all too often, or they sat vacant.

As Nathaniel stood to ponder it all, the crowd began to head for the exits and that voice from above soon said, "Thou must move on!"

The path led to the street, turned, and in a moment's notice, was upon the doorsteps of a church. Nathaniel recognized it to be Pastor Dan's place.

A church service was being conducted and Nathaniel followed the path through the lobby and down the aisle. It went past the pulpit, then turned to exit through the side door.

Nathaniel stopped down front, then for the longest time stood amidst the crowd along the front row. He was in observation of many that had responded to an altar call. Those who were before the altar were praying. Some were kneeling as they looked skyward. Others bowed their heads while they stood. Several cried with arms raised. They were accepting Salvation - the redemption of Christ.

Nathaniel left the church, not long after that, to tread upon

the path once more. This time he walked a great distance.
Nothing lay straddling the path anymore. Yet, several things
began to appear all about in the surrounding areas.

Directly to Nathaniel's right, only yards from the path, was a
small pond. Nathaniel had occasion to smile, for he saw two
older men fishing from a boat. He uttered to himself. "I never
went fishing till I spent some time at Lost Lake. I had every
opportunity to do so though. I lived next to one of the largest
lakes in the world ... A Great Lake ... Lake Michigan ... never
found the time ... I suppose."

In the distance, off to the left, was an amusement park.
Nathaniel could see people milling about and the rides were in
motion. He could hear the screams of excitement with every twist
and turn of the rollercoaster. "They look like they're having a
good time." He thought. "I've never been to one."

Nathaniel found himself walking with a stiffer pace. Along
the way he observed children at play, parents picking them up
after school, teens eating burgers at McDonald's. The kids in the
restaurant were joking around with each other, smiling, having a
good time. As Nathaniel stared through the window, in
observation of the teens, he commented. "I could not tell you
what a Big Mac tastes like ... let alone boast of having a friend to
share the experience with."

A sense of guilt was stirring within Nathaniel, its presence
felt, then he asked, "Lord ... what are these things I see?"

God's response was, "It is that of which thou hath not
experienced."

As he watched the teens through the pane, the tears began to
flow down Nathaniel's cheeks. He told himself, "I've missed

much."

That voice from above soon said, "Thou must go."

With that Nathaniel wiped away the tears, then he began to travel the path once more.

Nathaniel had walked, in his estimation, fifteen or twenty miles so far. He saw nothing for a time after that but planets and stars beneath him. Although it was a humbling sight, each ensuing step gave curiosity an edge to build upon. He soon asked of God, "Is the distance the same for every tour?"

The Lord replied, "It is not."

A bit of delayed hesitation ensued, then Nathaniel said, "You're of few words ... aren't you, Lord?"

When God didn't respond, Nathaniel said, in jest, "You're like a tour guide one never sees."

A moment later, God said, "Thou must continue ... the path of life beath different for all."

In short order, a hastening of harmony began to occur. A few individuals, then several, began to approach Nathaniel. Many walked alongside him. Others just shook his hand, then walked away. They seemed to appear out of thin air, yet, from all directions in staggered sequence. He recognized them all. A few were close friends. However, he considered many to be nothing more than acquaintances.

Nathaniel thought it was strikingly odd the amount of time each individual spent with him as he ventured down that marvelous path. Many of those, he recognized as a business acquaintance, stopped only briefly to give a greeting or hand shake. The opposite was true for those he considered friends. Those individuals spent time with Nathaniel, walking and talking to him, telling him how much they valued his friendship. When the procession of visitors adjourned, Nathaniel asked. "What was that?"

God's reply was, "Many thou hath come in contact with ... time spent with them was but a portion ... a measure of love thou had for them."

"I was going to ask you that ... yet ... what was I thinking." Nathaniel did so attest. "You're an all-knowing God ... with answer in hand ... several steps ahead."

Nathaniel then noticed something off to the side that seemed a little peculiar. Standing upon a hill, to the right, was a couple. They were holding hands and using the free ones to wave at Nathaniel. He said, "Those people act like they know me!"

God's response was: "They do, my child."

"Did they have a stake in my life as well?" Nathaniel asked.

"They are your great-grandparents, my child ... Eli and Mary."

A sense of overwhelming joy overtook Nathaniel. Then his composure faded. He asked. "Can I go over there ... talk to them?"

"Thy cannot."

With that, Nathaniel noticed the couple had begun walking toward him. As they drew closer, they began to run. As soon as they reached him, they threw their arms around Nathaniel to embrace him and then gave him an added kiss upon the cheek.

Nathaniel could do no more than cry. He was overwhelmed with emotion, to the point of being speechless. He then fell to his knees, hugging their legs. His great-grandparents in turn caressed his neck and shoulders - then, they were gone.

Nathaniel remained on his knees, sobbing, with face in

hand, long after realizing Eli and Mary had departed.

That voice from above did eventually say, "Thou must finish that which has begun."

Nathaniel could not bring himself to rise. So overcome by it all, he continued to weep harder.

God was moved by that display of emotion, and then revealed to Nathaniel: "Eli and Mary have been watching you for some time, my child ... praying for you ... asking that thou be used."

Nathaniel sobbed a short time more, then wiped his eyes and said, "I never knew."

With a gentle urging, God stated, "Thou must go."

Nathaniel was eventually successful in regaining his composure, but it was no easy task.

He had walked a moderate distance, setting out upon the path yet again, when he saw something astonishing upon the horizon.

As he grew closer, Nathaniel could see the outline of a large city. Before long he was in awe, marveling over her design. "Magnificent" was the word he used. It was nothing short of stunning to look at, all bathed in brilliant light.

As Nathaniel approached, that sense of reverence within him deepened. Waiting at a colossal gate was someone Nathaniel needed no introduction to. He knew who he was without speaking a word. Clothed in a full-length robe, one of pure white, stood the Gatekeeper. The Guardian greeted his guest with an outstretched hand. A surge of emotion began to flow through Nathaniel's veins, and his speech departed with it, for the Gatekeeper's hand was pierced through.

Nathaniel's curiosity was heightened all the while when he observed a large book, one held by the Guardian's side. When he inquired as to what it was, the Gatekeeper replied, "It's The Lamb's Book of Life."

Unsure of himself, or that his name would be upon the scroll, Nathaniel shifted his eyes from the book. As a ploy, he then tried to change the subject by inquiring of other things.

"What is this place?" He asked of the Gatekeeper.

"It's the City of Crystal ... the New Jerusalem."

Nathaniel was still in awe, yet somewhat nervous, when he pointed and asked, "That's a massive gate ... What's it made of?"

"Solid pearl" was the reply.

There was a total of twelve entrances to the city, all such as this. Gates always open to the invited, yet, it was Nathaniel's path that led to this particular one.

Nathaniel said, "Words cannot describe this place ... it's beautiful!"

In response, the Gatekeeper offered little more than a friendly smile.

An open gate revealed a never-ending street, one supported upon the clouds.

As Nathaniel's mind began to wonder, he surveyed the surroundings. He then made the comment, "The sun never sets here ... night has no place within these walls ... does it?"

The Guardian became solemn with that and gave a profound answer of, "Light cannot dwell with darkness."

With a glance upward, then to the side, Nathaniel added, "Those walls are really high... thick ... they're so ... beautiful."

"They're Jasper ... two hundred feet thick by your measure."

The Gatekeeper replied.

Nathaniel was taken back by the supporting foundations under the walls also. They were encrusted with precious jewels; a few he recognized, emeralds, sapphires, topaz, yet many he didn't.

Nathaniel could see from where he stood a great street running through the city and it was transparent as glass.

On either side of the street were trees blooming with fruit. Down the center of the great street ran a river - *The River of Life.* Its water was flowing crystal clear.

The Gatekeeper was none other than Jesus, and he could sense his new guest was still a bit apprehensive so he placed a hand, in a loving way as only He can, upon Nathaniel's shoulder.

When He said, "**Well** done ... thy good and faithful servant," Nathaniel dropped to his knees and the tears did fall.

Chapter Nineteen
Revelation

The weather over recent days had been quite pleasant and Nathaniel found it refreshing to leave the door propped open by day, the windows cracked wide at night. The cool breeze blowing through the cabin that morn reminded him of Navy Pier back home. Those memories of when he felt the wind blowing in off Lake Michigan while strolling the shore, enjoying the simplicity of a hot dog during a long lunch, were a mull. The more thought he gave to it, the greater his longing for Chicago was.

Restlessness was gaining a foothold upon Nathaniel's soul; the reason being he hadn't left the cabin for days. With elbows propped upon that old table, a rub to the face with his hands, Nathaniel pondered what to write. He then scratched out:

"July 3rd - The Year of Our Lord, 1990

I have been nursing a sore ankle for days.

I was surveying the property last week when I accidentally discovered an old root cellar - it had the indication of being such.

Its location is directly behind the cabin, to the side of the privy. I estimated the distance to be roughly forty yards. If it was once domed with earth, its round summit is no more. Its existence has escaped my detection all this time.

The entrance was covered with planks. They have since become rotten. The boards were covered with a few inches of dirt, accompanied by a blanket of sod. When I stepped upon that area it gave way and I fell probably ten feet or so. I twisted my ankle in the process, was bruised and scraped up a bit, I'm still trying to recover from that.

I found an old generator in that cellar, along with a container of gasoline. There were several other miscellaneous things down there, but none as important as the generator.

Once I'd gained my composure, with an injury, I tried to assess the functionality of the unit. I have determined it to be a lost cause however. When I removed the cap from the container the gasoline smelled foul. The generator was covered with dust, but I gave the pull rope a tug nevertheless. It broke off in my hand.

I have never professed to being a mechanic, but I'm afraid an effort to save that piece of equipment would no doubt be one in vain.

I left everything as it was, endured the pain, and crawled back to the cabin on my hands and knees. I'll deal with that hole in the ground later.

The batteries on the computer and phone are running low. I thought that generator might provide some electricity to charge them, but then I recalled having an adapter that can be plugged into the cigarette lighter of the SUV. I would attest that avenue is my only option now."

In association with a piercing memory that now weighed upon Nathaniel's conscious a moment of hesitation did follow. He then later wrote.

"I have been giving a lot of thought to something I saw a while back, that of which I've neglected to document.

I came across a grave sometimes back. It was in the middle of nowhere, at the base of the mountain, along an old trail, strange

I never saw it, all those times I ventured that trail, till I stumbled over it.

The grave was marked with an old headstone chiseled out of rock. It looked quite old, worn by the weather. I could barely make out the words etched upon its face, but they read: Here lies a good man.

I must admit, I was left gaping as to who he was. I wondered who dug the grave, put him there. How did he die. When did he die? Those and a host of other unanswered questions raced through my mind.

I have visited that grave a couple times since. Be it a foolish notion or not, I talk to that marker whenever I'm there. I've always been one to pay respect to the deceased. Be it odd or not, I find it reassuring to strike up a lopsided conversation when I visit. It's a purge to my soul, besides, you couldn't ask for a better listener.

I never gave much thought to death, or to the mark I may or may not leave until coming here. How fitting the characterization Lost Lake *bares - I've found renewal while residing here. I've begun to see things in a different light. I thought I had it figured out, a grasp of what life was all about, but the bewilderment of the world had its say and threw up an obstacle or two along the way."*

As Nathaniel sat to gather a few more thoughts, a stir within, he took notice of his reflection in a glass of tea he'd poured now resting upon the table. He took a drink from it, then raised the glass to examine its reflective properties. A distorted image bore itself now in Nathaniel's hand. The sight of it brought on a surge of self-examination that became exceedingly more prevalent the longer he stared.

Then, after a short sip, he set the glass down to pen, ***"How long shall I hover between opinions?***

The things of the world shall pass, that is a given, yet, building that of the unseen is a far greater task!"

Nathaniel scooped up the glass yet again, this time to finish its contents. With that he took a quick glance at the empty glass before setting it down, then said to himself, "I think I'll spend the Fourth on the Lake … maybe do a little fishing … toast the celebration with a nice glass of tea."

Nathaniel laid his pen down and pushed the journal to the side with that last entry. Much to his intrigue, he began to hear a cooing sound coming from outside. He recognized that sound. He'd heard it before. When he looked through the open door, he caught a glimpse of a dove waddling back and forth atop the handrail of the porch. It wasn't there long till it flew off. But Nathaniel enjoyed a view of the creature, be it one ever-so-short.

Nathaniel hobbled over to the stove, poured himself another glass of tea, then sat back down to write some more soon after.

With a flip through the Journal, he came across a blank page and then Nathaniel proceeded to fill it. With the writing of that usual illegible penmanship, he began: ***"I had a dream last night - its visualization was significant, not one easily expelled from memory.***

At the beginning of the dream, I was standing in the doorway of a factory. It looked like an older one, absent automation and the advancement of technology, built around the turn of the century it would appear, dusty, dirty, and the lights were dim.

I began a self-guided tour shortly thereafter, to assess the capability of the facility I would imagine. In the process, I came across several workers doing various tasks - spot welding, spray painting, and subassembly work. All of those who labored took notice of me, but never spoke. They glanced up, yet just gave a nod. Men and women alike. It was as they knew me, but lacked interest in interaction.

As I followed the overhead conveyor, that ran throughout the plant, I realized they were producing a finished product that resembled some sort of engine housing.

At the end of the line were two men. They were unloading parts from the conveyor. It appeared they were preparing the housings for shipment as well. Behind the men stood a large open door, it appeared to be some twenty feet in height. An assumption of course.

One of the men looked all-too-familiar to me, the other gentleman did not. For the life of me, I couldn't draw upon a name to match that face - that's a distinction that rarely invades my graces.

As a demonstration of cordial courtesy, I extended my hand toward the one I thought I knew. Instead of shaking my hand, he simply shook his head. His refusal to shake my hand bothered me. His attitude had surfaced, needing no words. His partner also shook his head, when I turned to extend my hand toward him. Like the first, his feelings, too, were on display. Then, both simply walked away.

Within moments, a bright shaft of light began to beam through the door. The focus of my attention then fell upon that.

*When I turned to look back, the men were gone and the
conveyor was no longer on.*

*Curiosity intervened thereafter and I went outside to find that
source of light.*

*I discovered a road out there. It ran past the back of the
facility. The thoroughfare was a narrow one. It was a single
lane that looked like it had just been paved.*

*I began a trek upon that road, and hadn't gone far when
curiosity overtook me once more. When I looked back the
factory was beginning to decay, slowly implode, until it was little
more than an ugly pile.*

*As I walked down the road it began to glaze over with ice. I
found that odd for it was a sunny day. It made me watchful of
my footing.*

*In the distance, to my left, I could see a woman. She looked
familiar as well, but a name escaped me. Of all things, she was
riding a stalk of corn!*

*The stalk was moving, plowing through the ground, but it hit
something and came to an abrupt halt - throwing the woman off.*

*I ran over to lend some assistance, but by the time I reached
her she was already standing. She appeared at the ready to
mount it once more. I asked her if she was all right, and then
she nodded her head as to say yes.*

*I couldn't help but stare at her for the longest while. I
eventually said something like, 'Do I know you?' She refused to
answer, only to look away. I thought to myself it looked like my
mother, but no words were exchanged.*

*Curiosity again came into play and I found myself examining
the stalk. I noticed it was broken at the base and the ears had*

been stripped away. For some unknown reason, I set out to repair it. As I did, another person came alongside. It was a man. He offered no assistance and kept his distance. It would seem he knew the woman, for she wasn't alarmed by his presence.

There appeared to be an electrical connection at the base of the stalk. Once I finished making the necessary repairs, affixing the broken shaft of the stalk to its base, it then stood erect.

No sooner than I said, 'There you go,' the woman took mount of the stalk in preparation to depart.

As I stood in observation of the woman's actions, I noticed an obstacle upon the horizon. It was something I had not seen before. A lake was now impeding the way.

I said, 'You can't go that way.' With hesitation, I told her, 'There's no way of knowing how deep the water is. That connection will short out anyway.'

With that offering of concern the man shoved the woman and shouted a persistent 'Go!'

I felt it best to leave after that, get back upon the road and higher ground.

The woman had an expression of sadness upon her face when I left, but that man was relentless in his endeavor to move her.

As they headed towards the water, I saw the sun break out from behind the clouds. That glaze of ice upon the road began to then melt.

(The dream ended there and I awoke)

I take the dream to have meaning. I feel it is representative of a past that has crumbled. That manufacturing environment is old and gray, dead and gone. The road ahead looked to be a treacherous one, but as I trod it *That Vision of Destination* **makes** *itself clear. Taking a familiar path will surely lead to destruction. There's no harvest to be found in traveling that way; after all, the stalk had no ears."*

With a slide of the Journal to the side, Nathaniel impulsively began to leaf through that John Newton biography till he came to a quote that grasped his intrigue.

He vaguely recalled glancing at the citing a couple times before, but a fresh visitation of the phrase, this time, had a lean towards influential.

"Man is not taught anything to purpose until God becomes his teacher," Newton wrote, "and then the glare of the world is put out and the value of the soul rises in full view. A man's present sentiments may not be accurate, but we make too much of sentiment. We pass a field with a few blades. We call it a field of wheat, but there is no wheat. No, not in perfection, but the wheat is sown, and full ears may be expected."

Nathaniel read that several times, digesting its implied meaning with studious interest.

An involving spin of thought crossed Nathaniel's mind once again and he reached for the Journal. With a flip of Newton's biography to the side, he cracked open the Journal to resume where he'd left off.

He then added a scribbling of, ***"I once read a quote by the English sculptor Henry Moore. It went something like: 'The** secret of it all is to have a task, something you devote your entire life to. Something you give everything to, every minute of the day for the rest of your life. And most of all, it must be something you cannot possibly do.'"*

With a mixture of feelings now a boil, Nathaniel further wrote, *"I must find ways to need less - share beyond belief - with passion, anything is possible. Albert Einstein once penned:* 'Only a life lived for others is worthwhile.'

I read a statistic once that claimed the World's richest 350 people have the same amount of money as the poorest two and a half billion. At the time, that blasphemous imbalance elevated my concern. I even boasted of being in the top ten of that lofty group. I must say I despise any reference to that statistic now. A passionate turning of the cheek to wealth would be symbolic of my disgust.

I classified myself as Stoic for a time, indifferent, unimpressed. I was free of passion - unmoved. I repressed emotion whenever I could. I was a fool. Now that I look back, I was characterized by an austere attitude, self-disciplined in a sad way, impartial to the point of being apathetic toward the larger scheme of things that life, and God, had to offer - no more!"

Nathaniel retired his pen shortly after that. In turn, about a half an hour later, he decided to turn in a little early. He tossed and turned for a while, pounded the pillow, threw the cover off and dragged it back on a time or two. Sleep was a scarce commodity for a bit.

When slumber finally came, Nathaniel began to dream again.

In the dream he was standing beside Jesus next to an immense cornfield. In the field were a few stalks that stood roughly five or six feet tall. They were green and had sprouted a few immature ears. The stalks didn't appear to be planted in any sort of grouping or row. They were just scattered about here and there.

Christ said, "Stay the course. The harvest hasn't come."

Those instructions were the only words spoken, and Nathaniel couldn't recall anything more when he awoke the following morning. He jotted down what he could recollect though.

The proceeding day was the Fourth of July, a time of celebration for many, and Nathaniel's restlessness would be put to an eventual ease. He would come to understand that calling of his, be privileged to that divine direction he'd sought, the purpose of life, a destiny defined.

That evening, shortly before supper, Nathaniel had an inaugural experience he'd never forget - *The Revelation* is what he christened it.

Nathaniel experienced a vision that night. It was something far different than any dream he'd had.

While sitting at the table, wrapping up a prayer with his eyes closed, Nathaniel's consciousness began to fill with fanciful sight. At first it was the appearance of fields, a landscape filled with various crops, miles upon miles of them, then some intriguing symbols flashed through his mind. He'd heard the term "In my mind's eye" before, but he'd never experienced the like. The symbols appeared to be molecular structures of some type. There were three in all.

Apprehension held Nathaniel in the beginning, but he soon understood what the experience was. It was meant to be; one in which God eventually spoke.

The Creator told Nathaniel those symbols were indeed molecular structure, one of soybean, wheat, and corn. Nathaniel then saw a stalk of corn. It had an ear or two per plant, sixteen to eighteen rows of kernels per ear, a total of eight or nine hundred kernels per ear. (The Lord called that average)

Then Nathaniel saw a branch of wheat. One was shining in the sun and the other one was covered with snow. Its season of maturity was dual, something of which Nathaniel didn't know, winter and spring.

The plant had various branches, main stems and others called tillus, and they all held a head of wheat. Each plant had three or four heads per, each head containing twenty kernels or so. (God called that average as well)

A vision of the soybean was then etched upon Nathaniel's mind. It was a plant that held anywhere from thirty to a hundred pods, each pod containing the beans, roughly three or four beans per pod. (The Creator of it all labeled that average too)

God then told Nathaniel the average crop yield could be doubled or tripled, that he was to feed the world with the surplus.

Nathaniel responded with an air of revolt. With a boast of reason, he spouted about how he knew nothing of genetics. "I'm not a botanist." He said. "Besides … even if successful … crossbreeding and molecular manipulation takes decades!"

When Nathaniel threw logic to the wind, venting with that verbal mutiny, God put a period on it by saying, "My Will has been revealed."

Chapter Twenty
Implement Of Your Will

"An Encounter
September 1ˢᵗ 1990
I can recall many a church service," the entry read, *"that I watched an interpreter for the deaf. The church had both male and female interpreters. They usually stood only a few feet from the pastor on the same platform and communicated with those who were deaf in the crowd. The interpreter would use body language, finger, hand, and arm movement, mixed with an occasional display of assorted facial expressions to speak in a magical way.*

The deaf, usually dozens in the audience at any given time, would watch the interpreter for the signing - they would do so with an added measure of concentration, quite possibly more so than those who could hear.

On occasion I saw the deaf cry, even though their world was silent. It could have been a testament to good preaching, but I don't think so. I attribute it to God's uncanny ability, those mysterious ways he employs in touching our souls.

It wasn't unusual to witness the deaf raising their hands in praise or kneeling before the seat, yet, they couldn't hear a musical beat or single word. (Odd that they're defined as handicapped)

The ones I observed displayed a more genuine longing for God's presence than the majority of those in the audience who bore a tag of normal. Those who weren't considered disabled were in reality the disadvantaged. Oh, how little we perceive.

I gave this entry a title of Encounter - I do so for a reason. In a sincere way I admire the deaf. They don't have to contend with the noise of the world and the accompanying distractions. It makes sense that with the departure of hearing the remaining senses would be heightened. It's a plateau that many in the adjoining sea of humanity ignore. Close your eyes for a while. Plug those ears and tune out the world. That encounter we rarely embrace.

My time spent here has been devoted to much thought, not so much of self but of God, His son, and the importance thereof.

I've held many a foolish prerequisite in the past, some dear, but the definition of a touching of the soul had evaded my concern until I came here. It was an escape of my understanding. God can't be defined by reason. I've been taught that. Our thoughts can be flawed, and not always to be trusted. I apologize for confining You to a plain of thought, Lord. You are so much more! My intellectual barbarism has brought shame. My logic has failed me. It's been a distraction to an intimate encounter with You - I'm truly sorry."

Nathaniel had since gripped the notion he'd become ordinary. Through self-will, he was living in an impoverished state. A first for him. Strange, for he couldn't be happier. The perception of being reduced to meagerness is what he thought he had accomplished. His stead was the gain of a fourth-rate being living a paltry existence, the status like many, and it made Nathaniel humble like never before.

Although he'd been contemplating a return to Chicago for a while, Nathaniel was convinced it was time to do so and planned on leaving Lost Lake the following day.

"I've decided to leave this place."** He wrote. **"I must say, it's been an experience that's changed me. How ironic it will be packing up and heading back, on Labor Day no less, unemployed and starting from scratch - I have no clue of things to be!

Faith can be defined as confidence or trust, a belief in something with a lack of proof, but Hebrews 11:1 displays an air of refinement, a more subtle point of distinction for my taste. *'Now faith is the substance of things hoped for, the evidence of things not seen.'*

I have little left, something like twenty thousand I suppose, yet I'm determined to start anew back home and work toward that vision of feeding the less fortunate with what I have. Lord, I've heard *The Call.***"**

A strafing of thought crossed Nathaniel's mind with the penning of that. Then he recalled having something in his possession that he went to retrieve. He had forgotten about a coin he'd brought and he began to search through his stuff for it.

Tucked away in one of his bags, sealed in a plastic case for protection, was a coin he highly prized. It was a *Good Samaritan Shilling*, a very rare piece, minted in the 17th century.

When Nathaniel found the coin he took it back over to the table, then sat down to study it.

He'd collected coins from the time he was a boy. As he examined the coin, he reflected back upon his seventh birthday. It was his father, Jessup, who gave him the coin as a gift that day. He told Nathaniel a hobby of collecting valuable coins was wise, and Nathaniel never steered from that advice.

Most of Jessup's wealthy friends and business associates knew about Nathaniel's hobby, the proud father often brought it up in the midst of small talk.

Nathaniel recalled a few years in which Jessup's friends made the giving of a birthday gift a heated competition. In buying an expensive coin to give Nathaniel as a gift, Jessup's wealthy pals would often stumble over themselves to best each other. Nathaniel was at a loss, because he failed to see anything humorous about those actions now.

The Shilling he held in his palm was minted in Massachusetts, during the colonial period. Its face value was a sixpence - an equivalent of six pennies. The silver coin was a rare one and Nathaniel understood its worth to be roughly around fifteen hundred dollars or so.

As Nathaniel stared at the specimen, its engravings struck a cord within. The coin revealed a neighborly man kneeling to bind the wounds of another in need of help, while the donkey upon which he rode stood quietly in the background.

Nathaniel's long-standing hobby had been little more than that, an interesting pleasure. Nathaniel hadn't made the assertion money was nothing more than an implement, something that shouldn't be worshiped, till he'd spent some time at Lost Lake. His priorities had all together changed since.

With the departure from Chicago Nathaniel left behind several safety-deposit-boxes containing the collection. For reasons he'd failed to grasp, Nathaniel left the valuables in a vault back home. It wasn't so much a lack of concern for the collection, for Nathaniel knew he was leaving it behind, it was the haste of taking it along or dealing with it that seemed less important at the time.

That line of thinking may have been a little rash though, for Nathaniel was now contemplating upon what to do with that vast collection.

Nathaniel recalled having other coins that boasted of religious engravings as well.

A French coin he owned bore the words, "Christ Conquers, Christ Reigns, Christ Commands." It was a common inscription up until Napoleon discarded it.

An English coin in Nathaniel's possession was an interesting one too. Edward IV minted it, calling it the "Angel." One side of the coin was the likeness of the Archangel Michael, winged and haloed, spearing a dragon, and on the other side was a ship bearing a cross as a mast, with the words, "By Thy Cross Save Us, O Christ Our Redeemer."

Nathaniel also had a coin from Holland that had the engraving of a Bible on it, and an inscription of, "This We Support; On This We Depend."

Then he recalled reading somewhere about America's adoption of a new coin in the early 1780's. It was one that bore the all-seeing eye of God for the first time.

Nathaniel thought the collection would fetch a hefty price, and he pondered selling it off upon his return to Chicago while he flipped the Shilling about on his fingertips.

Convincing himself the extra money would go a long way in feeding the poor came with little effort. Nathaniel then held, with determination, that's what he should do.

Nathaniel's mind drifted off to something else when he glanced at the Journal lying to the side. He laid his hand upon it, hesitated for a moment, then slid it toward himself with the cup of his hand and cracked it wide.

With a click of the pen, he began to jot down a few more thoughts.

He wrote, *"I had a ridiculous dream last week. On second thought, it may not have been so ridiculous after all - I wonder!*

In the dream I was wandering about aimlessly. But then I came across a small crowd, all of whom were gathering around for something of which I wasn't quite sure.

At first the crowd appeared calm. Then they grew restless. It wasn't long till anticipation began to erode and their nerves became frayed. I began to think I was standing in the heart of a mob that was beginning to form.

The mood of those a mix in the crowd soon shifted thereafter. For reasons I failed to grasp, one by one they began to form an orderly line.

In the distance, I then saw a large door. It appeared to be made of a heavy stone, and it was now protruding from a mist that I hadn't noticed before. Oddly enough, no one seemed alarmed by the sudden appearance of that door or the accompanying fog that surrounded it.

As each individual got closer, the door opened rather slowly toward them to reveal a curtain awaiting beyond the portal.

The young and old, male, female, and married couples alike began to file through.

On occasion the line was fast-moving, but at other times it was not.

I, too, found myself a part of that stream.

As I drew near, I could see the hesitation in many that were about to enter in. I also stood in witness of a few who refused to participate and dropped from the ranks.

I did observe during the wait that a variety of races were present. Some were speaking languages that were unfamiliar to me. Strange, for many were bowing their heads or raising their hands aloft - it appeared they were praying.

I have never been one to dive into the pleasures of the unknown, but I asked a teenage boy who stood in front of me where we were.

His reply was, 'We're in the divine line, man!' I recall being a little taken back by that, but then pointed a finger to ask what's behind the door. Before the young man could answer the question, I was quick to badger him with a hint of logic. I was arrogant and rude, for which I had no excuse, by grasping for reason when I asked, 'Why are so many willing to partake in something they can't see?'

The teen surprisingly had a demeanor absent anger. He simply smiled, then said, 'I call it the Leap of Faith Machine.' (I wasn't quite sure what to make of that at the time, but that particular reply would spur wonder then result in an eventual view of a young soul that was mature indeed)

It wasn't long till we both were standing before that door. I could see the anticipation building within that young man as he stood in front of me - it was now his turn.

He was bursting at the seams with enthusiasm when that door opened. The teen was bold and quick to rush through that curtain as soon as it was revealed. But before he took that step, the young man assured me it wasn't as crazy the second or third time. (I was a bit puzzled by that, but didn't have the opportunity to probe anymore for he was then gone)

At last, it was my turn. I was a bit apprehensive to say the least.

That thick heavy door began to slowly pivot open as to invite me in. When it swung wide, I could see that curtain on the other side. I hesitated a bit at first, but eventually inched forward a couple steps.

I got close enough to pull the curtain to the side with both hands. It was constructed of material like I've never seen. It was a heavy drape, well-made indeed, and it took some effort to move. It was an attractive thing to look at for it had a purple tint and the fabric shimmered with the reflection of the sun.

Oddly enough, when I pushed the curtain to the side the light revealed nothing. Past that curtain was the stirring void of darkness. I got scared. Fear now had a hold.

Others in line were growing impatient with me by then. They started yelling, saying things like, 'Come on!'

I considered turning back with each ensuring shout, but just could not. I was being driven somehow. Something was saying, 'Trust me.'

With that I closed my eyes and took a step or two in. When I did, I began to fall. Fear had a stranglehold on me by then.

I was falling at a rapid rate at first. Then, for some unknown reason, my descent began to slow abruptly.

I was hurtling down a dark shaft. The thought struck me that death was imminent more than once, but then I saw a faint light at the bottom of the shaft.

Others, of whom I recognized from being in line, were gathered about beneath me as my descent slowed even further.

Eventually I came to a stop at the bottom of the shaft. Surprisingly enough, it was a soft one at that.

When I landed upon my feet, I found myself in the center of a well-lit room. It was large enough to hold several thousand. I hadn't been there long till someone approached me. It was that same teen who had been in line before me. (I was a little shaken, but he didn't appear to be)

I thought it was odd that a young man, someone unfamiliar, was willing to befriend me by extending a hand of friendship then add, 'I've been waitin' for ya!'

I responded with a reply of something like, 'Where are we?'

I asked the teen if I knew him, but he said 'no.'

He gave me a simplistic explanation for the plight, one of which I thought was sincere, for he said, 'It's the thrill of the Leap of Faith Ride, man!' He went on to say, 'When you're in His will, you land on your feet.'"

[I then awoke from the dream]

With a desistance stroke of the pen Nathaniel flopped the Journal shut. His focus had been caught up in yet another glimpse of meditation. He slid the bulging Chronicle to the side, stood, then ambled toward the open door.

A shaft of light streaming through the cabin's inviting entrance engulfed the table at which Nathaniel sat. Its illuminating presence diverted his attention, but at the same time grasped his intrigue.

With an arm wrapped about one of those support posts, Nathaniel stood in thought of things to come. His mind was a ponder as he stared at the glitter of the sun's reflection upon the still waters faint ripple.

It was late afternoon and Nathaniel reasoned it would be dark soon. A hint of excitement, coupled by subdued concern, ran about Nathaniel's thoughts. The reality of leaving this place come morn was now a stir in the man.

A final leisurely stroll around the Lake Nathaniel did then take. The grassy banks gave way to a clearing paved with pebbles beneath those sloping cliffs on the north end. It had been there, most often, that Nathaniel discovered something of himself.

As Nathaniel gave host to reflection of days there, he knelt down to gather one of those stones beneath his feet. He then stood to gaze upon that rock of which he now clutched.

With a humbled bit of wonder, he murmured, "King David did much with no more than a stone."

Nathaniel then hurled it to the waters depth and made his way back to the cabin as the sun began its departure.

Supper was nothing more than some beans and a slice of bread that evening. Then Nathaniel had thoughts of packing after the completion of the meal.

He thought he might jot down a departing thought or two before leaving the following day, that being his reasoning for letting the Journal lay.

With the gathering of the few belongings he had, Nathaniel noticed, tucked away in a corner of the room, that martyr book he bought back in Chicago. As he held it, the idea of how odd it was he never once cracked it open filled his thoughts. But then he noticed something even more peculiar with an attempt to pack it away.

A slip of paper fell from the pages to the floor. When Nathaniel reached down to retrieve it, he noticed some writing upon it.

It read:

"Imagine yourself as a living house. God comes in to rebuild that house. At first, perhaps, you can understand what He is doing. He is getting the drains right and stopping the leaks in the roof and so on ... But presently he starts knocking the house about in a way that hurts abominably and does not seem to make sense. What on earth is He up to? The explanation is that He is building quite a different house from the one you thought of - throwing out a new wing here, putting on an extra floor there, running up towers, making courtyards. You thought you were going to be made into a decent little cottage: but He is building a palace. He intends to come and live in it Himself."

C.S. Lewis

With fascination Nathaniel sat at the table and began to leaf through the book. To his amazement he discovered several other slivers adrift in the pages. He thought that was quite odd for he was convinced it was a new book, its depths not yet explored or held.

For reasons that escaped him, Nathaniel hadn't cracked its spine or even had a fleeting interest in that book all this time.

The folded scraps were only a few, but their inscriptions were a vault of intrigue for Nathaniel.

Once he'd finished his search Nathaniel gazed upon that small stack, then he began to unfold each and read them one by one:

"For one human to love one another: that is perhaps the most difficult of all of our tasks, the ultimate, the last test and proof, the work for which all other work is but preparation."

Rainer Maria Rilke

"Where man is exploited, crushed, degraded by man, the Christian cannot avoid involvement by escape into the realm of spiritual values ... he is on the side of the little people, the poor. His place in the world is there ... because his communion with Jesus Christ is communion with the Poor One who knew total poverty, total injustice, total violence."

Jacques Ellul

"Jesus is the prophet of the loser's, not the victor's camp, proclaiming that the first will be last, that the weak are the strong and the fools the wise, that the poor and lowly, not the rich and proud, possess the Kingdom of Heaven."

Malcolm Muggeridge

"So, this is now the mark by which we all shall certainly know whether the birth of the Lord Jesus is effective in us: if we take upon ourselves the needs of our neighbor."

Martin Luther

"What we see, and like to see, is cure and change. But what we do not see and do not want to see is care, the participation in the pain, the solidarity in suffering, the sharing in the experience of brokenness. And still, cure without care is dehumanizing as a gift given with a cold heart."

Henri J. M. Nouwen

"If you can meet with triumph and disaster, and treat those two imposters just the same; if you can bear to hear the truth you've spoken, twisted by knaves to make a trap for fools, or watch the things you gave your life to broken, and scoop and build 'em up with worn-out tools, yours is the earth and everything that's in it, and - which is a more - you'll be a man, my son."

Rudyard Kipling

"Attempt something so impossible that unless God is in it, it is doomed to failure."

John Haggai

Were these the inscriptions of someone searching for ascension to a spiritual plateau? They were indeed a wealth of wonderful penmanship, sprawled about on a receptacle called expression. Who traced those penciled replicas of wisdom? Were these just a collection of humbling words, or were they more to the one who recorded their symbolic meaning, clipped each, folded them, then tucked them away - Nathaniel could only imagine.

Was this a divine impartation, conveyance of some kind? He pondered upon that for a while too. Perhaps it was. At times the answer evades our grasp, never to be revealed.

The experience lent way to a transfixing hold upon Nathaniel's thoughts nevertheless.

Needless to say, Nathaniel's eyelids were growing heavy by now. The day had been a long one and his tiredness, mixed with a drain of anticipation, thoughts of what tomorrow held, were getting the best of him.

That bunk in the corner looked all-too-inviting and he would curl up in its warming allure shortly, but not until he read a curious scripture he'd fumbled upon days prior.

"If you have any encouragement from being united with Christ, if any comfort from his love, if any fellowship with the Spirit, if any tenderness and compassion, then make my joy complete by being like-minded, having the same love, being one in spirit and purpose. Do nothing out of selfish ambition or vain conceit, but in humility consider others better than yourselves."

Nathaniel paused for a moment, reflecting, then thought to himself, "My, the opposite of indifference … indeed. A contrary slant for most."

"Each of you should look not only to your own interests, but also to the interests of others. Your attitude should be the same as that of Jesus Christ: Who, being in very nature God, did not consider equality with God something to be grasped, but made himself nothing, taking the very nature of a servant, being made in human likeness. And being found in appearance as a man, he humbled himself and became obedient to death - even death on a cross!" (Philippians 2: 1-8)

When he awoke the following morning Nathaniel got dressed and prepared for the trip back to Chicago. He sat at the table, took a few bites out of an apple, and penned the last Journal entry.

"September 2, 1990

This is my last journal entry before heading back to uncertainty. Chicago was home once. I'm not so sure anymore.

God said months prior, 'From plains of those less tread, thou will go!'

That thought has flooded my mind of late.

Although the phrase may seem simplistic, I'm swayed by the fact - He will lead, I must follow!

For it is impossible for a limited mind to grasp the unlimited. It's a theme, therefore, I must applaud.

A year has fallen by the way, more so a fog of distinction, yet in retrospect it has been the most memorable one of my life. The Creator bore grace upon this place called Lost Lake. I shall not soon forget the depths of those spiritual waters.

Lord, your wonder has a grasp upon my soul. Your never ceasing presence amazes me.

I vow to be an implement of Your will, a tool for service, till my days are at an end.

I'm heading back to Chicago with a vision to implement!"

Nathaniel was inclined to reflect upon what he wrote for a while. He prayed some, then finished what little packing he had left.

He murmured a few words of encouragement to himself as he gathered up what bags he had. He thought to himself, several times, "I can't thank You enough for bringing me here," as he made way for the door.

Nathaniel couldn't bring himself to depart immediately. Instead, he stood for the longest time on that porch staring at the lake. That post he leaned upon had been a worn friend for a while. There was nothing more than silence to ponder, yet that was more than enough, for time was unimportant at the moment.

Chapter Twenty-One
Reap the Magnificent

The sun had just peeked over the horizon and Nathaniel was on his way back home. That orange glare was a bit much that morning and he slaw relief from the orb's rays with a flip of the visor. A scrap of paper fell upon Nathaniel's lap with that. The folded note had been tucked away atop the seclusion of the visor. Nathaniel applied the brake, then came to a stop on the side of the road. He'd forgotten all about writing that tattered gem and he opened it.

It read:

"I'm Nathaniel Everett Irwin, forty-five, not too old to endeavor upon a new beginning. This spiritual voyage has been ordaining to say the least. But my departure will be one toward the unknown. The year is '90, Chicago's the destination, and with a realm of uncertainty looming before me I can only ponder the way as a shining definition of faith."

It seemed to be a quick trip this time, little more than uneventful, in comparison to the maiden excursion. Those accompanying speculative thoughts tumbling about in the recesses of Nathaniel's mind, although occasional, did help pass the time though. When he did stop to grab a bite, or rest, Nathaniel spent most of it jotting down notes. A few were simple journal entries, others were compelling thoughts he had, some personal reminders, and then there was a short list of contingency plans like selling the coin collection to gain revenue once home.

When he arrived in Chicago Nathaniel toyed with several ideas. Then he came to the conclusion it was best to pay Pastor Dan a call first.

When Nathaniel got to Pastor Dan's he parked out front, then leaned his head on the steering wheel to ponder for a while. After he'd gathered his composure, and rehearsed what his thoughts might be, Nathaniel got out of the vehicle and slowly walked toward an old friend's door.

It was late, after midnight, and there didn't appear to be any lights on inside the home. When Nathaniel stepped onto the porch, he twisted his knuckles and raised an inverted fist to tap on the door. He hesitated for a moment, then looked through an adjacent window once more before tapping heavily upon that glass storm door protecting the entry.

Nathaniel stepped back with that and nervously waited for someone to answer the door.

It wasn't long till a light came on in the rear hall. Nathaniel peered through the window for a short while, then he saw Pastor Dan emerge from one of the rooms with a robe clad about him while he rubbed his eyes as to remove that lingering sleep.

Nathaniel was a bit nervous and tried to pass that brief moment of anticipation by glancing over the bushes that surrounded the perimeter of the porch. That porch light hanging on the wall next to the door did then come on, illuminating the silent darkness where he stood.

The Reverend opened the interior door to peer through the exterior door's glass pane. He was quite surprised to see his friend standing there and with elation said, "Nathaniel!" He then swung the door wide, stepped out on the porch, and gave Nathaniel a big squeeze. As he was hugging Nathaniel, Dan patted his friend on the back and whispered in his ear, "I sure missed you."

Although Nathaniel wasn't usually speechless, he was that time. Yet the Pastor knew his friend was glad to see him. Those faint tears now welling in Nathaniel's eyes were a reflection of that.

The Minister released his grip on Nathaniel, held the door open, then yelled, "Betty! ... Nathaniel's here! ... Nathaniel's here!"

With a wave of his hand, Dan gestured, come on in. He then grabbed Nathaniel's arm to escort him inside.

"Can I get your bags?" The kind Reverend asked.

"I'm tired ... we'll leave them for tomorrow." Nathaniel replied.

The Pastor's wife emerged from one of the rear rooms, then greeted Nathaniel as he and Dan stood in the living room.

The gentle persuasion of the Minister was, "Sweetheart ... would you get that extra bedroom ready for Nathaniel ... I'm sure he's beat."

"I wouldn't want to intrude." Nathaniel blurted out.

"Nonsense!" Dan proclaimed.

"It's no trouble at all ... I'll see to it ... turn the sheets down and get everything ready." Betty said with a kind smile.

"I think it would be best if you stay with us for a while, Nathaniel."   The good Reverend did prod. "People were looking for you there for some time ... they probably still are." Dan did then pat Nathaniel on the back to say, "Why don't you get some rest ... we'll talk some more tomorrow."

Nathaniel thought about it for a moment, then nodded his head in agreement.

He didn't even remember his head hitting the pillow, and Nathaniel slept all morning the following day. Dan, nor Betty, had the heart to wake him. They let him sleep. It was sometime around two that afternoon when Nathaniel finally woke. When he emerged from his room, he found the good Reverend and his wife sitting at the kitchen table. Dan was reading the paper. She was knitting something.

When the Pastor caught a glimpse of his guest, he tossed the newspaper to the side and said, "Good morning … or should I say good afternoon." With a wave of his hand, Dan then said, "Sit … Would you like something to drink, a coke, coffee … or do you want something to eat instead … Betty can whip something up for you."

Nathaniel said, as he took a seat, "A sandwich would be nice … something with cheese and lettuce."

Dan added, "I'll take one too!"

As Betty prepared the snack, the two men carried on idle chitchat between themselves.

When she finished her task, Betty placed a plate of food in front of Nathaniel and Dan and left one sitting at the end of the table for herself.

When all three were ready to eat, Pastor Dan asked Nathaniel to say grace.

With heads bowed, Nathaniel said, "Lord … I want to thank you for changing me … only You could … I was a fool … a self-absorbed fool … you didn't create me to acquire things … you created me to love people … and that I fell short … I'm sorry … Forgive me."

With that, the tears began to well up from within Betty.

With the brush of a backward hand over his face, to clear any remnant of emotion, Nathaniel added, "Bless these people, Father … they're good people … bless this food which will nurture our bodies … we give You thanks … in all things … Amen."

When Nathaniel finished, Dan nodded his head, but Betty had to rub her face to dissipate the lingering tears.

None of them said much as they ate though. It was as if each were absorbed in their own thoughts.

When he had finished eating Nathaniel offered to wash the dishes, but Betty would have none of that. "You're a guest." She insisted.

The Minister asked his wife to leave the dishes in the sink so he and Nathaniel could have some time to talk. He then added, "Can you give us a bit of privacy, Dear? Nathaniel and I have a few things to discuss."

Betty countered by saying, "Of course," and left the room.

After his wife had exited the kitchen, Pastor Dan looked at Nathaniel to say, "I want you to be patient and hear me out."

Nathaniel's reply was, "Okay."

The Reverend had been rehearsing what he had to say in his mind all morning, and went on to say, "I consider you a close friend, Nathaniel."

Nathaniel shook his head in silence as to agree.

"First of all, it's none of my business where you've been for the last year. I'm sure that's between you and God and we'll leave it at that."

Pastor Dan hesitated for a moment, and then went on to proclaim, "For the last three months, I've been having the same recurring dream. I've had that same dream probably five or six times. In it, I'm standing in front of God's throne. It seems to be infinite in height and width. God's sitting on the throne, but his appearance isn't anything like what we can imagine."

Nathaniel's intrigue was beginning to escalate with that.

The Minister then added, "God was like a mist that glowed. It was beyond comprehension. It's hard to define how magnificent He is. Because God's a spirit … Nathaniel.

Nathaniel continued to be respectful of what Pastor Dan had to convey and sat in silence.

"In that dream, I then kneel in front of God's throne … bawling like a baby. The Lord then tells me you left Chicago with over $100,000 cash and you'll come home with a little over three thousand dollars."

Nathaniel blurted out, "My God, oh my God, that's right!"

Pastor Dan then said, "Let me finish."

Once again, Nathaniel shook his head in silence as to agree.

"God told me not to spend any of that money you wired the church, Nathaniel. There's still over $700 million dollars in the account. I haven't spent a dime of it. The Lord warned me not to touch it."

Although the good Reverend was tempted a time or two, he was faithful to never tamper with that three quarters of a billion dollars he was entrusted with. However, the church did benefit from the interest that principal investment drew for years to come.

By now, Dan was starting to succumb to the stirs of emotion.

As a tear welled in his eye, the Pastor said, "Betty and I have been saving for a new car, but God told me in those dreams to buy you a house in Mount Prospect instead. It's close to downtown. He said in the dreams that it's near where your ancestors once lived."

The tears were free-flowing by then from the Minister's eyes.

"God said you would need a place to stay when you get back and that house would come to mean a great deal to you."

Nathaniel was beginning to realize this was all in God's plan and, he too, was beginning to get emotional.

"I told Betty about the dreams and we talked it over. Three or four weeks ago, we drove to Mount Prospect and found a house for sale near downtown just like God said. The realtor said a businessman owned the home and that he felt led to sell it for $30,000. That was his very words. It went on the market that day … and guess what Nathaniel … we bought it right then and the transaction went quick … no problems … and by the time we paid the asking price … closing costs and all that … we still had $3,000.00 left over. And what a coincidence that you came back to Chicago with about that amount."

Nathaniel then blurted out, "I don't know what to say."

Pastor Dan held up a finger and added, "I'm almost finished with what I have to say. About a month or two ago, a man paid me a visit at the church. He said he was your lawyer and that he was looking for you. I told him I didn't know where you were … which was the truth at the time. He kept saying something about 'There's a deadline approaching.' He wouldn't say what that was though. I guess he's bound by attorney-client privilege … I would suppose. I think you should call him … when you get a chance."

Nathaniel took the pastor's advice and set up a meeting with Clarence Conn the following week, after he'd gotten acclimated to his new surroundings in Mount Prospect. That two thousand square-foot, three-bedroom, two-bath, ranch home with a fine backyard was quite a nice surprise to Nathaniel. It felt downright homely compared to that high-rise penthouse he used to occupy in downtown Chicago. You might say that rustic cabin on Lost Lake made the one-time executive view his living conditions in a much different light and with heightened appreciation.

When Nathaniel met with his attorney, he was quite shocked by what his counsel had to say.

The elderly Conn said, "Nathaniel, I've been your family's attorney for a long time. I've always gone along with your wishes, but I have to be quite frank. I thought you were having a nervous breakdown when you decided to step down and sell the company. I'm not near as bright as you, Son, but someone said you were having a *Come to Jesus* moment … and I can respect that."

The lawyer then said, "Feel free to interject your thoughts at any time."

The only thing Nathaniel could say was, "Go on."

"I knew it was your wish to hand over a Power of Attorney document to George Willis, your Vice President of Operations. Well … I hope I don't draw your ire, but I have a confession to make."

Once again, Nathaniel said, "Go on."

"Without your knowledge or consent … or that of George Willis for that matter … I included a waiver … a *Buyback Clause* in the legal wranglings when you sold Irwin Industries to Global Technologies. The Clause basically said you can buy back the company and its assets within 18 months … minus accrued interest of course. The revenue gained from the sale of the company, Nathaniel, is in an escrow account because no one knew where you went after that. It's something like 55 or 60 billion, Son, and it's drawing interest."

Nathaniel interjected, "And GTI went for that?"

Clarence's respond was, "Les McGree, their CEO, wasn't thrilled with the idea, but he and their board acted on it. Out of a blinding sense of greed … I would suppose."

Nathaniel said, "I see … go on."

"What I'm trying to say is … what I did was probably wrong by concealing that from you and George, but my intentions were noble … I assure you."

Nathaniel just sat there to intently listen.

"As I told your pastor, Nathaniel, there's a deadline approaching … that 18-month waiver that gives you the option to buy back the company and its assets will expire in four or five months."

The counselor then took out a calculator and did some figuring.

"It looks like $27.6 million would come due for that accrued interest that I was talking about … if you decide to reacquire your company, Son. If you decide to do that, I'm sure Les McGree won't be very happy. But it has legal standing and it's ironclad. The interest rate is generous, absorbent probably, but that's where we stand."

Nathaniel just sat there in silence for quite a while.

After enduring several minutes of dead silence, which hovered over the room, the attorney said, "Well … say something, Son."

Nathaniel got up from his chair and walked over to the window.

As he was staring out the pane, with his back turned to the counselor, he said, "I've never asked you if you believe in God, Clarence … Do you?"

The attorney's reply was, "Yes."

"Do you believe in divine intervention?" was Nathaniel added pry.

"I suppose God orchestrates things from time to time. I'd be a fool to believe otherwise." Clarence added.

Nathaniel then went on to say, "I'm not angry at all, Clarence. I know you were looking out for my best interest … I didn't know it until just now."

After a moment of hesitation, Nathaniel went on to proclaim, "I won't go into a lot of detail, Clarence, but I have been on a year's sabbatical … a spiritual voyage you might say. I've always thought that money and logic were everything … Boy … that was flawed thinking at best. Have you ever heard that term, 'God speaks the loudest when it's quiet."

The lawyer's reply was, "Can't say I have."

"God intervened in my life, Clarence. He didn't like the path I was on … so … He changed it … and I let Him. I gave up riches and what I thought was prosperity. In reality … it wasn't prosperity at all. There's a big difference between happiness and prosperity you know. I was miserable before, Clarence. I was of the opinion I was penniless, but I was happier in seclusion … and still am. Now you tell me I haven't lost anything. But you're wrong."

The Attorney then asked, "How so?"

Nathaniel said, "I've lost the biggest detriment to mankind."

The counselor then asked, "What would that be?"

Nathaniel simple reply was, "Pride."

After Nathaniel stood to stare out the window for several more minutes, the silence began to get to the lawyer, so he interjected, "How would you like to proceed, Son."

Nathaniel walked back over to his chair and sat down; and with that he began to sob.

His attorney was a little taken back by that, but thought it was best to enact sympathy and patience. In time, Conn said, "I've never seen you like this, Son. Is there anything I can do?"

Nathaniel looked upward towards the ceiling to say, "Thank you, Lord!"

Then Nathaniel instructed his lawyer to proceed with the enactment of the Buyback Clause. He ended the meeting by saying, "Restore Irwin Industries to what it was, but its mission will change from greed … to humanitarianism."

It took a few weeks, some heated verbal skirmishes with a horde of lawyers at the law firm GTI had retained, with a mix of concentrated legal maneuvering, but Nathaniel's attorney was successful in re-obtaining Irwin Industries. Clarence Conn saw to it that the purchasing price, $57.6 billion, used to buy Nathaniel's company, was transferred back to Global Technologies from escrow. Accrued interest was also paid to GTI during the transaction, and that amount wasn't far off from the counselor's calculated estimate he gave Nathaniel weeks prior.

Oddly enough, Global Technologies changed next to nothing concerning the company's structure. There were some personnel changes, but they hadn't sold any assets, liquidated equipment, or tinkered with any of the divisions nestled within the corporation. Nathaniel's lawyer attributed that plan of action to the *wait-and-*

see advice GTI legal counsel, no doubt, gave their CEO and Board of Directors.

An effort to restructure the Corporation ensued after that. Clarence Conn even undertook the painstaking task of interviewing the past members of the Irwin Industries Board of Directors. None of them were retained by Global Technologies to serve in any capacity. However, one of Nathaniel's previous board members had passed away, succumb to his battle with cancer, and all but one were still interested in serving on the board of Irwin Industries once more.

Betty Montgomery, Nathaniel's personal secretary of many years, who was now in her 80s, retired and drew her pension when Nathaniel departed Chicago for that seclusion of Lost Lake. It took a bit of coaxing, but Nathaniel was able to coerce his faithful secretary back into service for the company - he considered that unselfish act of Betty's a personal favor. She would prove invaluable to the CEO for it was a dubious task, a tedious endeavor indeed, to reshape the corporation into that God-guided image of which Nathaniel was determined to implement.

George Willis, the Vice President of Operations for Irwin Industries, wasn't old enough to retire. Global Technologies told George his services were no longer needed, and he found it difficult to find a job once GTI took over. He had contemplated bankruptcy recently because he'd been drawing a smallish weekly unemployment check, for about a year, when Nathaniel returned to Chicago.

Nathaniel paid George a visit at his home one day, and the two went out to lunch. The CEO thought it was important to fill his friend in on the numerous events that had occurred in the past year. It took Nathaniel an hour to explain everything, and another hour or so to convey his vision of what God had in mind for the company. George listened intently to the Executive the entire time, and was intrigued by what his CEO had conveyed. Nathaniel was never aware of George's personal spiritual convictions, but he did learn of those in his conversations with the VP. Mrs. Willis had been a Christian for many years, Nathaniel came to understand, and she had convinced her husband to convert to Christianity from Catholicism about six months prior.

Nathaniel offered George Willis his job back at full salary. He also threw in some incentives, if George could pull off what the CEO was about to usher forth in a restructuring plan that had painstakingly taken weeks to document.

In the coming months, Nathaniel and George Willis, along with their staff, would vigorously apply their knowledge of corporate identity and business savvy to enact a plan that so vast it took a few miracles along the way to accomplish. The Corporation, which many claimed to be a conglomerate, saw change in corporate vision, policy, and structure within its divisions.

Some of the smaller manufacturing divisions were sold to Global Technologies. They were no longer needed because Irwin Industries had a revised vision of corporate goals that had dramatically changed from the previous ones. The CEO and board of GTI were more than willing to accept that offering and bought up those smaller divisions with eagerness. Their CEO even went as far as to tell the Wall Street Journal, who wrote an article about the transaction, "It's a salve that soothed the pain of an open wound Irwin Industries created."

The revenue gained from that sale of assets to GTI was used to retool and implement the necessary conversion processes of the larger manufacturing divisions within the Corporation. Those sizable divisions were soon, thereafter, converted into food processing plants and others for the production of agricultural equipment.

The logistical division's primary mission was shipping and receiving and always had been. However, the revised overall plan for that administrative entity now consisted of a concerted effort to build automated warehouses, that had a footprint of a million square feet or more, within several supply chain enterprises that were formed around the world.

The transportation division, which had been of average size before, expanded rapidly with the implementation of Irwin Industries restructuring. The purchase of hundreds of cargo panel vans, as well as the addition of a large fleet of semi's, happened in three fiscal quarters alone. A vast inventory of locomotives and boxcars were already in the Corporation's possession, and they were used to a far greater extent in the coming years. A small fleet of cargo ships were also acquired to make Irwin Industries *a worldwide claim to fame*, as some in the press would come to say.

An additional division was added when the restructuring plan was implemented. A few mockingly called it *The Great Digs Endeavor*, because the sole purpose of that entity was to dig wells in impoverished areas around the world. Nathaniel went on record as to say, "The addition of well-digging equipment by our company is in line with our corporate mission to feed the world. Everything has to have water to live, and we shall stride to provide that."

That division, responsible for water supply, would buy small tracts of land when corporate scientists discovered underground aquifers in the countries they explored around the globe. They were able to accomplish that through advanced technology the Corporation had acquired.

The purchase of that land, in whatever country it may have been, was leased back to that nation for a dollar a year by Irwin Industries. Every agreement signed by a nation and the Corporation consisted of a stipulation. The stipulation was there would be no additional fees, other than the required dollar per year, the country of record would have to pay in order to have the water rights to those wells. That country would have to, in turn, provide the H2O to their people for free. If that nation broke the contractual agreement with Irwin Industries, the Corporation would reassume the water rights and then, in turn, provide the water supply to those in need at its own discretion.

Fittingly, Nathaniel was most intrigued with the genetic research the company's R&D department had undertaken since the restructuring had begun. Scientists within that division were successful in their engineering effort to manipulate genetic material in order to alter the hereditary traits of a cell in plant species. The biologists Nathaniel had on staff were ingenious in their efforts to produce higher yields in plants such as soybeans, corn, and wheat.

Within five years, *The Nerds in the Lab*, as Nathaniel jokingly referred, had made great strides in increasing crop yield by some 20%. Nathaniel made it a point to sketch those genetically modified cell structure images God gave him at Lost Lake. Those drawings would indeed proof to be instrumental to the success of the biologists he had working for him.

Many renowned scientists said that accomplishment was impossible, and were skeptical of any sort of success in such a short period of time. Nathaniel never failed to always counter their skepticism with, "But, you don't seem to fathom who my God really is."

Irwin Industries bloomed into something Nathaniel could have never envisioned or comprehend. The Corporation sold processed food and bulk grain to companies foreign and domestic. They also sold their sustenance to countries around the world. They sold those products to their customers at a drastically reduced rate, with a stipulation that purchaser would have to give away a tenth of each order to those in need. Many customers thought that was a noble enterprise to pursue, but several just viewed it as a loss or tax write off. Irwin Industries kept meticulous records and held their customers to that requirement. If they didn't keep their end of the bargain, it would void the contractual agreement between the two and further business between them would surely be in peril.

It was now the mid-90s, and the Company's successful conversion was now a reality. Nathaniel's personal secretary, Betty Montgomery, approached her employer one day to claim she's wore-out and was determined to fade into an existence of permanent retirement. Nathaniel told her he understood, and appreciated her dedicated service and friendship to him after all these years. However, Nathaniel was worried about replacing such a valuable lady as her. Betty lightened that anxiety of Nathaniel's, marginally, when she claimed she had someone in mind that her employer could trust - a niece on her mother's side, she said.

Betty scheduled the interview for Nathaniel, with that potential replacement, the following week.

At the start of the interview, Nathaniel said, "I see on your application that you have some experience, Becky."

She replied, "Yes, and I'm dedicated too."

Nathaniel then asked, "Why don't you tell me about your family."

Becky said, "My husband recently passed away … He had cancer."

Nathaniel acted genuinely dismayed by that, but continued to listen intently.

The Applicant then added, "I have two children … A boy and a girl."

Nathaniel blurted out, "Their names wouldn't happen to be Andy and Kim … would it?"

Becky was puzzled by that question. She sat in her chair, overcome by bewilderment, as she contemplated Nathaniel's intrusive pry.   She then said, "How did you know that?"

Nathaniel then asked her if she believed in God.

Becky's reply was, "Of course I do, but what's that got to do with this?"

The CEO then asked, "Do you believe God talks to people?"

Becky added, "Yes, but I'm finding this interview quite strange."

Nathaniel then proceeded to claim, "God's given me some insight, Becky, and I would like to hire you to replace Betty Montgomery as my personal secretary."

Becky said, "I need the work, Sir, but I'm wondering if every day will be as odd as this one?"

The Executive claimed, "It could be!"

A couple days later, Becky decided to take the job and become Nathaniel's personal secretary.

Within a month or two, the CEO told Becky he had been thinking about buying a place on the ocean in California. He added that he would like for her to accompany him there to help pick out a nice secondary home.

Nathaniel tried to coerce his secretary into it by saying, "Would you like to bring your kids on the trip with us … make it a mini vacation … you might say?"

Becky thought that was a wonderful idea.

Nathaniel did then claim: "It's settled then … and oh … by the way … do you like to fish?"